The Harder They Come

The Harder They Come

A NOVEL BY
Michael Thelwell

Grove Press, Inc./New York

First Edition 1980
First Printing 1980
ISBN: 0-394-50652-9
Grove Press ISBN: 0-8021-0191-7
Library of Congress Catalog Card Number: 79-2321

First Evergreen Edition 1980
Second Printing 1980
ISBN: 0-394-17599-9
Grove Press ISBN: 0-8021-4288-5
Library of Congress Catalog Card Number: 79-2321

Library of Congress Cataloging in Publication Data

Thelwell, Michael.
    The harder they come.

    I. Henzell, Perry. The harder they come.
II. Title.
PZ4.T383Har 1980   [PR9265.9.T5]   813   79-2321
ISBN 0-394-50652-9

Manufactured in the United States of America

Distributed by Random House, Inc., New York

GROVE PRESS, INC., 196 West Houston Street, New York, N.Y. 10014

In the
Memory and Spirit
of
Morris Matthew Thelwell, M.H.R.,
and
the people he loved and served
until the day
he danced,
And went to join the ancestors.

Author's Preface

It is necessary to say a few words about the relationship between
this novel and Perry Henzell's justly celebrated film of the same
title. Anyone who is familiar with that fine political film will see
at a glance that this book is not a "novelization" of the filmscript.
This is not said to minimize in any way the considerable debt that
the book owes to the movie, but in fact to affirm what I feel to be
an even more profound and interesting debt and relationship. The
recent practice of "novelization," by which is apparently meant
the adding of chunks of narrative and description to a film's dialogue, does not, to my mind, result in a novel. At least, not what
I think of as a novel.

The Harder They Come, as written by Henzell and Trevor
Rhone, is an intelligent, creative, and very successful cinematic
interpretation of an event in contemporary Jamaican history which
now has passed into legend: the life and exploits of "Rhygin,"
the first and most dramatic of the great ghetto gunmen. Henzell
and Rhone used events from "Rhygin's" career as the center of a
film about working class life and culture which probed the psychological, economic, and political roots, as well as the media
inspiration, of "Rhygin's" rebellion.

Their film is the inspiration for this novel.

While strictly adhering to that general vision of the meaning
of the event, I have added much historical and political detail
which, because of the inherent limitations of the medium, was
beyond the scope of the film. To that end, I have created characters and situations, as well as a personal and social history for the
hero, in such a way, one hopes, as to preserve, and indeed deepen,
the essential character and vision of the film while expanding its
historical and cultural range. For example, I have for reasons of
irony and sharpness compressed some sixty years of social history

and cultural change—some would say "progress"—into one generation.

What I had hoped to achieve was a broader new work into which the action, characters, and scenes of the film could be organically integrated and which would work as a novel at least nearly as well as the film did as cinema. Stated differently, I tried to write if not the novelistic equivalent of the movie then at least the novel from which the film might have been derived were the process reversed, as is more usually the case.

Having begun the process of acknowledging indebtedness, it is not easy to stop. I may as well go ahead and clear the ledgers of, as Unoka the father of Okonkwo would advise, at any rate the larger and more pressing debts.

This whole enterprise owes a great deal to Kent Carroll, the astute editor at Grove Press who thought it up and never lost faith. My children Tracey and Todd are owed a great deal, as much for their patience and forbearance as for their clear critical commentary pithily expressed ("Oh gross, Dad, raspy"). For willing and skillful work on a manuscript that seemed endless, I owe Meline Kasparian.

The book is dedicated to my father, as is appropriate. But there are, in the literary lineage, some senior relatives whose influence on the book has been profound and which in any case will be easily visible to whomever cares to look. So I acknowledge our indebtedness to Chinua Achebe of Nssukka, Sterling A. Brown of Howard, Sidney Kaplan of Massachusetts, and Andrew Salkey of Jamaica.

—M. T.
Pelham, Massachusetts
June 7, 1979

Behold my people: How violence does enfold them like a mantle. It sitteth upon their shoulders even as a garment.

Book of Lamentations

Jah Version

BOOK ONE

The Hills Were Joyful

And the hills were joyful together,
and the valleys clapped their hands, hallelujah

A glossary of Jamaican terms and idioms appears on
page 393.

1

Village Bwai Version

So me get it, so me give it . . .
Jack Mandora, me no choose none . . .

"Yoh! Ivan . . . Ivanhoe yoh!" Without pausing in her work in the open kitchen, Miss 'Mando listened to the echoes of her whoop bouncing back and forth against the hillsides and away down the valley, growing fainter as they went. "Ivanhoe . . . hoe . . . hoe . . ."

Wherever the boy was, she was confident he would hear. Even if he didn't know good and well when supper was, she was deservedly famous in the district for the clear, carrying qualities of her whoop. Not that you heard really good whooping anymore, most of the young people scorned to learn how—too old-fashion and country for them she supposed. But she didn't care; *she* remembered. At planting time, when she used to go with her father and brothers to the little plot of ground that fed them all, the hillsides would ring with the sound of machetes and the heavy rhythms of hoes. And the singing? Yes Lawd, the wild, beautiful, melodic lines and the steady beat of the songs that kept the tempo of the work. And the hillsides—in them days? She smiled at the recollection. The hillsides had been alive with activity like when you stir up a duck ant's nest, entire families laboring side by side to coax from their steep little farms the earth's riches. In those days you could stand on Jancrow mountain and call somebody slap down at Blue Bay. All you had to do was start it: "Tata Uttie ooee." And from the next hilltop, a neighbor proud of his own whoop would pick it up, and you would hear it carried on loud and piercing in the quiet mountains, each whoop resonating off the hillsides as though off giant sounding boards, and carrying incredibly long distances. In a few minutes the answer would come relaying back: "Uttie no dey yah oo" ° or "Uttie a listen oo."

° No dey yah: is not here.

But now Miss 'Mando listened to the echoes of her holler die away into silence, and went on peeling yams and green bananas for her "dutchpot"—the large iron stewing pot that hung over a logwood fire on the waist-high platform of clay and rocks in front of her. Where was that boy? She swept the peelings into a pile for the goats and turned to the entrance to look fretfully down the valley.

Amanda Martin, known to all and sundry as "Miss 'Mando," was a black woman past the prime of her life. The walls of her kitchen, a small three-sided shed set behind her house, were made of woven bamboo strips plastered with clay. The roof was thatch, the clean swept earthen floor packed hard by generations of bare feet. Smoke from countless fires had blackened the rafters, where strips of meat and the curling tails of pigs and oxen hung, spiced, salted, and curing. On the table where she peeled and washed her food was a huge clay bowl called a *yabbah;* under the table sat an elaborately carved hardwood mortar—a hollowed out wooden bowl with a heavy pestle. Drinking water was kept in a large thick jar of baked clay with a long spout like a teapot, made from an ancient design that somehow worked to keep the water fresh and cool.

Miss 'Mando looked down the valley that had been her home, and her fathers' before her, ever since they had abandoned the hot plains, the sugar plantations, and the cruel memories of slavery, to fashion for themselves a free existence in the rainforests of the high, rugged mountains.

The sun was setting behind Jancrow mountain, a purple blue shadow crept steadily down the valley. From the virgin forest— the standing woods—on the mountaintop, the plaintive lonely call of a peadove carried clear and tremulous in the still evening air, a single, pure, note of infinite and unfathomable sadness. Poor thing, thought Miss 'Mando, maybe she like me, calling her lost pickney.

Coming every evening as it did at the same time, just before the sudden tropical night fell over the forests, the peadove's cry was for her the sound of dusk. Some people said the bird was a ghost—a duppi—the minstrel and messenger of the night, ordered for some wrongdoing to signal the coming of its master each evening from the highest branch of the tallest mahogany tree on every mountaintop. The call came again—*co coo coooee.* The sound filled the shadowed stillness of the twilight, and as always reached Miss 'Mando's heart, causing her to tremble slightly with some ancient sadness of forgotten origin.

Her eyes, still clear and sharp, ranged over the valley, which in the evening shadow was blue black with a thick and luxuriant vegetation. A stranger might see there only an undifferentiated mass of lush tropical jungle. But to Miss 'Mando it was nothing of the kind—it was home and history, community and human industry, sweat, toil, and joy. Towering over everything was not jungle but trees left there for shade and someday timber. Mahoe, cedar, mahogany, fustic, trumpet, and the occasional dramatic blue-green bursts of bamboo. And food trees dense with leaves and hidden fruit—the purple leaved starapple, regal breadfruit, mango, pear, ackee, jackfruit—each with its unmistakable contours darkly silhouetted against the blue evening light. Here and there, the broad crowns of coconuts swaying precariously on impossibly slender sun-seeking trunks.

Beneath these giants she could make out the shrubs, the coca trees, apple trees, coffee patches, bananas, plaintain, and textured yam vines shooting up the poles that were their ladders to the sun. And hard against the earth the broad heartshaped leaves of coco yams, *baddoe, dasheen, yampee,* and patches of sorrel, of red peas and *gungo.* Occasionally through the canopy of leaves a tin roof glinted, or where nothing else could be seen, the smoke from a kitchen just like hers marked the place where people lived.

Between the various homesteads a network of footpaths and trails wound its intricate way, connecting homes and farms into a human community. The forest, that apparently random jungle, was in reality a testament to human tenacity and labor. For there were not to be found there six trees that did not contribute significantly to meeting the needs of the small community. They represented the product of a relationship evolved over many centuries, in a distant, almost forgotten country, between man and the land. The mountain valleys with the strong life-giving sun, heavy rains, and rich deep earth had been there fallow and waiting, it seemed, for them. And they had come—Akan, Ashanti, Yoruba, Mandingo, Wolof, Ibo, and Bantu—turning their backs on the slavery that had welded them together into a new people. They came with their ancient tools and processes, bring the foods they knew and their animals—goats, fowl, pigs, dogs, and a few asses and cows—and their sense of life and community, their songs, stories, and dances, and their sensitivity to life and respect for age and for manners. There on the steep sides of the valley all were transplanted and all grew and prospered.

They were almost self-sufficient. The few necessities that neither their land nor labor could provide—tools of steel and glass, cloth, oil for their lamps—they bought with money they earned by selling their surpluses at the government market in the nearest town. It was a new life in a different country but in its deepest rhythms and style it was not so different or so new.

As Miss 'Mando looked over the valley, her eyes kept returning to a place on the ridge where there was a gap in the trees. That was where her grandson would first appear on his way home. Where was that boy? It was just the other day, it seemed, he was a child. At suppertime she'd never have to call more than once and, before the echoes had died away, he'd be running up the path, eyes and face shining, breathless and shouting, closely trailed by a small big-eared mongrel known only as "Dawg."

"Supper ready, Mah? I hungry." His bright little eyes darting around the kitchen, fairly skitting with impatience to eat and tell "Mah" his adventures since lunchtime. Oh, but he was a blessed chile. Such an obedient and loving little boy. She would make him wash his hands and face in the enamel basin and say his grace and sit at the table.

"Bwai, you a somebody, y'know. I nah bring you up like no leggo beast." He would laugh at the notion of a boy growing up like a goat or donkey that had escaped to the standing woods, a "leggo beast" gone feral and totally uncapturable by his former owner.

But now she was no longer sure she could manage him any more. Pickney seemed to grow up so quickly now, filled with strange and alien notions, disrespectful of age and authority, seeming to share a rough and casual disdain for the manners and values of the elders. Now it was already night, dark and sudden and no idea where he was. Dinner was ready and no sign of Ivan. Her annoyance grew, as though to mask the glimmer of worry that tried to edge its way into her consciousness. What if he had fallen from a tree? Was lying somewhere with his back broken? He loved the river and spent long hours swimming and diving beneath the rocks with the sinuous grace of a water snake. But suppose something had happened? The rainy season was just past and the river was heavy and deep and could be treacherous.

"Serve him right if the supper cook 'way to porridge."

The kitchen was now filled with a rich yellow glow from the fire; ghostly shadows danced against the wattled walls. Miss 'Mando moved the pots back from the fire and with a machete reached into the glowing coals and retrieved a breadfruit that was in danger of burning. She set it on the edge of the coals to keep warm.

Yes, something was happening to that boy. And whatever it was, she didn't like it. The other day when she was at the river washing clothes he had been playing and wrestling with some of his friends in the water. She had not paid much attention to them until the noise changed. When she looked up Ivan was holding one of the boys round the neck and repeatedly pushing his face underwater. Each time the boy came up he screamed, "Chu, done no, Rhygin! Done no, man!"

She had stopped them immediately and summoned the victim to her. "What you name, bwai?"

"Me name Dudus, mam."

"Whe' you come from, son?"

"Blue Bay, mam." The boy was about Ivan's age and seemed mannerly enough. He said that he came from the neighboring town no more than five miles away.

"Who is yo' father, son?"

"Him name Maas' Burt, mam. Maas' Burt Thomas."

"The same one have a boat, and sell fish a Blue Bay market?"

"Yes'm."

"Ah know him. You come from good people, son. But tell me somethin'—what was that name ah hear you callin' Ivan?"

"Rhygin, mam. No so me hear the pickney dem call him."

"Well," she said sternly, "him name Ivan. Ah doan want hear you call him nuthin' else. All a you little bwais is too mannish."

Miss 'Mando did not know whether to be amused or concerned. There was something about Ivan that fit the name Rhygin. He was so full of life and energy, so full of questions. There was nothing that didn't interest him, and nothing that he didn't think he could master. Though he was quite small for his age, he seemed to give direction to his playmates. Maybe too much so for his own good. He was the first to swim across the river, to jump off the high bridge where the road crossed the riverbed. Lawd, what a fright! What a way did she frighten when the group of children tearful and screaming had come running up the river bank, where with a group of women she had been washing clothes. At first they thought that some animal was chasing the children. It was hard to tell just what they were saying, all running and screaming at once, but the sense of panic and disaster had been clear and the one word that stood out was Ivan, *Ivan*.

"Wait, what happen to the pickney dem?"

"Lawdo. Ivan dead."

"Miss 'Mando, Miss 'Mando, Ivan drownded!"

By the time she understood what they were saying—that her

grandson had jumped off the bridge into the deep powerful current of the river and failed to come up—and had had time to feel her stomach turn over and a heavy knifelike pain shoot into her chest, robbing her limbs of strength, so that she swayed and would have fallen without support from her friends; had just opened her mouth to give voice to the terrible throat-rending wail that greeted death when she heard:

"See 'im deh!"

She bit off her anguish, shut her mouth and blinked her eyes to clear the red haze from her vision. And when she could see again, there he was coming down the riverbank, a solitary, bedraggled, scrawny manchild limping painfully and reluctantly toward them, in manner and appearance suggesting nothing so much as a waterlogged mongoose.

She even forgot to be angry as she picked up the hem of her long dress and ran like a madwoman toward the small figure whose intense eyes shone with apprehension and a faint, tentative pride that only found expression after she had picked him up and squeezed him to her bosom.

"Ivan, Ivan, what Ah goin' to do with you?"

"Me do it! Ah said Ah could. And Ah *did* do it too." Eyes round and serious, he nodded sharply for emphasis.

"Bwai, you out to kill me, or what?"

She ordered him to pick her a bamboo cane, then holding him by the collar she marched him down to the road to see just what it was he had done. It was a strange procession that day. She, clutching the miscreant by the collar, accompanied by the women and the children, now serious and chastened, as much by the ominous switch that Miss 'Mando brandished as by the threats and maledictions of their own mothers.

"What a way pickney can rude, eh?"

"Ah tell you, if fe me pickney evah try anything like dis, Ah beat him till him fenneh."

"But that boy can't alright? Ah wonder if is obeah,° them obeah him."

This comment, said with an undercurrent of malicious speculation, did not escape Miss 'Mando's acute ear, which was attuned to even the slightest trace of any derogatory reference to her person or family. She was too distressed to respond, but she marked the originator for future reference. The suggestion that baleful spiritual forces were at work on her grandson was not one

° Obeah: malign use of spiritual forces.

she normally would permit to pass without vigorous challenge.

Soon the little band came to the bridge. It stood some thirty feet above the swirling dark green water where the river spilled its accumulated force through a narrow ravine into the sea. The swiftest and deepest point of the entire river, it was a place invested in legend with mysterious and supernatural presences.

"Dere," the children cried, pointing to the highest point, "is up dere so him jump off." They said it with a mixture of self-righteous accusation and no little awe.

Miss 'Mando saw in her mind's eye the small figure, solitary and determined, standing up there on the railing of the bridge. It was then, as she stood there holding Ivan's collar looking from water below to the bridge above, that her anger began to change to something else. Could the bwai be indeed mad? Surely no pickney, without being chased, without the spur of panic or madness, could summon the nerve or desperation that would cause him to launch himself into the air and the fast silent waters below.

"Mi Gawd." It was the same woman who had speculated on the possibility of obeah, but now there was no malice in her voice, only a quiet wonder. "What a way de pickney have heart, eh?"

"Well, Missis, dem say if you born to heng, you can't drown," said another.

And Ivan, somewhat frightened by the experience and the effect it had on the assembly, recounted how he had held his breath as the rushing water swirled around him, feeling himself swept along far below the surface by a current more powerful than anything he had ever felt, until he surfaced not far from a sandbank a hundred yards below the bridge. It was the pride that did it: the pride Miss 'Mando saw struggling unsuccessfully to hide beneath a show of penitence decided her response. In her fear and anger she beat him like she had never expected to beat any living thing, especially her own grandson—but even after her hand, almost of its volition, grew still, as though conceding the futility of any further beating—she knew that he had learned nothing.

No, him spirit really strong, she thought, sitting there in the glow of the fire, it really strong. But him is not a bad pickney at all, y'know. Him is just one of dem people who tink say them can box-box up the world an' spit in life face. But him wi' learn. She felt like the mother pig who, when asked by her pickney why her mouth was so long, merely grunted and said, "Aai mi pickney, you young but you wi' learn."

Deep in thought she got up, and almost absentmindedly took

her machete and pushed the fire together. As the rekindled flame sprang up it cast a red glow over her seamed black face. "Aaiie, mi pickney, you wi' soon learn."

Pickney can be funny sometimes. Where them get such a name for Ivan, like *Rhygin?* Did they really know what it mean? It wasn't a word you heard so much any more, only from old people. Raging, strong but foolish too, overconfident, not knowing where the limits were. Hmm, maybe the pickney did say true, the bwai had something in him that was rhygin. Mi father used to like that word. In every litter there was always one—as soon as 'im could walk good 'im be bringing fight to some larger animal. Strong natured before 'im time, poor precocious little t'ing you see 'im running up behind 'im own mother and mount her, 'im little backside just a' windin' and a' grindin' air, till she would get tired of the foolishness and jus' lick 'im down. But soon he'd be back again to jump on her, or one of his litter mates, just frantic and futile. And Maas' Joe, her father, God res' him spirit, would burst out with his bellydeep laugh and say:

"Look 'pon de little man hog (or ram goat or buck rabbit), look how him *rhygin.*"

"Is only a beast," her mother would sniff, "but you should know better."

Miss 'Mando smiled at the memory. So that's what them calling Ivan, eh? *Rhygin?* Well wherever 'im is, 'im grandfather must be killing himself with laugh. But the boy getting big. Only hope 'im not out there troubling somebody gal pickney. If Ah ever know that is so 'im doing, the kind a lick Ah give 'im, 'im piss straight like man rat. She laughed at her own crudeness, for she was in all things a moderate and respectable woman. Then she rose to go get her lamp from the house.

. . .

Ivan had never intended to be so late. In the first place he never liked to get Miss 'Mando angry or upset. In the second place—and this was by far the most pressing reason—the darkness of the valley was truly frightening, especially before the moon rose. A variety of spirits roamed the darkness and an encounter with one or more of them was to be dreaded. There were duppies, disembodied spirits of dead people, who could take any form they wished, a black dog, or a *pattu,*° or more commonly a human

---

° *Pattu:* screech owl.

form hideously disfigured. But you could always tell them by the sickening, nauseous smell that foreshadowed their appearance. When they struck, the victim was never the same. Like Maas' Zekiel, whose family found him lying unconscious beneath that trumpet tree coming up, his face twisted permanently from the force of the duppi's blow. Ever since that time his speech had been thick and he was subject to fits, unpredictable and frightening paroxysms that rendered him helpless. He had spent much money on visits to a famous obeah man but to no avail.

Ivan clutched the two large sea mullets and the string of breadfruit he was carrying, and walked faster. He was over the second rise now and for a few yards the path would be level. Everything was changed, mysterious and frightening in the darkness. A cool mountain breeze blew over his sweaty face and a tremor ran down his back. For courage he began singing—one of Miss 'Mando's beloved long-meter sankey ° hymns:

> Ah been down in the valley
> For a very long time
> But Ah ain't get weary yet.

The trumpet tree seemed larger, more menacing, its canopy of enormous textured leaves dark and unnaturally mobile. Ivan's eyes strained to pierce the gloom. His breath came in jerks, but he continued the song until the tune was reduced to shambles and noise and then silence. He sniffed deeply. The air was pure and sweet, filled with the natural gentle odors of the tropical night. When Maas' Zekiel had been found, so rumor had it, the strong, unmistakable smell of fermenting hog swill had hung like a cloud around the place. Eyes fixed on the tree Ivan advanced stiffly, the effort to control his impulse to run giving his gait the rigidity of a robot's.

"Do Jesus, just mek Ah reach home quick, Ah never be dis late again." He was almost past the tree now, containing with a massive effort of will the nervous tension that pulsed through his body and pushed him toward a state of mindless, instinctive, running, bawling terror. The motion in the tree seemed greater. There seemed to be a swaying independent of any wind. But Ivan was winning. He was walking past boldly and, so he thought, without visible signs of fear. But he should be singing, shouting, announcing his presence so that whatever was there would not know he

° Sankey: after Ira David Sankey, author of a popular hymnal. A common name for a hymn book was a "sankey."

was afraid. He wished he had a drum or even a tin pail. A song came to his lips, he bawled out *"Rock of Ages . . ."* and that was as far as he got. The topmost branches exploded in a sudden eruption of sound and fluttering. A shadowy shape rose from the tree with a raucous and discordant shriek: a family of guinea fowl, those noisy and contentious birds, had taken to roosting there.

But it was only when Ivan could see the glow of Miss 'Mando's fire that anything resembling coherence returned to him. As he climbed the last hill, reduced to a walk by the sheer steepness of the path, he fixed his eyes on the comforting glow from the kitchen. Strange, after the first few panic-stricken leaps he'd known what it was—the continuing clamor behind him was unmistakable—yet he could not stop running; once the dam broke, his legs no longer obeyed him. There was a strange pleasure, a release in just giving himself over to terror, to the blind unthinking energy that swept him over the path. What a strange thing fear was, "Big Fraid" as the people called it. As they said: "When Big Fraid tek man, him run from pickney an' buck down Bullcow."

But if it wasn't for that guinea fowl, Ah woulda mek it alright, he thought. Miss 'Mando loved guinea-fowl stew. He would surprise her with one real soon. "Yes," he vowed, "bet you me's the last one you going frighten so." It was funny, though, once he'd stopped running he was no longer afraid.

It had been a great day. Dudus's father had taken them out in his canoe to go pull his fishpots. Ivan had swum and played on the beach before, but to go out in a boat far beyond the reef? Dudus was sure lucky, he could do that every day. On the way back, Maas' Burt had allowed them to swim on the reef through the sparkling clear water. The wonder of it all! Dudus's father had a box with a glass bottom, and when he put it in the water you could see the floor of the sea, the strange shapes and colors of the coral. It was a new and different world of pure white sand with strangely shaped formations in purple, blue, and red. And thousands of fishes—spotted, striped, round, long, red, blue, and such colors as were never seen on land. There was so much that he couldn't look at everything at once. He could hardly wait to show his grandmother the two fat yellowtails Maas' Burt had sent and to tell her of this strange new world he had seen. He had decided right there, sitting in the boat that bobbed and rose with each successive wave, looking at Maas' Burt skillfully guiding the canoe, its bottom covered with wriggling fish and crusty crawling lobsters, that he'd be a fisherman, too.

Maas' Burt gave a slow knowing smile. "Bwai, you never see anything like dis, eh?"

Ivan could only shake his head in awe.

"Wonderful, Maas' Burt said, "it wonderful to raas,° man."

And the two boys and the man were united in a shared wonder and a sense of great well-being. The next moment a large wave hurled the boat upward over a submerged coral ledge and Ivan shouted with surprise as he wiped the salt spray from his eyes. Maas' Burt, laughing with pleasure, wrestled the small craft into the spray.

"Dat wonderful too," he drawled softly, wiping his eyes.

The sun was midway down toward the horizon when they dragged the boat up onto the warm sand. Ivan moved as if in a dream, his face and eyes glowing with the marvels of the day. After the constant restlessness of the sea, the land felt strange under his feet. The ruddy afternoon played over the small cove, bathing the boats and the sparkling ocean in warm golden light. Ivan was drunk with sensation, feeling the warm sand coating his ankles, the hot glow of the sun on his shoulders, and watching the geometric shadows of huge fish traps and hanging nets, the richly colored and strangely shaped fish that Maas' Burt sorted, identifying each kind, explaining their value, habits, and how they should be handled. It was so much to learn, maybe Maas' Burt would take him on and teach him the trade of the sea. He paid close attention to everything. Groups of people, other fishermen, women and children wandered by to see the catch. They praised Maas' Burt's luck, exclaiming over some of the rarer species that the sea had offered up. Ivan was fascinated by two in particular— a strange creature they called a "sea puss" with a round body surrounded by eight long tentacles, and an ugly grayish fish covered with vicious-looking spines, which without warning puffed itself up until it resembled an inflated hog's bladder with thorns.

When Dudus's father had finished he had three piles: the bigger table fish which would go to market, a pailful of smaller fryers, and a variety of odd fish of lesser value which Dudus and Ivan were allowed to distribute to the children standing around. Trying their best to look nonchalant but bursting with importance, they presided over the rapidly diminishing pile. It was then that Ivan's commitment to the life of a fisherman was confirmed

---

° Raas: a corruption of "your ass," used as an adjective or expletive; not to be confused with Ras (for Ras Tafari).

beyond question, though an hour later this commitment was to undergo a serious blow.

The fisherman's knife flashed in the afternoon sun as he scaled and gutted two plump sea mullets. He worked quickly, whipping the entrails into the air where they were caught by circling seabirds.

"Ivan, come yeh," Maas' Burt said.

"Yes, sah?"

The man looked at him closely. "So . . . you a Miss 'Mando granpickney? What a way you favor her to death? Ah want you to tek these two mullet to you granny, tell her Maas' Burt sen' dem wid respeck."

"T'ank you, sah." Ivan picked up the fish.

"Dudus, tek the sprats to the café. Tell Miss Ida Ah wi' see her later."

The fisherman picked up the big basket for the market and with a grunt heaved it onto his head. The two boys watched him walk down the beach, the heavy basket steady and unwavering over his erect back and strong ebony shoulders that gleamed in the sun. As he went clouds of smoke from his pipe billowed out around his head, and above him a couple of sea-hawks squeaked and gibbered, circled and dipped, but never had the nerve to actually steal a fish.

"You wan' come with me, Ivan?" Dudus asked.

"Where you going?"

"The café. You no hear whe' Pa say?"

Ivan hesitated. He was reluctant to end the warm, magical glow of the afternoon, but he knew it would take some time to get back up the hill to his home, and he didn't want night to catch him.

"Bet you nevah go a café yet? Come on man, Miss Ida have a music box up deh."

Dudus's manner was mysterious and somewhat superior as they made their way down the beach, slowly at first while he explained how Miss Ida had come from town to establish the first café ever known in the district, a place where some people went at night to drink rum and beer and to dance to calypso and other music that came over the music box. Dudus's eyes sparkled in his freckled brown face. "Some a the Christian people in Blue Bay, the postmistress and teacher wife and so, them no like Miss Ida." Here his eyes grew big and his voice sank in volume but increased in intensity. "Dem say she a *sportin' lady.*" He peered at Ivan, nodding his head for emphasis.

"Oh," said Ivan, then aware of the inadequacy of his response, "that awright."

"Yes," said Dudus, "dass jus' whe' me father say too."

Then their pace became more normal—they ran on, hollering, throwing stones into the breakers and sand at each other. But Ivan's thoughts raced. Drinking rum and dancing to city music, eh? The prospect seemed entirely as attractive as it was mysterious and certainly forbidden. The boys came around the curve of a headland and a little bay stretched before them. They charged shouting at a flock of vultures gathered around a pile of fish offal left reeking on the beach. "Jancro, jancro," they shouted, sending the large buzzards running, hissing, and puking, with bald heads bobbing awkwardly before they could launch themselves into flight on their creaking rusty-black wings. The boys stopped breathless, watching the ominous black scavenger birds cruising in large graceful circles on the sea breeze, their red heads glowing in the sun.

"An' you know what?" Dudus said. "I love Miss Ida. When Ah get big Ah going to beg her."

"Beg her what?" Ivan demanded.

"Beg her what? Beg her what?" With each repetition Dudus's tone was more scornful and incredulous. "You say beg her what? To married, a course."

Properly chastened, Ivan said nothing. Look 'pon Dudus though? Talking about married! Who woulda want 'im with 'im face round and speckle like booby egg? Always acting like 'im nice jus' because 'im live a Blue Bay. Talking 'bout him going married sporting lady? Spitefully Ivan timed his move and gently nudged his friend's foot, tripping him and causing the pail of fish to spill onto the sand.

As they gathered them up and washed the sand off, he asked, "What's a sporting lady?"

"Wait?" Dudus said, twisting his face into a mask of astonishment and contempt. "You is a *bungo?* You no know what sporting woman is?"

"You know?" Ivan challenged.

Dudus shook his head in disbelief and lofty contempt, as though in wonder that anyone could be so backward as not to know what a sporting woman was, and even more incredible, could accuse him, Dudus, of a similar ignorance. He stalked off as though he couldn't condescend to entertain such impertinence.

"Ah notice you don't say nutten," Ivan crowed.

"Me no have time fe play with pickney." He flung the response over his shoulder without breaking either stride or dignity. That was too much for Ivan. First by calling him a *bungo*—an ignorant and unsophisticated country bumpkin—and now a child, Dudus was attacking both his wit and his maturity.

"Who you a call pickney?"

Something in Ivan's voice told Dudus he had better steer the conversation into other, less hazardous directions.

"Is only pickney don't know what sporting woman is—the best woman in dis worl'. Every man love a sporting woman, but is not every man dem love." He started to add, for emphasis and to strengthen what he felt might be some weakness in his explanation: "Is only pickney don't know that." But, as the people said, "Coward man keep sound bones," so he did not. In any event Ivan appeared if not entirely satisfied with the explanation, at least willing to let it drop. So they proceeded.

But Ivan's curiosity had been pricked. Time was no longer important, nor was Dudus's newfound superior manner. He had to see for himself this café, and this mysteriously alluring "sporting" woman who had excited such differing reactions from Dudus on the one hand and the postmistress on the other.

Miss Ida's Rough Rider Café was definitely not what he had expected, but then what had he expected? Dudus's explanation hadn't been too exact. The café stood on the beach in a grove of coconut trees, the trunks of which were whitewashed to a height of about eight feet. It seemed like a huge building to him, and was open to the air with low cement-block walls from which jutted the posts holding up the thatch roof. The walls appeared multi-colored and as the boys drew nearer Ivan could see that there were people painted on them; women in long brightly colored dresses danced with men in shirts equally bright against the white background. They were people such as he had never seen before: they were black but the lips and cheeks of the women were blood red and their shoes were green or yellow or blue, as were the men's. When they got closer Ivan saw the figures were all grinning, though the various positions in which they were frozen seemed to him difficult and even painful if not outright impossible.

"*TChuh*," he exclaimed with an air of dismissal, "dem favor duppi."

"You is a real hillside bungo. After is not so duppi look."

"How you know whe' duppi look like? You ever seen one yet?"

"See dem yes," Dudus muttered as positively as he could.
"See what? You too lie. Whe' you ever see duppi?"

> *Dudus lie,*
> *mouth dry,*
> *suck matter*
> *outa donkey eye.*

Ivan sang tauntingly, savoring his small victory as they approached the entrance. He resolved to act as though cafés were entirely commonplace in his experience, and maintained his posture of exaggerated nonchalance when they entered the cool dim room with its smooth concrete floor covered liberally with red ochre. After the warmth of the sand the floor felt cool and smooth underfoot; he had to resist an urge to slide over the strange surface.

The café had electricity and a row of colored bulbs ran down the middle of the room. On both sides were tables with chairs made of wooden kegs cut to leave a back rest and a seat. There was the sweet wet smell that Ivan associated with rum shops. At a table at the far back a group of men were playing checkers and drinking white rum.

"What you bwais want? Oh, is you Dudus." The voice came from a figure moving out from behind the bar and wiping her hands on a towel. "What you bring fe me?"

"Some fish me faddah sen', Miss Ida."

Even before Dudus spoke Ivan knew that this could only be Miss Ida. She was a woman, as were his grandmother and her friends, but there the similarity ended. He couldn't take his eyes off her. Her lips were red, and when she smiled, as she seemed to do a lot, there was a flash of gold. A thick wave of black hair swung down to her shoulders, which were bare. And what shoulders they were—wide, smooth, black—and below them, outlined clearly under a tight red blouse, depended two round outthrust globes fighting against the fabric and coming to perfect points some distance in advance of the rest of her. When she walked her hips, which flared dramatically from a tightly belted waist, rolled with a majestic rhythm as though to call attention to themselves. And indeed, the checker game was temporarily suspended when she emerged from behind the bar.

"Lawd," one of the men breathed reverentially, but loud enough for the tribute to carry, "what a woman walk nice, sah?" He shook his head slowly in rapt devotion.

"Then, why 'im sen' you?" she asked Dudus. " 'Im couldn't bring it himself?" She accompanied the question with a toss of her head and a low musical laugh.

"Him say him wi' see you later, mam," Dudus explained.

"An who this?" She nodded in Ivan's direction. "I don't believe I know this little man?"

Ivan's eyes had not left her face. He didn't think he could speak.

"Is mi friend, mam—" Dudus began, but Ivan's voice cut him off.

"Mi name Ivan, mam. But dem call me Rhygin."

"Oh Gawd," Miss Ida bellowed. "If Ah laugh Ah dead." Her laughter came from deep in her throat, loud and easy, filling every corner of the big room.

"Bwai can't even piss straight," one of the men said. "Talk 'bout 'im *rhygin.*"

"Lawd, don't mek Ah laugh," Miss Ida implored. "Ah can't stan' it. What dem call you, sah?"

"Dem call me Rhygin," he said firmly.

"So . . . you *rhygin?*" Her voice was low and thoughtful, teasing as though she were contemplating this information. "Hm, Ah believe you too. If, ha ha, if you was little bigger Ah woulda have to see how *rhygin* you is. He he heeh. But look what I live to see, though eh?" And she dissolved in laughter again. "Both a you come on." She walked her swaying, sinuous walk back to a glass case on the bar. "I don't know when las' I laugh so good. Come yah, Maas' Rhygin; you too, Dudus. Ah must give *unu*° something, eh?" "Well—speak up," she commanded. "What you want? Unu want fish? Jerk pork? *Bullah,* coconut drops, *toto?*" As she spoke she indicated the goodies stacked in the case; small crisply fried fish, peppery and hot with the heads still on; a lump of pork, equally spicy, smoked black for days over a green wood fire; the sweet cakes known as *bullah* and *toto* and candy made from coconut. "Talk up, what unu want, Rhygin?" She chuckled over the name again and rescued them from the necessity of choice by loading a tin plate with pieces of everything in the case.

They sat at a table eating, shrewdly measuring the diminishing pile of food. Ivan was trying to decide between a large tempting fishhead or an equally attractive lump of candy. If Dudus

° *Unu:* plural *you,* like the Southern *you'all* or *y'all.*

went for a bullah, then he could have the fish, yet how to get the candy . . .

"But wait? How Ah could evah forget?" Miss Ida's voice from behind the bar cut into his calculations. "Two sporting man like unu can't eat without music, eh? Lawd!" She continued doing something to a little box behind the bar as she fussed at herself with a pretended distress that thoroughly amused the checker players. "Lawd but how Ah could forget eh? Missa Rhygin, you mustn't mind, y' hear, sah. Old age is a bad thing, it worse dan obeah. Gentlemen, you music."

And the café filled with music. Or rather, to Ivan, the café filled with Miss Ida around whom throbbing, heady, erotically insistent rhythms swirled and played. The big lady was light on her feet; the carnal exuberance of her breasts and hips seemed to engulf him. She seemed transfigured, not unlike the ladies at Miss 'Mando's pocomania° meetings, but the dreamy expression on her face, the smile on her painted lips were not very spiritual. Nor was her sweet, heavy perfume as she danced around them. Ivan's senses were assaulted in a new way. This was city music, café music, the music of pleasure and fleshly delight, and Miss Ida was its incarnation. She was a dancer moving effortlessly with the melody, anticipating the brassy variations of the trombone, but always coming back to the heavy rolling drumbeat that seemed to drive and control the bumping, grinding motions of those massive, insistent hips.

> *Oh Miss Ida*
> *Don't you lift up any widah!*
> *Seem to me that you set pon glidah!*
> *Oh Miss Ida . . .*
> *You a real rough ridah.*

With a final challenging, shuddering roll of her middle, Miss Ida's dance came to an end with the music. The café became quiet, echoingly quiet, as though some dynamic and elemental force had swept through and then was suddenly and abruptly gone.

"Ah see say you like that, eh Missa Rhygin?"

Ivan nodded his head, speechless.

° Pocomania: African-inspired religious sect noted for possession by spirits during ceremonies.

"Come back when you get little bigger, and we wi' see how you can dance. I believes you going be a dancing man, ha hah."

He was almost home now, crossing the low stone wall that marked the beginning of Miss 'Mando's home place. He had only to follow the path under the giant breadfruit trees planted by the first of his family. In the damp shade of those trees grew coffee plants and cocoa planted by his grandfather, and in the small area around the house the fruitful trees that were a botanical testament to the passing of generations of his ancestors. But Ivan hardly noticed the trees as he passed. Taking their presence and offerings for granted he passed by quickly, somewhat anxiously, knowing that his grandmother's concern frequently expressed itself in painful ways.

Were he a little older with more knowledge of history and a sense of irony, he might have reflected that no land was naturally so benevolent and hospitable to humankind. Then he might have understood that he was walking through history, that each tree represented the foresight and agency of a departed forebear, and the very availability of the species represented the supreme irony. In the days when sugar was akin to gold, and the metaphor for wealth in European society was "wealthy as a West Indian planter," that same planter class, anxious to increase profits, used the Royal Navy to scour the Empire for plants that would feed their slaves and so lessen their dependence on imported food. They had succeeded too well for their own interests, bringing yams, ackees, melons, assorted tubers and peas from Africa, mangoes from India, breadfruit, apples, and coconuts from the far reaches of the Pacific, finally bringing to the land the riches that helped to end slavery and their world. For the Africans, taking seeds and cuttings, had simply left the plantations to establish free communities in the hills.

But, young and untutored, Ivan passed heedless. The sweet rhythms of the drum and the intoxicating tunes raced around his head. He would be a singer of songs, a music-maker, a dancer. It was a strange and mysterious world, this city where such music came from. He didn't know how it would come about or when. Still he had been called. Meanwhile there was Miss 'Mando to be faced. He would tell her everything—except about the café.

But the kitchen was empty, the fire glowing red, scarcely more than a bed of coals. A tin dish was covered up beside the coals, a bad omen. It meant that his grandmother had eaten and retired, leaving his supper there to keep warm or get cold. He hung the fish where they would be cooled by the mountain breeze, put his breadfruit on the table, and approached the little house. A light shone through the window. He climbed the steps, tentatively opened the door, and stood looking in. The room was lit by a lamp. Miss 'Mando sat at the table next to the lamp squinting grimly into the open Bible that she held before her. In her seamed, black face her eyes were impassive; only the tight line of her mouth and steady rocking of her body betrayed her anger. A fireless pipe was clenched between her teeth and she seemed totally oblivious to his presence as her eyes searched the pages before her. The silence hung between them; Ivan's spirit quailed. He had expected a scolding, shouts, even a beating, but not this.

"Betake dy footsteps from dy neighbor's door, lest he tire of dee." Her voice was cold and rasping as the scrape of a coffin against the sides of the grave. She gave no sign of having seen him. For a moment Ivan could not even be sure she had spoken, that the sound, so sepulchral and grim, had not in fact come from her shadow that flickered against the wall, outlining her shape like some hovering spirit. "Ye children, be obedient to dem that are dy parents in de Lawd, that dy days may be long . . ." She continued to rock steadily, the gigantic shadow faithfully keeping time.

Ivan stood there in confusion, a guilty desolation sweeping over him. His grandmother was like a stranger, mechanically rocking, her face an inscrutable mask under the turbanlike head-cloth she wore to bed. Timidly he stepped into the room.

"You supper in the kitchen. Go get it. And wash you hands and foot dem?"

When he returned she seemed normal, her eyes following him as he entered on silent, tentative feet. Teary and apprehensive he sat trying to eat and be inconspicuous at the same time.

When she spoke her voice was normal, quietly and deceptively conversational. "Den, where you bin so long, Ivan?"

He told her, omitting the visit to Miss Ida.

"Oh? An' is you one come up de mountain?"

"Yes'm."

"Oh? You one . . . You do well, hm—and what you see?"

Ivan looked up puzzled. "Ah doan see nutten, mam."

"You doan see nutten'? You doan see nutten'? Keep it up. Tek care what you going to see don't blin' you."

The food was like dust in Ivan's mouth and the effort to swallow almost gagged him.

"You choke? You don't choke yet! Whatever you looking for will soon fin' you. But, it don't look like you hungry? You must be eat out, eh?"

"No'm." Ivan kept his eyes in the plate.

"You keep it up, bwai! Walk late! Love night—everyt'ing wi' happen to you. You hear me? Mark me word dem—I say *everyt'ing* wi' happen to you."

"Yes'm."

"Don't bother sit dere and play-play wid the food. Gwan to you bed—and say you prayers too."

Ivan crept away with a murmured good night and went to the corner where a straw mattress lay on a low wooden frame. He quickly undressed and put on a sleeping robe, the result of three holes in a flour sack made soft by countless scrubbings on a broad rock by the side of the river. Miss 'Mando sat watching him and the hangdog way he kept his eyes averted. Maybe this was the way to handle him, by keeping him off balance. Beatings only seemed to make him rebellious and resentful but her studied and withdrawn coldness did seem to chasten him.

She sat motionless in her chair, her eyes fixed on the small figure as he swiftly and silently prepared for sleep. The sounds of the night—the croaking of lizards and tree toads, and the high whistling of an insect chorus—came softly into the room. As she watched his slender black body, luminous in the yellow lamplight and velvet black in the shadows, her heart was pained by the strong but vulnerable beauty of his young life. He was the last of her issue. His mother, her only daughter that had lived to adulthood, was somewhere in the city. The only evidence of her existence, apart from Ivan, was a few letters and an occasional money order. The city, that alien, distant and unknown world, had taken Miss 'Mando's four sons, spewing them out into an even more distant and unknowable world. Rafael, the eldest, drowned when the ship taking him to England to fight the Germans went down. Isaac gone to Cuba to cut cane over fifteen years ago and no word for years. She knew he was dead, rest his soul. One night, years ago, she awoke cold and sweating in the hot darkness, with a dull weight laying on all her limbs. She felt his spirit take leave of her. He was gone, the second born. She knew, felt in her blood and spirit, the loss of the life she had brought. And she turned her head to the wall and quietly hummed the wild, mournful songs of death. The last she had heard of James he was in jail. Life imprisonment for killing that half-white, white-livered slut he had married. And the youngest she had buried herself. They had brought his broken body home to the mountain after he had been gored and trampled on the estate where he had sought work as a cattle drover—the only one she had had the meager satisfaction of burying decently, down beyond the stone wall, in the little plot under the giant breadfruit tree where the graves of her parents and grandparents lay. And now there was only Ivan, not yet twelve years old, and showing the familiar restlessness and hunger for roaming. Better, God forbid, that she put him in the ground next to his fathers than live to see him wander away heedless into the world's dangers. With a sigh she reached over and blew out the lamp. Instead of the familiar and comfortable darkness she was startled to find the room silvered with the pale ghostly light of a full moon.

Sleep would not come to Ivanhoe. He lay still, listening to his grandmother's breathing. Through closed lids he felt the lamp go out. Over the monotonous drone of the insects and the croaking of the small reptiles, he heard the hunting call of the pattu, a bird of ill-omen, people said. But he didn't listen to the sounds of the night. Pounding in his ears were the erotic drums of the café, the tune repeating itself hypnotically in his head. He didn't even smell the pungent khus-khus roots Miss 'Mando had put into the straw of the mattress. Still in his nostrils was the heavy and exciting perfume of Miss Ida, who moved sensuously and effortlessly on the swell of the music as the small canoe had ridden on the waves. There was no sleep in the little house for a long time that night. Miss 'Mando was troubled; she didn't know that the thing she feared, the thing that would take Ivan away, as all her children had been taken, had come to him that day, but still, her spirit was very uneasy.

Next morning Ivan was up before his grandmother. He dressed silently and crept out of the house into a spectacular tropical morning. The grass beneath his feet was cool and soaked with dew. A light mist, soon to be burned off by the sun, draped the mountain in silvery mystery. Down the valley in the distance the sea sparkled in a misty sunlight. In the trees around the house, small, brightly colored birds flittered and chirped. He ran down to the kitchen and took a basin full of corn and fed the chickens that came running out of the surrounding underbrush, small, tough little birds of bright iridescent plumage, descended from Spanish fighting birds and a bald-headed African strain whose antecedents were lost in history. Then he took the machete and chopped a pile of grass and savory bush for the family of goats his grandmother kept for milk and meat. He checked the water tins. There was enough water for a day's needs. Then he took the tin of boiled hog feed—the peelings of bananas and yams and other kitchen trimmings—out to a small shed where a huge sow, her belly heavy with young, was tethered. By the time he got back, still laughing at the way the pig slobbered and grunted over the slop, his grandmother was up. She stood in the kitchen doorway, an amused smile on her face as she watched him run up the path.

"Ivan, what Ah goin' do wid you?"

"What, mam?" He stopped, confused, checking mentally to see what his crime might be this time. "I was jus' feeding the sow. . . ."

"I know," she said, "but what you forget?"

"Nothin'. Ah don' forget nothin', mam. Ah feed the chicken dem an the goat too."

"What a way you helpful dis mawnin'! Don't think Ah don't be grateful." She was laughing quietly. "But why you don't go back and bring back the hog slop tin, eh?" She hugged him and rubbed his head. "Run go get it," she said, "an' when you come you get a good breakfast."

They ate in the kitchen, Ivan sitting on the edge of the wooden mortar and drumming his heels against its side. She pushed before him a hot mug of chocolate, rich with goat's milk and oily from the unrefined chocolate beans that came from their own trees. Miss 'Mando piled a tin plate with fried yam and breadfruit, topped off with a large piece of fish fried in coconut oil. "Eat hearty," she said. "Today we going to the groun'."

Ivan liked to go with her to the little piece of land where they grew their food. Already he was quite skillful with the machete and hoe and knew how to plant and care for the different food plants they grew. While they ate the sun came over the mountain, and they could feel the chill leave the air. He rambled on about the sea, and the strange and marvelous fishes he had seen, and about the colors and shapes of the coral. As she ate and watched the intense expressions play across his face, Miss 'Mando felt peaceful. She had forgotten after all that he was only a little bwai, a small pickney. This one would stay and be a comfort to her in her old age.

"The sow was alright?" she asked.

"Yes, Granny. Look like she soon drop."

"Boy, how you can know dat?"

"How you mean, Granny? Me know when her time come."

"Well, you right. You is a bright pickney. If you behave yourself, Ah wi' gi' you one of the litter."

"You mean fe meself?" He jumped off the mortar and ran toward her with his eyes shining.

"Yes, you getting big now. You can care you own animal. An' I will give you one of the goat kid dem too. You not too young to start. What? Bwai, is what you want?" Ivan easily eluded her half-hearted attempt to push aside his kiss.

The old lady wrapped some food in a broad coco leaf and placed the neat parcel in a large round *bankra*, a basket with an indentation in the middle of the bottom. Then she carefully arranged her machete and digging fork in the basket so as to achieve a balance, pulled on a pair of high black rubber boots which were traditional wear during the wet season, stuck her lighted pipe in her mouth, and was ready. After she placed the basket on her head she called Ivan, who had gone up to the government road to fill his pockets with pebbles for his slingshot. He came running back, picked up a basket that was a smaller replica of his grandmother's, and they set off down the little mountain track, the bankras framing their heads like gigantic Mexican sombreros.

At the bottom of the hill their path led into a wider track that ran down the valley, connecting with other small paths to other homes. On this wide path they met people similarly equipped, going to their own plots. They greeted by name everyone they passed.

"Mornin' Miss 'Mando. Glad to see you looking so well dis Lawd's day mornin'."

"Morning, Maas' Joe. And how is youself?"

"Healthy, thank de Lawd."

"An' you people dem?"

"Nothin' bothah them except hungry."

"Well," said Miss 'Mando, eyeing the huge bunch of bananas that Maas' Joe was balancing on his head, "hungry better dan sickness."

"Is true, praise de Lawd."

"Well, 'member me to dem."

"Ah be please to do dat. Walk good."

Ivan trotted on ahead, searching the surrounding trees for birds, the prey for his slingshot. He never failed to greet any adult he met with the proper respect. Boys his own age were greeted according to their status, friend or foe. If the relationship was not friendly and Miss 'Mando out of earshot, there would be an exchange of unflattering anatomical references.

"Beg you draw in you mouth mek me pass. You mout long like fe hog!"

"Chu, you head favor jancro pickney!"

None of this took place if the parents were close by. Girls were passed with an aloof and impervious dignity.

Invariably, when the person Miss 'Mando encountered was not a close neighbor, Ivan would be brought back for inspection: "Wait, Miss 'Mando? Den that mus' be you gran'son Ah jus' pass? What a way 'im grow out of me eye! Call 'im mek me know 'im."

Beaming with pride she would call Ivan back to be examined and commented on.

"Lawd, what a way 'im grow big? But Ah would know 'im anywhere, 'im is the dead stamp of 'im grandfather."

And Miss 'Mando would continue on, assured that should the boy be in difficulty or need, there was one more adult obliged by custom and friendship to come to his aid.

The plot was a large one for one woman and a small boy. But Miss 'Mando was known to be hard working and as strong as most men. She quickly checked to see if any stray animals had gotten onto the field, or as had been increasingly the case in recent days, human predators—"reaping," as the Bible said, "where they had not sown." But everything was intact. The yam vines, fat and healthy, thrust upward toward the sun on their tall poles. The sweet potatoes were lush and green, and the coco plants with their broad succulent heart-shaped leaves were bigger than she had seen them in many seasons. As she looked over the work of her hands a great contentment spread within her. Surely, as her daddy, dead and gone, used to say, this was a blessed land, rewarding the honest farmer. Ivan followed her on the tour of inspection, his comments matching hers, and again she marveled at the brightness and good sense of her grandson. They worked steadily, weeding, hoeing, occasionally digging into a yamhill to see the progress of the giant tubers swelling beneath the moist black earth. Caught in the familiar rhythm of the soil, the comforting damp smell rich in her nose, Miss 'Mando began to sing softly.

Suddenly she looked up from where she was squatting before a mound of earth, her skirts hiked up over her knees and bunched down between them modestly. Some small distance away Ivan, unaware of her attention, was singing a worksong. Pickney, dem full of surprise, she thought. She hadn't known that Ivan could sing that way. She wiped her face with a cloth, and began to clean her earthstained hands, listening to his pure young voice playing with the melody and styling it. But it was a different style—the melody and the words of the song were there, but not like she had ever heard them. The boy, skillfully excavating a yam root with his machete, was—apparently unconsciously—teasing and shaping the tune, biting off phrases, elongating notes, creating a new version. She listened for a minute until Ivan, conscious of the silence, looked up.

"Wait, Ivan. Is where you learn to sing so?"

He looked embarrassed. "Nobody learn me, Granny, is jus' so me feel it."

"Well . . . you good." She looked proud and thoughtful for a minute, then continued: "But singing is fe bird. Man mus' work. Nothing say you can't work and sing too but you *mus' work.* Unless—" She paused and looked at him searchingly. "You wan' turn preacher? How you would like dat—to be shepherd of a band?"

Ivan smiled and began to preach and whoop, punctuating each phrase with deep grunts and eloquent little steps. It was an accurate, slightly mocking, portrayal of a preacher. "So you mean, Granny? Dat wouldn' bad, y'know."

"Cho bwai, stop it." She half laughed, half scolded: "You cyan mock God, y'know." And the moment passed.

By midafternoon the work was done, and both baskets heavily laden with produce. They sat in the shade and ate their lunch, washing the food down with coconut milk. "Now Ah want you to lissen me. Lissen me good," Miss 'Mando said after a while. "When we reach home you can go play—shoot bird, whatever you want. But if you go a river Ah want you home by sunset. Don't do like yesterday. Because Ah want you come with me to a shelling match tonight. Now you know Maas' Nattie seem to like you. Him doan have no pickney you know, and no family neither. Is him one an' God, and all that lan' whe' 'im have."

Here her voice grew low and confidential, her expression very serious. Ivan had to lean forward to listen even though there was no one to overhear them save a speckled chicken hawk circling lazily on the updraft from the mountain. "I believe that 'im looking someone to leave all that lan' to when 'im dead. An'—'im seem to like you. You no see how 'im always telling you all kin' of story? An' you member when Ah tell 'im how you jump offa de bridge 'im laugh and laugh an' say 'Dat boy have de spirit of de young Garvey, a strong spirit, Ashanti spirit!' an' then 'im laugh so til water come to 'im eye? 'Im like you, definite! So Ah want you to show 'im good face, an' be on you best behavior. Treat 'im good, an' go laugh an' talk up wid 'im. You understand me?"

"Yes'm." Ivan ate in silence. He liked Maas' Nattie, who was the richest black man in the district. He was very small and very, very black and rode a big gray horse. All the people respeck 'im. He had been to Panama and had made a lot of money digging a canal. Ivan wasn't sure what that was, but all the white men that came to dig it got sick and died, so they had to send for black men. An' Maas' Nattie had gone and had not died. Even some of the black man dem dead off, even though everyone knew black man stronger than white man, otherwise black man would a did dead out long time, from all the pressure white man put 'pon dem. But Maas' Nattie had become a foreman, an' did the job and come back with plenty money which he used to buy up plenty land.

But Maas' Nattie was strange, kinda funny. Before going away he had been a tailor's apprentice, and every year he bought a big piece of black cloth from town and cut and sew himself a suit with a waistcoat. 'Im say is 'im suit to bury in. An' every year when 'im didn't dead, 'im bring out the suit at Christmas and get on him big ol' horse named "Hell-Dynamite-Lightning-and-Thunder" and ride through the district lifting his hat politely to all he met, saying real nice, like "The compliments of the season to you, sir, an' to you, madam. See, I am here for another year." Then he would come to dinner at Miss 'Mando's, in the black suit. He did this every year that Ivan could remember. At first he used to stare in fascination and fear at the black burying suit and would keep away from the man who wore death so easily on his back. But by evening he would be sitting on Maas' Nattie's knee listening to his stories about Cudjo the maroon warrior and Ma Nannie his sister who was a witch and a warrior too, and about the great Marcus Garvey who was "the black man savior" and who was born not forty miles away. Maas' Nattie never told Anancy stories or talked about duppi and evil spirits, but spoke of real black men like King Prempeh and King Chaka, and Ras Menelik whose black armies defeated the Italians and took back his country which was in Africa.

Everybody said Maas' Nathaniel was wise, and that he was a proud black man who knew many things because he had traveled to distant lands across the sea. Sometimes, when he was in a good mood, he'd take Ivan up behind him on the horse and they'd go riding around the district, Ivan clinging to the back of the saddle and waving proudly to the children he met. Every Christmas that he could remember Maas' Nattie brought him a paper money note, which Miss 'Mando carefully put away in the biscuit tin hidden behind one of the fireplace stones in the kitchen. Next to Miss 'Mando old Maas' Nattie was Ivan's favorite person in the world, so being nice to him was hardly a problem. What was new was what his grandmother had just confided to him, about her secret expectations and hopes concerning Maas' Nattie's land.

Having spoken rather bluntly, Miss 'Mando appeared to pay no more attention to the boy. She finished eating and reached into the folds of her tie-head for a length of what the people called "jackass rope," a pungent tobacco, cured and woven into a rope and sold by the yard. She cut off an inch which she carefully sliced into fragments and packed into her pipe. Under the canopy of the trees it was dark and cool except where the sunlight broke through in sharp contrasting patches of light. She lit her pipe and leaned back against a low stone wall. It was peaceful, the air still, the woods quiet except for the drone of insects. The old woman could have been asleep, her eyes squinted against the smoke from her pipe which made patterns of light and shadow in the still air. But she was watching the boy closely, wondering if perhaps he were not still too young for such discussions. He seemed to be deep in thought as he sat chewing reflectively some distance away. No, it was not too soon for him to begin thinking of the future. He would be a good farmer, loving and caring for the generous land as his fathers had done. She would give him his own animals, and as soon as he was big enough she'd talk to Maas' Nattie about a piece of land, not big at first, but good rich bottom land on which he could start his own cultivation. He'd stay. She would see to it that everything he could want or need would be here in these peaceful valleys and sunny hills for him to discover. She puffed contentedly on her pipe, lulled by the midafternoon stillness, and the comforting presence of her grandson eating his food.

When Ivan finished eating he in turn regarded her. She

seemed relaxed and at peace, blending perfectly with the shadows, the stone wall, and the land. He looked at her calloused hand, now earthstained, that held the pipe and as she raised it to her lips he saw the ridges of hard muscle in her arms ripple like those of a man. Miss Ida's arms, he remembered, were smooth and round, and it was as if he were seeing his grandmother for the first time. Even though he had just met Miss Ida he loved them both— but what a difference there was between them! He sensed they wouldn't like each other, and that somehow the arms told the story—one smooth, round and soft looking, the other knotted and muscular and very strong. He wondered what more was hidden in that difference.

Suddenly large drops of rain fell into the valley. The sun was still bright so they knew the shower wouldn't last, but for a few minutes huge drops crackled furiously against the leaves and fell into the cleared field with pounding thuds. Ivan ran out into the clearing and danced in it.

"The devil an' 'im wife fighting over fishhead!" he said, laughing, giving his grandmother the traditional children's explanation for rain and sunshine at the same time. Then as suddenly as it had started the rain stopped, and they loaded the heavy baskets on their heads and started up the mountain. A different, sweeter smell now came up from the soaked earth; leaves glistened in the sunshine. Miss 'Mando stepped carefully on the slippery path, bearing her laden basket effortlessly and smoothly up the steep hillside, a gaunt, erect, and timeless figure followed by her grandson. Overhead, very high, the solitary hawk spun and wheeled, occasionally sending his shrill hunting call keening into the valley.

"Hm," Miss 'Mando grunted, "massa hawk hungry." She steadied her basket and looked up. "See him dere, no more dan a speck way up deh."

"Why 'im crying so, Granny, look like 'im just warning all the bird dem?"

"Come," she said, "Ah goin' show you something." She set down her basket. "Look 'round you, you notice anything?"

"No." he said, looking around puzzled.

"Thass right," she said, "nutten'."

"What you mean, Granny? What Ah suppose to looking for?"

"Fe what you don't see," she explained. "Usually you wi' see plenty plenty little bird, bird flying up and down. What happen to dem?"

It was true. There was no activity in the trees or in the sky.

"Dem all hear de hawk an' tek bush, just hiding in the thickest tree dem can fin'. An' ol' Massa hawk him hungry, probably have pickney in 'im nest so 'im trying to frighten them out of the tree dem."

They watched as the hawk circled nearer, emitting the angry sounding shrill cries.

"Look," Miss 'Mando said, "over on the hillside see dat guava grove? Ripe guava deh over dere, is it him watching."

The hawk came gradually closer, until Ivan could see the red markings under his tail and his white neck as he rode the updrafts in crisp, patterned circles.

"No. Don't watch 'im. Look at the guava tree dem."

Ivan looked at the trees. Nothing moved.

"Watch," the old woman said confidently.

The hawk wheeled and screamed. The valley was quiet, even the insect chorus seemed to be silent. Then suddenly there was a flash of green and yellow from the grove of trees and a parrakeet broke cover and started across the valley with frantic, desperate wing strokes. It seemed to be heading for the tall trees on the hillside where they were standing. But halfway across, the bird gave a sharp squeak and changed direction, almost falling into a clump of low bushes as the hawk swept silently across his line of flight.

"Him get 'way, Granny," Ivan cried.

"Maybe," she said, "watch no."

The hawk swept back in a wide unhurried circle, high above the little bush. It seemed in its flight quite unworried and confident. Ivan could see its wide tail flexing as it steered itself delicately on the wind. *Kreee. Kreee:* the sharp, bitten-off call seemed louder and was so highly pitched it set Ivan's teeth on edge. In the bush the parrakeet began a lamentation of its own, not its usual raucous, contentious noise but a broken, uncontrolled sound like the whimper of a creature mad with terror.

"Poor little t'ing," Miss 'Mando said, "im see 'im death now. 'Im so 'fraid 'im jus' a bawl."

Ivan pulled his slingshot as far as he could and fired at the hawk. For a second the stone seemed dead on course but then it rapidly fell away, passing below and a little behind the predator. The bird turned its head slightly, almost disdainfully, as the whizzing stone arced away into the valley. Then the parrakeet flew out again, trying to get back to the guava grove where the rest of the flock huddled in uncharacteristic quiet. The hawk, moving with arrogant grace, made three powerful, unhurried wing strokes, then locked his wings and went into a dive so fast and steep it appeared that he must crash into the hillside. At the last second the parrakeet cut sharply, looking slow and awkward. The hawk veered, extended talons hammering the smaller bird. Then everything was blurred in whirling wings and a puff of green feathers. There was a loud shriek, abruptly ended by the flash of the great acipitor's head striking down with a vicious jab, and then the predator spread its wings against the updraft and went into a long, swift glide just above the trees and down into the valley; then it pulled out of the glide and with powerful strokes started climbing toward its nest on the mountaintop.

The last anguished shriek of the parrakeet had been very loud and piercing. As if it were some kind of signal, a discordant chorus arose from the flock in the guava tree, a raucous, noisy, indignant, screeching cacophony of protest and outrage. Then the flock took to flight, at first a bright confusion of green and yellow noise. Then without any lessening of the frightful din they came into formation—a V-shaped line of flight which cursed and threatened as it went, as though they were swearing never to return to this valley of death.

"Never min'. You think is hawk kill that parrot?" Miss 'Mando asked, when speech was again possible.

Ivan felt a little weak. It had all been terrible and beautiful in all its terribleness. "Yes'm. Don't we did see it?"

"We see ol' hawk *ketch* 'im. But is *'fraid kill* 'im. If 'im did stay ina the guava trees wid the rest of 'im generation dem, the hawk never coulda catch 'im. But is 'fraid 'im fraid cause 'im to fly out. You see?"

Ivan saw. It must have been terrible to sit there watching the shadow of death circling over, hearing that grating scream until you couldn't stand it anymore, couldn't force yourself to sit still any longer, until nerve and control went and panic took over. Yes, 'fraid can kill you. He remembered his trip up the mountain the previous night and felt very sorry for the dead parrakeet.

"Well," said Miss 'Mando, picking up her basket, "that mek two t'ings you learn today."

"Yes'm," agreed Ivan, wondering what the other thing was.

• • •

That afternoon just before the sun set he came into the kitchen where Miss 'Mando was fixing an early supper. She always insisted that they eat before going out at night, even though on an occasion like this shelling match, lavish refreshments were always provided.

"What you want?" She recognized from his expression that some request, the favorable disposition of which was not certain, was forthcoming.

"Ah just going down the bottom?" he said vaguely. "Ah soon come."

"Where you going? Dinner almost ready."

"Cho, Granny, Ah jus' goin' down the bottom."

"You not telling me where you going? Well then don't go."

Ivan started to pout and plead.

"Alright, Ah don't care where you go. But if you not back in a half hour Ah leaving you one here tonight. You hear me?"

"Yes'm, t'ank you, mam." And he was gone, leaping like a goat down the path.

The sunset found him crouching, hidden by undergrowth, at the base of a stone wall some distance from the trumpet tree where he had been so frightened the night before. His slingshot was in his hand and in its leather pouch was a carefully selected, almost perfectly round, river stone, smooth and heavy. He expected to have one shot at close range. That would be enough. The shadows were lengthening and he knew it was just about the time that chickens and birds sought the safety of their roosts. The smaller birds were already in their nests. From where he lay he had an unobstructed view of the base of the tree. Everything—the trunk, the dead leaves—took on a rich, brown glow in the ruddy twilight. He lay motionless, eyes glued to the area where he expected the guinea fowl to appear. He felt an insect crawling erratically up his leg, but did not move. A dozen times he tensed, catching his breath at some sound in the underbrush. A dozen times the sound wasn't repeated.

As he lay there the swift, deadly tableau that he had witnessed that afternoon flashed across his mind. The unerringly merciless swoop of the hawk had been so accurate and so certain that it was beautiful in a dreadful kind of way. But he had fired at it. Why? He wasn't fond of parrakeets. Last year a flock of them, maybe the same flock; had eaten all the ripe guavas on his special tree, and then they had damn nearly messed up all the starapples and naseberries, too. And those were his favorite fruit. Maybe the pitiful cries of the bird as it huddled in the bush had affected him? It had sounded so lonely, so afraid and so hopeless.

But anyway this was something different. Miss 'Mando loved

guinea-fowl stew, and besides he could still hear that malicious *kut kut kut* of the bird, laughing at his headlong flight last night.

It came again, the *kut kut kut*. Then Ivan saw them. A cock, heavy and fat, strutting with a slight sway as he approached. He was a round, stocky bird, his blue-black feathers edged in white. Ivan's blood raced with a hunter's excitement. Behind the cock came a hen, and behind her, in stately procession, eight or nine young birds, tiny replicas of their parents. The cock appeared bald, with pronounced white markings like a mask around his eyes, and as he walked he twisted his little head snakelike, from side to side, peering in all directions with those hard, suspicious eyes. Every few steps he'd stop, his head cocked to one side as though listening, his yellow eyes glittering. Ivan waited; already he couldn't miss but he wanted to make sure. Two more steps, then another. The bird froze, one leg raised tentatively. Slowly, taking steady aim at the still head, Ivan pulled back the stone. It would have to be a head shot, for the birds were legendary for their toughness, their thick feathers sometimes smothering even loads of birdshot. Impulsively, Ivan stood up. With a startled squawk the cock leapt into the air, its stubby wings flailing. The stone thudded into his chest, knocking him down. He hit the ground scrambling and scurried into the underbrush, voicing as he went the earsplitting scream for which guinea fowl were famous.

"Go find anedah roos'," Ivan taunted. "If Ah was a wicked man, you woulda dead now. Ah bet you nevah hide an' frighten me again." Feeling very good he started home.

It was not quite dark when they set out on the road to Maas' Nattie's. Ivan knew that Miss 'Mando wanted to arrive early so as to assist the old man in his preparations for the shelling match. She had wrapped her head in a new plaid headtie and was wearing a bright apron of the same material. Her most precious possession, a pair of gold hoop earrings which Maas' Nattie had given her years ago when he came back from Colon, and which she did not always wear, adorned her ears, the yellow metal seeming to glow with life against her black skin. She carried a small wooden stool, while the boy balanced a bunch of green bananas on his head. From the pace she set, Ivan knew she wanted to get there before any of the other women. Barefooted, he occasionally stumbled painfully on the broken stone surface of the road.

As befitted his prominence, Maas' Nattie's house was a larger, more imposing version of Miss 'Mando's: a neat little woodframe cottage with a shiny tin roof and three or four rooms. It sat back from the road on a small plateau, after which the land dipped sharply into the valley. A hedge of hibiscus and red aurelia set the yard off from the road. Maas' Nattie's skill in woodwork was evidenced by ornately carved cornices, flutings, and finishings that edged eaves, doors, and windows of the cottage. The wooden sections were painted in intricate designs of red, blue, green, and black so that the overall effect was bright and quite startling. Rich people and tourists passing in their cars frequently stopped to take pictures of the house and gardens. One bearded white man, much to the old man's delight, had become quite excited, repeating, "How utterly marvelous," over and over and something about "an African sense of color."

One of Maas' Nattie's favorite sayings was "Tek care of the land and you wi' nevah hungry," and in keeping with that precept he had transformed the land around the house into a garden in which just about every indigenous fruit and herb and many varieties of flowers were to be found. He also constantly experimented with crossbreeding plants and produced exotic and unusual fruit which he exhibited proudly. "A blessed lan', blessed—is nothing it can't grow," he'd say as he pointed to his dwarf banana tree which bore deep purple bananas, or the tree with podlike fruit in which were bitter nuts he called *bizi* or kola.

Wearing a freshly ironed khaki suit and shiny black boots, the old man seemed to be waiting for them as they approached the gate. "Miss Amanda an' little Ivan! Well an' good. Well an' good. How you do?"

"We hearty, thank the Lawd, Maas' Nathaniel." They always called each other by their full names. The two old people shook or rather held hands warmly, each looking intently into the other's face as though to discover any changes recorded there.

"You hearty?" he repeated. "Dat do seem so. You look fine as silk, Miss Amanda, and plenty stronger." Miss 'Mando glowed like a young girl. "An'—what's dis?" He asked, turning to Ivan with his bunch of bananas, *"Bwai,* you was worried say you wouldn't get what to eat, yah?"

"No, sah, me'n Granny done eat supper."

"Ivan!" Miss 'Mando's voice was sharp, cutting him off.

The old man laughed out loud. "So I was right, you eat aready, eh?"

"Is not that we didn't think say you have what to eat. . . . Is just dat the bwai want to bring you dis few-few banana knowing how you like young banana. An' is offa 'im own tree it come too."

"Oh? Look what I live to see!" Nathaniel exclaimed. "Dis little baby can bring me what 'im grow himself, to eat from mi own godson's han'." He took the bananas with exaggerated ceremony and carried them behind the house to his kitchen, where a great many pots were on the fire. Miss 'Mando immediately began a tour of inspection, looking under lids, beneath white cloths, and stirring and testing pots still on the fire.

A short distance from the kitchen was a flat concrete area, called a barbecue, used for drying and curing corn, coffee, or cocoa beans, castor oil seeds, or any crop requiring that process. Tonight one end was heaped high with bags of corn: it was here the shelling match would take place. Nathaniel placed three large kerosene lamps along the side of the barbecue. He also brought out huge *yabbahs* filled with fermenting gingerbeer for the women and children, and a demijohn of raw, white estate rum known locally as Joe Louis or *rude-to-parents* because of its potency. As he set down the huge wicker-wrapped bottle the old man grunted with anticipation. "Hm, smell yah, boy," he said, removing the cork and sniffing the pungent sugarcane smell that filled the air. "All dis now, y' know, it not safe to smoke while you a drink it. It wi' explode. Dem don't call it Joe Louis fe nothing, y' know."

"I jus' hope that unu man don't hope to drink all dat," Miss 'Mando said from the kitchen. "Anyhow dat drink up, no work can't do, an' fight must bruk out. Definite."

"Man can't work without a little heat ina 'im belly, you should know dat Miss Amanda." And he winked at her.

"If is dat kinda work you talking, some man don't need nothing," she said. "And you, bwai, what you laughing about? You too mannish. Don't be listening to old people talk."

"Oh don't bother the bwai, 'im be of size before you know it. Why soon 'im be looking wife."

"Nathaniel Francis, bite you mouth and don't be giving this force-ripe pickney any idea into him head before time, y' hear?" She turned back into the kitchen with a furious rattling of spoons and implements.

The people began to arrive, each group as they came in greeting Maas' Nattie and Miss 'Mando formally. The men wore their work clothes: dull gray shirts and pants made from a heavy English cloth known as "ol' iron" for its color and durability. They carried their machetes, thirty inches of steel razor sharp and silvery, and as much a part of them as their hands. Their hard-working, child-bearing, women wore fresh dresses shiny from the iron. The gold earrings and bangles bought with money hoarded bit by bit from their market profits gleamed against the coconut-oil-smooth blackness of their skins. Most wore bright new head-cloths, lending a festive air to their appearance. Soon there were about twenty-five people gathered around the barbecue. The lamps were lit. Maas' Mattie took a seat on a tall chair. The lamps cast a yellow circle of light around the group. In the dark trees, hundreds of fireflies punctuated the shadows. The surrounding mountains were dark, dimly outlined shapes, and a cheerful warm glow came from the kitchen fire.

The old man picked up an ear of corn and said, "Ah t'enk de Lawd for a good crop." There was a murmur of assent. "And Ah'm t'ankful for mi good frien' dem who come yah tonight to help a ol' man." With a powerful twist of his wrists, he stripped the kernels from the cob. "What you see to eat, eat. What you see to drink, drink. Is nutten much, but whatsoever you see, you welcome to." There were a few snickers of rejection at the disclaimer because everyone, even had they not seen the pots of food in the kitchen, knew that Maas' Nattie's generosity was beyond question. This generosity was obligatory; people who got the reputation for cutting corners on the refreshments found that their neighbors tended to be otherwise committed when they announced a shelling or digging match. There was no danger of that in Maas' Nattie's case. No payment was ever considered for these events but whenever one had a major project needing many hands, one simply made preparations and announced it. You were then obliged to attend the functions of all who came to yours. "So and so owes me a day" was an obligation that had to be honored. The other attraction beyond economic necessity was the social aspect of these occasions.

For the first half hour the conversation was a friendly murmur punctuated with bursts of laughter. Apart from Maas' Nattie, who sat in a chair at one end of the barbecue like some Biblical patriarch, the people were ranged on low stools on both sides of the concrete. There was a kind of informal contest between the sides, largely pushed by the children and younger people to see which side would do the most work. They watched the pile of cobs and the kernels to see if they were winning and urged the adults on. The women talked among themselves and the men discussed weighty matters like crops, prices, and techniques of farming. Soon flirtations among older boys and girls and the teasing among the younger began to distract from the work. A few squabbles broke out, and were quickly suppressed by the women.

Maas' Nattie cleared his throat. "You know I always have reason fe everything Ah do. You know why Ah chose tonight for this shelling match? Hum, you don't know?" Here he paused and a silence fell over the gathering. "Well, today is de anniversary of de battle of Adowa."

"Teach, brothah."

"Yes, sah."

"Knowledge, yes!"

The old man proceeded to recount, to the admiring interjections of his audience, how in 1896 in Ethiopia the poorly armed, supposedly ill-trained peasants of Ras Menelik defeated and put to the sword the Italian armies of conquest. "Black man like we, from the rising of de sun to de setting dereof, slay or put to flight over ten t'ousand of de enemy."

The end of the story was greeted with shouts of "Words, sah," "Wisdom, yes." "So black man fe strong." That was the signal for stories to be told, songs to be sung, riddles and proverbs and rhymes to be exchanged, each side trying to outdo the other in eloquence and wisdom.

Ivan liked shelling matches. He enjoyed the warmth and sense of community and the stories, which no matter how often they were heard never seemed to get stale. Everything was done according to a set way, no one seemed to know why. But at the end or beginning of an Anancy story the teller would always say

> So me get it
> so me gi' it
> jack mandora
> me no choose none.

Nobody seemed to know who or what jack mandora was, but everyone always said it. Or in giving a riddle it always was

> Riddle me dis
> Riddle me dat
> Guess me dis riddle
> or perhaps not.

The stories were very dramatic, with songs in them, and when the various characters spoke they all had different voices; when they were angry they bellowed, afraid they quavered; when they were trying to fool someone, the voice became sly and confidential. Some people were better storytellers than others. A good storyteller could keep the audience entranced for an hour. They were singing a song now about a great tragedy. A young policeman, done some injustice by his officers, had brooded on the wrong. It was a slow melancholy song telling how he decided that only blood could discharge the dishonor to his name and manhood. It described in detail how he got his pistol and

> *That young policeman*
> *with revolver in hand*
> *Sought out those who had done*
> *Him a wrong.*

Ivan sang lustily. His flesh crawled with shame when the injustice was done. His spirit soared as Roy walked through the police station on a Christmas morning, shooting his tormentors. His heart sank as the last sad verses—describing how Roy was hung high on a gallows as the sun came up—and the last solemn dirgelike notes hovered in the night air.

There was a song for every major tragedy of that sort. Very soon after the event a music man would come through the district, singing the song that preserved the story, and selling printed copies of the words for two pence. Soon that song too would be a part of the communities' repertoire and thus part of the legend of the land. The songs were all sad and tragic. Young women would become tearful as the handsome, brave young heroes ended up on the gallows, which it seemed most of them tended to do. Sometimes, depending on the incident being related, the man or woman would be wicked and heartless and in those songs they would eventually pay for their wicked deeds.

But the song about Roy Maragh, the young policeman, was the saddest and Ivan's favorite. It was sung in the slow tempo known as the common meter that was usually associated with funerals. During the singing, Ivan heard a steady thumping. He knew that one of the women was using a mortar and keeping time to the song. He knew what she was crushing. The first corn shelled was always parched in the fire until it was crisp and brittle. Then with sugar, salt and some spices it was pounded in a mortar into a fine delicious brown powder called *asham*. This was a special treat for the children on these occasions.

"You ha' you wise man, you ha' you fool. But the answer to dis no teach in a school." The speaker was Maas' Joe Beck. Ivan knew that Maas' Joe, a man of brownish red complexion of the type the people called red-ibo, was usually very quiet. The challenge that he was now issuing to the other side was in good part due to his frequent visits to the demijohn of Joe Louis. From the introduction Ivan knew that the story to follow was not a frightening duppi story about travelers encountering the dread spirits in lonely places, or a story about the trickster Anancy outwitting Tiger, Lion, *Tacumah,* or other animals. It was a problem story in which the audience would have to decide what the wise and just ending should be. He liked those stories best. Maas' Joe who, behind his back, was called "Fire-pon-sea" or simply "Fire," began.

"One time dis king had one daughter dat was very pretty. Every man who see her wanted her fe wife. Ah say the gal did pretty, she pretty, she pretty, she pretty so 'til. But she did also *faastie* ° so that none of the man dem she see satisfy her. So one day the father get vex, 'im say,

" 'So . . . no man no please you nuh? We gwine see. Any man who can ketch me a wild bull without use rope or gun or anyt'ing but 'im hands dem, gwine get you fe married. An' Ah don' care if 'im ugly, Ah don't care if 'im fool. Any man who can tame wild bull can tame you.'

"None a the young man dem in dat place even bother fe try. Dem say,

'Bull a trouble an' the gal worse, so why even put yourself to that botheration?'

"But one day two strong-looking, good-looking, young black men dem walk in an' say *dem* a go ketch de bull. So dem tek bush after bull. Two weeks pass an' no word of dem. The people dem decide say bull musbe kill dem. Or else dem fall into sink hole or ina quicksan'. But one evening, the younger one 'im stagger in. 'Im scratchup-scratchup and 'im clothes tearup-tearup, and the whole of 'im batter-batterup so till 'im could barely walk. 'Im say,

'I come to claim mi wife. Ah know Ah don't ketch the bull but is over a hundred mile I run 'im. Ah run through bush. Ah swim over river. Ah run up mountain. Ah run down mountain. But Ah couldn' ketch him. The las' Ah see the bull, 'im an' me breddah drop down over a cliff. Both a dem *mus'* dead. So since me don't love dead, me turn back. And since is only me lef', I claim the gal.'

"Well the king an' all him people dem reason together an'

° Faastie: arrogant, impertinent. Pronounced "fay-stie."

since it didn't look like anyone was gwine ketch the bull an' come back alive, dem say dem will give the bwai the gal to married to. So dem kill plenty fowl an' goat an' gather yam an' banana an' get out plenty rum. Den the king invite up all the people dem and all the musicman dem an' the dancer dem an' announce big feas'. Dem just sit down to start to eat an' drink. The bwai him sit down next to the gal an' both a dem look well please wid each other. The king heart glad, it glad, it glad so 'til . . . Just then dem hear a voice cry out,

'Not a man eat, not a man drink. Ah say not a food taste, not a rum drink. I come to claim mi wife.'

"Everybody frighten an' look up an' what you think dem see? Dem doan see a t'ing but the older breddah. An' 'im was a big, strapping, *tallowah* ° black man. 'Im clothes tear off 'im, an' 'im body chopup-chopup all over like somebody take machete an' cut 'im. An' 'im wrapup in a bloody bullskin with the head an' the tail still pon it, want to favor *Joncunnu*.°°

'Unu say whosoever ketch the bull supposed to get her and see it yah . . . is me ketch the bull.'

"So the king him say, 'Is true I did say dat an' Ah can't break me word. But see the trouble yah, me done already tell you brother say him can get mi daughtah. You see, we all t'ink say you dead. Is almost a month now an' you no come back.'

'Well Ah come back now. An' Ah want mi wife.'

"An' wid dat him don't say another blessed word only cut 'im eye an' grit 'im teeth dem like him vex. So the king call all 'im people dem an' go discuss de problem with dem. Now, 'im done give 'im word to two man, an' anything him decide one *must* vex. What 'im fe do?

"So the king 'im gone ina the house a whisper and reason with all 'im chief man dem, an' the people outside dem a talk too. Some say doan give the gal to none a dem is the only thing to do. Others say dat the one who ketch the bull deserve fe get her. Some more say is not fair: look how the young gal and the little breddah love each other, and look how the young man dress up 'imself an' get all ready fe married. Is not fair to stop it at the las' minute so. And the gal she, well she doan say a word. She just take one look at the big breddah him wrap up ina the bloody bullskin wid fly dem a crawl 'pon it and open her mouth' a give out one

° *Tallowah:* sturdy, muscular.
°° *John Canoe:* Masked dancer with a bull's head.

hell of a bawling. She put her han' on her head an' bawl and *bawl*. One confusion! One *kass-kass!* ° An' so Ah lef' it up to unu, what is de solution?"

As Joe Beck's words died away there was a momentary silence over the group. The picture so vividly created by the storyteller sat before Ivan's eye: the people all gathered together and festive, the couple first sitting together in happy expectancy, then the girl distraught and weeping. In the center of attention the victorious brother, dirty and bloody, eyes red with fatigue and anger, locks matted with gore and with the grisly trophy sitting on his shoulders, a dread specter with two heads, both glowering defiance and rage at any who would deprive them of their painfully won reward. It did not seem like much of a question to Ivan; a promise was sacred and valor and sacrifice demanded its reward.

Then the argument started. The older people said nothing. Perhaps, thought Ivanhoe, because they knew the answer. But there was usually no "answer" to these riddles. The same problem, depending on the mood of the audience or the emphasis of the individual storyteller in outlining the situation, frequently found a different consensus with each telling. The young women and girls felt that the choice should be the girl's. Joe Beck said that it was the father's responsibility to decide. They argued. Identifying with strength and success, the young men argued for the older brother. Joe Beck at length told what happened:

After a lengthy consultation the father came back and addressed the three. He told the daughter to cease weeping and to remember that it was her haughtiness and foolish pride that had brought them to this predicament. Then he addressed the brothers. He told them that the entire town was impressed with their worth and valor. The younger one had chased the animal longer than anyone else. Thus they knew that he was strong, determined, and loved their daughter. But having subjected himself to great hardship and finding himself in distress and without hope of success he had turned back, as who wouldn't? Thus he had proved himself to be human, with human failings. But in turning back he had not completed the task, and had therefore failed.

The older brother on the other hand would not accept defeat. With a fanatic singlemindedness, no doubt inspired by love, and with a strength and endurance that was greater than anything in living memory, he had persisted and ultimately succeeded, nearly

° *Kass-kass:* noisy contention, argument, confusion.

killing himself in the process. It was a deed that would live forever in legend and song, bringing perpetual credit to his name
and the memory of his fathers. Here the father took up a bag of
money and, as though at a signal, his young men—all armed with
machetes—casually drew near. He told the victorious brother,
that the wealth and fame he had won would be his reward, but he
was to take it and leave immediately and never return, for a man
like him, loved strongly and hated even more so. He had demonstrated that once his mind was set on an idea no suffering, priva-
tion, not even death itself could sway him. It was awesome but it
was inhuman. Every married couple had their fights; every family
their disagreements. If the king gave his daughter to him he
would live in fear for her safety and worse, would know that there
was no reasoning with him.

On the other hand the younger brother was a man like them—
brave enough but with limitations and frailties. Such a one could
be lived with, but there was no living with a man whose will
knew neither fear nor limits. He should take his money and his
fame and go his way. The elder brother sprang to his feet, looked
at the young men's machetes, at the bag of money, and at the
weeping girl. Without a word he left, taking nothing but the
bloody hide.

Again there was silence. Then old Maas' Nattie spoke. "Is trut'
the man talk y'know, the livin' trut'." The older people nodded
their heads in agreement and a murmur of assent rose up. Age had
taught them that a spirit of compromise, to bite one's tongue, to
"take low," to be flexible, was the most important quality that life
taught if one was to live in human society.

"Strong man never wrong," Miss 'Mando murmured. "Weak
man can't vex."

Ivan was on his feet, inarticulate and stuttering from his sense
of outraged justice. His fury was focused on Joe Beck, who regarded him with a tolerant smile. "Dat wrong. . . . You is a wicked
man. Is not justice dat."

"Ah, mi son," Joe Beck said. "You young but you wi' see. If
you was a king or a faddah you would see different. Justice is not a
straight t'ing you know, is a crooked and curvy t'ing. It have to
twis' an turn and ben' up"—here he made a sinuous, twisting
motion with his pipe—"to get to where it mus' get to."

"Sit down an' cool you temper, young bwai, is only a story,"
another man said. Embarrassed at his outburst, but with anger
still seething in him, Ivan sat. He picked up an ear of corn and

attacked it viciously, keeping his head down and looking at no one. Where was the justice in that story? How would Joe Beck—wicked ol' red-ibo brute—like it if it was him did ketch the bull an' the people cheat him so? It woulda did serve dem all right if the older brother did come back by night an' burn the town down like Samson an' the Philistine corn. Anyway, he reflected angrily, he didn't really like shelling matches: too much woman and pickney and petty talk. Bet you if it was a digging match nobody would agree with such a decision. But those were men's events, when new land had to be cleared and plowed by hand. No woman, pickney or old man, but only strong young man dem who could work hard, hard.

He remembered when they were clearing Miss 'Mando's new farm it had taken two days. The men had gathered early, bringing their machetes and heavy forks—a line of men naked to the waist, their huge muscled torsos shining in the sun; hard-handed black men, proud of their strength and their ability to do muscle-tearing, heart-stopping work under the merciless sun, and to sing defiantly as though challenging the work as they did it. Ivan remembered the excitement as they gathered boasting and teasing each other, surveying the seemingly impenetrable green wall of the jungle that had to be cleared. Then when they were together, the leader, his heavy baritone echoing in the valley, raised a song. And with the chorus, the line of machetes flashed in the sunlight and the men threw themselves against the green wall:

> Me say . . .
> Hill an' gulley ridah
> Hill an' gulley, huh.
> Me say, hill an' gulley ridah
> Hill an' gulley, Huh.
> You bruk you foot, you tumble down
> Hill an' gulley, Huh.
> You tumble down, you bruk you neck
> Hill an' gulley, Huh.
> You bruk you neck, you go to hell
> Hill an' gulley, Huh.

The solid rhythm of work songs, men's songs, bawdy and violent, silvery machetes streaking, the grunted chorus punctuated by the ring of the blades falling as one. The line of men like a single, many-handed machine setting a brutal pace in the tropical heat. And Ivan running up and down the line, bringing tins of cool water to the men, who paused only to gulp down gallons of it. Although the water seemed to pour immediately out of their skins in streams of sweat that made them glow in the sun like polished ebony carvings, soaking trousers and forming small puddles around the feet. On their shoulders, along their backs, cords of muscle swelled up, popped out, like a bag of snakes writhing beneath the skin, and veins stood out like lines on a map. The brush retreated steadily before the onslaught of flashing blades, and the boisterous exuberance of songs that stirred the heart and drove the arms. Ivan loved it, the raw physicality of it, the sweet smell of the damp black earth being opened up to the sun, watered with sweat and quickened by the songs of the men.

In the middle of the day, when the sun was overhead and the heat on the valley floor was like an oven, the men broke for lunch. Then Miss 'Mando and the women had come, almost staggering under the heavy tins of food—yams, bananas, dense cartwheel dumplings called *tie-teeth* and huge pots of curried goat so hot with pepper it caused eyes and nose to run and beads of sweat to pop out on the skin. Sitting in the shade the men consumed enormous quantities, sweating from the pepper and washing the hot food down with gulps of white rum. When Ivan tasted the rum it burned his mouth and settled like fire in his belly and the men had laughed at his gasping and tears.

"How you can eat food so hot, and drink rum too?" he asked when he could talk.

"Is alright, young bwai," they explained, sweating. "One heat drive out the other." It made no sense to him.

It was after lunch that day that Joe Beck got his nickname. When the meal was over and the women had taken the pots and gone, the work began again. Joe Beck started up the singing with a song that they never sang when the women were around.

> *Huh! Pussy ketch a fire 'pon sea,* huh!
> *Make it stan' deh burn,* huh!
> *It too bad,* huh!

Joe was recently married so the men laughed when they heard the song he selected. But what Joe didn't know was that his young bride, a tall, spirited, black girl called Pearl, had forgotten a pot, perhaps deliberately so that she could come back to admire the strength of her husband at work. Her voice cut through the laughter.

"Sing dat song again, Joe Beck, Ah didn't hear it."

Joe Beck turned and found her standing there, arms akimbo, eyes flashing.

"Ah—Ah never say nuthin', mi love—" Joe began.

"You *dawg* you, Ah hear what you was singing, Well since it so bad ina daytime when you wid you friend dem—just 'member at nighttime, say it burn up a sea, you hear, mi love?" she said sweetly. And turning her back she strolled off with a proud indignant rolling of her hips.

"But—but Ah nevah say nothin', mi love," the men teased in squeaky falsettoes. "Lawd, Joe Beck pussy burn up. It burn up; you 'member that, Joe." And from that time if you wanted to get Joe angry you only had to hide and shout as he passed, "fire pon sea." Or squeak "but Ah nevah say nothin', mi love."

The memory soothed Ivan's outrage somewhat and he again took an interest in the events around him. People began to bring out the tin plates that they brought with them, for food was being served. This was light refreshment since the work was not heavy. Ivan was torn between his wish to sulk in solitary disdain and the urge to go get a plate and thus rejoin the group. A soft voice cut into his deliberations.

"Ivan, Miss 'Mando sen' this for you." He looked up silently. A young girl stood there holding two plates. He hesitated. She held out one of the plates and her eyes glowed warm. "Cho! Never mind—take de food, Ivan man," she urged gently.

Ivan was defeated. "How come is you she sen'?" he asked ungraciously, as he took the plate.

"Is me ask her," the girl said simply, "because Ah like you style." There was nothing flirtatious or coy about her. her matter-of-fact statement was simply an admission of truth. "I believe say you was right 'bout dat story too, an' Ah did want you to know dat." Her smile was warm with admiration as she settled down on the edge of the barbecue.

Ivan knew her slightly. She went to the government school which he attended when he felt like it, and he had noticed her there. He had never paid any attention to her, or for that matter, to any of the girls. But now her unexpected support and frank offer of friendship touched him deeply. He watched her as she ate. She was about his age, slender as a sugar cane stalk except where a gentle swelling about her chest and hips indicated the promise of the woman that was to be. She was wearing her school uniform, a white blouse and blue skirt and her feet were neatly encased in white canvas shoes. There was something very neat and clean about her appearance. Her hair was braided away from her face, exposing the clean, pert lines of her cheekbones and nose. Against the sooty blackness of her skin her even teeth gleamed startlingly white. Her eyes were the warm honey brown color that the people called "maroon" eyes, after those legendary African warriors who had held these hills for a century and a half against the military might and clever schemes of the British.

"If you see me again you wi' know me?" she murmured, to tell Ivan that she was fully aware of his appraisal. Her gently teasing tone told him that she didn't really mind.

"Yes, y'know," Ivan drawled making his voice as deep and contemplative as he could. "Yes, Ah will know you, too." And it was her turn to look away.

From the kitchen where she was observing the conversation with amusement, Miss 'Mando mused, "Hm, Maas' Ivan getting along well! Ah woulda give anything to hear what dem a say to each other." But the girl was polite and helpful, clearly well brought up, and was such a pretty little pickney too. She was not at all displeased. Whatever they were discussing seemed serious and totally engrossing as they sat together in the thin moonlight. Ivan had almost finished his food. He especially liked the dish— the popular name for which was *dip-and-fall-back*—salt mackerel simmered in the meat and oil of coconuts and served with green bananas and cassava pancakes called *bammies*. Miss 'Mando watched the young girl lean forward to slide the rest of her food into Ivan's plate. *"Hai,"* she thought, "she ketch him now! Mi grandson have another woman fe feed him. What is dis I live to see?" Still chuckling she turned to another woman and asked, "Who dat pickney sitting over there wid me grandson—Ah can't mek her out."

"Is no me little grandpickney Mirriam, she get so big is no wonder you no know her." The two women looked at each other and began to laugh.

Ivan hardly remembered the rest of the evening. There were only a few bags of corn left when the people gathered again around the barbecue. Mirriam made no move to join her grandmother on the other side. Ivan was hopeful but anxious. Would she stay with him in plain sight of everyone? She didn't seem to share his sense of the delicacy of the situation or his nervousness. She picked up the empty plates and started slowly toward the kitchen.

"Where you going?"

"Nowhere—to de kitchen."

"Oh. You coming back?"

"You want me to?"

"If you want."

"No, only if *you* want."

"Well," began Ivan but she had slipped away. Suddenly he was very lonely and wished he could have told her that he wanted nothing more than for her to come back. He was sure she would go sit with her grandmother and he wouldn't be able to talk to her again that night. Miserably he sat there shelling corn trying to puzzle out how a man could feel so good one minute and so bad the next. He was barely listening to the general talk which was about the weird spirits of the night, duppies that appeared in many forms: the old *Hige*—a malevolent vampire that left its skin and sucked the soul out of people in their sleep until they wasted away and died or became zombies, spiritless robots without will or desire. To kill the ol' Hige one had to find where it had left its skin and sprinkle it well with salt and pepper so that when the ol' Hige returned it couldn't slip back into the skin and would be dissolved by the sunlight. The conversation hardly improved his mood. Now a woman was telling of her meeting with the dread rolling calf, a particularly malevolent species of duppi which appeared as a ball of fire rolling over the ground accompanied by the clanking of chains and sulphurous fumes.

"Ivan, hol' out you han'." A hoarse, ghostly command came from behind him.

"Wha'?"

It was Mirriam with a coconut shell full of *asham*. "Ah fin' it in the kitchen," she said gleefully. "You frighten, eh?"

"Me frighten? No—me know it was you," he lied and smeared her face with the powdered corn. Ivan's happiness was complete. Mirriam sat near to him sometimes giggling dutifully or shivering at the fearsome tales. He pretended unconcern. Young children who started to doze drew nearer to the safety of their mother's skirts, where enfolded in warmth and safety they listened, their little eyes popping with the pleasure of terror perceived in security.

The pace of the work was desultory now that only a few bags were left, but no one seemed in a hurry to bring the occasion to an end. The mountain of empty cobs was so high that people on one side could hardly see over to the other. The power of "Joe Louis" was evident in the slurred voices and bawdy jokes of some of the men. The evening was winding down. Ivan and Mirriam talked earnestly, Ivan telling her about the ocean and about Miss Ida's café. Mirriam was appropriately shocked and disapproving.

From the vantage point of his tall chair Maas' Nattie still presided over the gathering, but full of rum and ripe old age he would doze off from time to time. Diplomacy required that people pretend not to notice. Except Maas' Nattie's mind would wander and he would utter phrases in different languages picked up in the travels of his youth. A couple of Spanish sentences might conclude with Marcus Garvey's *"Rise up ye mighty race and accomplish what ye will."* Each interjection was met with admiring murmurs since talking in tongues was much respected as a sign of wisdom. Maas' Nattie had also spent some time in a place called Alibami where he had developed certain enduring and inflexible ideas about the nature and proclivities of white people, along with some incantations in a tongue that sounded tantalizingly like English, except that no one could quite understand them because of the way he intoned them through his nose. On these occasions, whenever he lapsed into this "mericanman talk," it was a signal that he was "charged" and was about to go to sleep.

He sat up suddenly and glared at the group, the abrupt action securing everyone's attention. "Whin-the-gawin-gits-taff-the-taff-gits-gawin," he admonished. "Winnas-nevah-quit-an-quittahs-nevah-win." He punctuated this with a sly nodding of his head and looked around to see if anyone would challenge the sentiments thus expressed. Then he gently lapsed into sleep.

The people then carefully carried the old man into his house, put the lamps out, and went home. They went in small groups, in different directions, and carried torches made of strips of truck tire—not only for illumination but because the pungent odor of the burning rubber was felt to be a repellent—equally effective for mosquitoes as for duppies and evil spirits.

2

Big Bwai Version

In the mornin' you fresh an' bloomin'
In de evenin' you widder away

—Rasta Chant

Ivan awoke at the first pale light. He could hear the hoarse
breathing of his grandmother from her corner of the room. It was
still too dark to see her, but in the quiet darkness her breath
seemed labored and raspy. He lay in bed a few minutes and listened to the sounds of the morning—the chirping of birds and the
crowing of roosters echoing in the quiet valley. Today was an
important day. Quickly he dressed and slipped outside. Miss
'Mando did not appear to awaken and he was happy. He couldn't
stand the way she looked at him with silent accusation ever since
he had come home with the cheap transistor radio, and she discovered that most of the money in the biscuit tin behind the stone
in the kitchen was gone. After all it was his, given him by Maas'
Nattie, and he could use it if he wanted. True, he hadn't asked her
permission—but it wasn't as if he had stolen anything either.

Moving swiftly, he scattered corn for the fowls, chopped grass
for the goats, and slopped the hogs. The water drum was low, so
he fetched a kerosene tin full from the standpipe down the road.
He did the chores quickly without thinking or pausing to admire
the animals that belonged to him, the offspring of the animals
Miss 'Mando had given him two years before. In the kitchen he
didn't bother to eat but made a small package of salt and pepper,
which along with his radio and a small knife he wrapped in a
piece of cloth and dropped into a tin pail. He took his slingshot
and examined the strands of rubber for any small breaks that
could cause the rubber to snap. He changed one of them, filled his
pocket with small round stones, and set out.

He went up the side of the mountain toward the standing
woods, climbing steadily for a few minutes until he stopped and

looked back. Below he could see his grandmother's house nestling on the ridge, and stretching below that the green valley running down to the sea, which was a pale misty blue in the morning light. The sky was clear and cloudless; it was the kind of morning that was so infinitely clear, the air so sparkling, that some people said that from the mountaintop one could see Cuba. Ivan felt happy and free amid the lush beauty of the green and silent mountains where the slightest sound rang clear and pure. He wished he could play the radio to listen to the slick talk of the DJ's and the music they called *ska*. That was really the issue between him and his grandmother. He had stopped going to school and divided his time equally between tending his animals, working the small parcel of land that Maas' Nattie allowed him, and hanging around the café listening to the sinful and ungodly music that Miss 'Mando disliked so. She did not mind too much about school, because although she could read enough to read her Bible, and had a peasant's respect for schooling, she felt that too much education would serve to pull Ivan away from the land.

He approached the standing woods, the uncultivated virgin forest that crowned the mountain. He liked the dark woods, thick and mostly impenetrable, where one could get the feeling that no man had ever walked there before, and in the quiet mysterious stillness of which he sometimes felt very close to a calm presence, an inscrutable spirit that seemed to talk to something deep and unknown in him. But this morning he hoped to surprise a family of partridges, fat, russet birds that avoided the lowlands, but could sometimes be found scratching like chickens in the remote shadows of the woods. Silently Ivan moved down the goat track, stopping to listen every few steps. He didn't see anything this morning and emerged on the other side of the mountain. Well, he knew where there would be birds. An overgrown cornfield lay midway down the hill. There he would find a flock of doves waddling over the powdery earth, seeking grains of corn left by the reapers. He bent down and crawled up to the stone wall that enclosed the cornfield and with his slingshot in hand, cautiously peered over the wall. He could hear rustlings in the dried stalks.

There they were—ground doves—tawny gray birds with black markings on their sides, and bigger pinkish gray peadoves strutting their stubby bodies on pink legs. Ivan was very efficient. He carefully chose a target. At the snap of the stone's release the birds flew up, their wings making a whirring sound. The bird he hit seemed, after a little quiver, to be dead. He stayed behind the wall so that the flock would return. They did, showing no curiosity over the body of their fallen comrade. He shot another. This one wasn't dead, so he recovered the fluttering bird and killed it, picking up the first one on the way. An hour later he had four birds, now headless—taking off the heads prevented stiffening—tied by their legs in a feathery bundle hanging by a vine from his waist.

He left the cornfield, and started down the mountain. He was descending into another valley, this one enclosed almost completely by mountains. The lower slopes were cultivated in bananas and here the carefully turned soil was loose and soft. In the soft soil he gave himself up to the momentum of the slope, running rapidly down, his legs churning, leaning back at an impossible angle to keep his balance and avoid falling forward on his face, leaping sideways to avoid trees, and shouting and whooping in exuberant glee.

At the bottom of the hill he came to the river, green and sparkling in the sunshine. He lay catching his breath on a sandy shoal and felt the sun warm on his body. Lazily he turned on his back, looking up at the sky and the steep hillsides that enclosed the little valley. He turned the radio on and an alien electric voice broke the silence, the voice of "Numero Uno," the voice of glamor and sophistication that Ivan never tired of listening to: "This is the cool fool with the live jive with mah mojo workin' and the music perkin', coming at you this bright sunshiny day from Kingston, Jay Aye."

But today, with the warm sand at his back and the silent green mountains towering above—well, after the quiet of the standing woods Ivan didn't really want to hear it. He turned the radio off and started down the riverbed toward the sea. He rounded a bend and came to a grove of bamboo under which a number of rafts were beached. One was his and he pushed it into the current, put the birds and the pail on it, and began to float downstream, searching the shallows for *janga*, the brown river shrimp, which could be found clinging to the mossy undersides of rocks or surprised in open water as they darted frantically for the shadows. These he caught with deft swoops of his cupped hands and dropped into the pail. He was in no hurry. Sometimes he'd leave the raft and swim and dive in the green cold pools around rocks. At times there were no banks; the mountains plummeted down into the water, creating rocky cliffs. In the deep water beneath these cliffs he dived for the big grandfather *janga* that filled his hands, wriggling powerfully and attacking with their claws. Soon his pail was almost full and he lay down on the raft and allowed the slow current to carry him while he listened again to the lively and insistent music on the radio. He passed groups of children splashing in the shallows, an occasional lone woman beating her clothes on the rocks, flocks of jancrows—black scavengers sunning their bald red heads on sand bars—and fields cultivated to the water-line in yams, coconuts, and bananas.

Drifting silently around a sharp bend in the river he came to a sandbar that was entirely deserted except for a solitary figure kneeling on a rock. Hugging the bank, a sly little smile on his face, Ivan quietly guided the raft under the overhanging rock and toward the figure. Silently he beached the raft and climbed on the rock which hid him from her view. Then he stood quietly watching, a unexpected lump growing in his throat. He had known Mirriam would be there washing her clothes, but the picture she presented couldn't have been more effective had it been deliberately posed. Naked except for her drawers, she was draping some clothes over a low shrub. Perfectly and unselfconsciously at ease, she appeared a creation of the landscape as she stood there, her slender young-girl legs so long and gently curving, her small virginal breasts rising as though to greet the sun. Her skin glowed richly black against the green background. Ivan stood in near awe. She gave no sign of having seen him but returned to the rocky ledge where she continued her work.

Nor did she make a move to cover herself or in any way to acknowledge the intrusion. The natural grace and modesty of her movements completely negated his presence, and shrouded her in a dignity that couldn't have been greater were she wearing regal robes. Then, without hurry or embarrassment, and without any apparent concession to his presence, she casually pulled a loose shift over her head.

Ivan chuckled. So she still wasn't talking to him, eh? Ignoring her he returned to the raft and got the things he had left on it. He walked past her and made a small fire on the bank. He put the pail of shrimp on to boil and began plucking and cleaning the doves. These he seasoned with salt and pepper and hung over the fire. During this process no word passed between them; in fact they behaved as though they were entirely alone. When the birds were cooking Ivan disappeared into the bush. Soon his voice came back, shouting up the hill.

"Maas' Buttie ooh!"

From somewhere up the hillside a response came. "Who dat?"

"Ivan, sah!"

"What you want?"

"Ah begging you a breadfruit, sah."

"Tek it, nuh."

Ivan could have taken it without asking but he was Miss 'Mando's grandpickney and no thief. When he came back he carried a breadfruit and a few coconuts. Mirriam watched him covertly out of the corner of her eye, a faint smile playing about her mouth.

"Wait," Ivan mused as though to himself. "Look like somebody turn me food. Ah wonder is who? Hope them no poison it."

"Go dead a bush," Mirriam said smiling, though it was the worse curse one peasant could give another, wishing him the death of an animal, alone and in the bush.

"Oh, is *you!* I didn' see you," Ivan said. "Would you care to join me for a little dinner, mam?"

"Perhaps," she said, and continued washing. "Ah have to decide if Ah want to eat a bush with any *bungo* whe' doan go school and only want listen to foolishness on radio all de time."

"Suit yourself. I know say I hungry and the food almost done. Soon as the breadfruit done cook is feas' I a go feas'."

So far things were going much better than they might have. Ever since he had stopped school and bought the radio, Mirriam had become distant and critical. Her coldness was in its own way as bad or worse than Miss 'Mando's vocal and continuous disapproval. Between them, life for Ivan had not been comfortable in the last year. It was Mirriam's ambition to go to the Teacher Training College and to return to the district as a teacher. She had no patience or understanding of Ivan's plans to go to the city to become an entertainer, thinking that a worthless and empty dream inspired by Miss Ida's raffish café. But today she was at least talking to him. When the shrimp were red, the doves golden brown, and the outside of the breadfruit black, he called her to eat. She reached into her clothes hamper, brought out a large alligator pear and a piece of bread, then approached the fire and took over the sharing of food onto the basinlike leaves of the coco yam.

"Bwai, the food look good, eh," Ivan said. "Ah was looking a pear too, you know, but none never ripe at our yard."

"Dis one come offa the tree by tobacco pond. You know dem ripe early."

"Yes," Ivan said. "Everyt'ing ripe early at your yard."

She looked up quickly and away. Ivan watched the precise movements of her hands as she knelt in front of the fire, eyes squinted against the smoke. A great tenderness rose in him. Something in him wanted very much to spend his life providing her food and sharing his life and meals with her.

"Alright, come eat."

"You know dat Ah was looking fe you," Ivan ventured, looking down at his food.

"Cho, is must lie you a lie . . . What a big entertainer man like you coulda want wid poor me?"

"Cho, Mirriam. No bother start dat argument again, man."

"Alright." Her tone softened. "Is no use talking 'bout dat now. Thank you fe the dinner, y' hear?" She raised one of the plump birds to her mouth in a kind of salute. Then her strong white teeth sank cleanly into the crisp breast and the succulent juices trickled over her chin. "Ha." She grinned, wiping her chin. "When corn time come all bird fat."

"True," Ivan agreed, "but it look like is more than bird fat." He ran his eyes slowly over her bosom. "Everything fat up, yes."

"Ivan, you too rude."

"Pickney rude, me no rude; me *rhygin.*"

She looked at him with a mocking respect. "Oh, is so me hear." Her tone heavy with awe.

"You hear? One day you wi' know as well."

"Ah so? But dah day deh no come yet. It may nevah come too."

"You believe so?" Ivan questioned softly, and Mirriam busied herself with the food in front of her.

It was shady and cool under the trees on the bank. A sea breeze, salty and fresh, caressed their faces and rippled the surface of the green river, creating choppy crests that sparkled and shimmered in the sun and foamed against the banks. They lay, shoulders propped on a log, listening to the gentle lapping of the water. Mirriam's face was pensive.

"Dat was nice, Ivan."

"Is awright."

"You see like now . . . ?"

"Now?"

"How everything calm an' pretty, you know, the river an' the sun an' the hillside . . ."

"What 'bout it?"

"Well—" She seemed to be groping for the right words. "Well—you know mi cousin Raphael?"

"You mean black Raphael, the one dem call River King?"

"Same one, say him is the King of the River—is a very funny man, you know. Some people laugh after him an' call him fool-fool but I doan believe so, you know. 'Im spen' all 'im time 'pon the river, say is nothing 'im need that 'im can't find right hereso. One day 'im tell me, 'im say, 'Mirriam gal, mek people say what dem want to say. Me know dat when the sun bright and the breeze cool an' the mountain dem purple, an' the sky blue, an' river water heavy an' cold an' green, an' me go up to seven mile green where de dock deh? Listen no, gal. Me say me just all smoke up a long mellow spliff,° yes, one stick of me own personal, mellow, mountaintop, goatshit ganja, you know? An' me head jus' come clear, clear an' vision increaset', you know; an' a spirit of love an' reasonin' jus' fullup me head, y'know. An' Ah jus' stan'up ina the raft an' push off for de sea, seven miles down de valley? Cho! Me one an' Gawd on the river? Have Mercy! Just the wind ina me face an' the sun 'pon me chest, an' on both side is mountain and cliff-face just a rise up sudden so? An' under you foot the bamboo dem jus' a creak an' roll an' buck like wile mule with the power of the river? Me say, dem time deh, when Ah coming down, me one an' the river? Man can hear Gawd voice, you know? Yes, an' see him face too. Yes, dem say that we poor, dat we black, yes an' ignorant too—an' it even could be true y'know— but dem time deh, when is just me an' me raft an' the river an' the mountain dem, is nobody deh a world who is better off than me. *Nobody, me say.*' "

Mirriam finished and looked expectantly at Ivan, her eyes shining.

"Him say all that?" Ivan muttered. "I nevah sure say 'im could even talk." He was jealous that this man had seemed to make such an impression on Mirriam. He had seen Raphael, a huge black man of solitary habits and massive build, with shoulders and arms of great size and strength from life on the river. He owned nothing save a number of bamboo rafts and some fishing nets, rarely sought human company and, apart from a polite greeting when absolutely necessary, rarely spoke to anyone. The word was that high in the remote fastness of the mountains he grew and smoked a particularly potent strain of ganja which was

° Spliff: long, cone-shaped marijuana cigarette.

responsible for his strange ways. He was famous for his ability to pull—no other raftsman could—a fully loaded raft *up* the river. And he did it casually, almost contemptuously, never leaving the middle stream where the current was strongest, his slender bamboo pole and giant shoulders defying both load and current in a way that seemed effortless.

"So him can really talk, eh?" Ivan repeated.

"Not only can talk but ha' more sense than you an' all a dem whe' call him fool," she said hotly. "Anyway, on a day like today I believe I can understan' just what it is Raphael see."

Though he didn't admit it, so could Ivan. Where Mirriam lay, her face in shadow, its clean angles gleaming like soft velvet and her golden maroon eyes glowing with dull fire, she was framed by the river and, behind that, the bright green foliage of the opposite bank. She seemed relaxed and contemplative, unaware of him or the growing intensity of his gaze. Slowly, almost involuntarily, he drew closer to her, his eyes never leaving her face. She seemed almost asleep, lulled by the gentle breeze, the steady afternoon drone of the insects, and the distant murmur of the sea.

But then she sprang up abruptly and with a mocking laugh pushed Ivan over with her foot, leapt lightly to the top of the rock, and casting off her loose shift posed briefly against the sun before diving cleanly in. They swam and wrestled, chasing each other in and out of the water. Then Ivan tripped her on the bank and followed her down into the soft grass. He looked into her eyes. She ceased struggling and returned his gaze, her eyes excited, apprehensive.

"No, Ivan," she said, as his arms went around her, "no. No, Ah say, you can min' pickney?" But the voice was weak and her arms were like bands of iron around his neck. Her breath came hoarsely, caught convulsively in her throat, and a single tear snaked over the delicate curve of her cheek and lost itself in the sand.

They lay intertwined, very still for a long time, the breeze cool on their hot damp bodies. Then Ivan sat up and turned on the radio. Mirriam was crying as she leapt up and shouted, "Turn the damn somethin' off, Ivan—you mean say even at a time like dis—?" She became inarticulate with rage and began snatching her clothes from the rocks and bushes. Guiltily, Ivan turned the radio off, but it was too late. He stood there looking sheepish and feeling worse. When he offered to walk with her she didn't answer.

He stopped to catch his breath at the crest of the first hill, just as the sun was about to begin its final plunge into the sea. The fiery fingers of the Caribbean sunset splashed the hills and valleys with a reflected blood red light. So intense was this light that when Spanish seamen, full of Catholic guilt and superstition, first saw it, they believed they were approaching the world's end and were looking at reflections from the satanic furnaces.

Jeasas Chris'! Ivan thought. What a way woman troublesome, eh? *What* was wrong wid Mirriam? What she really want, anyway? She an' Granny, bwai, dem never stop, man, nevah stop. Any little t'ing that remind dem of me plans, dem jus' swellup and vex. Uh uh. Wait? Dem think say man a go pen up yah 'pon mountainside like goat-kid all 'im life? Cho, them wrong dereso. Definite! Why, dem can't even understand that it for dem too, mostly for dem, in fack, that ah going turn meself famous. Everybody, since me small-small, talk 'bout how me *rhygin* and have plenty heart, so why now dem have fe go on so, jus' becausen me want follow me heart? Look, Mirriam! Look how nice everything go today. Today she prove her love. Is really a hell of a thing she do, an' Ah know it. Is one young gal dat who no take herself light at all; she not to be confused with dem little droopy drawers, fuck-a-bush gal that Granny always talking 'bout. No, she definitely love me, and prove it today too. Mek me feel like a man, a lover-man, yes, a king to raas, an' then bam! Everyt'ing crash. Ivan swore, shook his head, and turning his back to the bloody sea, started up the hillside.

Miss 'Mando was even worse. For about a year now he'd had to endure her stony disapproval of just about everything he did, especially those hours he spent at the café. "Den Ivan, is what you looking in dat place, eh? You t'ink say is a nice place dat?" How could he explain to her about the music, the hold it had on him—the thrilling completeness he felt in moving to and singing along with all the latest songs, the eagerness and longing with which he pored over city newspapers with their pictures of singers and bands, their accounts of dances and clubs, envying the glamor and fame of the entertainers. His granny couldn't understand that. How could she? She never was further than fifteen miles from her mountain in her whole life.

Miss Ida understood, though. She told stories of the clubs and entertainers she had known, the great dances she had been to. And sometimes she would leave off whatever she was doing to watch him and challenge anyone around: "Tell me say dis young

bwai doan ha' a gift. Listen to the bwai sing Calypso, no?" Then
Ivan's joy would be complete.

Still, it was hard not being able to share his dreams with Miss
'Mando anymore or even to rush home as he used to, to tell her of
the day's adventures. But ever since that day she had grown steadily more remote, more cold and uncommunicative.

She was in the kitchen on that day. And, like a silent accuser,
the empty biscuit tin sat in the middle of the table. "Granny,
look—" he began, thrusting his prize toward her.

". . . BRINGING TO YOU SWEET STTRAINNS UH, ANN SOFT UHH
REFRAINS . . . NUMERO UNO . . ."

"Get dah damn foolishness out de house," she had snarled,
without looking up. He had turned it off and she merely said in a
lifeless voice, "So is dat you tek the money for? Hmm, you do
well," and turned her back again. He couldn't even get her to
listen to the Sunday programs of devotional music, since she regarded it as sacrilege to play God's music on the same devil's
instrument that brought the sinful music of Babylon. So he
couldn't play the radio within her earshot. Her general manner
became one of ponderous grief and visible disappointment. Her
nightly recitation of the Scriptures was dominated by references
to prodigal sons wasting their substance with harlots, scarlet
whores of Babylon, and the well-deserved destruction of Sodom
and Gomorrah. Almost perceptibly she grew feebler and seemed
to lose interest in things. Nowadays when she spoke it was mostly
to herself. To the accompaniment of heavy sighs, she would give
voice to dark mutterings, usually from her large store of proverbs
about the foolishness, selfishness, obstinacy, and inevitable ruin of
children. "Hmm, chicken merry, hawk near," or "Pickney ears
hard; him skin better tough," "Who can't hear will feel," "Hard-
ears-pickney kill him Mummah," or "Pickney *nyam* Mummah,
Mummah no *nyam* pickney." ° These proverbs, while they could
only be intended for Ivan, were never addressed to him. The
closest she came to direct address on these occasions was to look
at Ivan with her eyes full of tears, shake her head sadly and wail,
"Lawd, look 'pon me good good pickney—is must obeah, somebody obeah him."

Well, Ivan thought, we going see who dem obeah, because
obeah or no obeah, is great I going to great. Then see if she don't
glad . . .

° The child devours the mother, the mother never devours the child.

He came over the last low stone wall and approached the home-place. Everything seemed as he had left it that morning. The hogs had not been slopped, the goats neither fed nor milked. The kitchen was empty and the ashes of the fireplace were cold. For the first time in his memory there was no hot meal awaiting his return. Could his grandmother be at Maas' Nattie's? Recently she had been spending more time than usual with her old friend. He didn't know what these visits were about, but she always seemed to return from them with an aura of serenity and quiet satisfaction.

The door of the house was closed, which meant she wasn't home. Suddenly apprehensive, he ran to open it, calling, "Granny? Granny? Is me, Ivan." There was no answer. He entered. The room was hot, the air stuffy with a faint smell of old flesh, sweat, and stale urine that wasn't usual. She was still in bed, sitting propped against the wall, motionless. "Granny? You alright? You doan feel good?" She didn't answer and appeared to have fallen asleep while reading her Bible, which had dropped from her hands. "Granny—" Ivan began again, and knew even as he started to speak that she was dead.

It was more than the rigid and unnatural stiffness of her posture that told him. It was something in the appearance of the room itself, the uncharacteristic heaviness of the air, a terrible kind of stillness as though some intangible spirit had gone from the wood and stone. Through the slotted jalousies, rays of red sunset streamed, striping the still figure with alternating bars of color and shade. Miss 'Mando seemed to have prepared herself. Instead of her usual plaid bandanna, her head was covered with the pointed white turban of a pocomania queen mother and she wore her white baptismal robe. And in her ears, illumined by a bar of light, Maas' Nattie's earrings glowed like bands of gold fire against her black skin. To Ivan, standing paralyzed at the door, she seemed strangely shrunken and very frail. He saw that she had cleaned and swept the room, changed both beds, put her house in order as though for the coming of an important visitor. The only things marring the order were a small pile of ashes on the floor, where her pipe had fallen from her mouth, and the crumpled and torn page of the Bible lying on her lap.

Ivan approached slowly like one drawn against his will. As he got closer he could see more. Despite the signs of preparation, her expression was startled. The eyes wide and emptily staring, mouth gaping slack-jawed in an expression of idiot astonishment, with a dribble of dried spit snaking from its corner and into the crags of her withered neck. Already ants were congregating at the corners of the eyes, a few crawling over the cloudy balls. In the red beams of sunset, the familiar lines and creases of that ancient face became alien, an inhuman mask grinning stiffly in the eerie light.

Ivan wanted to run and bawl but something kept him there, forced his reluctant feet toward the bed. When his shadow fell across the face, two large flies came buzzing furiously from the open mouth. He laid her down, wiped the ants from her eyes and gently closed them, then wiped the spit from her chin and pressed her mouth closed. He arranged her hands, removing from them as he did so, a torn piece of paper. When he had done all that he could think of to do, he draped a cloth over the corpse and then ran stumbling from the now dark room.

He knew that he was in the kitchen, leaning with his head and shoulders resting in the cold ashes of the fireplace. He could not tell how long he had been standing so, or if it had been his voice that filled his head, echoed in his chest and seemed to fill the world with an awful howling. *"Waaiie, Miss 'Mando deadooe . . . Granny dead! Granny Dead! Granny deadooee . . . Waaiioo . . . Deadooe . . . Granny deadoe."* Had he really hollered like that, or was the voice only in his head? No! He knew that he couldn't have given voice to his grief in that time-honored and spontaneous way, because if he had, the neighbors would have already begun to gather, joining their voices to his in a clamor of fear and loss, while the hills rang and the valleys filled with the shrill, discordant ecstasy of woe. Even now there would have been lights bobbing and flickering through the trees on the hillsides, as others rushed to the house of mourning in answer to the obligation of death. So the bawling must have been in his heart.

Over the yard a thin ineffectual moon was rising. Even the animals seemed desolate; neglected all day they huddled silently as if they sensed that something had forever changed. They didn't sleep or move around, goats neither bleated nor pigs rooted. Only the pattu's ominous screech disturbed the low hum of the night insects.

Granny dead! Granny dead! She dead alone! She one! Granny dead alone! Not a soul to close her eye dem! To even han' her a drop a water! Granny dead! Dead, she one! The words repeated themselves in his head as he started down the dark road, moving like a zombie, without conscious will. And the beat of his feet against stone, the rhythm of the insect chorus, the tree toads and croaking lizards, echoed: *"Granny dead. Dead alone. Granny dead. She one."* He was oblivious to everything—the darkness, the overhanging trees, the rocks that savaged his bare feet—he was aware of no purpose, destination or direction, he was just stepping. *Granny dead. Dead alone. She one.* Then he realized that he was in Maas' Nattie's yard. Light shone from the windows.

"Maas' Nattie? Maas' Nattie?"

"Who dat?"

"Is me—Ivan."

"Come in nuh, door open, man." The old man was fully dressed, his manner neither surprised nor hurried as he met Ivan at the door and with one look took in his ash and tear streaked face. "Come in, young bwai, and siddown." He put a protective arm around Ivan's shoulder and led him into the room.

"Here, young bwai, siddown an' calm yourself. Here, tek a likkle bush-tea, steady you nerve dem—maybe a likkle white rum 'pon it." Muttering more to himself than the boy, Maas' Nattie bustled solicitously around.

"Is Miss 'Mando—" Ivan began.

"Ah know. Soon as Ah see you Ah knowed," the old man said. "But you calm yourself, me son, tek it easy an' tell me how it go." As Ivan tried to pull himself together and to organize the events into some coherent pattern in his mind, the old man said, "Bwai, your Granny was one hell of a woman doh, eh?" He shook his head with a kind of admiring wonder. "One hell of a woman. You t'ink she nevah know, long long time? She well know, man, an' mek all her plans dem as proper as you please."

There was another silence as Ivan tried to bring his mood into line with the old man's calm matter-of-fact acceptance. "Yes sah, one hell of a woman." He spoke softly to himself. "And Ah bet you anyt'ing she wasn't surprise neider? No sah, nor 'fraid too? Not Amanda Martin, not even ol' Massa Gawd self coulda frighten her. She done fix up her business, mek all her arrangement dem, an ready to go long time. Ready an' waiting cool as you please. You b'lieve say that woman stop, yah? You t'ink say she easy?"

The bush-tea and rum, as much as Maas' Nattie's untroubled manner, calmed Ivan enough so that he could repeat what he had found. He finished the story and looked to the old man as though for assurance of some kind.

Maas' Nattie had followed the story with a squinted concentration, as though wanting to impress the details on his memory. At the end he seemed strangely satisfied, almost pleased. "Ah tell you! Ah tell you she nevah surprise," he said, slapping his knee sharply for emphasis. "But you, you do well," he said to the boy, "you well able fe you size, y'know. Now gwan go saddle de horse, mek we go keep her company, nuh." As Ivan started to rise Maas' Nattie noticed the paper sticking out of the pocket of his shirt. "What?" he said, pointing. "Wha' dis?"

"Wha'? Ah don't know—" Ivan began and fumbled with the paper. "Oh, is must be the paper Granny did have in her han'."

"In her han'?" the old man roared. "In her han', an' you don't say nutten? But how you nevah tell me dat, bwai?"

"Ah did forget, sah," Ivan said meekly.

"Forget? *Forget?* Bwai, how you can forget a t'ing like dis? Paper ina dead woman han', an' you *forget?*" His voice rose on the last forget, his face twisting in a grimace of incredulity. "Give me it." He took it gingerly as though it were a sacred relic or a talisman of fearsome and unknown power. Gently, almost reverently, he smoothed out the crumpled fragment, muttering agitatedly about "Young nagers not having the sense Gawd gave a bedbug," and fixing a pair of wire-rimmed glasses on his nose, he began to pore over it.

"Hmm." His eyes opened wide with an expression somewhere between surprise and significance. "She tear de Bible—Genesis 37, hmm." In the flickering lamplight his face was a study in serious concentration as he read: "Conspire against 'im to slay 'im . . . an' dey said behold dis dreamer cometh. Come now derefore let us slay 'im . . . Hmmm hmmm hmmm . . . and we shall see what wi' become of his dreams." He sat frowning and reading it over and over. "An' you say dis was in her han' eh?" Ivan nodded. "Is mus' a message dis, somet'ing she did see at the las'. Ah going to keep dis—go saddle the horse." Ivan left him sitting, a troubled expression on his face. When he returned the old man was ready. He was wearing his most recent burying suit and carried his Bible and a large brown envelope that was frayed and worn.

As he had done so often as a child, Ivan sat behind the old man on the tall stallion. In the crisp night air the beast was skittish and nervous, dancing and plunging against the tight reins, biting at the bit, wanting his head in the darkness. His iron-shod hoofs clattered over the rocks, striking an occasional spark and setting up metallic echoes of their passage in the blue night. People in dark cabins turned in their sleep and wondered what rider could be abroad and what possible mission had forced him to the road at that hour.

"Is mus' Maas' Nattie. But is what coulda happen? Is where him could be going so late? Somet'ing serious happen, yes." They turned and again sought sleep; whatever it was, tomorrow would be soon enough to find out.

Tired, perhaps of fighting the big horse, or out of his own anxiety to get to Miss 'Mando because it was dangerous for a corpse to be alone, Maas' Nattie said, "Hol' awn, bwai," and gave the stallion his head. The animal snorted, shook his head testing; Ivan felt the huge muscles tense, then a surge of power as the horse leaped forward in furious passage across the mountain. The wind whistled past his ears, stung his eyes, and in the darkness, under the cold stars glittering through the thin clear air, his spirit soared in exultation and fear.

"Ha haa, bwai! You see horse?" the old man boasted, and then very quickly they were there. Maas' Nattie handed him the reins. "Go tek care a de animal, bwai; my place is wid her."

He was beside the bed when Ivan came in. He had turned the sheet back from the dead woman's face and was standing, head bowed as though in prayer, looking into her face, his lips moving soundlessly. Finally he spoke. "So, me dear, you gone, eh? You really gone. Fe me time now fe mourn you. But don't fret 'bout nutten. We soon meet again. Soon to meet again. Soon soon meet again, me dear. Res' easy. Res' easy—everyt'ing goin' be jus' as you did want it—in the propah way— like in you grandfather time, jus' as Ah promise you. Res' easy—take you res' in peace, in blessed peace." Gently, gently he touched the face and gave a formal little bow, then turned away, his eyes shining unnaturally in the lamplight. "Come *yah*, bwai. Come here, mek Ah tell you 'bout dis woman, you gran'mother. Tomorrow we wi' tell de people dem, but jus' fe tonight me and you will have de watch dead."

With a quiet emotion he told Ivan that he had long loved the girl Amanda and she him. But being very poor and proud, he wanted to have something before they married. With her reluctant blessing and the encouragement of her father he had left; first for Cuba where he had cut cane, and then, hearing about high wages in Panama he had gone to build the canal. Many died but he survived and prospered. By the time he felt that he had earned and saved enough, eight years had passed. He returned to find that, years earlier, his name had been published among the list of the canal dead, even that services had been held in the district for the peace of his soul. Amanda was married, the mother of three and pregnant with Daisy, Ivan's mother. He invested his money in land and left again and was gone another twenty-five years, returning the year Ivan was born so that he could end his days at home in the hills.

Ivan understood then the great friendship between the two old people, and the irony behind the New Year's day ride in the burying suit and the quizzical greeting "As you can see, I am not dead."

Maas' Nattie was now talking about business. Something about a loan, and the story of James his uncle who had chopped up his wife, the pretty half-white barmaid of easy habits. It was an oft repeated tale in the district. "Das why it was dat time when you uncle James was in dat trouble is to me she turn. Money had to fin' fe the lawyer dem . . . Is me, you Granny come to. Is all down here." He pointed at a paper. "An' las' year when she see say you was bound an' determine to go a town, she sell me the house, lan' an animals—see here." He rummaged in the tattered envelope, producing all kinds of papers. He had a peasant's respect for records and documents and as he outlined the state of Miss Amanda's business, he produced paper after paper from the large envelope.

What it amounted to was that she had sold him the land before she died, partly to repay the old debt, partly to get the cash for the kind of funeral she wanted, a traditional old-fashioned one. Maas' Nattie had in turn promised never to sell the land, and if Ivan wanted he could live there and work it forever. If he was determined to leave, then the old man would hold it against the time when he would come to his senses. "She want everyt'ing done propah, accordin' to ol' time ways." His eyes glowed as he visualized it all. "Bwai, wait til you see dis yah funeral—is goin' be like when a ol' time maroon queen maddah dead. Bwai, you did know say you come from cromanty people dem, yes Miss 'Mando father was a maroon-man, y'know. *Yes,* wait til you see dis yah funeral, y' hear me? Miss 'Mando did know how t'ings suppose to do. De right way, man."

With a kind of excitement he began to go over the things that had to be done. Telegrams were to be sent to all relatives; an elaborate coffin, ordered and paid for months before, had to be fetched from the town; neighbors had to be informed. The next night there would be the traditional wake, the watch dead, the next day a large and spectacular funeral followed by eight days of sober observance and silent vigil, and on the last night, the night when the spirit of the dead returned for its final farewell, the great leavetaking feast and celebration called the Nine Night. On that night there would be a *Kumina* dance in honor of the dead woman and all her ancestors, beginning at sundown and ending at sundown the next day. It would surpass anything seen in the district, Maas' Nattie vowed, in the entire parish even, in recent years. Miss Amanda had left her instructions and the funds to see it done, and done well.

Old Nattie talked on and on through the night. His voice was quiet, barely louder than a whisper as was fitting in the presence of the dead. He spoke reverently, but also compulsively, as though he felt driven to purge himself of a heavy burden of history and memory, to entrust it to Ivan. At times he half-turned and seemed to address himself to his old friend. But mostly he spoke to the boy, urgently, insistently, as though by the force of his words, by his evocation of the spirit and greatness of times past, he could hold back the chaos and disorder that was abroad in the spirit of the present.

3

Nine Night Version: Dreams And Visions

*And they entered into the house of mourning and saw
that she was dead, they raised a loud wailing and tore
their garments and wept. When they had finished they
wiped their tears, arose and went back to their houses.
After that they wept no more for her that was dead.*
— Mystic Revelations of Jah Ras Tafari
Royal Parchment Scrolls

On the hillside across the valley a tall figure moved quickly over
the dark path like a man filled with purpose. A peasant he
seemed, from his gray loose-fitting clothes stained with earth and
sweat. From the ease with which his legs took the steep track, he
was born to the hills. He made no sound and carried no light but
his ascent was fast, although nothing in his manner suggested
haste. Near the summit, directly opposite Miss 'Mando's little
house, he stepped from the path into the dense and rugged underbrush. Still he went in an almost straight line, scrambling over
shrubs and rocky outcroppings until he came to the base of a
giant breadfruit tree. When he entered the dark shadow of this
tree he stopped, looking toward the gnarled gray trunk, mossy
and ancient. He stood staring at the old giant expectantly like
someone listening for a faint but important signal. Only his open
mouth and harsh breathing, and the sweat that gleamed on his
tense face and made him tremble slightly in the damp air, suggested the exertion of his long climb. He stumbled forward until
he was standing against the rough trunk with his arms spread
wide and the palms of his hands lying lightly on the bark. He
stood for a moment, just like that, motionless except for the heaving of his chest, until another, more violent tremor shook him.
When it subsided he stepped back and leapt, catching the lowest
limb and swinging himself into the branches. He climbed swiftly

· 77

and steadily without having to stop and look, as though his hands and feet were following a familiar path. He climbed into the upper reaches of the tree above the ridge of the hill and emerged from the shadows into a faint moonlight, still climbing and now muttering a steady chant until he was high above the hilltop and any other tree, where the branches, now dangerously thin, bent and swayed under his weight. Then he stopped, feet braced against a cross limb, grasping the center shaft which was so narrow that his hands completely encircled it. Then he threw his weight back, pulling the branch with him until it stopped and whipped back. He rocked back and forth, making the top of the tree sway as if in the grip of a soundless storm, and turned a rapturous gaze to the sky. And with the veins in his neck swelling and bulging, he began a howl that filled the night, silencing the crickets and setting the dogs to barking and howling too, a drawn-out unearthly sound: "BRIMSTONE AND FIRE!"

In Miss 'Mando's house, Maas' Nattie had long been silent, his face immobile in the shifting lamplight. Except for his unblinking gaze he could have been asleep. Ivan's head kept sagging onto his chest, until something snatched him out of a deep nod and he sat up quickly, looking at the old man across the table.

Maas' Nattie hadn't moved. He seemed small and thin, his clothes hanging loosely on him like a garment draped over a black skeleton. "Mad Izik," he said. "Ah was wondering if 'im would come."

So is that. Ivan listened to the night but all he heard was the chorus of dogs dying away in the valley. He looked again at Maas' Nattie.

"Wait! You will soon hear 'im."

"You mean 'im still deh bout? I t'ink 'im dead by now. Is a long time me no hear 'im."

"Dead?" Maas' Nattie said and sucked his teeth. "Listen no."

Then it came again, quavering and echoing with a lunatic fervor: "BRIM STOOOONNAH ANNN' FIAYAH! BRIM STOOOONNAH ANNN' FIAYAH!"

Again Ivan was glad of the old man's presence. That wild voice sounding so close, echoing into the room, would have been more than his nerves could stand tonight. He looked out the window. The top of the breadfruit tree, sharply silhouetted against the moon, dipped and swayed with unnatural regularity in time to the demented cadences of that howl: "BRIM STOOOONNAH ANNN' FIAYAH!"

Ivan knew Izaac by sight and reputation. A wiry man of closed countenance and haunted eyes, he was one of four brothers known to be good farmers and hard workers. He didn't drink and was never known to be in contention with anyone or to takes sides in the periodic disputes and feuds which added spice to the spartan life of the community.

Ivan had been very young the first night that that frightening sound from out of the darkness had sent him shaking to his granny's bedside. Crying with terror he had thrown himself into her arms.

"Is duppi Granny? Is a duppi, eh Granny?"

"Hush, pickney, hush. Is jus' Mad Izik. Moon mus' be full." She had to get up and light the lamp and hold him until he stopped crying. "Never mind 'im,' she said, "is jus' so 'im go on when de moon full sometimes." Then she took him to the window and showed him the tree swaying and dipping on the hill. She told him how Izaac from time to time moved from hilltop to hilltop, covering in one night over half the parish, stopping at certain trees from which he would proclaim his message.

"Me 'fraid 'im," Ivan had sobbed. "Den is why dem don't stop 'im?"

"For what? 'Im no hurt nobody an' who know wha' spirit call 'im?" And the first time she pointed him out, it was hard to believe that the same quiet-mannered man whose face carried such a gentle, distant smile could be the source of those powerful and frightening noises.

They said that many years ago the youth Izaac had been very bright in school and a devout reader of the scriptures. His father—some said he was proud and ambitious—had sold some land and sent the boy to Kingston to "study Parson" at a seminary. He was said to have boasted that Izaac would surpass the sons of the gentry and become a bishop in the Church of the King of England. What had happened was not really known, for Izaac had never said. But not long before he was to have finished, Izaac returned quietly and without fanfare. In place of the bright, friendly youth a silent man returned. For nearly a year he did nothing but sit on a hill and look toward the sea, rarely speaking even to his family. Then one day he picked up a machete and, working alone, began to clear corn land. But he never talked about his experience at the seminary.

His father swore that envious people in the district had put obeah on his son. Others said that it was Izaac himself, seeking greater and forbidden knowledge, who had sought supernatural aid only to have it run afoul of the power of the church and turn against him.

"You t'ink say de white man church is a play-play? You t'ink dem power stop yah?" they would ask, nodding their heads gravely to emphasize the mysterious knowledge they were talking about. There were those who felt that the answer was simpler. Izaac had found the studies too "high for 'im brain" and had resorted to the use of ganja, the "wisdom weed," to deepen his understanding. Everyone knew that deep thinkers and men of brilliance who engaged in weighty studies used ganja to strengthen their brains. But if "de brain couldn't tek it," as was clearly the case with Izaac, it would turn them mad. It was a lesson to Izaac and his father for their reckless ambition, for flying, like the bird in the story, "past their nest."

There was yet another school of thought, to which Maas' Nattie subscribed, which whispered bitterly that Izaac's misfortunes were the work of the "white and brown man dem" at the seminary. They were threatened by Izaac's brilliance and piety. Besides which, in their pride and arrogance of class, they resented the effrontery of the young peasant who had the nerve to sit among them and aspire to the cloth and pulpit. According to this school of thought, the cause of Izaac's trouble was not obeah or anything mysterious, but the accumulation of gratuitous and ingenious insults. What outrage finally tipped the balance wasn't known, but speculation was that it had to do with the beautiful and haughty daughter of a prelate. In any case it was an Izaac broken and injured in spirit, who limped home to the hills after a short stay in the lunatic asylum. One day, these people whispered fiercely, the brown and white gentry would pay for their wickedness. They nodded grimly, one day.

The first time, Izaac's family had tried to restrain him when the moon was full, but the spirit was not to be denied. So great was the fury and so unnatural the strength that surged in that slight frame that they were forced to leave him alone when his spirit was on him. Apart from that he was as normal as anyone else except when certain deaths occurred in the district. Whatever the cause, people agreed that Izaac's spirit was no *peaw-peaw* duppi of the bush, but a higher spirit of vision and even prophecy. It was that same spirit that now howled and lamented over the valley.

"Ah knew it. Ah knew it. Ah jus' had the feeling dat Izik

would walk fe Miss Amanda dis yah night," the old man said, and seemed deeply satisfied.

Soon a morning, before the sun had burned the dew from the grass, they came in numbers. Mostly women at first, in twos and threes—old friends and church sisters of the dead woman—wearing death sullen countenances, dirge-hymns of mourning not far from their lips, asking almost challengingly after the manner of her going, listening carefully to the story, noting the exact position in which she was found, what she was wearing, what she had in her hand, regretting the absence of any "dying words," but nodding and exclaiming over the torn Bible, and then finally nodding judiciously as if to express their satisfaction with the account before going in to "take their leave," quite as if Miss 'Mando would be sitting up in bed to receive them.

On arrival, each new group waited until a number sufficient for another telling of the story was gathered, then they went to take their leave. No one entered the house before hearing of the manner of the death. The women took over the house and kitchen while Maas' Nattie spoke to the men.

In the house the close friends and distant kin of Miss 'Mando washed and anointed the body, dressed it and laid it out on the cooling board. They moved the deathbed outside the house to "fool the duppi," built fires and went for water and firewood. The "dead water" that washed the body was carefully collected and this was brought and thrown at a certain place in the yard. Thereafter people were careful not to step on that spot. Maas' Nattie explained to a group of the older men that in accordance with Miss 'Mando's last wishes, "Everah t'ing gwine to be in de ol' way as 'cording to the elders. As it was with de ol' time people dem." After some discussion they dispersed to their several tasks.

Ivan was sent to catch up two goats and a hog which were quickly butchered and hung to drain by a group under the direction of Joe Beck, who butchered and sold meat in the district. Small children accompanying their mothers were set to chase and catch the chickens scratching round in the underbrush. The men constructed a large arborlike shelter, a palm frond roof raised on posts, beneath which the body would lie until burial and where the singing meeting and wake would be held at night. One group dug a pit over which the hog would be roasted, while others dug the grave next to the old graves down by the stone wall.

A cart was sent into Blue Bay to pick up the coffin, the arrival of which brought all work to a stop as the rich polished wood, the blue satin lining, and the brass handles gleaming like gold were admired and exclaimed over. Maas' Nattie beamed and nodded every time he heard someone saying that never before had a coffin so fine been seen in the district.

People continued to arrive, those coming from farther away who were not as close to the dead woman. Wishing to pay their respects, they all took some small part, if only symbolically, in the work. Most brought some contribution: a chicken, or some yams or bananas fresh from the field. Everything went into the pot. Soon the cooking spilled out of the kitchen and fires were built in the yard. Children were kept busy running home to bring pots or fetching pails of water from the standpipe. Miss 'Mando's piety, industry, and decency, and that of her family was praised repeatedly, the praise growing more lavish with each speaker.

Ivan accompanied Maas' Nattie as he moved from group to group inspecting the work and greeting folks. Despite himself he gloried in the attention as the next of kin, accepting the condolences and expressions of sympathy. From time to time he heard Maas' Nattie mutter:

"So you want it, me love. You please? Dis yah funeral is one whe' people going to remember an' talk 'bout fe generations."

And indeed, Ivan agreed, it was something. The ever increasing crowd, the varied and bustling activity.

"Yes, sah," one old man kept saying to any who would listen, "any how Miss 'Mando duppi don't well satisfy, den nothing no name satisfy again." Each time he said this it was with a strange kind of pride as if he were talking about his own final ceremonies, or as if taking a deep personal comfort in the scale and correctness of these preparations in a world growing daily more changed and uncertain. Maas' Nattie certainly seemed to share that sentiment, beaming every time he heard it.

As soon as it was dark and cooler, the coffin was taken into the house to receive the body. Before it emerged there was a rustling among the people sitting under the shelter. Izaac had walked in and quietly taken a seat next to the stand on which the coffin would rest. That was traditionally the place of the chief mourners, but Izaac seemed not to be aware of any breach of custom. He merely sat and smiled on the gathering, the smile of benign serenity which he wore when his spirit was not on him.

When the coffin was brought out and placed on the stand and the candles set at the head and feet, Maas' Nattie, in a departure from tradition, substituted a red, green, and black cloth for the usual white one, and the "set-up" or "singing meeting" began. Drawn-out melancholy notes of long-meter sorrow songs hung over the mountains and valleys like a rich velvet shroud textured by passion. There were tales, mostly of death or about the character and deeds of the departed and her family. But there were also riddles, word games, duppi stories, and much eating and drinking. Ivan, as next of kin, sat near to the coffin with Maas' Nattie. Mirriam and her grandmother were close by. Dudus and his father arrived from Blue Bay.

People, moved as much by the white rum and singing as by their remembrance of the dead, rose choked or even weeping to testify to their special relationsip to Miss 'Mando. However, even with the frequent and dramatic outbursts of tears and wailing it could not really be said to be a sad occasion.

Miss 'Mando had been old and had no known enemies so nothing sinister was suspected. The description of how she was found suggested resignation and acceptance; it didn't seem that she had "died hard." Everyone agreed that they could feel the presence of her spirit and that it was one of good-will and contentment. Izaac's serene smile at the foot of the coffin was seen to be the best omen of all since it was generally known that he could "see duppi." Joe Beck, a little carried away, got up and insisted that even the "dumb things" showed a spirit of peace. He had never, he said, slaughtered any animals that demonstrated so easy an acceptance of the knife. Ivan wondered if he could be talking about the bawling, struggling hog that had almost escaped twice with gouts of blood foaming from its ruptured throat. He and Mirriam nudged each other, whispered, and smiled.

"Ivan, Ivan look pon Dudus." Mirriam whispered.

"What?"

"You no see say him drunk?"

"You mad! Maas' Burt wi' kill 'im."

Dudus was standing at the edge of the shelter, his young brother Othniel looking at him with concern. Dudus was noticeably unsteady on his feet and was clapping his hands loudly and out of time to the song

> *Ah bin down in the Valley*
> *For a very long time*
> *I ain't get weary yet*
> *But . . .*

Great tears rolled glistening down his freckled cheeks. Ivan and Mirriam led him away to the pit where the hog was filling the night with the rich, toasty smell of roasting pork. Dudus was overcome. He bawled lustily and embraced Ivan.

"Ivan, Ivan, whaaiooo, me bes' fren'. Me good *passiero*. Lawd, me sorry. Me sorry, you hear? Poor Ivan, what you going do now? What to become of you?" He suddenly broke off his lament, belched, and an expression of astonishment came across his face as he ran quickly into the darkness.

Embarrassed, Ivan laughed when the sounds of retching came back to where he and Mirriam waited. "White rum lick 'im."

"Cho Ivan, don't laugh—you t'ink rum is a nice t'ing? Besides 'im is right, you know."

"You mean fe go black up° 'imself?"

"Don't play fool. I mean 'bout what you going to do."

"Oh, me? I goin' to town."

It was out before he could stop it. He had not in fact consciously made any plans or thought about his answer. But now it seemed to hang between them in the silence. In the glow from the pit he saw her face harden and small lines of tension form beside her mouth. He knew she was thinking about what had happened by the river and the thought that he might have given her a belly came to him for the first time.

"Den," she whispered almost unwillingly, "—den what 'bout—what about—us?"

"Me wi' sen' fe you—soon, soon."

She looked at him, something strange and very old in her face. "You know say me not goin' to live dere," she said quietly. "You done know that a'ready."

Ivan didn't know what to say. She hadn't changed her position, but she seemed to have moved a great distance off as she stared with glistening eyes into the red pit. He thought that her mouth trembled. Dudus reappeared, much more steady on his feet but with an expression on his face that reminded Ivan of when you beat puppy. He turned to him gratefully, "Wha' happen, man, you survive?" Mirriam moved away and Ivan didn't see her again that night.

The first pale streaks had begun to show over Jancrow mountain and roosters were crowing to each other across the valley when Maas' Nattie announced that the burying would be at noon.

° Black up: to get drunk.

Soon the only people left were stalwart and tireless ladies, laboring over fires on which was cooking food for the funeral feast, later that day.

The sun was almost directly overhead and the people had reassembled; there were more of them now as folks came from distant villages to be present at the burying. Miss 'Mando's sisters in the pocomania band were in full regalia: dazzling white robes stiff with starch and the peaked turbans which were the emblems of their sect. Maas' Nattie, resplendent in this year's burying suit made even more impressive by the red, green, and black sash with the letters UNIA embroidered in black, was ready to give the command for the pallbearers to pick up their burden. He had earlier spent a lot of time in earnest discussion with four old people whom Ivan had never seen before, three men and a woman all dressed in rusty black, who had suddenly appeared on foot. They seemed tired as though they had come a long way. There was something formal, almost military about them and they were especially interesting to Ivan because of the shiny brass instruments they carried. They were introduced by Maas' Nattie as "You granny loyal comrade dem" and Ivan wondered what unknown part of Miss 'Mando's life they represented. But Maas Nattie wouldn't explain more than "You wi' see, bwai, you wi' see."

Flanked by these ancient and mysterious presences, Maas' Nattie was just about to begin things when an unusual sound interrupted him. From the distant coast road came the unmistakable noise of a car turning onto the rocky road that led up the mountain. Maas' Nattie paused. Ivan felt a rush of excitement. Surely it had to be Miss Daisy, his mother, from the city. The drone grew nearer as the engine labored up the steep and twisting road. Everyone was listening. A whisper of speculation ran through the assembly. Sure enough, the sound approached the gap leading into Miss 'Mando's place and stopped. Ivan stared toward the road.

An elegant figure, dressed in black and wearing a hat with a veil and shoulder length black gloves, came toward them, her high heels skidding and buckling on the slippery rocks. She was carrying an impressive floral wreath which in its storebought and modern symmetry and perfection represented an unheard-of sophistication in those mountains.

"Is mus' de daughter from town?"

"No. Is not Daisy dat."

"Lawd, look 'pon de flowers dem Missis! Is can who?"

Identification was made more difficult by the veil fluttering from the stylish hat. Ivan recognized her a split second before Maas' Burt, looking stiff and almost unrecognizable in his suit, started up the hill to meet her.

"Pappy-Show!" old sister Anderson exclaimed loudly, twitching her shoulders to demonstrate that she was not impressed by the finery. "But Lawd me God, what a nerve de woman ha' doh, eh?" Mother Anderson was Miss 'Mando's closest friend and confidante.

"Do Missis, no talk!" one of the sisters agreed. "We poor sister mus' turn ina her coffin."

If Miss Ida heard she gave no sign. She walked easily and with dignity to where Ivan was and handed him the wreath.

"Ivan, bwai, Ah so sorry. When Ah hear Ah jus' had to come." She embraced him and stood back, completely ignoring the hard stares from Mother Anderson and her clique in their white robes.

"Thank you, Miss Ida," Ivan muttered, being careful not to look in Mirriam's direction. Maas' Nattie moved into the silence easily but with authority.

"You are welcome, Missis, to join us in our last farewells to our beloved sister."

Miss Ida nodded formally, then stepped up to the coffin, bowed, and said "Res' easy, Miss Martin. Res' easy. Take yo' blessed an' deserved res', in God's perfect joy an' peace."

"Ahmen!" roared Joe Beck, and earned a glare from Mother Anderson. Miss Ida gave a little curtsy and stepped back, a look of righteous piety on her face. Ivan thought her eyes twinkled just a bit.

Under a broiling sun, they carried the old lady in stately procession three times around the small yard, past the pig sty and the goat pen, over the low stone wall and through the coffee walk, to the new grave beside her husband's. The old-comrade woman beat a muffled drum roll on her Salvation Army drum and Mother Anderson and her pocomania sisters hummed slowly the tune of the lugubrious funeral standby:

> *Sleep on, sleep on*
> *Sleep on an' take thy rest.*
> *We loved thee true,*
> *But Jesus love thee best*
> *Good-bye . . . good-bye . . . good-bye.*

It was hot by the graveside. Even the shade of the huge tree gave little relief. They set the coffin down and looked to Maas' Nattie. He held up his hands in a priestly gesture as though asking for silence, even though the only sound was a few stifled sobs from the sisters.

"You all know dat our dear departed sister was very dear to mi soul—to all a we."

"Ahmen."

"Praise Gawd."

"Before she go, she leave me wid two las' wish. She say dat she want a big funeral, an' praise be to Gawd an' the love and respeck of all of unu she have dat." He looked at the gathering approvingly.

"Ahmen. Praise His holy name."

"Den she say she want to bury in the spirit. An' you can see dat. All a' unu is witnesses to dat."

"Hallelulah!"

"But next to her Gawd and her people dem, de t'ing that was mos' precious to her was the vision an' inspiration of the honorable Marcus Mosiah Garvey, the Leader an' Redeemer of de People." Maas' Nattie spaced each syllable of the name out like an exhortation. On the word "Garvey" the four old people pulled themselves smartly to attention and the old woman whispered fervently,

"Allelujah!"

"Many of unu will be too young to know dis," Maas' Nattie went on, "but the woman you burying was one of the *staunches'* and mos' *steadfast* and *earlies'* members of the Universal Negro Improvement Association in these parts."

Again a stiffening among the four ancients and murmurs of agreement.

"So Miss 'Mando's, res' her soul, 'las wish was to bury like a soldier of the Lawd and of Garvey." He stretched out his hand and the old woman marched forward and handed him a cloth somewhat smaller than the one he had draped over the coffin during the wake. It had embroidered on it in shaky gold lettering AMANDA MARTIN 1880-1950, and in smaller letters *Rise up ye mighty race*. Maas' Nattie exhibited it proudly so all could see. There were approving cries from the crowd as they read the inscription. He reverently draped it over the coffin, saying something that no one could hear. Then he drew himself up, faced the people, and in a voice throbbing with feeling and heroic fervor he declaimed:

> *Ethiopia dou land of our fathers,*
> *Dou land where the Gods love to be,*
> *As de storm clouds at night suddenly gadders,*
> *Our armies come rushing to dee.*
> *We must in de fight be victorious*
> *Our swords are outthrust to gleam*
> *For us will victory be glorious*
> *When led by de red, black and green.*

Here, the four rickety remnants of a dispersed army raised their reedy old voices in the passionate litany to a dead leader, a scattered movement, and a dream deferred but not forgotten:

> *Advance, advance to victory*
> *Let Africa's power be seen!*
> *Advance, advance to victory,*
> *With de might of de Red, Black and Green!*

The thin and ancient voices swelled with affirmation and a wistful grandeur on the last lines. Then, after a suitable pause, the men raised their instruments, the brass gleaming like dull gold in a shaft of sunlight. They stood there, Miss 'Mando's guard of honor, trembling right hands holding the brass to toothless lips, left fists clenched over their hearts. For reasons that he didn't understand Ivan felt a rush of hot tears behind his eyes. The old lady began a steady, low beat in a military cadence. The trombone missed the beat and started first with a windy wheeze, not unlike someone breaking wind, but quickly recovered and the brassy notes of the anthem quavered out, tentatively and discordant at first, then filling the valley with a broken grandeur that was nevertheless stirring. When the echoes of the last note died away, they buried Miss 'Mando.

• • •

Afterward everyone, even Mother Anderson's pocomania band who could have justifiably argued that their role had been slighted somewhat, agreed that it had been very fine indeed. Maas' Nattie wore the righteous satisfied look of a man who had seen his duty and performed it.

The afternoon was spent eating and drinking. That night there was a silent wake, but the crowd for this was much smaller, consisting mainly of close friends and neighbors and Mother Anderson's indomitable band, who would not be outdone in their devotion to tradition, piety, or the departed. Although Maas' Nattie would maintain with his last breath that the observations for Miss 'Mando had been strictly in accordance with tradition and "as 'cording to the old way dem," this was not quite true. And, while no one would annoy the old man by saying so to his face, there were a few old disputatious *tatas* around, who, holding themselves to be no less authoritative than Maas' Nattie on questions of tradition, whispered among themselves that there had indeed been lapses from strict orthodoxy.

At issue was this: everyone knew that the spirit of the dead remained in the grave for nine days after death, emerging at night to wander around the familiar places of the departed's life. This being so, it was necessary to have some formal activity—set-up, singing meeting, or a quiet watch—on each of those nights when the spirit would be wandering. But even more than the first night feast or the burying, it was the ninth night that was of significance. On this night, when the spirit finally departed the world, taking its last leave of the living, there was a great celebration from sundown to sundown. This included aspects of a wake, a singing meeting, funeral feast, and the ancient and mystic *Kumina*, a dance in which the spirits of ancestors took possession of the living and spoke through them so the last wishes and concerns of the departed could be revealed. On this occasion it was important for anyone who had known the dead person, or who could in any conceivable way be important to them, to be present to take leave of the spirit, lest it become angered or insulted by their absence.

It was not unknown for a spirit so offended to disrupt the proceedings completely, sowing rancor among the celebrants which resulted in fights and quarrels, or even for the spirit to bombard the gathering with stones and hard missiles. This was why Ivan had been kept busy running down to Blue Bay to send telegrams to the last known address of his mother.

It was the days between the burying and the Nine Night that the old men argued over, but quietly and among themselves. But if Maas' Nattie could be said to have neglected this period, it had also to be said that the important days were extraordinary. It is true that after the funeral feast had been eaten and the leftover food divided among the neighbors, the old man, who had not slept since the night three days previous when Ivan came knocking at his door, went home and took bed. When he came out it was to consult with Joe Beck and others about preparations for the Nine Night. Then he saddled his stallion and was gone for a day and part of the next night. No one knew at that time just what it was that had taken him away.

It was this hiatus that the strict constructionists pointed to in arguing that everything was not on the scale of the old days. Most felt that that was a quibble, because Mother Anderson and her flock of poco jumpers held loud sessions at the balmyard * every night and there was no law that said the celebration had to be held at the compound of the dead person, and who could imagine that Miss 'Mando's spirit would not be the central presence at such meetings? Also, as was pointed out, since the wake and burying had been so lavish and spectacular, most conversation in the district was about those events, especially the "Garvey business." So, clearly, the spirit if not the letter of tradition had been upheld.

Maas' Nattie seemed unconcerned. This was most likely because he did not hear the debate, or if he did hear of it, because he knew that the best was yet to be. The spectacular success of the funeral would be a hard act to follow, but he, Nathaniel, was up to the challenge.

Preparations for the Nine Night feast were even more extravagant than the burying and set-up. Despite the spontaneous contributions of the neighbors—even Miss Ida sent a bag of rice, considered town food—it was only Maas' Nattie's open-handedness in digging his own yam hills, cutting his bananas, and opening his pens, that prevented the total wiping out of whatever slim margin against hardship Miss 'Mando had managed to accumulate in a lifetime of toil through good years and bad, on the small holding. As it was, when the preparations were over, there was little left to reap in her ground, and there were few animals left in her pens save for those descended from the ones she had given Ivan when he was younger. Folks said that such extravagance—bordering on folly—was only possible because of the absence of groups of relatives counting the "dead leff" ** with acquisitive eyes. Indeed, this was noticed and there were speculative remarks passed to the effect that it seemed as if Miss 'Mando had given instructions to "done everyting" as though she knew she was to be the last of her line to live on that land. If Maas' Nattie heard these

* Balmyard: sanctuary of a pocomania shepherd where healing is done and religious ceremonies are held.
** Dead leff: estate left by the departed.

speculations he gave no sign but busied himself in the supervision of the preparations. All of this only meant that an even greater attendance was ensured for the old man's final production. As the people said, *"Bwai,* hear say is one t'ing; see fe self is somet'ing else."

People began to arrive in the afternoon, as soon as those domestic chores which couldn't be avoided or postponed were out of the way. With the cooking fires, the roasting pig, and the greeting of friends, the atmosphere was relaxed, almost festive, not unlike a small county fair. A current of expectancy—nothing somber or funereal—filled the air, in part due to Maas' Nattie's growing reputation as a producer of ceremonies. Almost everyone— even the "sanctified" sisters from the pocomania band—was seen to visit the demijohns of white rum, taking as Mother Anderson explained, "a little spirit to draw the spirits." Some of the older people, after the first little sip to "test the power," would casually spill a little rum on the ground to " 'member their dead," mumbling a string of names in a singsong undertone as they did so. The fragrance of wood smoke, roasting meat, and the pungent rum fumes mingled in a heady combination in the evening air.

The mystery of Maas' Nattie's earlier disappearance was cleared up as the sun was setting, when four men strode into the yard. They carried drums and had their heads wrapped tightly with bands of white cloth. Their leader was a squat fellow whose "cast" eyes looked disconcertingly in different directions, and who carried himself with an air of mystery and importance. He carried a large and elaborate drum called *Akete,* the granddaddy of drums. As he stood surveying the area a whisper ran through the crowd, the dread name *"Bamchikolachi, Bamchikolachi"* soon brought the children wide-eyed and nervous, quietly staring at the man of "power" who called spirits with his drum and who could see them approaching in the air. His drum was over four feet high and very elaborate, completely overshadowing the "female" drums which were its attendants. The group was greeted with respect and curiosity as they set up their instruments. Ivan was fascinated by the leader with the sonorous and mystic name, the power of which was such that people tended to say it only in whispers. *Bamchikolachi* even *sounded* powerful.

He politely refused all food, saying that he was on a *mission* and had purified himself. He did take a large measure of rum, which he accepted in a gourd decorated with feathers and carved designs. This he drank without pause after rubbing a quantity into the head of Akete to feed it. Then he sat quietly, hands resting easily on the drumskin, his mismatched eyes glowing in the fire-light. Having taken that position he remained motionless while his assistants busied themselves with various arrangements. One drew a large "holy" circle in the space that the people opened up under the shelter. The others set up their drums in a semicircle in front of the leader. Tassels of white and blue—the symbolic colors of the band's spirits—were tied to posts and rafters. Then the assistants went to sit in front of Bamchikolachi; they chatted among themselves and occasionally drummed out playful little rhythms as they waited. They seemed to enjoy the way the people tensed at each burst from the drums. The waiting became unendurable, and braver and more irreverent folks muttered, "Wait, is pose off dem come to pose off?" with some impatience.

But nobody said this loud, and the more prudent were quick to silence such outbursts. Just as the attention of the crowd had begun to wander, Bamchikolachi gnashed his teeth and shook his head as though stung by a scorpion.

"Hmm," grunted Joe Beck knowingly, "spirit deh yah strong, strong." Then Bamchikolachi sprang to his feet and paced around the circle, sprinkling holy water and rum from his gourd, and muttering fiercely in an unknown tongue. After each circuit he stopped, facing one of the cardinal points, throwing his fist forward and yelling something that ended with *"kumina hah!"* While he circled he studied the faces of the crowd, lightly touching several people who were thus chosen to "carry" the spirits in the dance. Ivan felt the light touch on his forehead and was immediately afraid. The first person chosen was Mother Anderson and the last was Izaac the madman. That Bamchikolachi, without prior knowledge of the community, had included in his selections the next of kin and the closest friend and spiritual associate of the dead woman, as well as the one person who was known to be regularly touched by spirits, was taken as a sign of the power of his vision.

In the intense and watchful silence, Bamchikolachi returned to his drum and filled his mouth with rum. He sprayed it in a fine mist at the fire which flared with a pale blue flame.

"Ago deh yah," he chanted.

"Ago deh," responded the assistants.

"Ago deh yah,"

"Ago deh." °

° Traditional beginning. It either means "I am going there," i.e. to the land of spirits, or is a fragment of some African language, the meaning of which is lost.

In a blur of speed his large hands raced across Akete's great head and the deep voice of the drum rolled out over the hills. The lighter voices of the female drums fluttered in and out of the rhythm and *Kumina*, the dance of the spirits, began. If nothing untoward happened, the sound of drums would greet the sun as it rose over Jancrow mountain in the morning.

As the throbbing rose around him Ivan felt his fear ebb away. His heart pounded to the beat of the drums, his blood raced, his feet—indeed his entire body—began to move, to lift itself on the swell of the rhythm without conscious volition on his part. He felt himself drawn into the sacred circle. It was not possible to resist the hypnotic beat that seeped into his bones, took over his heart, and emptied his mind of thought. He found himself chanting words without meaning as he danced:

"*Ago deh yah,*"
"*Ago deh.*"
"*Ago deh yah,*"
"*Ago deh.*"

At first they danced together in the steady almost monotonous *Nagah* ° shuffle around the circle. Akete controlled the pace while the female drums speeded up, slowed down, and explored polyrhythmic variations. The dancers became sharper and freer in their movements, breaking the circle and dancing into the center, captive to one or other of the minor rhythms that took their spirits over. Different beats served as vehicles for different spirits, and dancers responded when these rhythms appeared and the associated spirit reached out to touch them.

Ivan's head felt very light and as though it were swelling, growing immense, but there was no pain, just a sensation of airiness. His limbs were weightless too, moving and responding to nuances of the beat without thought or energy on his part. It was as if the drums had taken possession of his body and from some independent source had supplied it with the energy to dance in their service forever. He never tired, in fact he felt nothing save a great detached calm as if his mind had floated away and, emptied of the thoughts and concerns that usually rattled around in it, was at complete rest. In this dreamlike condition, Ivan felt that all the dancers, when they moved as one in the pulse and ebb of the rhythm, merged together and became a new, single being, sharing

° *Nagah:* either a corruption of the old *Nago,* refering to a Yoruba person or custom; or, in the dialect, a version of "nigger," from the plantocracy's pejorative description of the slaves dance.

one mind and moved by a single great will. But these moments alternated with the feeling of floating slowly, silently, and alone in some unknown place. It was a feeling of pure peace, of serenity, and a strange easy warmth.

Then the beat began to intensify. It didn't exactly speed up, but in some way he could not name it seemed to be more powerful, more urgent. Bamchikolachi leapt to his feet. While his hands continued to pound a steady pattern on the skin, his unbalanced eyes peered up into the dark air and he uttered affirmative little grunts from time to time. He was watching a spirit in the air, something no other drummer was able to do. His feet began to dance from side to side behind the drum, his hands flashed, his face contorted, his grunts became more explosive, then suddenly with a sigh the tension left him and he slumped down as though drained.

"Aiie, 'im tu'n back." His voice was heavy with fatigue and disappointment. Akete's huge voice stuttered, then fell silent.

The women standing among those who were not dancing—at least in the circle—let out a chagrined sigh, echoing his disappointment, and then spontaneously they were singing:

> Bright Soul,
> Wha' mek you tu'n back?
> You come a River Jordan
> An' you tu'n back!
> Bright Soul,
> Wha' mek you tu'n back?

In the sudden vacuum the female drums rattled on, seeking another potent beat, but their voices were uncertain, lacking authority. The circle of dancers turned inward. They looked toward the center of the circle, barely shuffling their feet in relaxed time to the singing, waiting for the direction and authority of the big drum. Ivan came to himself. Under his clothes he could feel cool rivulets of sweat against his hot body. He could hear the hoarse breathing of the other dancers, saw the bright white of the women's headcloths vivid against the sweat-shiny black skins. The throbbing, driving flow of warm energy that he had been riding was gone and he felt his limbs again. They were heavy.

In the center Bamchikolachi's shoulders sagged, his chin lolled forward onto his chest. His eyes were hidden and he seemed almost asleep. Around him a hum of conversation began.

"Cho," Maas' Nattie grumbled, "is what dis doh, eh? Bamchikolachi, hmm?"

" 'Im a try too hard," Joe Beck said. "You can't force dis t'ing, you know."

"Can't force it. Can't force it. Spirit mus' tek over drum, drum no call spirit. Is spirit tek de drum."

"Is aright doh," Maas' Joe soothed, "plenty-plenty power deh, yah. You will soon see who name Bamchikolachi dis yah night." He puffed on his pipe and settled comfortably on his seat. "Cho," he added, "is jus' de warmup dis. 'Im jus' a get warm."

Baroom. Pow. A horny palm exploded against the drumhead. *Baroom pow pow pow.* The sharp sound rang against the mountain and came back. The force of the sound fired the dancers' excitement. Bamchikolachi was like a man possessed. He grimaced and gnashed his teeth and his hands blurred in violent flurries against his drumskin. The voice of Akete seemed frenzied, the barely controlled fury of the rhythms rising rapidly to an almost hysterical pitch. The dancers grunted and whimpered, whirling and leaping with a desperate exultation. Old Mother Anderson began to wheel and dip. White foam appeared at the corners of her mouth.

"*Yes,*" she assented, "*ayah,* yes, yes," and she began to yelp and gibber as she spun and whirled across the circle like a great, white airborne bat, her robe fluttering in the firelight.

"Ah tell you! Ah tell you!" Maas' Joe Beck cried, barely able to keep his seat. "She gone now!"

Fast bursts of ecstatic language came from Mother Anderson as she swept in fluid sweeping turns back and forth across the circle and then collapsed into the arms of some onlookers. She lay rigid for a moment. Ivan's mind was clear, focusing on the old woman. He had sense of what his body was doing, but the circle of dancers was just a blur of urgent motion around him. A great tremor shook the old woman. Her chest heaved as the breath burst from her mouth in hollow honking gusts. She was "trumping and travailing in the spirit," the first step in possession. She trumped with great force, emptying her lungs exposively and refilling them with agonized-sounding wheezes that twisted her body as if she were having epileptic seizures. Then she became calm, almost comatose, and as the spirit took complete control she began to talk in the voice of an old man.

"Shepherd Anderson," muttered Maas' Nattie, nodding in approval. Shepherd Anderson was Mother Anderson's grandfather who had died some fifty years earlier. A luminary of the pocomania cult, he was a man famous in his time as a healer and prophet and his voice frequently was the first—and often the only one—to be heard on these occasions. Sometimes he brought messages from people's departed family, sometimes he foretold disasters and brought warnings. Once or twice he sounded as though he were drunk and was not easily understood. Now he spoke about a breeze-blow that was coming though it did not seem urgent: houses would be blown away but no lives would be lost. For the next few months fishermen would be well advised to read the moon carefully before going to sea, especially when the moon was waning. "Yes," he volunteered, "Miss 'Mando is here an' well please. Well please except for one thing . . ." Then the voice fell silent and another dancer began to wail and then started to trump. Mother Anderson lay still. She was being fanned by some women, who also administered smelling salts. Suddenly she sneezed and sat up, accepted a drink of water and calmly, supported by her helpers, took a seat and watched the dancing.

Ivan hadn't stopped dancing, though he had regarded everything with a detached interest that surprised him. When the second woman began to trump, he suddenly became chilled: the sweat that trickled over him felt cold in the mountain air. He felt vaguely troubled and stopped dancing and went to stand by Maas' Nattie. The sense of well-being and relaxed warmth was gone and he was suddenly afraid.

"Wait—Ah see you tu'n poco jumper," the old man teased about his dancing. "Ah was waiting fe spirit to tek you too." Noticing that the boy was shivering he gave him his black coat and a sip of white rum. The overproof liquor ran into Ivan's belly and gradually he became warmer, but he was still vaguely apprehensive. The woman who had been trumping had stopped. Evidently it was not her call, for she said nothing. She merely stood motionless with her face fixed in a rigid smile.

"Watch Izik," Maas' Joe whispered in wonder. The madman had entered the circle. He did not dance, trump or do anything dramatic, he just walked slowly into the center, but every eye was on him. He bowed solemnly to the transfixed woman as he passed and there was something funny, something familiar about the way he walked. What? Ivan couldn't place it. Izaac's mouth was open but he wasn't smiling. In fact his face seemed drawn and strained and seemed in the flickering light to be aging. Deep wrinkles etched themselves into the skin around his eyes and mouth.

"Lawd Jesus—is Miss 'Mando self," Joe Beck whispered hoarsely.

And it was, indeed, his grandmother's voice—Ivan could never mistake it. It was at first the friendly, slightly formal voice she used when greeting acquaintances on public occasions. She called the roll warmly, greeting and thanking many of those present, especially Maas' Nattie who was weeping openly. She inquired about a few that were absent, particularly Daisy, her only daughter. She had, she said, intended Mirriam to have her gold earrings but those were now in the grave. Would Maas' Nattie . . . ? Yes, he said, he would. And Mother Anderson, she had promised her some chickens, were any left? Maas' Nattie should make a point of thanking Miss Ida for the rice, but if it were already cooked he should send her another bag, but politely with many thanks.

The madman was silent for a while, walking about shaking hands, moving with that erect grace which the old woman had never quite lost. Then the voice changed. It became grating and metallic, the grim disapproving voice that Ivan had come to know.

"Ivan, mi gran'pickney. Whe' him deh? Is gone 'im gone a'ready?"

"No no," people called. " 'Im is right here, how you cyant see 'im?" Very reluctantly Ivan approached the edge of the circle. Again his head felt swollen, his knees weak.

" 'Im is right yah by me," Maas' Nattie called out placatingly.

Ivan wanted to run, and, despite the comforting arm that Maas' Nattie had draped over his shoulders, would have done so if the madman had started to approach him. But Izaac just peered at him nearsightedly and began to weep, pounding his head with his hands in the timeless female gesture of distress.

"Aaiee! Mi pickney, mi pickney. Mi pickney. Fire an' gunshat. Gunshat and bloodshed. Bloodshed and gunshat, waiee oh." The madman tore at his clothes and wept.

Then the voice, again cold and without emotion: "Behold dat dreamer cometh . . . let us take an' slay 'im . . . an' den we shall see . . . what shall become of his dreams. Yes, what shall become of his dreams. . . . For behold your young men shall dream dreams and your young men shall see visions. . . . Where dere is no vision the people perish. . . ."

Beside him Ivan could feel the old man stiffen. He heard him catch his breath and utter what seemed like a groan. Maas' Nattie's thin arm tightened on his shoulders.

"Talk plain, I beg you. Talk plain," the old man implored.

But Izaac said nothing more. He merely stood in an attitude of utter despair, shaking his head and weeping. Murmurs of sympathy rose from the people, though the cause of the spirit's distress was far from clear.

"Poor t'ing doh."

"Lawd, what a crosses, eh?"

"*Oie*, Missis, you see how trouble stay."

The drumming was like a distant accompaniment. Izaac wept bitterly and the people murmured sympathetically. After a while his behavior changed abruptly. He straightened up; the lines and creases left his face. He began to dance and frolic about in an idiot's dance full of grotesque gestures and poses without meaning, laughing and giggling and occasionally slapping himself on the head. The woman again began to trump and convulse and collapsed in a heap on the ground. At that moment Izaac's antics ceased and he walked out of the circle in his normal way with his usual serene smile and preoccupied manner. Without looking at anyone, although all eyes were on him, he walked to a fire and accepted a large helping of curried goat and Miss Ida's rice. Rice was considered a great delicacy, not being grown in the mountains, and the madman would accept neither bananas nor yams. He was the only person present who seemed completely unaffected by the night's events.

The drumming began again but it was perfunctory. When it was clear that no one was really moved to dance more and that no other spirits would visit, Bamchikolachi stopped. He took his drum, nodded to Maas' Nattie, and walked into the darkness. His assistants stayed to eat and drink and to tell strange tales of the wonders they had seen from the shadow of their leader's mystic drum.

It had been expected that the general festivities—singing, telling riddles, seeing who could create the biggest "Nine Night lie," and feasting—would continue until sunset the next day. But the dramatic appearance of the dead woman's duppi, for clearly that was what it had been, cast a pall over the gathering. Nobody spoke of anything other than the strange and troubling message and all its possible meanings. Ivan felt that they were all talking about him. Even Maas' Nattie seemed withdrawn and thoughtful in a troubled kind of way. The situation might have been saved, for there was good company and large quantities of food and drink remained, and a festive mood was just beginning to reassert itself—when the stallion reared up, broke its halter, and galloped snorting and whinnying around the small yard. It kicked a pot off the fire and knocked down one of the posts supporting the shelter before it leaped the low stone wall and galloped down the road, its shod feet clattering over the stones.

"Is arright," Maas' Nattie said to some men who were preparing to go in pursuit. "Is arright, 'im nah go nowhere but to 'im yard." Which was true—but his unusual and portentous behavior coming at such a time caused people to remember pressing obligations at home. What was at first a trickle became a general exodus, and the sun rose on a scene of desolation and emptiness. The fires had smoldered and died, the grass and shrubs were trampled and bruised, and only two drunks lay under the broken shelter when the old man and the boy went to sleep.

BOOK TWO

Another Generation Cometh

*One generation passes,
and another generation cometh:
but the earth abideth forever.*

—Ecclesiastes

4

City Bwai Version

Behold that dreamer cometh . . .

They came on foot out of the hills before the sun had risen, when the chill mist from the sea still billowed among the dark trees, softening their outlines and making the leaves damp and shiny. Ivan, Dudus, and his younger brother Othniel came through the empty streets past the silent two story wooden houses and the old Spanish brickwalled square, headed for the piazza in front of the china shop where the bus stopped. The brothers were along, not simply to see Ivan off, but to help carry the three heavy boxes of "membrances" that along with advice and benediction were showered, as a matter of course, on anyone going from the country to the city.

" 'Member me to Miss Daisy, Ivan. See few little pear an' one bunch a banana yah. Tell her Maas' Joe Beck sen' dem wid respeck."

The little town was silent as they entered the square, the only sound the distant roar of the waves breaking on the sea wall. They were not the first to arrive. On the concrete piazza two market women were already sitting asleep against the wall, surrounded by baskets and boxes of food for the city markets. They seemed at first lifeless bundles of clothes amid the clutter of commerce that surrounded them. The boys waited, talking in low voices as the sun rose behind the mountains, tinting the world with a delicate pale pink light, and the piazza began to fill with travelers. These were mostly women, the sisterhood of hagglers, traditional grass-roots merchants with their plaid headcloths, heavy men's shoes and wide straw hats. The masters of a sophisticated and myste-rious pricing system, they represented—from time immemorial—the link between the small farms and the hungry city, and thus controlled the peasant economy on which the daily food of the country depended. Some arrived singly, erect under the weight of huge head-balanced baskets. Others came accompanied by their menfolk and children, each carrying, according to their age, bundles and baskets of appropriate size. Soon the area was filled with baskets of yams, bananas, strings of colorful fruit, mangoes, tangerines, coconuts, starapples, red peppers, long cords of sugar cane, chickens firmly trussed with heads tucked under their wings, and even a suckling pig or two bound and squealing.

Ivan's excitement mounted as the time for the bus's arrival came and went. He tried not to keep turning in the direction from which it was expected, and hoped that his anxiety wasn't visible to the hardbitten and casual travelers around him. With his new clothes and the little stingy-brimmed straw hat he had bought to give him what he hoped was a look of urban sophistication, he didn't want his nervousness to betray him. So many people. But all of them couldn't be intending to get on the bus? How was everything going to hold? One thing sure, though, he wasn't going to be left. He moved his boxes nearer to the road, thereby calling attention to himself and precipitating a general movement in that direction.

"Bus comin?"

"Me no see nutten."

"Is wha' do dis big head boy, eh?" demanded a fat lady in an irritable voice, "Him must be t'ink say him pay more fare dan everybody else?" Ivan pretended to be deeply interested in the horizon as if the woman could not possibly be speaking to him.

"Yes, is you Ah talkin' to. You wid the hat favah poor parson pickney. Why you t'ink say you mus' first, eh?" The reference to the hat elicited a few snickers because the poverty and consequently ill-fitting clothes of certain of the rural clergy was a traditional source of irreverent humor. Ivan's cheeks burned.

"Cho. Lef' off the young man, Mathilda. How you cantankerous so? Mawning jus' light an' you soun' like you wan' fight already?"

"How you love *kass-kass* so, eh?" another voice remonstrated with the speaker. There was a general murmur of assent attesting to Mathilda's bad temper.

"But wait . . ." Mathilda drawled with deceptive calm, "but wait? Is me unu ha' strength for dis mawnin'? Unu t'ink say Ah nice, no? But Lawd," she appealed dramatically to Providence, "you see mi trial here dis mawning? I beg unu lef' me out dis here mawnin' yaah! *Lef'* me out, Ah say!" Her tone was both threatening and challenging, as if she dared the universe, much less any one in the group, *not* to leave her alone. Further developments were aborted by the arrival of the bus.

That was also an event of no little drama. Long before its appearance, its roar destroyed the peace of the countryside as the driver double-clutched down through the gears, over-revved the engine to a tortured howl, and with exquisite timing came around the corner to the accompaniment of a series of deafening back-fires. The bus, a decrepit red and green juggernaut of indeterminate vintage, rumbled up to the group, belching thick clouds of black smoke, shuddering and jerking on creaking springs as it skidded to a stop with a loud hissing of air brakes. Emblazoned on the side in an ornate gold script was the legend FERVENT PRAYER—GOD IS MY CO-PILOT, a claim which no one observing its progress over narrow mountain roads could reasonably doubt.

"Aaiee! Drivah! Drivah to raas, man." This admiringly from a group of loafers standing in front of the rum shop. The crowd began to mill and jostle around the door while the "pilot," an intense, thin East Indian, sat majestically behind the wheel as though savoring the adulation that was his due. Ivan stared at him. So this was the legendary "Coolie Man," or "Coolie Duppi," so-called because people swore that only powerful supernatural aid could account for the many accidents from which he had walked away. Not all of the passengers were so lucky, but he was the only driver ever known to regularly beat the morning train into the city, although that was when both he and FERVENT PRAYER were younger and less battered. To Ivan the bus seemed close to being dangerously full already. The baggage racks on top were invisible under a clutter of boxes and baskets.

"Open de door, drivah!" a man yelled imperiously.

"Wha' you a do? Siddown deh like you nice, watch 'im nuh?"

"Open de raas door dem."

Coolie Man ignored the clamor and flicked his cigarette disdainfully through the window. Carefully he peeled off his gloves, removed his dark glasses to reveal bloodshot eyes, and turned a baleful gaze on the crowd. He regarded them impassively for a minute, then bellowed, "Stan' back. Unu out to bruk down de raas door? Stan' back, Ah say."

The crowd surged against the door defiantly. "Me say, open the raas door!" one man shouted, punctuating his remark with a resounding slap on the metal side.

"Unu nah move, no?" the driver taunted, and raced the motor, engulfing the crowd in acrid black fumes. The people were driven back choking by the cloud and the driver's assistant, a burly fellow known as "Drunk A'ready" who served as loader, collector of fares and enforcer of order, took over.

"Unu mus' ha' manners. One at a time now!" he bellowed as he emerged. Muttering, eyes tearing, the crowd began to pay their fares. Ivan was the first to enter, dragging the box with his clothes and most of the money Maas' Nattie had entrusted to him. He had heard tales of clever city pickpockets and was taking no chances. There were no seats so he sat on the box in the aisle just behind the driver. The passengers already seated were divided about the disagreement between the driver and the people.

"But dis man mad?" a woman speculated loudly. "Is why him have fe handle de people dem so?"

"De drivah right," a man maintained. "Dem mus' ha' manners. If is me, Ah lef' everyone a dem."

"You see you? Is all like you whe' wrong wid black people. Jus' because you ha' fe you seat, you wan' lef' de rest a we."

"All Ah say," the man said pedantically, "is dat dem *mus'* ha' *manners*. When Ah was in London, people always line up orderly. English people ha' manners," he sniffed.

"G'way," the woman jeered, "you face favor manners. Is English man you love, eh? All a unu too bad-minded an' wicked. Look 'pon you too, a talk 'bout manners, you teeth tusk like fe hog." This sally was greeted with a ripple of laughter in appreciation of a certain cruel accuracy of the description. The advocate of manners and the English grimaced in an attempt to stretch his lips over his protruding front teeth and lapsed into silence, the most unkind cut of all being the laugh of the driver whose actions he had defended. The latter then stepped out of the bus and strutted grandly into the shop, ignoring the jeering descriptions of his person and the unnatural sexual practices to which his conception was attributed by the crowd.

The processing of passengers was a lengthy and lively business, since fares were computed not only on the basis of destination, but on a variable scale which took into account the number and size of the passenger's goods, whether they were animal or vegetable, and apparently whether the gigantic assistant liked the "style" of each individual.

"But it look like say is two fare unu have—one fe young gal an' one fe me?" the heavy woman who had challenged Ivan objected.

"How fe you *batti* ° fat, you shoulda pay double. All like fe you batti can' hol' ina one seat," the assistant said with a nasty laugh.

° *Batti:* buttocks.

"Go look 'pon you maddah batti how it fat," the woman spat, hands on her hips belligerently. "You faastie bitch you, who fa batti you a look 'pon." And with a twitch of the massive posterior under question she entered the bus. Two women entered without incident, but the third had a different grievance.

"What? How it can be two dollar fe go a May Pen, an' you only charge three fe go Kingston? Unu too damn t'ief, man."

The liveliest dialogue concerned another issue, the impartially rough treatment of the merchandise at the hands of Drunk A'ready.

"Maastah! It coulden' be mi yam dem you dash down so. Wha' happen sah, you trouble wid your head now?"

"Ah beg you try no mash up me mango dem, y'know sah!" a woman said.

The assistant grunted, and replied sweetly and with indisputable truth, "You lucky is not egg in dere, mi love," and threw the bag up with the same cavalier disregard to contents.

"Ugly black brute," growled the owner, as she stomped into the bus.

To Ivan's great relief, the loading was finally complete. Miraculously, it seemed that every person, box, bundle, chicken, and pig was aboard the bus, which had settled ominously low on its springs. Despite the open doors and the cool morning breeze, it was somewhat stuffy in the packed interior. The driver hadn't returned and the assistant too had disappeared, presumably to track him down. The passengers were not in good humor, nor were they inclined to patience. Complaints were voiced loudly, irritably: "Is whe' dat coolie man gone to, eh?" Warnings were uttered: "Dem don't want I get ignoran' out yah today, y'know?" The expressions became more angry and frequent. A long arm reached over Ivan and pressed the horn, which blared out with raucous urgency.

The driver appeared at the door of the shop, wiping his mouth and blinking in the sun. He sauntered up to the door, cleared his throat, spat, wiped his chin, stuck a cigarette in the corner of his mouth, and then climbed up to his seat. With studied deliberation he pulled on his gloves, wiped his sunglasses and put them on, adjusted the rear-view mirror, then turned and silently regarded the passengers, for a long time. He spat through the window again and closed the doors. "So . . . it look like unu deh 'pon haste, eh?" He laughed hollowly and said, "Watch me nuh," and with a flourish, started the motor.

"Drivah, to raas, yes," came from the back. It was a sentiment Ivan shared. Whatever the driver's obvious social shortcomings, and they were many and grievous, there was a dramatic quality to the way he carried himself, and style was style. Now he was perched on the edge of his seat, head cocked to one side in a listening attitude as his right foot stabbed at the gas. His right hand nonchalantly rested on the gear lever as the pistons pounded and black smoke from the exhaust filled the square. The driver seemed to listen a moment, then in one incredibly quick, almost stylized motion, his hands and feet blurring, he came off the gas, depressed the clutch, slapped the lever into first, came up off the clutch and went back down on the gas. The bus lurched forward; had it been less heavily laden, it might have leapt, but under the circumstances a lurch was no mean accomplishment.

From his vantage point Ivan could observe the driver's technique as well as watch the passing landscape. He wanted to pay particular attention to the driver because among his first projects, after establishing his fame as an entertainer, was to get himself a motor vehicle of some sort: a shiny sleek American car preferably although at first a motorcycle might have to do—after all one had to be realistic.

Coolie Duppi's technique was well worth observing if not emulating. They were passing through a moderately curvy section of road. On the level the bus could not go over forty-five miles an hour, which, given its load and the condition of bus, driver, and road, was entirely too fast. On the frequent downgrades, however, there seemed to be no limit. Coolie Man's approach to cornering was as simple as it was effective. He would race toward the narrow blind curves with his horn blaring. This, clearly, was intended to warn any animal, human, or vehicle that might be around the corner to climb the bank, for, having given what he considered suitable warning he would wait until the last possible minute to gear down and skid the heavy bus around, using every inch of the narrow road in the process, the shouts of the more nervous passengers seeming only to goad him on. He was a study in motion. He didn't sit on the seat so much as brace himself against the edge, in a kind of splendid tension between his body and the instruments. The left hand held the wheel, except for when he needed both hands to wrestle the bus around a curve. The right hand flashed between the busy gearshift, his mouth with the ever present cigarette, and the horn, while his feet danced between brake, clutch, and accelerator as he geared up and down on the hilly, twisting, narrow road. It was exhausting just to look at him.

Outside the landscape flashed by in a greenish blur—Ivanhoe had never gone this fast in his life. As the telephone poles flashed by like a row of soldiers, as the top heavy bus swayed to a chorus of groans and wails, he experienced the same fascinating mixture of exhilaration and fear that he had felt as he plummeted toward the dark river, the day he leapt from the bridge.

Then they entered a long plain where the road became relatively flat and straight, the driver's performance less dramatic, and the motion of the bus steadier, almost monotonous. Everyone relaxed. Ivan's excitement ebbed away and he sank back on his box. He felt an exhausted calm creep over him as though he were going to sleep. So much had happened so quickly. Like the landscape outside, recent events flashed through his mind in rapidly changing impressions. Gradually his mind too slowed down, and the general conversation that swirled around him receded to a distant hum.

. . .

Two evenings ago, after the tumult of the Nine Night, the little yard had seemed very empty, even desolate. The animals—those that had escaped the demands of traditional hospitality—had been moved to Maas' Nattie's pens. Down by the stone wall under the breadfruit tree the mound of fresh turned earth, like a scar on the face of the mountain, marked Miss 'Mando's last resting place. Ivan had been tying up the last box when he heard the clatter of hooves on the road. He listened; it was not the urgent staccato of a gallop, but a more stately almost processional gait, somewhere between a canter and a walk. He met the old man at the gate. A small, almost tiny figure atop the huge beast, Maas' Nattie regarded him gravely without speaking.

"So you goin' to fin' you mother, den." It was not a question and Ivan nodded. "Well, is a shame she miss de funeral—but what to do . . ." There was a note of proprietary disappointment in his tone, as though he were personally pained that everyone had not been at the funeral. "An'—after you fin' her—you not coming back?" There was a questioning inflection at the end, but this too was no question. Ivan nodded again. The old man sighed, and slowly, with an air of tired resignation, dismounted. "Well, can' say Ah surprise. Mek we tek a walk, bwai." Ivan was not surprised either when after a seemingly aimless stroll around the yard they arrived at the group of graves. The old man bowed his head and his lips moved; then he began to speak out loud, not looking at Ivan or appearing to address him directly. He could have been talking to himself, or to the spirits of those that lay in the earth.

"Y'know," he began musingly, "dem say 'a fly that no tek advice will follow dead man mouth into grave, huh'? Listen me, an' listen good to dis poor ol' fool. Ah been almos' everywhe' an' done almos' every t'ing. Ah nevah sorry when ah lef' an' then Ah wasn't much older dan you—an' Ah nevah sorry when Ah come back, eider."

"Bwai—you a somebody. You come from some whe'. All you generation dem is right yah." He gestured emphatically toward the earth. "You Granmaddah, you Granfaddah, you uncle Zekiel whe' de bull kill down a Duncans—him dey yah too. All a dem right yah. Good people—respectable. People say all kin' a t'ing— some say dem did proud. Some say dem did quick to anger an' love fight. But Ah nevah hear nobody say dat you people evah t'ief. No sah, not a man can say dem evah tek nutten, not a *penny*, not a *fowl*, not a *pin* whe' dem nevah work, sweat an' pay fe. You hear me bwai?"

"Yes, sah," Ivan murmured, tears in his eyes.

The old man nodded as though satisfied. "Good. Good. Well don't you evah forget dat. You come from somewhe', from decent people dem, people whe' nevah ha' no heap a money—but dem nevah poor neider. And you raise up decent, to know what right an' to have manners. Bwai, don't grow 'way from you raisin', eh?"

"No, sah."

"Now, dis place you a go—Kingston? What you know 'bout it? You t'ink say it stop yah? You a go see t'ings whe' you nah go believe. Me say even *after* you see dem with you own eye, when you rub you eye an' *look* again an' see dem *again*, you nah go believe dem. Me know." He shook his head slowly with a kind of sad emphasis.

"Town people dem *different*, different bad, you *hear* Ah tell you? Dem no stay like we. All kinds a people you a go meet dere. Some whe' no know no law at all, *atall*. Lie? Mi Gawd! T'ief? Ha' mercy! You no see t'ief yet. Wait, you see! Dem *love* fe work dem brain fe get what is not fe dem, to reap where dey have not sown, to pick up what dem no put down. Uhuh. Some a dem—if dem tell you run—stand up. If dem say stand up, run. If dem ready fe tell lie 'pon you, you must hang. Dem come a courthouse, kiss Bible, *tek oath*, shed tears, Ah mean dem cry de *living* eyewater, an' look dead ina you face an' tell lie send you to gallows." Maas' Nattie fell silent as though he could find neither words nor emphasis to express the unfathomable level of iniquity to be found in the city.

"Courthouse is not a nice place—no go deh. Me say *no go deh!* Thirty years me deh out a world—Cuba, Panama, 'Merica, Kingston. But to dis day Ah can' tell you how de inside a courthouse stay. Is not a good place—no go deh, me say." His voice rose sharply, and staring fixedly at Ivan, stamping his foot after each word for emphasis he repeated, *"No go deh, me say."*

He continued in that vein for a while, then his voice became reflective, gentle. "Ah always did have a special likin' fe you, bwai. Y'know, you granfaddah was a maroon man. Y'know dat? Ah been telling you so from you small. A cromanty man from Accompong maroon town. Well, Ah always say you tek after him. Dem is a funny people, y'know. Do some funny t'ings. But it look like to me you have dat same spirit. But bwai—" His voice sank almost to a whisper. "You gwine have fe careful. . . . No matter how you heart big, sometime you have fe take low. Have fe tek low sometime. So de worl' stay, me son. When you black an' no have money, you have fe tek low sometime. Is so life go—strong man nevah wrong an' poor man can't vex. Use you head, boy. Dem say 'coward man keep sound bone.' Now Ah not saying you fe let people piss down you back an' you call it sweat. No. Not so! But you have fe use you head more dan you mouth. You gwine have fe wrap up heart burn in a you chest and force you mouth to smile. When hot word come a you mouth, you gwine have fe swallow dem down so burn you belly bottom. Use you head, bwai, you head more dan you mouth." He was silent for a long time, then he breathed a heavy sigh and said, "Arright, pay you respeck to you Granny, an' come let we go up." Together they bowed their heads in silence before the grave.

When the old man was again on his horse his mood seemed to change, become lighter and more expansive. "Oh, me nearly forget. Now how Ah coulda forget a t'ing like dis? Old age worse dan obeah ° fe true." He reached into his pocket and produced a small bag which he casually tossed to Ivan. "Here take dis—is fe Miss Daisy. But be careful wid it, is plenty money. Tell her say is

° Proverb.

her legacy what lef' after the lan' sell an' everyt'ing pay fe." He kicked his mount into motion and started away. Then he wheeled around and came back, a huge impish smile on his face, looking at Ivan appraisingly, his eyes glowing with mischief. "Bwai, you full a you self now, eh? Money ina pocket an' a go a town. Yes, you jus' a dead fe somebody call you man, eh? Well you gettin' dere, me lad, you gettin' dere. You live long enough, everyt'ing wi' happen to you. So Ah talkin' to you as a man now, not as no more pickney. Dis is somet'ing Ah couldn' tell you down deh." He gestured toward the graves and his voice became conspiratorial: "One mo' t'ing—bwai, you *can'* done pussy. You gwine ha' fe tek some an' leave some. You *can' done pussy* so don't mek it rule you. You can' done it *a raas.*" And with a rich, lascivious chortle, he turned the horse's head around and galloped off.

Ivan stood open mouthed for a minute before he too started to laugh. "Yes, Maas' Nattie say you can' done pussy." Lost in his reverie, Ivan did not realize that he had spoken, until his quiet laughter was interrupted by a sharp, suspicious voice.

"What you say, young bwai?" The woman was frowning at him, her disapproving face daring him to repeat what she seemed to think she had heard.

"Me nevah say nutten, mam," Ivan said meekly.

"Hmm," she sniffed. "Den is what sweet you so?"

Ivan didn't feel he needed to answer so he shrugged and looked outside. There wasn't much to see. The bus was still rumbling easily through the rolling plain, the road bordered by an unbroken monotony of cane like a green ocean.

But suddenly he was fully awake and staring at the road ahead. There the entire world seemed to be on fire. A wall of orange and yellow flame crackled in the air above the cane. A dense cloud of black smoke billowed into the sky, screening out the sun. The bus began to fill with acrid fumes. All Maas' Nattie's stories of slaves in revolt burning down the plantations rushed into Ivan's mind and filled him with fear and excitement. But he knew that there were no more slaves, so what was this enormous fire? An accident? No one seemed worried. What if the bus were to catch fire?

The man on the seat on the other side of him noticed his agitation. He smiled at Ivan kindly. "Wha' happen, young bwai? You nevah see dis yet?"

"No, sah," Ivan admitted. "Is what?"

"Nutten," the man said." Is just burn dem a burn off de leaf dem. Mek it easier fe cut de cane."

"Den, it no burn up de cane too?"

"Dem say it no harm it. But sometime when de workers dem strike, or if dem have some dispute dem will burn up de cane still."

Ivan watched the raging, apparently uncontrollable fire until it was no longer visible and wished Maas' Nattie were present. So black man was still a burn down the canefields dem? Maas' Nattie would want to know that. He would write him. . . . Excitement flooded him: he was really on his way to Kingston, at last, to a place of excitement, of possibility; to a great unknown future where anything could happen. What was it really like? He had no clear picture, only a vague image of broad streets, grand houses of stone, glass and brick, and stores in which wonders were to be had, money in large quantities and dance halls, and all just waiting for him.

The first thing would be to find Miss Daisy; after that there was a blank. What then? Where would he live? In an upstairs house with a room on the second floor, he sort of hoped. How did one become a singer man? As Miss Ida said, a *"recording* artis'." He savored the phrase: Ivanhoe Martin, recording artis', how sweet the soun'. Now all dese people on the bus, dem didn't know him. The lady who jus' tek him on, she didn't know who she was talking to, but one day, *bwai*, one day she might see him picture an' maybe remember de country boy who was sitting on de box. One day dem wi' all know me. He straightened up, flicked his hat back, and tried to look worldly and mysterious.

Around him a babble of conversation floated as people commented loudly and freely on whatever caught their attention. They would boldly enter a conversation going on two seats away to venture an opinion or confidently correct a misstatement. There were sharp exchanges of wit as arguments developed between strangers, with other strangers taking sides. Clever remarks were greeted with laughter and applause, foolish or unpopular ones with derision and ridicule. Though a faded sign said LOADED CAPACITY 44 there had to be, not counting chickens and pigs, at least sixty souls aboard. The very crampedness eliminated any sense of privacy or isolation and every shudder, creak, or groan from the laboring bus was occasion for graveyard humor.

"Ah wonder," speculated a loud, quizzical voice addressed apparently to the universe at large, "why dem a jam up all dem little pickney under me batti, eh? Bwai, if Ah evah fart, dem mus' dead, y'know."

"Well, Ah sure hope say is not ripe pear 'im eat fe breakfast," another voice said, followed by a loud, vulgar sound. The only people who didn't join the laughter were three small children crowded behind the tall fellow who had first spoken. They made futile attempts to pull back out of the danger zone and the smallest, a little girl, began to whimper.

"Cho, unu too damn wort'less," a seated woman scolded. "See how unu a frighten de pickney dem wid unu slackness. After you wouldn't want nobody handle fe unu pickney so—dass if unu can ha' any." She glared at the tall fellow and reached out to the child. "Come yah, mi dear, come sit 'pon mi lap." The other children were similarly rescued from the possibility of a bout of sudden flatulence on the man's part.

Once safely seated, the little girl glared at the tall man and piped up clearly, "You wuthless, hugly brute, you."

"Dass right, mi love, cuss him," a voice encouraged and even the saturnine Coolie Man joined the laughter.

Although no one else could fit on the bus, and nobody seemed to wish to get off, it stopped in every town they came to. "Engine ha' fe cool off," Coolie Man said tersely as he made for the rum shop the first time they stopped.

"Engine a cool off, drivah a hot up," someone observed.

"Hope him no bother drunk up 'imself so kill we off, y'know."

"Drunk up 'imself? Ha! Drunk up 'imself? Wait, you no see say him drunk from mawnin'?" another asked.

"Yes," someone else agreed drily, "we ina de copilot hands long time."

When they came to the mountain called "Diablo," Coolie Man floored the accelerator and developed as much speed as he could. But the steep winding road slowed them down gradually, and less than halfway up they ground to a halt. Ivan looked at the man next to him inquiringly.

" 'Im a go try reverse. If dat no do it, we wi' get out an' walk up to the top."

Slowly, on a road flanked on one side by the face of the mountain and on the other by a steep chasm, the bus was turned around. Then Coolie Man opened the door, and standing—one foot on the running board, the other on the accelerator—he inched the bus around the steep curves. The engine shrieked and pounded and Ivan could feel on his face hot blasts of oily air from the exhaust. Everyone seemed to be straining, faces tense with concentration as though willing the sluggish vehicle over the hill. Then with a heave, like a laden mule gathering its muscles and forcing itself over a wall, the bus lunged up the last incline and onto a level plateau. There was a collective expulsion of breath from the passengers.

"Bwai, you can' beat Englishman when it come to motor, eh?" the tusk-toothed fellow observed in a voice bursting with anglophilic pride.

"Yes," the fat woman taunted, "we know long time say Englishman a you God. But is how come dem bus couldn't go over front way, eh?"

He gave her a pitying look and treated the comment to a haughty silence. They stopped while Drunk A'ready poured water into the steaming radiator. Ivan looked around in some astonishment. There was something very different about the landscape which at first he couldn't figure out. Then it struck him: they had turned inland and for the first time the familiar blue of the sea wasn't visible in the distance. He had never been completely out of sight of the sea before—from his mountains the sea was always visible. But from here, on all sides, he could see nothing but a great plain, with bleeding slashes like raw wounds on its green face, where precious red earth was being scooped up. He had always assumed that on this "small island in the Caribbean sea" as he had learned in school, the sea would be always in sight. To his eyes now, as he looked around and saw in one direction distant mountains shrouded in clouds and in another, a horizon where the sky met land rather than sea, he was filled with a sense of vastness and size beyond anything he had imagined.

"Bwai, an' dem say dis yah country small?" He felt a twinge of exultant and proprietary pride.

When the bus had cooled to Coolie Man's satisfaction, he resumed his seat and again, with his usual finicky attention to detail, went through the ritual of gloves, glasses, and mirror.

"Arright now, we late," he announced. "Time is money, so unu bettah hol' on good," he added, with the familiar mirthless laugh. At first he inched down the steep road with a restraint that was as exemplary as it was surprising. Then they came to the foothills where there were relatively long stretches of straightway punctuated by deep curves. It was as though he had been waiting for this road, as if there were between himself and the road some private grudge or covenant which now possessed him. If Ivan had been impressed with his skill and daring earlier, that paled to insignificance in the face of what now happened.

Taking advantage of the straight downslopes, Coolie Man allowed the heavy bus to hurtle forward unchecked, attaining speeds way beyond the normal capacity of the abused engine. For a brief time, Ivan was carried away by the freedom and excitement in the sensation. Then just as the speed seemed excessive, the bus beyond control, with a corner rushing to meet them, Coolie Man geared down and stood up on the brake, so that they could feel the grab of brakes and compression resisting the pull of gravity. With a rush of wind, a shriek of metal, and the squeal of tires, the ponderous bus seemed to be struggling against a force that was pushing them outward toward the puny-looking restraining wall, and into the chasm beyond. Coolie Man—his slight, tense body wrestling with the wheel—seemed at the last minute to fling the bus into the turn. The rear swayed sickeningly each time and once sideswiped the wall with a crash before bouncing back into the road. When he cut the inside corner too close, shrubs and low-hanging branches banged explosively against the sides, and each crash was greeted with a wail:

Bang! "Whaaiio, Ah dead now!"

Bang! "Whaiooe. Stop de bus!"

"De man mad ooe'!"

Ivan felt no exhilaration now; now he was terrified, as were the rest of the passengers. The pandemonium was complete.

"Ooh, mi maddah . . . mi maddah . . . mi maddah," the fat lady sobbed.

But shouts of anger and fear merely added to the other noises and seemed to feed the drunken obsession of the driver. He was either laughing or shouting but what he was saying was lost in the tumult. Once when he skidded around a particularly vicious curve, the sides of the bus brushed against the face of the mountain. "Dis a Coolie Man to raas!" he shouted boastfully, and banged his knee with an exultant hand. On another curve Ivan felt the inside wheels leave the surface of the road, and the top-heavy bus seemed to teeter for a sickening second before settling back on four wheels. There were shouts of "Lawd Gaad, Ah dead now!" and "We a go tu'n ovah, we a go tu'n ovah!" Ivan clutched the seats on either side to avoid being thrown violently from side to side as around him people sobbed, cursed and prayed.

When Coolie Man eased the bus into the plains the shouting didn't immediately subside.

"Stop de bus, you ol' drunkard, you."

"Ah six pickney me lef' a yard, stop de raas bus, Ah say."

"Dem fe lock you up, you wicked coolie brute, you."

The anger of the people was real, and the general sentiment was for stopping the bus and summoning the nearest police. Ivan was sure that if the driver were to bring the bus to a halt for any reason he would be mobbed by the crowd. Coolie Man, clearly sensing this, did not stop. He proceeded at a reasonable pace, the very model of circumspection as the bus rumbled over the plain. He never once answered the abuse and threats that poured over him. Except for the intermittent sobbing and the continued grumbling, and the sweat-soaked figure at the wheel, Ivan could almost believe that the last ten minutes had been a dream. Then without warning Coolie Man pulled over and slowly eased the bus to a stop in the middle of a canefield.

"Dis is your captain speaking," he said mockingly. "Ah go open the door. Who wan' leave, leave! However, dere can be no refunds."

Ivan looked at the unbroken walls of cane stretching into the distance and made no move. Neither did anyone else. Coolie Man waited expectantly with the doors still open, then said,

"Nobody wan' leave? De way unu bawling, Ah t'ink say everybody woulda gone by now. Arright, den." He shrugged, closed the doors, and drove onto the road.

The bus proceeded in silence. Then, gradually, conversation returned—a hushed, almost gentle hum. People began to talk in awed whispers of the experience they had just shared, their voices taking on an element of grudging and proprietary pride.

"*Bwai*, you feel when it lick de wall?"

"Wah do you? Ah t'ink Ah dead done."

"Missis, me heart stop, *bram*."

Shaking their heads in wonder, they began to savor the experience, to rehearse the language that would do it justice when they returned home and regaled friends and neighbors with the tale of their miraculous escape from death. The fat woman who had been calling for her mother gave Ivan a moist shaky smile, rich with shared intimacy, and whispered, "You t'ink say him mad?"

"It well look so," Ivan said.

"True, but him can sure drive." She sighed and settled into her seat with a satiated smile. Curiously enough, the look she lavished on the sweat-streaked back of the driver was of a strange and transcendent gentleness.

—Hmmn, Ivan mused, he was not even in the city yet and he had seen and been a part of so much that was new. What more could happen in Kingston? What was it really and truly like?

They had passed through a number of towns, none seeming much different in character or appearance from Blue Bay. Was that what Kingston was like, only larger? The same rusty tin roofs, wood and concrete houses with unpainted wooden frames? No it had not only to be larger, but somehow more. Just how he wasn't certain; grander in some way, perhaps?

In some of the towns, especially as they were approaching or leaving, they passed areas where large houses were set back behind smooth lawns dotted with shady trees and well-kept flower beds. Sometimes there were cars parked in front of the houses and children playing on the lawns. Besides the children, Ivan saw only an occasional black man watering a lawn or polishing the car. He knew, without having to ask or speculate, that these men were not the owners. Who those fortunate ones were, and how many people lived in such enormous and rich-looking houses remained a question. Maybe that was what the city was like?

And the people? At home they always talked about "Kingston people," marking by that term a very real difference between them and ordinary folk. How would they be different? Certainly the people on the bus seemed no different from the ones he knew. There was a lady sitting behind him, pipe in mouth, who reminded him, uncomfortably almost, of Miss 'Mando. But then, these were country people going to the city. Absently he picked out a huge and luscious mango from his box, one of the 'membrances for his mother. It was her favorite kind. He stroked the smooth skin and sniffed its rich ripe smell.

"You carryin' a lovely mango from country, man—you have any more?"

It was the friendly man who had explained the burning cane to him. Maybe he thought Ivan was taking mangoes to market. "No, y'know," he replied. "Ah teking dis fe mi mother."

"Oh . . . Put it up den," the man said with a nod of approval.

As if in answer to Ivan's wish to know what the city looked like, they came to a place where men and machines were at work digging long trenches in the road, and were diverted onto a small, unpaved road which curved up a low hill before rejoining the main road. When they topped the hill the man pointed, whispering hoarsely, "See it deh, bwai, see town deh."

Ivan looked. Just for a few seconds it was there, stretching before them in the distance, the place that had haunted his thoughts and dreams since that first day in Miss Ida's café. He had a swift impression of a great sun-splashed blue bay with a long narrow halfmoon of low land jutting from the east and curving around to the west, encircling the bay and separating it almost completely from the ocean, then the plains—on which the city sat—sloping gently and then rising sharply toward the surrounding mountains.

In the split second that it flashed before him, Ivan had the impression that the city rested in the intersection of two great arches, the wide curve of the bay and the low land that ran out to sea and the vertical arc of the land that swept gradually back toward the mountains. Then it was gone, as the bus started down toward the plains. Ivan closed his eyes and tried to hold the image in his mind's eye, but it was sharp only for a minute before fading.

The traffic became increasingly heavy even as the road grew wider. There was an unceasing stream of cars, buses, trucks, motor bikes, and animal-drawn conveyances: heavy mule drays, donkey carts, handcarts, which—with hundreds of bicycles in ceaseless and random motion—slowed the bus to a crawl. Suddenly, even this snail's pace was too fast for Ivan. He wanted to stop the bus altogether and slow down the traffic so that he could have time to absorb fully every new image. He was drawn to the cyclists bobbing in and out of the traffic like fish around a coral reef. Clearly there were two classes of bicycle, two distinct and opposing schools of thought so far as style, function, and appearance were concerned. One approach was Spartan. Slender, swift, mean-looking, no-nonsense machines, these were stripped of all nonessentials, leaving only the frame, seat, wheels, and rakishly low-slung handles. They were ridden by young men who maneuvered their mounts with a reckless intensity that seemed at one with Coolie Man's approach to his bus. In pairs or singly they swooped down on the congested traffic, riders pitched forward heads over handles, legs churning, power-kicking, as they zigged and bopped in and out with a casual and skillful abandon, shouting gleeful defiance at each other and the larger traffic.

"Cho," said the man sitting near Ivan, as a pair shot out from behind the bus and narrowly missed an oncoming car before flashing out of sight. "Dem t'ink is play dis. Little more you see dem lay down a roadside crashup."

"Dat happen plenty?" Ivan asked.

"Every day, man, every day . . ."

The other school of cycle lore went to the opposite pole. Where the first were dangerously spare, the second were elaborate, ornate, expensive. The first operated on the principle of elimination, of unending reduction, the pursuit of pure function; the second was an expression of accretion, of endless accumulation. Their frames were hardly discernible under a profusion of knick-knacks, baubles, talismen, medallions, ornaments of metal, glass, and even fur, ingeniously attached. Elaborate patterns of colored wire wrapped the frames, producing a beaded effect. Tall, mastlike projections of wire, lined with fluttering pennants and crowned with flags or the furry tails of small animals, rose majestically above the traffic. In motion, the wheels of these bicycles became technicolor light shows, their patterns made by the colored wires, mirrors, and reflectors strung through their spokes. Where the first were wasps, these were butterflies; where the first danced and tacked through the traffic like frigates through the fleet, these threaded their way with the stately and ponderous grandeur of tall ships, like great masted galleons with pennants aflutter, taking the tide.

The pride and joy of their owners, these were no mere vehicles of transportation but works of art, deeply personal statements. The kings and emperors of cycledom, the products of a boundless ingenuity and a spectacularly uninhibited aesthetic, they resembled, in strange atavistic coincidence, the great masked festival dancers of West Africa, and like those avatars, their awesome progress was not silent, but was accompanied by the jangling of many bells, the clatter of rattles, and the musical notes from car horns. Ivan followed the progress of one of these apparitions until it was lost from sight, straining his eyes as though reluctant to be robbed of so extravagant and unexpected a treat. "Jeesas," he murmured. "Jeesas Gawd."

They were now on the outskirts of the city. The canefields and pastures had given way to scattered houses, then shops and bars behind crowded sidewalks. Then, off in the middle of a field so flat, so dusty, and so desolate that it seemed to have lost any ability to nurture even the most miserable weed, they passed something for which nothing in either Ivan's experience or his wildest imaginings had prepared him. He was first attracted to a cloud of black smoke in the dusty air; as they drew closer, he saw that what was burning was huge, sprawling, and shapeless: piles and small mountains of what? The air in the bus began to smell like burning rubber. Then he could see broken boards, dirty newspapers, rags, bottles, tin cans, bloated corpses of animals, the rusty and rotting shells of cars, and worn tires all thrown together in a chaotic jumble.

Ragged people were digging in the rubble, pulling and tugging, while over their heads squadrons of vultures wheeled in the smoky air. The mountain of trash seemed to stretch very far, then gradually without perceptible demarcation or boundary it became something else. But what? A jumbled and pathless collection of structures. Cardboard cartons, plywood and rotting boards, the rusting and glassless shells of cars, had been thrown together to form habitations. These shanties crowded each other in an incoherent jumble of broken shapes without road or order. Out of the detritus of urban life, they made a dense mass, menacing in its ugliness and carrying in its massed, sprawling squalor a meanness and malevolence that assaulted Ivan's spirit. Looking at it, he felt joy and excitement shrivel within him, and he began to be afraid. Most of the people on the bus were looking straight ahead, sullen shamed expressions on their faces, though some, like Ivan, couldn't take their eyes away.

The man nearby was looking at him again.

"Is the firs' you seein' it, young bwai?" he asked quietly.

Ivan swallowed and nodded.

"Das whe' dem call de Dungle," the man said as if that explained everything.

Then, mercifully, the ugliness was past and the city began. Buildings lined the road on both sides. They were a disappointment to Ivan: worn wood and cement structures, they seemed in need of paint and were certainly no larger or finer than those of the small towns they had passed. They were only more and closer together.

"Wes' Kingston dis," the man explained.

Ivan nodded, looking out at the crowded sidewalks. What a heap a people! It seemed as if all the people who lived in all the houses that he could see stretching back down the sideroads, had for some mysterious reason gathered on the sidewalks, to make a packed, jostling, boisterous river of black humanity. It all seemed overwhelming, out of control—the throngs lining the road, the noisy traffic, sometimes jammed bumper to bumper and barely moving, then suddenly in chaotic motion as though racing to the next jam-up. It was not exactly a different country: looked at individually the people seemed no different. But the number of them—so many, many more than he could ever remember seeing in one place. And collectively, the crowd, as an entity, seemed tense, nervous, and moved by a single and alarmingly unpredictable will.

There were even animals in the city and they too were different from their country cousins: nervous, sullen-looking, scrawny, urban beasts. He saw pigs rooting along gutters, goats mincing arrogantly across lines of traffic, and gangs of dogs, unbelievably meager and predatory-looking. Slinking stealthily through the litter of the side streets, they seemed both cowed and vicious, with tails curled guiltily between gaunt flanks as though in recollection of the last kick or anticipation of the next. They nevertheless bared their teeth and snarled and snapped at each other and at the pigs and vultures that contested with them for edible scraps.

"*Coo 'pon* the *nyaman* dem! What a way dem *boasie,*° eh?" the fat woman exclaimed suddenly. She was calling attention to a band of cyclists advancing in dramatic formation. Some forty men, they were led by a grizzled old patriarch clad only in shorts, the raffia hair around his head like a cloud of serpentine white locks. His black face, with deepset eyes glowing beneath beetling brows, was framed by a long, strikingly white beard. His wizened frame seemed disproportionately small and thin beneath that leonine head. Behind him two riders, no less impressively bearded and locked, stretched between them a banner in red, green, and gold with the inscription INRI in black, and some smaller legends Ivan couldn't read. Behind the banner in disciplined ranks, dread and matted locks framing their faces, in prideful oblivion to their surroundings, came the band chanting in unison:

> *RAS TA FAR iie . . .*
> *Let the POWAH . . .*
> *from ZION fall on I. . . .*

The rest being lost, as they swept out of sight and earshot as suddenly as they had appeared.

It had been so unexpected and startling a sight that Ivan's face must have reflected his wonder. The man beside him laughed as though he were personally pleased with Ivan's response, and said in explanation: "De Emperor man dem—Warriors of Nyabhingi, Men of Dreadlocks, Ras Tafari—dem call dem anyt'ing."

So that is what Rastaman dem look like? Ivan had heard vague and contradictory stories about a new sect that had emerged from the shanties of West Kingston. And a few men in his district— whom nobody took seriously—had announced that they "had

---

° *Coo 'pon:* Look at. *Nyaman:* from Nyabhingi Warriors, another name for Rasta Farians. *Boasie:* boastful, proud.

turned Rasta." But nothing had prepared him for the sternness and pride, the sheer drama of their appearance. No wonder dem call dem 'dread,' he thought. Bwai, dis yah city going be a hell of a place.

"Cho, ol' dutty criminal dem," sniffed the fat woman, unimpressed. She gave a short disdainful laugh and added, "Dem fe go look work. And cut dem head too. If dem head dem evah ketch a fire, de whole a Kingston no mus' bu'n down."

The laughter that greeted the fat lady's words bothered Ivan. It seemed disrespectful. There had been something strange about the group he had just seen, but also dignified and proud, like the people from Maas' Nattie's stories as he imagined they would look, Maas' Nattie's beloved black warriors. Also something religious, and back home no one would dare laugh at something religious. Bet you, he thought, if dem was up in her face she wouldn' talk so. The woman was smiling with smug self-satisfaction at the success of her wit. Ivan gave her a stony look.

They were now in the city and traveling really slow. Passengers began to stir and stretch as though in anticipation of the end of the journey, and the bus finally rolled to a stop at the top of King Street opposite Coronation market.

Despite his anxiety for the journey to end, Ivan now found the prospect of getting off the bus into the dusty heart of the city profoundly unsettling. The old bus had become familiar, comforting even. He had begun to recognize the voices and idiosyncracies of the passengers. Even the cantankerous fat woman and the erratic Coolie Man seemed a crutch, a link with the past only reluctantly to be relinquished. Also, he had only had to sit and look down, from a detached height, upon the surging chaos of the streets. Now, at the point of stepping down, of actually entering and becoming a part of that crowded confusion, he felt isolated and apprehensive.

5

Babylon

The dust and reflected glare from the sun hit him. The heat rose
off the pavement in waves. Ivan was surrounded simultaneously
by the din of the crowd and pounding bass rhythms from the
sound system of a music shop across the street. He could see the
bobbing heads of teenagers dancing in front of the store, and for a
moment he felt as if the entire street was pulsing and rocking
with an energy that ebbed and flowed with the music's insistent
beat. Even a portly grandmother trudging about her business
stopped and cut a lively step or two when the music *nice* her.

Clutching the box on which he had sat, Ivan stood in the
middle of a jostling crowd of market women and some young men
who had suddenly materialized, and watched anxiously as Drunk
A'ready handed down the baskets and packages. Seeing a box that
looked like one of his, Ivan forced his way forward. "Ah believe is
mine dat, sah," he called tentatively, reaching up. Just as he was
about to receive the box, he was roughly shoved aside by a burly,
fast moving form.

"Beg you no baddah gi' way me foodstuff dem yaah, sah," the
fat lady hollered to the assistant as she glared at Ivan.

"See me name deh." She pointed triumphantly. "Since when
you name Matilda Guthrie, sah?" she demanded as she flounced
forward to claim her box.

"Well—Ah sorry, but Ah did t'ink say it was mine," he
explained.

"Hmm, of course, sah. Non a unu young bwai woulda t'ief
nutten, eh?" she mocked.

The crowd laughed. Ivan was resentful, feeling certain the
woman knew it was an honest mistake on his part. But as he stood
there he could see why the market women were so suspicious,
apparently of everyone. The gang of youths, stridently volunteer-
ing their services as porters and agents, were adding greatly to the
general confusion by muscling their way into the crowd to claim
in the names of the owners stuff coming off the bus.

"Is yours dat, lady? Mek Ah get it fe you. Ah wi' carry it go a market fe you." Legitimized only by their own offer they fought their way forward without giving the owner a chance to accept or reject the service.

Finally Ivan was successful in retrieving the two boxes that were his. He set them down in the shade of a tree and with his belongings in a protective heap at his feet tried to get his bearings. The midafternoon sun heated the tin roofs and radiated from the pavements so that at street level the temperature was higher than anything he was accustomed to; and the light came off the white walls of the buildings with a painful intensity unknown in the green mountains. Wiping the sweat from his face and the inside of his hat, he looked around.

Across the street was the huge tin roof of the market, a group of sprawling shedlike structures from which came the hum of commerce, rising and falling in waves like the distant roar of the sea. A second, unofficial market was also in progress, in the shade of the giant flowering tree under which he stood. From what he had seen so far, everyone in Kingston was a seller of something or other. From a loaded donkey cart a man was selling green coconuts, slicing off the tops to get at the cool milk inside. Next to him another sold balls of shaved ice covered with syrup. One woman dispensed spicy meat patties from a portable tin oven. From a glass case another sold fried fish. Young men walked around with boxes slung from their necks in which were nuts, candy, dried shrimp, popcorn, guava cheese, and assorted confectionaries. Others had little stands where they hawked glittering trinkets: pocket knives, key chains, earrings, bracelets, and novelties of all sorts. Some vendors, aggressively seeking business, pressed their offerings on passersby. Others contented themselves with bawling out the virtues of their wares, while some, displaying an artist's pride in their creations and performances, sang witty verses in praise of theirs to tunes that were clearly original.

The nonsellers added to the general noise by shouting greetings to friends and acquaintances across the wide streets. Quarrels unfolded publicly and noisily. Men called amorous suggestions to women; sometimes a women took offense and replied at great and bawdy length. Traffic rattled and roared in the street. Drivers shouted at cyclists and honked their horns. Cyclists shouted at pedestrians and rang their bells. Pedestrians shouted at everybody and shook their fists. Several times Ivan was convinced, from the force of the exchanges, that bloodshed—or at least physical violence—was inevitable. The glare, the heat, the stifling crowd and jammed traffic seemed to add up to a dangerous level of irritation and frustration. But somehow a sense of humor combined with cautious discretion dissipated the rancor into verbal sallies, before it became physical.

He realized that he was very thirsty. Leaving his possessions in the care of an elderly woman selling mangoes, he went to buy a snowball. It was cool and delicious, but when he was finished he was still thirsty. He bought a coconut; that was better. Then he realized that he was ravenous. He bought some patties and another snowball. They tasted especially good to him, his first meal in the city. He ate slowly, watching with fascinated eyes the life unfold around him.

When he was finished eating he decided it was time to go. He was listening to very careful directions from the snowball man and keeping a watchful eye on his boxes when two young "dreads" came up the street. As they drew abreast of the old lady mango-seller, one stumbled over Ivan's box, staggered as if to avoid a fall, and swore loudly, drawing all eyes to himself while his companion's hand flashed into the old lady's basket.

When the staggerer regained his balance, the other asked, "You alright, Jah?" °

"Yes, y'know Jah, I man survive."

"One love den, Jah," his companion said, and handed him a mango.

Instinctively Ivan wanted to challenge the thief, but though he stared he thought better of it.

Seeing Ivan's look, the thief gave him a crafty, almost conspiratorial, grin and said loftily, "De world is de Lawd's an' de fruits dereof."

"Truly, Jah," the other agreed, and took a bite.

May be, but 'Im nevah sen' you to reap dem though, Ivan thought.

"Cho!" the snowball man sneered. "You can' judge by all like dem yah, sah. Dem a no true Rasta. True Rasta is a jus' man. Dem yah a jus' ol' criminal whe' beard-on fe hide from police yaah." He looked at them angrily and shouted with a gesture of dismissal, "G'way, unu too dyam t'ief. Unu mus' be no ha' no maddah. Unu fe go shave you head an' look work, man."

The shaggy youths merely laughed and walked away eating the mangoes.

° Jah: one of the mystical Ras Tafarian names for God. Also used as a form of address to the divinity in every man.

There was much in the incident that disturbed Ivan. Not that a couple of mangoes was a major loss to the old woman. But the open arrogance of the youth and his own failure to do anything made him angry. Also the idea of people stealing fruit which, in his village during the season, could hardly be given away, was strange. And to steal from an old lady, and to do so openly? It was clear to him that it would be no easy task to master the ways of this city. It was bigger, hotter, dustier, noisier, fuller, messier, and more confusing than he could possibly have expected.

But if it was intimidating Kingston was also exciting, full of unknown possibilities and mystery. Ivan set his hat at a jaunty angle, with some difficulty picked up his boxes, and set out to find Miss Daisy. His pace was slow both because of the cumbersome boxes and from the effort to remember and follow the directions, which had sounded so simple and direct when he was listening to them but now seemed vague and intricate. Also, every few steps presented some new spectacle to distract him.

He was just about to admit being lost and to begin seeking new directions, when he came to a corner on which a group of young men were milling around in easy cameraderie. It seemed to him that all conversation among them ceased as he approached. He imagined their city-wise, street-tough eyes studying him critically. He quickened his step so as to appear purposeful. Then feeling the effect to be wrong, he slowed down to appear at ease. It took a supreme effort for him to turn his head in their direction as he sauntered past, but he felt it would be more natural to look in their direction than to keep his gaze straight ahead. When, with studied unconcern, his glance fell on them, he found that no one was looking at him. They were all grinning widely and looking either at a point directly behind or just in front of him. He jerked his head around and walked faster, feeling his cheeks and ears burning. He felt awkward and conspicuous, as though he had developed some visible deformity. There was a burst of laughter behind him and he thought he heard the phrase, drawled in simulated amazement, "Laawd—country-come-a-town doh!"

Mek dem laugh, man. Dem t'ink say I *nice,* Dem wi' soon see say Ah not no ordinary country bwai dis. One day dem, alla dem town people, gwine ha' fe see me an' wish me well. Me go show dem who name *Rhygin,* to raas, y'know. For a moment Ivan's angry embarrassment blinded him to where he was. He already was a great singer, famous and sophisticated and adored by the same boys whose laughter he could still hear ringing in his ears.

BEEP! BEEP! He was in the act of leaping from the path of the oncoming car when he heard a mocking and imperious voice.

"Hey country bwai, come outta de way, man, *move*."

That word again. He whirled furious to find, not the speeding car of his imagination, but a stocky round-faced boy his own age pushing an elaborate handcart shaped like a truck and equipped with a steering wheel and horn.

"Wait," Ivan drawled. "Must be you own government road now?"

"Cho. You mus' look whe' you a go, man," the boy said more pleasantly.

Ivan was struck with the boy's physical resemblance to Dudus and his anger left him. "Hey. You know de way to Milk Lane?" he asked.

"Maybe, Maybe not. Is beg you begging direction? Or is hire you wan', hire de transport?" he said, eyeing Ivan's boxes. "You 'ave money? If you ha' money you go anywhere, y'know. But if you no ha' money, you fart. Better you stay home."

What a boasie little raas, Ivan thought. Talk 'bout ha' money? Suppose him see what money I have? He resisted the impulse to flash his roll. Instead he asked noncommittally, "Arright den, how much?"

"Fifty cents an' help me push."

Ivan calculated rapidly. If Milk Lane were close by, then the boy was taking advantage. If it were far, then the price was fair. On the other hand the boxes were heavy and cumbersome and with a guide he could avoid the double humiliation of being lost and having to admit it to strangers.

"Talk up man, talk up!" the boy demanded with the air of a man being kept from important appointments.

Ivan laughed. "Cool yourself, young bwai, you in business."

"Sceen, man," the boy agreed.

It was a relief to throw the boxes into the cart. The boy proved an engaging guide even if his manner was patronizing. He maintained a running commentary on the places and people they passed. He seemed to adopt Ivan and was full of warnings and advice on how to avoid the pitfalls of the city, especially the hustlers. Ivan listened carefully with no response save an occasional grunt.

"Whoa. Hol' down, man," the boy suddenly shouted and threw his weight against the cart, bringing it to a sudden stop. "You no see red light, man? Dat mean stop, y'know? Dass why country bwai always a come a town come get dead, y'know." Indeed, a line of cars was now racing across the intersection.

"Wha' happen, Winston?" the boy shouted to another who was sitting in a cart at the curb. "Winston" didn't answer and the boy's manner became agitated.

"See wha' Ah dey tell you, man?" he said to Ivan. "You can' trus' nobody, y'know. You know how long da bitch deh owe me money? But him nah dodge me today, y'know." He grew more indignant as he spoke. "Hey, me wan' mi money now *today*, y'hear, sah?" he roared, and started toward the boy, leaving Ivan and the cart in midtraffic. Then he stopped and stood in frustration, clearly torn. "Hey," he cried to Ivan as though suddenly inspired, "me know. *You* go on fe it, man. Five dollah, you gwan fe it," he urged.

The sudden confidence flattered Ivan. He was quite eager to prove himself, to demonstrate his own cleverness and toughness against the slickster, "Winston." "You don' ha' fe worry, man. Only way you doan' get it is if him no ha' it," he assured the boy, and started off. He snapped the brim of his hat and moved through the traffic with a slight swagger and considerable difficulty. But as he drew closer his confidence wavered. He half hoped the guy would run off and so avert the confrontation, but "Winston" appeared unperturbed. He lounged in his cart and chewed contentedly on a stalk of sugarcane, paying absolutely no attention to Ivan's approach.

"Hey, Winston!" Ivan called.

The boy looked past Ivan as if he had not heard.

"Yes man, is you Ah talkin'," Ivan insisted.

"Winston" looked up curiously. "Me?"

Ivan realized with sudden confusion that he didn't even know his new friend's name. "Yes, you, man—uh, me fren'—Ah, de guy over deso—" He pointed over his shoulder. " 'Im sen' me fe him money, man. Yes, man, him say you ha' de money." Ivan's tone grew insistent as "Winston" looked at him in noncomprehension. The boy seemed retarded—fool-fool—at least was acting that way, "playing fool to ketch wise," as Maas' Nattie would say. Suddenly Ivan was furious. All the jeers. All the contemptuous attitudes of these town nagahs—just because he was from the country didn't mean he was a fool. "Winston" would find that out.

"Hey, Winston, man. De man sen' me fe de money." He stretched out his hand.

"But is not me who name Winston, man. Whe' him is? De

man who sen' you?" He was looking in a puzzled way at the street behind Ivan.

"See him deh, man." Ivan gestured behind him again and, following the other's blank gaze, turned to see a moving stream of traffic where the cart had been. Across the intersection, disappearing on the other side of the stream of traffic he thought— imagined, *hoped*—he saw the small hand truck.

"Hey! Come back wid me t'ings. Hol' down! Come back!" He started across the street but was driven back by the traffic.

"Wha' happen? You raas mad?" an angry voice demanded from the speeding van that had almost hit him.

"Is no use kill yourself, maastah," the boy who was not Winston said, placing a restraining arm on Ivan's shoulder. "Is what happen?"

Ivan was dancing in frustrated desperation as he waited for a chance to get across the street. The look of concern on "Winston" 's face was worse than the laughter he knew he deserved, and he wouldn't tell him how he had been fooled. "Is arright, man—me jus' ha' fe find somebody," he explained.

When the light changed, he sprinted across the street. "Me ha' fe find dat raas bwai . . . Every gawd t'ing me have deh ina 'im cart. How me could mek such a t'ing happen, eh? Up dis road yah? No, down so? No. Every Jesas t'ing. An' me maddah money too—most a it anyway. Me a go fin' dat bitch bwai. Me must find him. Cut up him blood claat, y'know."

He ran aimlessly down crowded sidewalks, into deserted alleys, across wide streets, growing more desperate with every passing minute. Then he suddenly stopped. "Wait. A police—Ah bettah fin' a police." He looked around him for a policeman, in the process describing two complete circles and attracting attention to himself.

"Wha' do you, mi son? You arright?" a matronly woman standing behind a novelty stand asked.

"Police—Ah looking fe a police. Dem t'ief me t'ings," Ivan told her.

Her eyes darkened with immediate and spontaneous sympathy. "Poor t'ing," she said, 'an' you jus' come from country nuh? All dem police know is fe come roun' an boddah people 'bout pedlar license; you can' fin' one when somet'ing bad happen," she fussed, looking around. Not seeing a policeman she raised her voice in an ear-splitting bellow. *"Help! Murdah!! Police!"* It was so loud and unexpected that Ivan stepped back in surprise. "See if

dem no hear dat," she said confidently and continued conversationally to Ivan, "Tell me is what really happen?"

As he related the tale, a curious crowd gathered around them.
"Is what happen, mam?"

"Nuh dis poor yout' yah," Ivan's ally declared, gesturing
towards him, "some t'iefing ol' brute nuh *samfie* ° de poor
fellow."

"What a shame, an' such a nice decent lookin' yout' too."

Thoroughly embarrassed, Ivan became the object of much
clucking and head-shaking and philosophic consolation.

"Help! Murdah! Police!" the lady bellowed again, drowning
out the well-meant sympathies.

"Tek heart, young bwai, everyt'ing is fe de bes'."

"Cho, t'ief nevah prosper, y'hear."

"What a life, eh?" another pondered. "How people can t'ief
so?"

Ivan was surprised at the speed with which the crowd had
gathered and transformed him from a lonely and ignored stranger
to the center of much sympathetic attention. The spontaneous
warmth and fussing of the lady was comforting, though hearing
himself described as "dis poor yout'" and a "decent young bwai"
was somewhat embarrassing, as it gave rise to an indignant self-
pitying kind of emotion that brought a mist to his eyes. He might
have lost the struggle against unmanly tears had not the arrival of
a constable introduced a practical line of action.

After hearing the story and carefully noting a description of
the culprit and his truck-wagon, the constable, with Ivan in tow,
set out to tour the usual haunts of the handcart boys. They were
accompanied, to his great surprise, by a fair sized crowd who
seemed to think nothing of wasting an afternoon just to see what
the end would be. They kept up a stream of commentary on the
generic iniquity of "all dem handcart bwai dem" and seemed to
be in competition to devise the most original and exquisitely painful punishments, which "if it was up to me," would be the fate of
the thief, and all like him. With Ivan and the constable at the
head they visited the Park, the market, the train station and other
centers of commerce where groups of handcarts and their drivers
could be found waiting for hire. There was no sign of the stocky
youth nor his truck among them.

It was growing dark when Ivan, tired, hungry, footsore, and

° Samfie: to con, trick.

dispirited, arrived in Milk Lane. He saw a narrow dusty trail flanked on both sides by high tin fences surrounding tenement yards, the residences of the city's more fortunate poor. The lane was poorly lighted. From behind the fences came the murmur of conversation, the sound of music from radios, and the smell of cooking as people prepared the evening meal. Under a single street light a group of young men were playing a loud and dramatic game of dominoes.

Bwai! Ah can' believe say is dis' mawnin Ah leave Granny yard. It couldn' be, is too much happen. Maas' Nattie, Dudus, Mirriam—dem seem so far, not even in de same country. All dat a history now. Hmm, somebody a fry fish—smell good. *Bwai,* if Ah deh a country all now, Granny ha' food cook, supper ready—Wha' do you, bwai? Look like you tu'n fool, you no know say Granny dead? Dah life deh done, finish . . .

But, it look like is de place dis? It look so, yes! Wondah if Mama is dere? Is wha' kinda place dis Mama live doh? She must ha' somet'ing to eat. Bwai, Ah tired. Is how much mile I walk today, eh? So de road tough—an' hot, me Gawd. De shoes dem tough too, burn me foot dem. But it must be yahso—mek Ah ask dem bwai over deh."

Ignored by the players, Ivan limped toward the game. Youths somewhat older than himself, they seemed to him entirely at ease in their loud talk and easy laughter. Their wit and style, their air of being where they belonged in the urban evening, made him feel shy. Especially the tall black one who looked even blacker behind his dark glasses. He was clearly the leader; with his bearded face set off by a black beret and a single gold earring, he dominated the conversation with his loud assertive voice, and the game with his flashy style of play. Ivan was impressed. But, me nevah know say man wear ears ring, he thought, an' nobody say nutten? Any man whe' can do dat must be bad no sore. The board rattled as this fellow slapped a domino down with spectacular force.

"Hai! You evah see a play like dat?" he boasted. "How much card you have?"

"Two!"

"Two? Really? Two? An' you partner, how you stay? Huh? Ah see. . . me can' lose, y'know. Can' lose to blood." He had his dominoes cradled in one palm, the other hand raised above his head with his next play already selected and threatening, and turned his head slowly as he rechecked the board, "reading an' counting" with elaborate and conspicuous care.

"Hey, you know if dis lady live 'round here?" Ivan asked timidly, pushing forward the paper with Miss Daisy's address.

The tall fellow barely flashed a glance at the paper, and with his eyes still on the board motioned with a preoccupied air toward a zinc fence opposite.

"Ovah dah yard deh." And with that quick gesture Ivan was dismissed. "Oh is my play? Well, I *draw*. Yah! Yah! Yah! With deliberate drama and a kind of triumphant snort between each play, he slapped down the three remaining dominoes that he held.

Ivan couldn't help being impressed as he walked away. So he had found his mother, who lived, if the young man was right, behind that gate in the zinc fence. He hadn't seen her very often in recent years. Would she recognize him? His memories of her were few and vague. As the moment of meeting approached, not knowing what reception to expect, he became apprehensive. Also, how could he tell her of the loss of most of the money and all the 'membrances from the people in the district? Passing through the gate he entered a long yard, in the middle of which was a sprawling house that seemed to have grown in fits and starts, without shape or plan, section by section as materials and chance permitted. The middle section of wood seemed the oldest. There was another section also of wood but that seemed newer. The wooden sections were sandwiched between cinder block wings, obviously the most recent additions.

The yard was of packed earth, dry and bare except for two huge leafy mango trees that shaded the house. Ivan faced a row of doors, each with wooden steps leading up to them. Some were open, spilling light into the yard. Women sat in these open doorways, or on the steps, watching suppers cook on small coal stoves set on the ground. They looked up silently as he approached.

"Ah lookin' a lady dem call Miss Daisy."

"Miss Daisy? What you want wid Miss Daisy?" one demanded suspiciously.

"Is me maddah, mam," Ivan said.

The woman's attitude changed immediately. "Oh, you is Daisy pickney? Me nevah know. She going to glad to see you. Down deh." She pointed to a closed door with a crack of light beneath it.

Miss Daisy lay back on the bed which all but filled the small room. She stared at the bare lightbulb hanging from the ceiling and felt the weight of her body sag heavily on the springs. She felt leaden, almost numb, as though she had lost all feeling and could never move again. Today was Thursday, cleaning day, and she'd had to cook and serve the family's supper too.

Kneeling on hardwood floors, while she scrubbed and polished them with a coconut brush, had left a burning ache in her knees, which were covered with an ugly pad of calloused skin, leathery and discolored. Her back and shoulders throbbed. The back was painful and stiff and getting worse and none of the medicines she tried seemed to help for long. She twisted and squirmed on the bed, trying in vain to find some position that would ease it. Suddenly the pain hammered her spine and she caught her breath sharply. It was so hot! Maybe she should open the door and try to catch a little breeze. No. Too much wickedness out there. And getting worse every day the good Lord sent. Better the door stay close.

She reached behind her for a damp cloth to wipe her sticky face. The cloth felt warm too. She looked at the big framed picture of Jesus on the wall. It sure was pretty. Preacher got dem from 'Merica. It pretty, fe true. The bright blue eyes glowed and the yellow hair shone with a saintly luminescence. He stood there cradling a little lamb in one hand, in another a long hooked stick. Jesus, The Good Shepherd. His expression was filled with ineffable compassion and love and sadness. He must be sad because of the pain. For his heart was visible; a bright red, it was encircled by vicious thorns. She understood pain. Her heart was suddenly full of a sympathetic ache for his suffering, and she began, without really being conscious of doing so, to sing in a slow sad long-meter time,

> De King of love my Shepherd is
> Whose goodness failet' never
> I nothing lack if I am his
> An' He is mine for ever.

She relaxed and closed her eyes. Yes, the door be better close. Too much wickedness and sin in dis yah Kingston. Yes keep de door close. Massa Jesus was her company.

She should be hungry, at least she knew she should be. Her fatigue-wracked body was too tired to feel it, but she should eat. What was there in the room? A tin of sardines. Yes, she was sure there was a tin in the box under the bed. That and some soda

crackers. A little more and she would get up and eat. But first she'd rest her back. Imagine dat woman doh, eh? She'd had to tell her she was a Christian, born-again, saved and baptized, and didn't t'ief nutten from nobody. Hear her nuh, talkin' 'bout she could see dat Daisy was feedin' herself wid her food anyway, even doh she was paying her two dollars more, so she was to find her own food. But what a wicked, faastie woman dat, eh? 'Bout she going tek two dollah off her pay? Well, if it did true say she was takin' de food right now she'd ha' a big plate of rice and peas an' beef an' gravy dat was lef' over from dinner. T'ief food! Imagine, me Daisy Martin, t'ief food? Suppose she evah go back to me "bush" an' see what food deh at mi maddah yard. She well faas'? °
Dese last few days Ah doan even feel like eat anyt'ing too much. *Aaiie*, but is true wha' dem say, "to poor is sin an' to black is crime." Her insulted dignity filled her with rage and took her mind off her aching back.

First time t'ings like dat used to really vex her, bring de hot-hot eyewater to her eye. But now she couldn' even bother vex no more. Dem kind of liberty jus' mek her tired—so tired. All day today her ears was a ring. Dat mean somebady callin' her name—who? An' her lef' eye was jumpin'. She goin' see somebody. Cho! But is who goin' come see poor me? Miss Daisy drifted into a fitful doze, that not-quite-asleep state in which strange images flicker against the walls of the mind, and dreamed she was being called in a familar voice she couldn't identify.

Nervously Ivan called louder. "Miss Daisy. Miss Daisy." Still no answer. But the light was burning and when he put his ear to the door he thought he could hear a hoarse breathing.
"Miss Daisy—*Mama.*"
"Uh what? Is who dat?"
"Is me Mama, Ivan."
"Ivan . . . *Ivan?* Arright, Ah comin'."
The door opened slightly and a sleepy incredulous face looked out at him.
Then the door opened wider and she stepped back. "Arright, come inside."
Mother and son stared at each other. Her face was puffy from sleep and fatigue, but underneath that unnatural softness there

° Faas': fast, impudent, insulting.

was something drawn, taut lines of exhaustion and pain. And her movements were stiff like someone very old, older even than Miss 'Mando at the last. The words came out before Ivan could stop them: "Mama . . . You sick."

"Ivan, where is you gran'mother? Why you leave country? What you come town for?" Her rapid-fire questions fell into the awkwardness that hung between them.

"Granny dead."

"Dead? How she can dead an' I nevah know?"

"We tried to get you—the telegram come back."

"Den when she going to bury?"

"She bury already."

"Bury already? *Bury already?*" Her voice cracked as understanding came to her. "Bury *already* an' I nevah get to go to the funeral? Oh God, Oh God, OOh God." She seemed to lose strength in her legs and collapsed on the bed, sobbing and moaning in gusts of inarticulate grief.

Ivan stood by, patting her shoulder awkwardly. "You don' ha' fe cry so."

"But is me *maddah. Ah mus' cry.*"

He felt clumsy and helpless, embarrassed that his words sounded lame and weak. He wanted to comfort her, to hold her, but couldn't put his arms around this tired, weeping stranger, his mother, sprawled across the bed heaving tearless sobs.

"Oh mi Gaad. Oh mi Gaad."

Ivan stood fidgeting. He surveyed the room to avoid looking at her. It seemed small, stifling hot, and crowded. Not a place to live, it was a place to sleep or to die. He gazed in amazement at the picture of Jesus. How bright the blue eyes. How pink the skin of the face. It seemed to glow and make his eyes water. The single growing thing in the room was a flower in a jar on the table. One single flower. But it too was strange, something about it. What? He had never seen a flower like that, so stiff and waxen. He'd look at it more closely later. Softly, softly music came to him as from a great distance. Kumina music? Wait, dem have Kumina in town? He'd have to ask. But surely that drumming and the chanting coming to him softly like something imagined or remembered, was Kumina. But it was different too. As his mother's sobbing subsided the sound became clearer, but still very soft and plaintive. A haunting melody and heavy beat. An old tune with new words:

De wicked carry we away
Captivity
Require from us a song.
How can we sing
King Alpha song in a
strange lan'!

Miss Daisy was asking, "Den what happen to de place?"

"Granny sell it before she dead."

He saw the sudden fleeting shock in her eyes as she digested the knowledge that there was no longer that piece of earth in the "bush" to which she could return, the traditional place, the center of their family's existence in this world. Quickly he explained about the agreement with Maas' Nattie. But he could tell that her questions had now become mechanical, that somewhere deep inside she didn't really care about the answer.

"An' what happen to de money?"

"She say she wanted a big funeral."

"Den? She tek all the money to ha' a big funeral? An' I didn't get to go? Oh Gawd." She shook her head in sorrowful resignation and for a minute looked as though she was about to begin sobbing again. But she resumed her questions in the same lifeless voice.

"Den, de money finish?"

That was the question he had been dreading! How could he tell her that he had lost a good bit of money and the food? From the appearance of her room she didn't have very much of either. Maybe he should say the money was all gone?

"Little bit lef'." He stalled.

"Wha' happen, you have it?"

He nodded, still undecided, then fumbled in his pocket and thrust a crumpled wad of notes at her. It was half of what he had been carrying. He felt guilty, but some sense told him to keep the rest for himself.

But she barely looked at the money. "Is only dis leave?"

"Yes."

She looked at him. He felt a guilty flush burn his jaws, but she was not thinking about the money. She took in the hat, the new clothes, and she knew that despite her pain and her exhaustion, she had to summon from somewhere the long relinquished maternal authority as well as the energy and the strength that would get him to heed her.

"Den how you going to get back to country tonight?" she asked disingenuously, pretending that he could be nothing else but a messenger though even as she spoke he was shaking his head.

"Ah not goin' back to country," he said softly.

"Where you goin' to dwell? You can't stay here y'know—" She gestured toward the crowded cubicle.

"Ah stayin' in town."

"You t'ink town easy? How you goin' live?"

"Ah can sing y'know, mama, I could mek a record."

She sucked her teeth in annoyed and total dismissal, looking at him as though he were crazy, a fool-fool pickney. "You tek dis t'ing fe joke?"

"Well den, Ah can get a job." His voice was sullen and stubborn.

"Ivan, *Ivan*, mi pickney—what you can do? What kin' a job you t'ink you can get? Outside a turn criminal—go pop lock an' bruk inna people house an' shop?"

"Why you have to say a t'ing like dat to me?" he demanded hotly, his voice rising. "Me not no criminal."

"Don't ask me any faastie question. You goin' back to country tomorrow." Her fear gave her a sudden burst of energy and eloquence. She described graphically and passionately the hardships and pitfalls of life in the city. She outlined her own life, the loneliness and fear, the hard work that sucked the life and youth from her, the pitiful pay, the gratuitous daily insults.

But he insisted that he wasn't leaving, whatever she said. He was going to make something of himself; she'd be proud.

"Aaiie, mi bwai," she wailed, "no so *aall* a dem say, all de young bwai dem. Likkle more you see dem gone a jail, gone a *gallows*. Dead a gun' shot, dead a knife woun', or dem tu'n drunkard."

"Mama, it *nah* happen to me, y'know. It *can't* happen. I know from I small-small say I a' go do somet'ing ina dis worl'. Is my chance dis. Ah can' go back. Me *can'* do dat." He stood before her, hurt, and defiant but very determined.

"You hungry?" she asked softly. "Ah don' cook much any more, but you can get somet'ing."

He nodded.

She opened the tin of sardines and placed the small fish with a few crackers in front of him. Then she went into the yard and brought him back a mug of water into which she mixed some brown sugar. She sat on the bed and watched him eat in silence. He was finished eating very quickly. She arose and began poking around in her box.

"Arright," she said resignedly, the same dull tonelessness back in her voice. "Since you determine, Ah wi' give you de name of a person who will try an' help you." She leafed through her Bible and came up with a small business card. "if you behave yourself 'im wi' try an' get a little job fe you. See it here."

He examined the card. "A preacher?"

"Yes. 'Im can help you."

Ivan looked dubious. "O.K. Mama. T'anks." He started toward the door.

"Ivan, wait!"

Silently he turned to where she was lying limp on the bed.

"You ha' any money? Tek dis." She held out a few of the bills he had brought.

"Is arright, Mama, Ah sell de few goat an' pig dem Ah did have. You tek dat."

"Well, an' you nevah bring as much as a mango from country fe me?"

"Mango season was bad dis year," he lied, and shamed he stepped quickly into the night.

When the door closed behind him, Miss Daisy lay still and silent for a long time. Then she rose from the bed and got down on her scarred and calloused knees, facing the picture of Jesus the Good Shepherd. Kneeling and rocking and rocking and kneeling, Miss Daisy Martin fixed her eyes on the Bleeding Heart of Jesus and prayed for her son, that "even doh a t'ousan' devils may tangle his feet, none should hol' him fas'."

The air—warm, dark, and rich with the smell of cooking, fragrant woodsmoke, and from somewhere the sweet smell of ganja—caressed Ivan's skin sensuously. The drumming and chanting had stopped, but the textured purple night was alive. From a neighboring tenement a song came from out of the darkness, a woman's voice, deep-throated and husky with sex. A man's voice said something indistinguishable. The woman laughed, a pleased teasing laugh.

The heaviness that had come on him left Ivan. His blood was fired by the vibrant sounds and smells. There was an overwhelming relief from the oppressiveness that he had felt in his mother's closed-off room. He realized that he was glad to be out of the presence of that worn-down, sad-eyed woman and was quickly ashamed of the feeling.

The warm breeze that touched his body brought also the murmur of the woman's low voice. A radio played softly. Ivan felt wistful, alone in the darkness, lonely in a way he had never known. A rush of blood-heat pulsed through his limbs and filled his head, then settled in his loins. He felt himself hardening, growing long, throbbing with almost painful urgency. He had never felt a sexual longing so sharp and undirected, so needy.

Nevertheless, he quickened his pace even though he had no real idea where he was going, for he was young and strong and hadn't yet learned fear—or even what there was to fear.

He saw that the domino players were still there. Maybe he could get to know them. Especially that tall flashy black one they called Jose, who seemed to be almost everything that Ivan aspired to become: city-smart, stylish, self-assured. But how to approach them? He remembered the snickers of the boys on the corner so he walked up to the game slowly, prepared to keep going at the slightest hint of ridicule. It wasn't necessary.

"Wait?" Jose asked casually without looking up. "You fin' Daisy?"

"Yes, y'know," Ivan drawled and, encouraged, eased to a stop. A player slapped down a domino arrogantly.

"Wait. 'Im boasie, eh?" Jose's partner jeered.

"What 'im play, *four?*" Jose asked laughing. "Jesas, Ah can' stan' it." He played. "See it deh! Cho, de game no done?" He looked at Ivan with a conspiratorial grin. Ivan laughed and nodded his appreciation.

"Den . . . Daisy is you ol' lady?" Jose asked.

"Yes."

"Dem call me Jose, is me control on yah. Anyt'ing you need, ask fe Jose. Is me dat, jus' ask anybody, y'hear?"

"Cool breeze," Ivan said, betraying his rustic origins. "Me name Ivan, but dem call me Rhygin."

There was a beginning undercurrent of laughter which Jose cut off. "Is your play, man. Whe' you a laugh 'bout?"

Ivan felt a rush of gratitude.

"So," Jose mused, checking his hand, "you sell de lan' a country an' come live a town now." It was half statement, half speculation. Behind the shades he watched Ivan with a care his voice didn't betray.

"Yes, you could call it dat," Ivan agreed.

"Ah see whe' you mean," Jose said thoughtfully. "Ah see whe' you mean?" He "bowed" his hand by playing his last three cards in succession. "Look, Ah not goin' play one more game until unu pay me. You owe too much now. Too much action roun' town fe me play wid no bruk sport who can't pay me. Right, Rhygin?" he appealed to Ivan.

"Righteous, man," Ivan agreed.

Again the muffled snickers. Jose glared at the offenders.

This openly offered alliance flattered Ivan. He wanted to say something to impress on all of them that although he was new he was no dum-dum. But what? He had a timely inspiration. One of the great attractions of the city, and a source of speculation and wonder back home, was the moving picture shows advertised so tantalizingly in the newspapers. What was the name of a theater? The first one that came to mind was Rialto. Keeping his voice as casual as possible, he asked, "You know wha' showing at Rialto?"

"Oh." Jose looked up surprised. "What you know 'bout Rialto an' you jus' come from country?"

"Read 'bout it, man. Read 'bout it," Ivan said and shrugged disparagingly.

Jose looked at him as though to say pretty good country boy, you alright. "Wha' happen, breddah, you wan' go Rialto den?" he asked.

"Dat wouldn' bad," Ivan drawled as though it were better than nothing but of no pressing interest. What could be better than to see his first picture show on his first night in town and to see it with the urbane Jose. But he wasn't sure exactly what Jose was offering and didn't want to seem too eager or presumptuous.

"Well, come den." Jose stood up.

"You mean—come wid you?"

"Yes man, why not?" Jose said.

Ivan was so happy that he didn't think about the sly smiles that the other players exchanged. Jose, walking in a loping stride with a slight insolent hitch of the left leg as though it were somewhat longer than the other, started down the lane accompanied by Ivan, who put a hip bounce into his own gait.

"Yes, breddah. I see right away say you is a righteous bredrin, guy. I a go show you de ropes. You only want little training. Nobady know dis town like me—is right yahso me born an' grow."

"Bwai," Ivan said, "Ah feel say I a go like dis town, y'know."

"No mus', man," Jose agreed, and turned into a tenement where a motorcycle was chained to a tree. "See de chariot deh," he said proudly.

"Aat," Ivan murmured in admiration. He looked at the sleek machine, its metallic curves gleaming beautiful in the moonlight, and caught his breath. "Den, Jose," he breathed, "is yours dis?" His respect for Jose increased even as he wondered how Jose could have accomplished such a prodigious feat of ownership.

"In a way," Jose said carelessly. "Ah use it in me work." He didn't explain.

"It nice bad, man."

"Jump awn, man, forward up yourself," Jose directed, kicking the engine to life. He lit a long "strato-cruiser," a paper cone filled with a mixture of ganja and tobacco, while Ivan settled himself on the back. "Show time, breddah, show time. Ay man, you evah bin on one a dese before?"

"All de time, man," Ivan lied easily.

"Good, well den you know fe keep you foot offa de muffler. Bu'n off you ankle dem, you fart!"

The bike bounced over the rutted lane, raising clouds of smoke mixed with swirling dust, before it burst with a stuttering roar onto the smooth pavement. The acceleration drove Ivan backward, almost unseating him completely as the bike surged forward. "Hol' awn, breddah," Jose warned, and swooped into the lighted street. One hand holding his hat, the other clutching the seat, Ivan peered over Jose's shoulder into a blinding glare of headlights, enthralled by the heady sensation of speed from the back of the bike, purer, more exciting than on the bus, and on the asphalt effortless and very smooth, like flying. Wind whipped into his eyes, stinging them with particles of dust and soot, so that the world was seen through a blur of speed and a veil of tears.

And what a world it was! The city's aspect had changed too. In the afternoon it had been stark and mean, with every blemish, every eyesore revealed plainly; it had seemed threatening, indeed even dismaying. Now the cosmetic darkness concealed all that under its cloak and only the sparkling oases of light and color shone like jewels set against black velvet. Purple, blue, and red neon lights shimmered from shop windows; the sidewalks were still crowded but in the electric night even the crowd was different, no longer a flowing river. Pockets and eddies of people formed in the lighted doorways of bars and clubs, or danced in front of music shops where the sound systems pounded the night with blasts of electronically amplified excitement. The operators poured on more power, mobilized more wattage, deployed more and bigger speakers in the traditional war to obliterate, by sheer volume, the competition across the street. When he entered these contested areas the level of sudden sound almost took the top of Ivan's head off, and he could feel, physically, on his face, the vibrations from the bass. *"Sounds an' pressure."*

Intoxicated by speed and power, the bombardment of new sensations, and the smooth throbbing of the sleek machine between his legs, Ivan—nerves raw and tingling from technological overkill—cruised apparently cool as ice and laying easy.

"Welcome to Babylon, Breddah!" Jose shouted.

The theater came into view while it was still some distance off. The tallest, most impressive structure Ivan had ever seen, it was not so much a building as a magical fantasy made real. An illusion of light and color towering up out of the night, its white-washed concrete facade was transfigured by the multicolored searchlights that beamed upward into the sky and surrounded the white walls with a soft rainbow. A marketplace of dreams, it was designed to appear fabulous, more magical, more impossibly brilliant than the illusions it dispensed so cheaply. Each gigantic letter in the name glowed richly out of a pool of deep and vibrant colors. Ivan's teary eyes opened wide in wonder. It was hard to believe that such a building existed at all, and that anyone with the price of admission (and almost any price would have seemed modest in the face of this splendor) could enter. Not twenty-four hours away from Miss 'Mando's hillside farm, and here he was about to discover the Rialto's mysteries. He wished Mirriam and Dudus were there, especially Mirriam. How could she, seeing this, ever doubt that he was right in coming?

He followed Jose to the front, unconsciously imitating his loose, slow, stoned swagger. Jose was flying easy. "Bwai, dis yah line too long again, y'know," he observed thoughtfully. "Watch me."

The waiting crowd was young, some couples—the girls shiny-lipped, red or green or blue or purple, depending on which ring of the rainbow they were standing in, their hair pressed straight and gleaming with oil, shoulders bare and darkly seductive, tight bright jerseys molding their breasts. They smiled coquettishly at the young men in their cheap bright sport shirts hanging loose. Everybody just styling—but mostly small groups of both sexes extremely conscious of each other, the girls aloof and seemingly unconcerned, the boys assertive and rowdy, eyes hot, hungry and challenging when they looked at the girls.

Ivan was glad to be with Jose, who didn't get on the end of the line. Cool, seeming preoccupied behind his shades he prowled along, a big black cat, greeting people like a politician bestowing a special grace on those fortunate or worthy enough to be acknowledged.

A group of younger boys passed along, imploring likely prospects. "Maastah," one said, holding out a palmful of change in evidence, "Ah need a smalls fe mek up de fare; let me go, maastah!"

"Ease me no, maastah, I'd a all like reach a show too, y'know."

Jose stopped, beckoned them over with a nonchalant gesture, and handed out coins with all the extravagant casualness of a bored Spanish grandee dispensing largesse, combined with the crafty calculation of a politician buying the vote. Then he resumed his quietly conspicuous passage along the line until he saw what he was seeking. Conveniently placed near the front, he found a group of friends and a rush of animation. Joyous laughter, slapping of hands, the elaborate rituals of reunion.

"Wha' a go on, breddah."

"Ah see you, Jose, hail up, man."

"Is me back, breddah."

"Nice. Nice."

"Ah a bring out a new breddah, y'know. Is me new walkin' partner dis." He pulled a thoroughly flattered Ivan forward: "Him name Rhygin." Jose introduced the group: " 'Bogart', 'School Bwai,' 'Easy Boat,' 'Peter Lorre.' " Low, cool murmurs of acknowledgement. Ivan attributed the easy and affable acceptance to Jose's patronage. They stood talking, Jose completely ignoring the people behind him as if breaking the line were the furthest thing from his mind. But after some short time had passed and he made no effort to move away a challenging voice shouted.

"Wha' happen, maastah, is bruk unu out to bruk de line?"

Jose turned, slow, deliberate, a study in understated danger, all the more menacing because it was so cool, so controlled, so stylish. "What you say, sweets?" he asked with a mocking sneer calculated to sharpen the insult.

"Ah say it look like you out to bruk de line," a tall youth with a scarred, hardbitten face said flatly, and glowered at him.

"No y'know, breddah." Jose laughed affably, after they had exchanged a long stare. "Why you t'ink I'd do somet'ing like dat?" With a disarming shrug he strolled off, drawing all eyes and leaving Ivan unnoticed in the middle of his friends.

Ivan bought the tickets.

"Cool, man," Jose murmured as he joined him at the entrance. "Ah like how you handle yourself."

Ivan reckoned the ticket a small price to pay for that compliment. They entered a big room with rows of seats facing a large, shimmering, red curtain that hung in long folds on the front wall. The room was crowded with more people sitting together than Ivan had ever seen. After they found some seats near the front he looked around with eager eyes and discovered to his shock that he wasn't in a building at all. There was no roof and when he looked up the moon was clearly visible coming from behind a cloud. He experienced a brief, unexamined sense of letdown, of being cheated. All that towering, gleaming exterior was just a big wall. What if it rained? He started to ask Jose, but didn't. Such a question might make him seem too raw and fool-fool.

In the semidarkness Ivan felt a current of infectious excitement, something shared, uniting the huge crowd. Taking his cue from Jose, he sank back in his seat and tried to relax. This proved impossible. He watched the curtain as it shimmered and changed color magically. There were a few minutes to go before the program started, but the entertainment began immediately, provided not by the management but by elements in the crowd who could not resist a captive audience. The unmistakable smell of ganja floated over the seats. Ivan looked up and saw clouds of smoke weaving through the glare of the searchlight and into the tropical darkness. A man down front was calling the roll.

"Caesar?" he shouted over the hum of conversation. For some reason everyone laughed.

"Caesar de yah," a voice came from the back.

More laughter. After a minute, "Bungo Jerry?"

"I reach, Jah," came from a far corner. More laughter.

A little later a shrill falsetto, seemingly near to tears, rang out. "If Ah did know is so you stay, Ah woulda nevah did come wid you. Cho, gi' me back me t'ings, man!" Sobs.

"Yes, gi' back de daughter her t'ings, man," a deep voice yelled.

"Arright, mi love, no cry," said a loud soothing voice, obviously addressed more to the crowd than the wronged lady.

"Why you ha' fe' shame me so?" the sobbing falsetto sounded again.

"See it yah, tek it no," the man's voice shouted triumphantly, again addressed to a crowd that was now listening and chuckling over the unfolding drama.

"See it yah." The man stood holding something up into the beam of the spotlight. All eyes were fixed on him as he waved what appeared to be a large piece of fabric over his head. A tentative titter began but most people were quiet, trying to see the object of the dispute. What this was had just begun to dawn on Ivan when a woman's voice was heard, clear but plaintive and querulous with subdued shock and disbelief and obviously not intended to carry:

"Mi Gaad, Dolphus, *is no de woman drawers dat?* It woulda hol' six like me."

It was hard to say which was funnier, the perfect but unintended timing in a crowd on the verge of laughter, the obvious shock and outrage in her voice, or the ambiguity? Was she more shocked at the coarseness of the incident, or at the improbable and absurd size of the garment? As soon as the laughter began to die down, somebody else would shout, with that remarkable gift for parody and mimicry that everyone seemed to share, *"Mi Gaad, Dolphus . . ."* and that would be enough.

Ivan was roundly enjoying the rowdy, uninhibited freedom and humor.

"Is Kingston dis," Jose growled, "everybady is a clown."

Ivan immediately stopped laughing and tried to copy the bored indifference that Jose wore like a cape. He observed two women down the row who with considerable effort, had composed their faces into expressions of stiff and disapproving sternness.

"But what a way dem awful, eh?"

"Dreadful, mi dear, dreadful," her companion sniffed, trying hard to control the trembling around her lips. She failed and dissolved into uncontrollable giggling under the other's reproachful looks.

Slumped low in his seat, surrounded by the crowd and enclosed within the towering circle of the walls, Ivan felt transported to a different world. He could hear the noise of the traffic outside but it seemed remote and unreal, even the moon rising directly over the mysterious and promisful curtain with its changing colors seemed different, not quite the familiar moon of his childhood hills. "Show time" someone yelled and commenced a slow clapping. More people joined in, in perfect time, and soon the entire audience was moving to a steady rhythm that grew in volume and intensity.

Suddenly the theater darkened and the clapping gave way to victorious cheers. Ivan became aware of a different tension now, a slight electric rush of anticipation, spontaneous and powerful, running through the audience. Young, black, poor, "sufferahs" and the children of "sufferahs," they constituted an audience so rapt and attentive, so impressionable and apparently uncritical that their identification was almost total. Accustomed as they were to a world of mystery, of street-corner visionaries, seers, and prophets, of dark and powerful forces, what they were about to receive was merely a dose of a new and greater mystery. One that revealed to them new worlds, alien and totally different from the grinding reality of their daily lives, but worlds that were in a strange, tangential way no less real and compelling, different realities but realities nonetheless. That was the meaning of the current that Ivan was captured by. He felt his palms grow cold and damp, a prickly feeling danced down his spine. The martial and portentous strains of "God Save The Queen" filled the theater. The curtains parted slowly and dramatically much as Jehovah must have parted the primeval darkness, and a giant technicolor Union Jack appeared, swirling folds of imperialist grandeur, every fold and flutter rippling and crackling in close-up detail as though quickened by a high wind. Then just as suddenly lines of red-coated soldiers in tall fur hats. Then a small woman in military uniform sitting erect on a huge horse. The Queen. A few loyal souls stood up automatically. Ivan himself started to rise until he heard shouts of "unu siddown."

"Look 'pon de bungo dem!"

"G'wai, unu siddown!"

"Wait," Jose drawled, "you really was a go stan' up fe dat white woman?"

"Wha' do you man?" Ivan said it as though Jose were mad even to suggest such a thing. He shifted his position ostentatiously to make it clear that he was only getting comfortable. The handful of standees were made of sterner stuff, however; they stood, ignoring the jeers and insults that swept around them, at stiff and determined attention until the last notes died away.

But it was wrong to call these *pictures*. No these weren't pictures; the movie was a flowing reality, unfolding like time made visible before one's eyes. With the parting of the curtains a wall had collapsed and Ivan was looking into a different world, where pale people of giant dimensions walked, talked, fought, and conducted their lives in a marvelous and quite convincing reality.

That was certainly how the audience around him took it. They laughed, cried occasionally, conversed with the characters, shouted warnings and abuse, and had been known to pelt the screen with beer bottles and to duck away and even run from cars crashing toward them at high speeds or guns that blazed fire into their faces. The identification, however *willing* a suspension of disbelief, was also spontaneous and damn near total.

Ivan found it marvelous enough, but strange. He was in a world of tall gray buildings peopled by unnaturally white men in long coats, who talked tersely through one corner of their mouths while squinting in the smoke of cigarettes dangling from the other, who robbed banks, escaped in big cars, fought each other and the police, and died sudden and violent deaths. In what seemed no time at all it was over. He sank back hoarse and drained, completely overwhelmed by the experience. Nobody moved, however, and suddenly another movie began.

It totally swept away the first. Only after it started did Ivan realize that the first had had no color, and instead of trees only gray and black concrete. But this one was in bright and satisfying color, in a land of big unbelievably blue skies, vast plains and towering mountains inhabited mainly by horses and cows. It was, incredibly, even better than the first—not just because of the color but because the world it revealed, although just as alien, was more recognizable, not morally chaotic like the first, but simple, direct, and clear, a world with a sense of honor in which unfolded a story of justice and righteous retribution.

The movie concerned a man named Django, a simple and peaceful man who was forced to fight a ruthless group of marauders. The action was swift, the detail stark and violent. Men's faces erupted like gory mushrooms under the force of well-placed bullets which struck with an audible, sickening smack. Knives flashed lethally; under a booted kick a mouth dissolved in a spray of splintered teeth and blood. Closeup of bloody mush. Ivan ached with the stoical, taciturn Django through vicious physical beatings, grieved with him over the murder of his woman, shared his humiliation and growing anger under the accumulation of outrage and injustice.

When finally a small army of the enemy, their cowardly faces hidden under red hoods, advanced behind a picket of rifles pointed at the hut where they thought they had Django trapped, it seemed like the end.

"Oh Gaad, dem gone wid Django now," he wailed, unable to control the fear and anxiety that gripped his belly.

"Why you no shet you mout'? You t'ink hero can dead? Starbwai can' dead, y'know." Jose's voice was impatient. No sooner had he spoken than Django stood up, almost miraculously, from a position *behind* the gang.

A low, approving, anticipatory, visceral growl rose from the audience, becoming a joyous, hysterical, full-throated howl of release, of vindication and righteous satisfaction as Django, grim-faced and alone, the very embodiment of retribution and just vengeance, raked the masked killers, hot, bloody destruction spitting from the Gatling gun on his hip. Men were torn apart, picked up and flung to earth in grotesque spinning contortions. The giant bearded face, tight jawed, crazy eyed, each line and furrow magnified 100 times, glared out at the audience, a powerful and primal force, an avenging angel in a sombrero.

Then the orgy of destruction was over. *"Ayah. Django tek no prisoners."* A long shot of a single standing figure and a hillside strewn with corpses. The audience danced and howled in gleeful transport long after the screen went dark. Ivan sat without the power to rise, aware of Jose's exultant voice.

"You ti'ink hero can dead—til de las' reel?"

Gradually the howling subsided, and the crowd, muttering excitedly, some running and acting out the ending, filed out in a rush of nervous energy that crackled around them, each nine feet tall, feet barely touching the ground, feeling no pain.

His ears still throbbing with the metallic staccatto of the gun, images of violence dancing before his eyes, a dazed and blinking Ivan followed Jose into the night.

"Not bad, eh?" Jose said. "Plenty action?"

"Truly," Ivan murmured. "Truly." But great as the action was, it was something else that intoxicated him. The world of the movie was harsh and brutal, yes. But it was also one where justice, once aroused, was more elemental and deadly than all the hordes of evil. He thought Maas' Nattie would approve of such a world.

"Well breddah, it look like you an' town going to get on arright," Jose said as they reached the bike.

"Yes, y'know," Ivan drawled. "Ah feel so, y'know."

"So . . . what now? You wan' go try some beginner's luck den?" Jose's tone was offhand.

"But yes, guyo. But why not?" Ivan's agreement was equally casual. He intended his tone to hide his complete mystification at what Jose could possibly be talking about. He hoped it involved some of the slick-looking, saucy-walking girls he had seen at the movie, but even if it didn't he was willing to follow Jose anywhere after that experience.

The same noisy group of boys who had been hustling "show fare" before the movie watched Jose rev up the bike, their eyes dark with envy.

"*Rahtid!*" ° they breathed, as Jose swung the bike around. "Lion, lion to raas."

With the wind on his face, the roar in his ears, technicolor images still dancing on his retinas and Jose's friendship and the admiration of the boys warming his belly, Ivan felt very fortunate indeed on his first night in the city. Riding behind the infinitely sophisticated street-tough Jose, he remembered none of the feeling of being an ignorant outsider only a few hours ago. "Ride on, breddah Jose! Wha' sweet so?" he shouted in his head.

The low concrete-block building seemed to be throbbing from the pressure of the heavy bass beat pouring through giant speakers.

"Ah yah so, y'know," Jose drawled as he skidded the bike around in a spray of gravel and dust. Ivan saw a bright sign on which PARADISE TILE GARDENS flickered in blue letters.

"Is here we goin' to try some beginner's luck," Jose said, as he saluted the gateman who waved them through with a grin.

"Is me new walking partner dis," Jose said, slapping Ivan on the shoulder. "Dem call 'im Rhygin. 'Im jus' come a town an' me a show 'im de scene, beginner's luck, y'know."

"Well good luck den, breddah." The man laughed and nodded to Ivan. "Hear what—since you new, de firs' drink is on de house 'cause Breddah Jose is a righteous breddah."

They passed through a room with enameled tables and tin chairs, to the dance floor which was not a room at all but a tiled area surrounded by a cement-block wall. It was jammed with people dancing to the loudest music Ivan had ever heard. When he passed in front of the speaker he could feel a wind and see the

---

° *Rahtid:* an expletive, possibly from "wrath."

cloth pulsing. Even though there was no roof, it was steamy hot on the floor. To Ivan's country nose the smell of sweating flesh, tobacco and ganja smoke, rum and heavy perfume was both stifling and erotic.

As his eyes adjusted to the semidarkness he saw a bar at one end of the room and at the other a kind of kitchen where curried goat and patties were being sold. He followed Jose through a long dim corridor to a closed door.

"Is who?" a voice demanded.

"Jose."

"An' who?"

"A new breddah—is o.k., 'im wid me."

The door cracked and then opened. Groups of men and a few women sat or stood around wooden tables on which there were cards and a lot of money.

"Wha' a go on, Jose?"

"You lucky tonight, Jose?"

"All the while, man—but I just a show dis breddah the scene."

A few eyes turned briefly to Ivan. "Well dis ah *de place*," Jose said with a proprietary air. "Anyt'ing you could want right here— wappi, tonk, poker, blackjack, crown an' anchor, domino, craps, everyt'ing. You feel lucky?"

"Bwai," Ivan said, looking apprehensively at the hard-eyed, intense faces of the gamblers. "I doan know, y'know."

"Cho—you look like a lucky breddah too, y'know. Yo coulda all mek a nice little stake fe begin you life a town, man."

"True, breddah, but later fe dat. I'd all like check out the music an' the daughter dem y'know, guy."

"Ah see why dem call you Rhygin, you is a flesh man."

"Yes, if you say so, an' a dancer too," Ivan said.

Lounging against the wall and sipping beers, eyes slitted against the smoke, they watched the dancers juking and grinding to the heavy heavy rhythms. Fats Domino complained about a lady who was never satisfied, Bill Doggett stomped out an instrumental called "Honkey Tonk." Big Joe Turner hollered about "Corrinna" and someone else was "sick an' tired foolin' 'round with you."

"Ayah sounds an' pressure," Jose said, lighting up a stratocruiser. He passed the weed to Ivan, who tried to handle it nonchalantly but the smoke burned his throat, choking him. He struggled to keep from coughing, sucking the smoke through his

teeth as he had seen Jose do. After a while he had a rush: he felt relaxed, but tingly in his limbs and in an easy, unhurried way very attuned to everything around him, engulfed by a great, swelling sense of confidence and well-being. The beer tasted less bitter. He couldn't keep from dancing as the music broke hot and funky around him, and every throb resonated along his spine.

"Contack," Jose said with a grin, seeing that Ivan was charged.

"Grounds." Ivan nodded and smiled dreamily. The music surged into his limbs as it had done at the *Kumina*. He seemed to be hearing it with his entire being, in a way he had never heard music before. Some of the dancers were very good, moving effortlessly in and out of the crevices of the beat, marking with the lines and patterns of their motion the contours of the sound. His attention kept going back to a tall, black girl wearing a shiny red dress that clung voluptuously to her well-proportioned young flesh.

Jose, watching Ivan checking the girls, said, "so you is really a flesh man den. You ha' de right spirit but you raw. You want educashan."

"How you mean?" Ivan said a little hotly. He felt he was at least as cool in his manner as Jose.

Jose drew him close and talked into his ear. "Cho man, you new to de scene. Ah mean, look here now—where you lookin'? All you min' deh pon is de daughtah dem. Dass de firs' sign say you no know how dis t'ing go. See," he instructed, "first you must check out de man dem. Certainly Jah. You mus' check out de man dem. Dat is where trouble deh. You see dat slim guy over dereso? Is a badman dat. Dem call 'im Needle. You no wan' mess wid any daughtah dat him ground wid. Remember dat—Needle. An' check dis one here, de semi-Rasta looking one. Doan mek de locks fool you, is a total *desperado*. 'Im name 'Stimulus.' Keep clear from 'im, I doan even sure say 'im is not a madman. An dah Chiney-Royal ° bwai in de corner? 'Black-China' dem call 'im. Me did t'ink say 'im was still a jail fe cut out a man belly. So dass de firs' lesson—check out de competition *first*. You get it?"

Ivan nodded, impressed and somewhat let down. The thin and

° Royal: In this usage denoting a racial mixture including African, e.g. Chiney-Royal (Chinese and African), Coolie-Royal (East Indian and African). Also humorously used, as in Monkey-Royal or Jackass-Royal.

dangerous "Needle" was dancing expertly and with a casual, proprietary insolence with the striking girl in red.

"Arright," Jose drawled after surveying the room, "dat seem to be de *iron* in de place tonight. But doan mek the youth dem fool you, neider. Some of dem might be young—but dem eagah, out to mek dem name. So you don' play nobody easy in dis town."

"Sceen," Ivan agreed.

"O.K. den. Now you can check de 'beef.' Now—is three kinda man de woman dem go for. Firs' is what you call a *faceman*. Hmm mek Ah see, yes. Yes, dah youth over deh by de bar. You see how 'im have face? Pretty bwai, nice in 'im face? Is a faceman dat. But dass all 'im have. Pure face. You see 'im don't dress too cool. Dass the second kind, what you call a *dude*, or a *stylis'*. You see dah ugly bwai in blue. You see how 'im dress soft, everyt'ing just match? Carry 'imself wid style? Dass a stylist but 'im no have face. An' den," Jose said loftily with the air of a man about to reveal a great truth, "You 'ave de heights—dat is to say when you fin' a faceman who 'ave *style*. An' if 'im 'ave mouth, an' heart, dat is what dem call a *star-bwai*." He stepped back and bowed with a flourish. "A *star-bwai*. Dass why I control on here, you see. Here endeth de lesson." He bowed again. As he straightened up, his hand flashed out and intercepted the hand of the girl in red whom Needle had just flung into a turn. Needle froze, a look of disbelief on his hatchet face as he looked at his empty hand stuck foolishly out in the air. Jose twirled the girl expertly for two beats, moving with that catlike insolence, then he thrust her away with a flourish, bowing to Needle as he did so. The girl's expression hadn't registered any change and she hadn't missed a beat. Needle said something that was lost in the music and continued his dance.

"Ah t'ink you say 'im so bad?" Ivan asked.

"Im bad yes," Jose grunted, "but I worse—an' 'im know dat. I *worse*."

So Needle was bad but Jose claimed to be worse. Looking at the lean planes of his face behind the cold glint of glasses, Ivan believed him completely. It was good that Jose was a friend. But the girl in red still fascinated him. *Bwai*, Ivan thought, I really like dis yout' style. She seemed young but there was something about the way she occupied that full body that was challenging, defiant, and beyond age. Her full lips pouted and her sleepy-looking eyes stayed almost closed. She never dropped off the beat or missed the slightest nuance of a signal from her partner. Yet there was a heavy langour to her movements that could be taken for boredom or intense weariness and which created the illusion that she was moving in slow motion through some dense, liquid medium. As he watched her Ivan felt she was the most desirable woman he had ever seen. A sharp lust filled his belly and pulsed between his legs.

Jose's voice was gently mocking in his ear. "Rastaman have a song, y'know:

> *You cannot go to Zion*
> *Wid a carnal mind.*

"Cho lef' off de flesh business, man, too much woman deh a town fe dat tonight. Is a pure money mission Ah on tonight. Mek we go try some beginner's luck, man. After dat—wid big money in you pocket—you can get six glad-time gal like her if you want."

Floating on a cloud of lust and grass Ivan followed Jose into the back room. "Mek sense," Ivan murmured, getting interested.

It all happened at the same time. Angry shouts and the sickening unmistakable thuds of violent blows. Grunts. Screams and the blind rushing of people stumbling over each other, pushing and shoving, unable to see what was happening. The sense of panic in an enclosed, too crowded area.

Ivan stiffened, staring around wildly. The crowd fell back from the middle, clearing a space the way a jet of air will part a pile of leaves. Except Jose; his bearded face lit up. He snatched off his shades to see better; his eyes shone with gleeful excitement.

"Fight, fight to raas!" he shouted grinning, then ran and pushed his way to the scene. But it was already over, being now a matter of wild swings, windy misses, and viciously swung feet that came nowhere close to target. The men were separated and were being held apart, sobbing and howling with rage.

"Let me go! Let me go! Ah gwine kill his raas!"

"Ah mark you face! Ah mark you face, ol' man. Ah wi' see you again."

"Cho," drawled Jose, putting his glasses back on. "Dem a mek joke. Dem t'ink is so fight go?" He sucked his teeth scornfully and turned away.

"Wha' happen? Who win? You see who win?" a latecomer asked, rushing up.

"Shiit," Jose said, "both a dem lose." He seemed to be disgruntled, as though personally offended at the failure of the combatants to provide a better show.

Ivan felt relieved and a little disappointed too, although at first, before he could tell exactly what was happening in the milling, screaming crowd he had felt deep fear. But the show wasn't completely over, a new element had entered.

He was a little man with a glazed, drunken look to his eyes. His manner was solemn and judicious with a pompousness that was comic. "Fool'nish." he proclaimed. "No damn fool'nish dis? Two man a fight over a woman?" He appealed to the crowd which was beginning to laugh. "Mi dear sah, you evah see such fool'nish?"

"No breddah, preach," Jose called mockingly.

"Yes, like de ass preach to Balaam!" someone else agreed.

The drunk nodded owlishly and raised an emphatic forefinger. "Daas right! Wha' sense it mek fe two man kill-up each other sake of a woman? No sense at all, cause look!" He paused with the air of a man about to deliver the clinching argument, then: "Listen me—if your woman don't encourage de other man nothin' couldn' happen. Nuh true, sah? Yes, dass why I always say—" Here he turned to the two fighters with a Solomonic air and spaced each word carefully. "Dass why I always say, *beat—de—woman first*. Always beat de woman."

A very lighthearted mood had been achieved; people laughed and shouted mocking agreement. The drunk was looking very pleased at the reception of his wisdom. Then a large figure bore down on him. The drunk, oblivious, was just repeating "always beat de—" when a tall, extremely sturdy woman snatched him by the collar and jerked his face close to hers so that the drunk's feet were barely touching the floor.

"You raas you, beat who? A which woman you wan' dem beat?" she demanded.

The drunk was having trouble breathing so that whatever answer he might have had was not forthcoming. He scratched weakly at the grip on his collar and squirmed.

"See me yah—beat me nuh?" the woman hissed before shaking the drunk and dropping him contemptuously on the floor.

"Is what you was saying," Ivan asked Jose slyly, when he could speak, "about not fe look at de daughtah dem?"

"Well, some a de daughtah terrible too," Jose conceded.

The drunk shook his head as though dazed. With painful effort he managed to regain his feet and stood swaying from side to side. "But Lawd," he said plaintively, " 'Ow me was to know say dem was a fight over such a *hefty* daughtah?"

6

Naked in Babylon

"But what is dis? Wake up man! What de raas you doing here at all, eh?"

The voice wouldn't go away. It had a rough tone, an anger, and an unpleasant intrusion that wouldn't stop. Ivan covered his ears. He wanted to sleep some more—forever. But the voice kept grinding annoyingly at the edge of his consciousness.

"Ah say get up to raas, man! After all." A hand was shaking him, causing little pricks of pain to shoot across his head.

"Cho raas, man, whe' you—" Ivan sat up peevishly. Bright sunlight assaulted his eyes. He quickly closed them again and tentatively shook his head which seemed to be spinning.

"Cho raas? *Cho raas?*" With each repetition the voice got shriller and more outraged, "You *raasing me, bwai?* Ah going call de police. *Dem* will show you raas!"

The word police cut through the fog. Ivan sat up and looked around. He was in the back seat of a car and nothing was familiar. A jowly brown face was scowling through the window at him.

"Ah want to know what de raas you doing in my *car?* Eh? Eh? *Eeh?*"

"Sleeping, sah, sleeping," said Ivan, scrambling out the door opposite the man. "An' Ah wasn't looking nothing to t'ief, y'know, sah." He backed away from the car and owner, who seemed quite upset. The car was mounted on blocks and had neither wheels nor engine, but the body was shiny and well-polished.

"Is wha' kin' a car dat? Better you tek it mek fowl coop," Ivan shouted from the safety of the road.

"Fowl Coop? Fowl Coop!" the man squealed, beside himself with rage. "You—you dutty little street Arab you."

"Beg you a ride go Spanish town no, sah," Ivan teased. "Ah pay you fe carry me go Spanish Town."

The confrontation with the man had taken his mind off his

immediate situation. But his head still hurt. His mouth tasted bitter and seemed to be coated with a furry film, and a spreading nausea filled his belly. He had no idea where he was. He was certain he had never seen this road before and he wished he could wash his face and body and rinse the foul taste from his mouth. His clothes felt damp and sticky.

What had happened? The events of the previous night seemed unreal, very distant, and tantalizingly hard to remember like the details of a dream that refused to be retrieved. As though through a fog he remembered gambling, a girl in a shiny red dress, a growing pile of money, his money in front of Jose . . . He seemed to remember people slapping their backs, buying them drinks. . . . How had he ended up in the car? Where was Jose? Something had happened, but what? The money . . . what had happened to that? He searched his pockets. And again . . . Frantically for a third time . . . No, that was all . . . a few crumpled notes and some coins. Not quite enough to buy a ticket back to Blue Bay. But where would he find the mouth to go back and admit that in twenty-four hours he had lost everything . . . money, clothes, food . . .

Ayah, it bitter, sah. He sat on a tree root and gazed emptily down the wide street at people coming out of the tenements, children on their way to school. It was all of little interest to him now. In the glare of the sun the city looked tawdry, dry, and dusty. Where had the magic gone? He felt sick and weak . . . alone, and very vulnerable.

He tried to collect his thoughts but had difficulty sorting through the memories, deciding what was real and what wasn't. He knew in his heart that something had happened, that his friend Jose hadn't robbed and left him. But it could be . . . why else would such a slick guy want to be his friend except to *samfie* him. No, it was not a dream . . . the movies, the dancing, the motor bike, ganja . . . all real enough. But something had happened afterward . . . what? Why couldn't he remember, cho raas . . .

Bwai, it was hot and getting hotter even in the shade. A dry wind stirred up the dust and left his eyes watery. Heat eddies began to shimmer in the street. What to do? Fin' Jose. That would clear up everything. But where? Milk Lane—don't that was where he met him? Yes but, which way to Milk Lane? Which direction to town . . . *Bwai*, if Ah could only wash out me mouth an' drink some water.

"Excuse, sah . . . please, you can tell me de way to Milk Lane?"

"Milk Lane?" *Bwai*, dat far no raas, y'know. You ha' money? You can tek bus? Is not no easy walk inna de sun hot, y'know, breddah."

Night was falling. Ivan stood under the tree across from the market sucking on a piece of ice he had begged from the snowball man. The mango lady had given him a few small mangoes and some advice: "Bwai, go on back a country yah—nothin' no deh yah fe you in town."

At that moment, footsore and dispirited with the night descending around him, he would have if he'd had the fare. . . . If Ah wasn't so big I'da jus' cry, he thought. . . . But no, Ah going to stay an' Ah going to mek it too. Going to mek it."

He leaned against the tree and tried to shut out the din of the passing traffic so as to consider his situation. *Bwai*, is so town big an' hot. Ah never so tired in me life an' so hot an' grungy. Maas' Nattie sure did know what 'im was a talk 'bout, eh? Me can' believe Jose rob me . . . my spirit really tek to de bwai too, y'know. If Ah evah fin' out for certain say is rob 'im rob me, one of we mus' dead, y'know. Mus' dead.

A constant stream of pedestrians passed. Many didn't seem to see him. Some looked at and over him as though he were part of the tree roots. Others looked with what seemed to him hostility or suspicion, and some with aimless curiosity. A few looked at the sweaty and dust-streaked youth with the worried face and showed something close to sympathy. Ivan felt exposed and again vulnerable. He longed for the security of four walls—any four walls and a roof—within which to hide for the night. He certainly couldn't sleep where he was. Maybe—maybe when it got darker he could slip up into the branches of the tree and hide among the leaves until morning? Nobody would know he was there. The idea seemed better the more he thought about it. Nobody would look into a tree. One thing was the constable, who kept patroling back and forth swinging his baton against his red-seamed trousers and, so it seemed, giving Ivan hard looks.

But it was soon dark. The snowball man swept up his area and wheeled his cart away. Ivan helped the mango lady lift her basket to her head and she stepped stiffly off into the night with a parting, "Tenk you, me son. G'wan back a you bush, y'hear. Dis yah place no good yaah."

The area was now deserted except for Ivan and a rather curious fellow engaged in animated conversation with himself, who had sat down a short distance away and now was busy going through the contents of a large crocus bag.° He was a shaggy-haired old man, short and stocky with sloping shoulders and bowed legs, and his dress was somewhat peculiar, consisting of a short belted tunic crudely fashioned, also from crocus bags. The policeman was nowhere around.

Now, if this strange fellow would take his bags and his mutterings elsewhere, Ah could slip up into the tree, Ivan thought. Aaiee, me—Ivanhoe Martin fe go asleep a tree like fowl! He was about to do so when the old man scampered past him, tossed his bundles into the lowest crotch of the tree and climbed like a monkey after them. Ivan stood with his mouth open, unable to choose between crying, laughing, or cursing.

There was a rustling of the leaves and the gnome's bearded face grinned down at him, cackling with malicious triumph. "He, he heaw, young bwai! Ah firs' you—you t'ink Ah never see say you was out to capture me resident, no?"

"Who me? You mad?" Ivan's indignation was as genuine as the quick flush of shame that burned his cheeks. "After me is not fowl? Man no sleep a tree!"

"Cho climb up nuh, man, you can get a room. In me faddah's house dere are many mansions—but you mus' ha' manners and ask fe one. An' you don't ha' fe shame. You wouldn't be de first y'know."

"Is market me come wid me granny," Ivan blustered defensively, "an' Ah better go help her now too."

"Yes, but don't tek long because Ah might change me min'."

The old man's mocking laughter followed him across the street, but a new idea took shape as Ivan approached the market. He found a piece of cardboard and lay down as inconspicuously as possible near a group of market women, hoping that if anyone else noticed him they would assume he was associated with someone in the group. It seemed to work. He lay stiffly at first, barely breathing, pretending to be asleep but really waiting to be challenged. Then gradually he relaxed and fell into an uneasy slumber.

Ivan was leaving; the market was eerily quiet and still in the pale dawn. He saw an open basket that seemed unwatched. He

° Crocus bag: bag made of rough sackcloth.

looked around. No one was stirring, but from within the concrete lavatory he heard a toilet flush. He grabbed a handful of bananas and an orange and ducked into the doorless entrance marked MEN, realizing as he did so that if anyone had seen him he was trapped. He ran into a booth and closed the door. His heart was pounding as he tried to control his hoarse breathing so he could listen. There was no outcry and no one came in. The place reeked of stale urine and the antiseptic odor of Jeyes fluid. The smell was sharp and overpowering, causing his belly to heave and fill his throat with sour slime. He controlled his breathing and his belly, then washed his face. And rinsed his mouth. The water was cool but tasted strange—it had a metallic, slightly bitter, unpleasant flavor.

He felt somewhat better when he sat in a little park to eat his breakfast. He had meant to eat only two bananas and to save the rest for later, but he couldn't seem to control himself. The orange was juicy and its tartness cut through the stale fuzz in his mouth. When he was finished he felt much better. He decided that he would spend the day searching for Jose and the handcart boy. If he didn't find either he would waste no more time in the search but get on with finding work, for if he stayed in the city, they would meet again some day . . . and he was staying.

If Ivan had stolen his breakfast that day he fully earned his supper. He was walking along the street that led from the heart of the city to the suburbs in the foothills when he came to an intersection where a steep side street swooped dramatically down to the main road. He glanced idly up the street and into one of those moments when time seemed frozen. Poised almost motionless on the slope was a huge, unpainted handcart piled high with bottles. Behind and above the cart, he saw in that instant a man's straining torso, and gaunt, darkly-bearded face, tense with effort. The dreadlocks' eyes were bloodshot and bulging, his face furrowed by anguished lines. He and the cart were frozen in a desperate tension as the man strained against the weight of the load and the pull of the slope and the cart edged gradually out of control. His torso glistened in the sun, muscles corded, veins swelled in the thin neck and shoulders. His eyes—filled with a baffled, defeated rage mixed with hopeless appeal—met Ivan's.

"Hol' on, breddah, no let go!" Ivan yelled, and dived at the front of the cart, throwing all his strength against the pull of the hill. He took enough of the weight so that the man behind was able to reset his feet, and together they wrestled the cart down the slope.

The Rastaman slumped onto the grassy bank at the side of the road, his bony chest heaving. His breath came in sobs and his eyes seemed to glaze over and lose focus. He was wearing only a pair of khaki shorts and his angular limbs gave the appearance of a jumbled pile of gleaming black bones randomly thrown onto the grass.

"T'enk—you—breddah." Each word came separately and with obvious effort.

"Res', bredrin." Ivan motioned him to silence. With his long limbs, bony frame, and spectacular matted hair he seemed to Ivan to be the tallest, blackest, most striking figure he had ever seen.

After a while the Rastaman sat up and looked at the cart with something like hatred in his eyes. "Ah—couldn' hol' it, Jah. Ah t'ink Ah was going faint 'way."

"Is arright, man."

"Jah, if it wasn't fe you—is mus' Gawd sen' you." He shook his head. "Or else my six pickney no eat tonight, y'know, Jah. An' dem faddah good fe sleep a jail too. Bwai, little more an' my pickney dem sleep a dungle tonight wid wind full up dem gut."

"Yes, I see say you was under pressure," Ivan said.

"Jah, me say. Me never know say de road was so steep. An' when I all come over dah hill deh—" He pointed up the road to a spot about forty yards up. "Is like de cart jump 'way from me, Jah. Like it get five time as heavy. Is all de way I man wrestle it, y'know—watch me han' dem." He showed his palms where the wooden handles had been slipping inch by inch, in his grip. The rough shafts had burned their way through a shield of heavy callous leaving smooth, raw channels.

"An' look yah." The man gestured to his right foot. He had lost his sandal and the abrasive surface of the hot road had flayed the skin from his sole.

"Bwai, me woulda did ha' fe let it go," Ivan said, looking at the mangled skin.

"Let go? *Let go?*" The man gave a short bitter laugh. "Kindred, you no understan' how dis t'ing go?"

Ivan ran up the hill and came back with the lost *shampata*—a piece of car tire cut to the shape of a foot and kept in place with two rubber thongs. The Rasta spat on his bleeding foot, rubbed away some shredded skin and bloody gravel, and attempted to replace the sandal.

"You say let it go, eh? Breddah, you understan' say is every penny whe' I man own inna dah cart? Anyhow it gallop down dah hill an' crashup, I man finish—*done* y'know. Den how my pickney dem to eat? Dem maddah have pot pon fire fullup wid bare water waiting fe me to bring somet'ing fe put in dere. How me fe let go? Ah dead first. An'—watch me—supposin' it rush down into dis road an' lickup a big man car? Is jail sufferah sleep tonight, y'know." Yes, Jah, jail—an' police good fe tek baton bust open me head an' shave off I man locks and beard too."

He spoke with a quiet intensity which only magnified the rage Ivan could see trembling like some beast trapped within the thin body.

"Aye, check me eye how dem red. You t'ink is so me born, Jah? When sun hot an' de cart heavy, I man can' even free up one han' to wipe off de sweat y'know. Is it burn up me eye dem so."

"Den, you couldn't get somebody fe help you?"

"My oldest bwai big enough, y'know, but 'im ha' fe go school—you t'ink say I want my bwai grow up to dis?" He gestured toward the cart.

Even without his injuries the man seemed to Ivan incapable of handling the load, especially in heavy traffic. "How far you going wid it?"

"De factory over on de west—'bout ten mile or so."

Ivan looked at the man and the heavy cart. Suddenly he had a sense of what it would feel like to push that cumbersome load through the baking, crowded streets. For the first time since he had lost his money and clothes his mind was on something other than his own predicament. "Me wi' help you push," he offered.

The Dreadlocks looked at him more closely than he had at any time during their conversation. "You know where de factory is?"

"No, but is arright."

"Kindred, you help I man aready—is plenty man woulda stand up and watch de crash an' laugh, so I man grateful still. But why you a go help I more?"

The man didn't seem suspicious exactly, just uncomprehending. Ivan was surprised at his response. "Is not anyt'ing I looking from you, y'know. But look 'pon you foot an' you han' dem, an' tell me how you one a go mek it wid dis yah load?"

"Truly," the man said, "people call me Ras Sufferah."

"Dem call me Rhygin."

"One love,° Jah."

Slowly, the Dreadlocks uncoiled his lank frame and gingerly put weight on the injured foot. He hobbled a few paces, swore

° One love: "One love, one heart, one destiny," or variations, traditional Ras Tafarian greeting taken from a Marcus Garvey slogan.

under his breath, then took his place between the shafts. Ivan grabbed the front and together they started toward the bottle factory.

It was a long slow journey over the melting asphalt, through the chaotic traffic with a desert wind swirling dust into their sweating faces. Ras Sufferah listened to Ivan's story and from time to time gave him advice on the various ways work, or at least subsistence, might be obtained. His view of the city, indeed of life, was very grim compared to that of Jose. In a perverse way he seemed to accept, even embrace, pain and distress since the city was "Babylon" in which "black man *must* suffer." But though he had written on the side of his cart SUFFERER #1, and appeared to take a bitter, somewhat fatalistic, approach to misfortune, there was a coiled, lurking anger within his meager body—but it seemed unfocused . . . directed to the universe at large.

Late that afternoon they pushed the cart through an iron gate onto the bare earth of the factory yard and up to a little wooden shed where the buying of bottles was done. A clerk was there, locking up. The cuffs of his white shirt were turned back and his tie hung open casually at the neck. His eyes were hidden behind cool-ray shades but Ivan could see the scowl that crossed his face when he saw them. He seemed about Ivan's age.

"Wha' happen, Sufferah? You know what time we close." He sucked his teeth and went back to locking the shed. "You know what—come back tomorrow, eh?"

"Cho, maastah, gimme a break, no sah," Ras Sufferah whined.

"No man, all you damn Rasta is the same—lie down under mango tree an' smoke unu ganja all day, den come talk 'bout 'gimme a break'? You must be no believe I have anything better to do wid my time, eh?"

"Maastah—Missa D, I man no ha' nowhere to keep dem bottle, y'know sah, by mornin' everyone of dem t'ief 'way. Maastah, I man need de little money, y'know sah—I *need* it, sah."

The clerk tested the door and turned with a gesture of dismissal. "Ah say come back tomorrow."

The Dreadlocks towered over him. His expression didn't change, but in some subtle say, because he neither raised his voice nor adopted a menacing stance, and indeed his language became one of begging, something threatening entered the encounter.

"I *begging* you, maastah. Because y'know, my pickney dem *hungry* an' I man *nah* go home widout sell dem few bottles, y'know. Me *can't* do it."

"But," said the clerk, opening the door, "understand that is only because of de pickney . . ."

Ivan and the Rasta sorted the bottles and packed them into crates, while the clerk sat in the shed and smoked a cigarette, frequently brushing back his cuffs to consult his watch.

"Well, what do you have?" he called gruffly.

"I mek it thirty-one dozen an' four, sah."

"Yes—an' how much a dem crack, eh?"

"Ah wouldn't bring you any crack bottle, sah. No say dat, sah."

The clerk came out of the shed carrying a slender ruler. Gesturing with it, he walked slowly around the boxes. He examined them silently for a moment, looked at the Rasta, then called over one of the gatemen.

"We don't tek these." He gestured to two boxes.

"Since when, sah," Ras Sufferah began.

"Ah say we don't buy dem, move dem."

The gateman pulled the boxes aside. The clerk walked flicking the ruler contemptuously. "Tek out dis—an' dis. Dis one, dese two . . ." The ruler moved continuously, rejecting at least two bottles from each box. Ras Sufferah looked at Ivan and at the growing pile of rejects.

"What wrong wid dese, sah?"

"Cracked, tek dem out," the clerk barked. The gateman followed the ruler pulling out bottles. When they were through, the pile of rejects was considerable.

"What about dese, sah? Is pay I have to pay fe dem, you know."

"Sorry, can't use dem." He offered Ras Sufferah some money. Sufferah just looked at him. "Come on, you going tek de money?"

Sufferer reached out his hand. "You really nah go buy dese?" he asked again.

"Wha' happen, you deaf? We can't use dem."

"No, sah," Sufferah said dreamily, "I man not deaf. Not deaf at all."

The two men looked at each other, the clerk with his hands on his hips and an expression of overbearing smugness on his face.

Then the Dreadlock's face twisted suddenly into an unexpected and enigmatic smile. "Arright, den," he said, and limped quickly across the yard, returning with a small boulder cradled against his chest. With a grunt, he heaved it up over his head. The clerk and the gateman scrambled out of the way. Sufferah strained to keep the rock aloft, weaving back and forth under the weight, then he flung the rock into the pile of rejects. Breathing hard, he stood looking dreamily at a long red line on his shin where a splinter had laid it open.

"But this raas man is mad to raas," the clerk said, "and ungrateful besides."

"Yes, is so dem stay, sah," the gateman agreed.

Outside the factory Sufferah looked at Ivan.

"Heh, breddah, tek dis," he said, holding out a dollar. "Ah wish I man could do better—but you see how it go."

"Yes," Ivan said, his voice trembling. "Yes, Ah see how it go."

The construction site was hidden behind a tall plywood fence. The metal gate at the entrance was chained and locked. A couple of security men wearing hard hats and pistols at their waists patrolled the gate. Ivan's heart sank when he arrived at six o'clock. Already the line of men stretched from the gate and out of sight around the corner.

"Line up," one of the security men bawled unnecessarily. "One line dere."

Men continued to arrive, look at the line, shake their heads, and take their place anyway. Like Ivan, most were dressed in the eclectic style dictated by poverty and chance. None could have been said to look particularly hopeful—not even the elite minority who wore efficient-looking work clothes of blue denim, and who appeared, with their hard hats and lunch boxes, very experienced and professional. At eight-thirty a jeep with four policemen arrived. They carried pistols on their hips and in a rack behind the driver the shiny squat butts of riot guns were clearly visible. They sat in the jeep smoking and drinking coffee, occasionally directing a cold stare at the line of men through the lenses of their aviator-type glasses.

At eight forty-five, three men came out through the gate and set up a table, at which one of them sat with paper in front of him. The foreman, a beefy fellow in a steel hat and heavy boots, stood next to the clerk's table. The third man, casually dressed in loafers and sports clothes, seemed different to Ivan, not like a worker.

"Who dat?" Ivan asked the man in front of him as they approached the gate.

"Shh," the man said, then whispered, "Das de party henchman."

"Oh?" said Ivan.

"You no understan'?"

"Not really."

"Is government work, dis—only dem party member dem get work here."

As they crept toward the table Ivan could feel the tension mount among the men around him. His own belly tightened. The man in front of Ivan, one of those in work clothes who had been talking confidently of the various buildings he had worked on, began to mop his face. His metal lunch box trembled where he had it cradled against his side. Ivan's stomach started to hurt. He had eaten the last of the bread and sardines he had bought with Sufferah's dollar that morning. Now it felt like a lump of sour lead in his belly. The man in front didn't look at the foreman. For some reason he seemed to be standing at attention.

"Whe' you used to work?" the foreman asked sharply.

"Mullers, sah."

"What kinda work?"

"Carpenter work, Maastah carpenter, sah."

"Why you leave?"

"Job finish, sah."

The man gave his answers in a low voice and stood gazing at the middle distance. Ivan could see a muscle in his temple twitching. A sheen of sweat coated his face. He stood rigid as the foreman paused and then said:

"All right, give you name to Mr. Jackson."

"Yes, sah!" the man shouted and started to the table, a huge smile cracking his face.

"One minute, dere!" The party representative's voice was commanding.

The carpenter stopped in midstride in an attitude of comic surprise. "*Me*, sah?"

"Yes you, sah." The party henchman's expression was hard and suspicious. "Yes you, sah—don't I see you somewhere before? What party you defen', eh?"

"Me no support none, sah."

"You damn lie! You's a big unionite—don't I see you over Mr. Maxwell headquarters de other day?"

"Me, sah? Me, sah? No, sah, don't run dem kinda joke deh, sah . . ." The man was out of control, his voice shrill with outrage. "Is t'ree month me no work, me have to get de little work yah today. What my baby fe eat, eh, sah? 'Im deh a yard now sick wid hungry knot up 'im tripe. No, sah, no run dem joke deh at all, *at all.*" If the man was acting, he was a hell of an actor because the desperation in his voice sounded very real.

Two of the policemen approached. The foreman looked uncomfortable. "You sure?" he asked the party man. "We need carpenters, you know."

"All right. 'Im can go through—but jus' fe today." He pointed at the carpenter. "An' you don't t'ink you get way wid nutten, y'know. Ah going check you out."

There was a movement in the back of the line. Some of the men were leaving. They went and stood some distance away and were talking excitedly among themselves. The party man looked at the police.

"Move dem! Don't make no crowd congregate here!"

"Either get on line or leave!" the cop shouted.

Ivan stepped up to the foreman.

"What party you follow?" the henchman asked.

"None, sah," Ivan answered truthfully.

"Well, choose one," the man said. "You mus' follow one."

"What kind of work you do?" the foreman asked.

"I can do anyt'ing, y'know, sah," Ivan answered, trying to smile.

"Anyt'ing? What name anyt'ing? You can pour concrete? You is a mason? You do carpenter work? Eh? Eh?"

"Ah never do it before, y'know, sah, but—"

"You can lay brick?"

"Ah can do anyt'ing, sah, jus' gi' me a break!"

"How you mean give you a break?" There was anger in the man's voice that Ivan didn't quite understand. "Leave de place, man."

"But Ah can do it, you know, sah. Ah only need a chance."

"How you mean you can do it? You ever do it yet?" He was shouting. "Ah say leave de place. Leff' de place, man. We need experienced people here. Don't bother waste my time. Next." He peered into the face of the man behind Ivan. "You again—don't I run you away yesterday?"

"Is not me, sah," the man began to whine as Ivan walked away.

Silver spray dances above the neatly trimmed hedge, its fine mist creates a rainbow in the sunlight. It makes Ivan's throat feel even drier. The sun beats down on the road causing the tar to bubble and stick to his shoes. Lines of heat shimmer on its surface, giving the illusion of little pools of water in every indentation.

The houses are large and cool looking, set well back behind spacious lawns dotted with minature fruit trees, flowering shrubs, and beds of flowers. From the road it is hard to see into these homes, their privacy ensured by tall hedges and fences. The ornate iron gates are all locked. Most have forbidding signs warning of bad dogs. The signs are not fake as he quickly finds out when he approaches the gates. Great well-fed beasts, barking and slavering, rush out, snarling and baring their teeth at him.

He hears a voice behind the hedge. A boy his own age is watering the lawn with a hose, singing a blues and dancing. Idly he twirls the nozzle and creates a shining pattern in the air.

"Psst, ay breddah."

The boy stops dancing. He flashes a glance toward the hedge and at the house. "Wha' happen?"

"Beg you a drink a water, no?"

"Bwai—" He looks at the house. "De woman in deh miserable *bad*, you know, guy."

"Thirsty a kill me, man."

The boy hesitates again. "Arright." He slips the hose into the hedge. The water is warm and tastes of rubber, but it is wet.

"One love, guy—aah, you t'ink Ah can raise a mango?"

"Is lose you wan' me fe lose de work, nuh? A gi' you de water, now you want mango." He shakes his head.

"Bwai, is since yesterday I don't eat, y'know. See mango on de ground, man. Dem can't miss two."

"Leeroy, Leeroy! Who you talking to out there, eh?"

The boy leaps as though stung by a bee. The voice did sound querulous and suspicious, or as he had said, "miserable bad."

"Nobody, mam," the boy sings out in a voice that manages to sound both innocent and half-witted. "Ah not talking to nobody, Miss Lillian, Ah not talking to nobody at all, mam."

"Old bitch," he hisses between his teeth. "Wait." Still spraying the hose he casually edges around so that the mango tree is between himself and the house. "Ah jus' a water the lawn," he bawls out again, sprinkling the sunlight, "Ah jus' a water the lawn." Ignoring the fallen fruit, he picks two of the largest and ripest and lobs them over the fence.

"Aye, man, no get in no trouble," Ivan whispers, catching the mangoes.

"Is arright." The boy grins. "Me tell her say me can't eat mango, say it run me belly."

"T'enk you, breddah."

"Jus' a water de lawn, Miss Lillian," the boy sings cheerfully, making a rainbow in the sky.

He was tired but it was more than that, inside him something was happening. He could feel a shrinking, a constriction, a closing up and sealing off of something that had always been part of him. A numb feeling spread into his limbs and made him heavy. He didn't like the place where he was. Street after street lined on both sides with forbidding hedges or walls. Gates with spikes jutting up, chained and locked; silent sentinels eloquent with hostility, unapproachable. In one afternoon he had come to hate and fear dogs, to see them in a new light. They hurled themselves against the iron gates with a frenzy that was incomprehensible to him. Why would people want to live with such savage animals? Then someone would open a door or peer suspiciously from behind the iron bars which were inevitably present on every window.

"What you want?" In reply to his courteous and suitable "Good afternoon, mam."

"Stan' back from the gate. The dog will tear you up. Come, Brutus." And Brutus wagging his plump rump and bounding like an overgrown puppy would obey, sweet as milk.

Nobody said "good afternoon." Nobody spoke in other than a cold, and for some reason that he couldn't understand, hostile tone, as though he were personally guilty of some offense against them. Sometimes, uncalled, the dogs ran along the fence barking and snarling, often in their fury snapping at the plants, until they ran out of yard and the task would be taken up by the "Brutus" in the next yard.

The feeling that his presence was unwanted, alien, and despised, was as inescapable as it was depressing. He knew he had a right to walk the road and look for work, but his progress was nerve-wracking and hurtful.

This gate was open, hanging ajar. His first pleased surprise gave way to apprehension. Did it mean that there was nothing between him and one or more of those wolf-like creatures? No—if they had those kinds of dogs, the gates would have to be shut. Or would it? Anyway, he didn't see or hear a dog. A yard apparently without dogs and with a gate open? He started to knock, hesitated. Why not go in—maybe if he could talk to someone? He looked at the yard. It was well kept; almost certainly they had someone already an' the damn dog was probably watching, lick-ing his teeth and waiting for him to take that one step that would put him out of reach of the safety of the street. The garden was where a dog could be sleeping too. Too big with lots of bushes. He stood in the open gateway and stared at the house. It was so big, so substantial, so beautifully painted. No—he'd better knock! He had an unobstructed view. For the first time he was not peeping between the bars of a locked gate, or through a hedge or over a wall. Jesas, this is what rich mean. Everything so clean, so fancy, so expensive. He took his first step, paused, then another. Nothing happened; he advanced well down the drive, his eyes fixed on the verandah. It was shady with green ferns on stands, it seemed a cool and delightful place in the hot afternoon. He realized that he was walking with a kind of apologetic tip, placing his battered shoes gently on the gravel walk, as though by a visible diffidence of posture and step he would negate the boldness of his presence. When he realized this, he forced himself to quicken his pace and place his feet down more firmly.

He could see a woman on the verandah. She was reclining on a rattan settee, her back turned toward the road. She was intent on something she was doing and didn't hear him approach. She was not white. But he couldn't think of her as black either, though there was not much difference in their color. *He* was black. *She* was rich.

He stands and watches her. She is wearing a loose shirt and well-pressed slacks of the same material. Her clothes are spotless. Her hair is oiled and styled and there is not a lock out of place. She seems cool and fresh. She is painting her nails. She is perfect. He clears his throat diffidently. She starts up and nearly spills her nail polish on the gleaming tiles of the verandah.

"Excuse, mam . . . Good day, mam?"

"What you doing here?" Her voice is not perfect. It is sharp, not at all gentle on the ear, there is an unpleasant tremor in it.

"Ah looking work, mam." He doesn't have to work to make his voice humble. He is intimidated by the opulence of the house and the conspicuously elegant grounds. He tries to smile.

"How did you get in here?"

"The gate was open, mam, so Ah come to see if—" His tone is even more self-effacing while trying to be hopeful.

She hasn't said no to the work. She looks at him—a hard, appraising glance— and seems less startled. "Close the gate when you leave. I have no work for you." She turns her back and picks up a magazine.

He understands that the conversation is over but he can not bring himself to turn around and walk away with so curt a dismissal. "Ah can wash your car, mam," he calls entreatingly, though he understands that there will be no work for him here and that the tone of his voice will make no difference.

"My husband has that done downtown," she snaps, looking up with a frown which arches her symmetrically plucked brows and threatens to crack the make-up on her cheeks.

"Ah can tek care of the garden," he says quickly.

"We have a service for—"

He cuts her off with "Ah can do anyt'ing, *anyt'ing*, mam."

"Look. You better go! There is nothing you can do for me, *nothing*. You understand that you taking a chance? We have two Rhodesian Ridgebacks. They could tear you to pieces."

"Well den, beg you a ten cent, mam . . ."

"I don't believe in young healthy boys begging—that's what's ruining this country. Beg, Beg, Beg. You should be ashame—go try to make something of yourself. And lock the gate behind you, too. Go on."

She watches him walk away with a certain defiant deliberateness. "Who left the gate open?" she shrieks at the servants in the house. "Those people really getting bold though, eh? Imagine how the boy look at me, like 'im want to beat me if I didn't give him work! You know the gate must be locked at all times!" she shouts. "Next thing you know someone break in and kill us all in our sleep!"

Sea-cow wears a white pith helmet. He is both tall and fat although his white-drill Indian army uniform makes him appear fatter than he is. He stands just inside the glass doors where he can admire his reflection, see arriving limousines, and take advantage of the air-conditioning. Despite his bulk he is very good indeed. He never appears to hurry, yet he usually has the doors open before the cars are fully stationary and, after handing the guests out, he beats them back to the hotel doors and has those open when they get there. He is inordinately, if understandably, proud of his smile. More than one guest, writing to compliment the management on a marvelous stay, has specifically mentioned his smile. One elderly lady with a touch of poetry in her soul said it was "as warm and bright as the Caribbean sunshine." The manager liked that. He designated Sea-cow "Employee of the Week" in the Chain's house organ. Sea-cow's enemies, the gang of boys who haunt the hotel parking lot, whom he disperses routinely and who named him because of his size, now call him "Sunny Sea-cow, the Caribbean Smiler." That seemed to the doorman to be going too far, making as it were a mockery of his greatest asset.

The glass doors slide open and a brown man walks out of the great white facade. He is wearing a tropical-weight business suit and the damp, satisfied grin of a man who has too well enjoyed the cocktail hour. Sea-cow bestows the famous smile like a benign black buddha, open palm at the ready. He murmurs something pleasant but does not accompany the man to the car; that is a service reserved for foreign visitors, government ministers, or local captains of industry.

From the shadows Ivan studies the businessman's face as he shifts his bulk to find a comfortable position behind the wheel. He seems very pleased with himself, so Ivan is encouraged to approach, trying to sound the way he has heard the other boys. "Ah was watching you car fe you, y'know, sah, begging you a ten cent no, maastah."

The man smiles with a crafty drunken indulgence as if to say, who you think you fooling? You'd as soon steal the car as watch it. You think I don't know you?

"Beg you a ten cents, sah?" Ivan repeats hopefully.

"No, man, the steward watches my car. Is him I deal with."

"But 'im not here all de time y'know, sah, and—"

"No, buddy, if you want ten cents, go ask the steward." For some reason this amuses the man, who chuckles as he drives off.

Ivan feels a heavy hand on his shoulder. He staggers forward from the shove. "Ah don't want to see you boys congregating out here bothering the guests; get away, man." Sea-cow is big, and not smiling.

It was late; Ivan didn't feel able to walk across the city to get back to the market. But he had been in the streets long enough to know that he could not hope to spend the night in this area with its tourist hotels, expensive restaurants, and night clubs. He sat in a tin shelter at a bus stop and tried to look as if he were waiting for a bus. When it got late he curled up on the seat, turned his back to the street, and hoped none of the police passing in their cars would notice him in the shadows of the little shed. Toward morning it began to rain steadily. The rain didn't bother him, it was warm and its steady gentle drumming shut out the sounds of the city so he was able to fall into a deep, exhausted sleep.

He was awakened by a sheet of muddy water sprayed from the overflowing gutter by the wheels of a speeding car. The driver seemed to be deliberately steering into the gutter for the pleasure of raising a plume of water behind him like a motor boat.

"T'ank you, you bitch," Ivan muttered, and stretched his stiff limbs.

Gradually he began to lose track of time. The days and nights ran together in his mind and he couldn't say on what day a certain thing happened or whether it was two weeks or three since he had stepped down from Coolie Man's bus. The only thing that was always, indisputably real was the day-to-day hassle in the teeming streets; finding a place to sleep and something to eat. He seldom thought about Blue Bay. His plans to be a singer lay dusty and unused on a back shelf of his mind like a favorite book which has been misplaced and forgotten. Now his aspirations extended no further than to his next meal. The hope of a job, any job, and a room of his own—a hope once so present and tangible—faded and receded. What little energy remained after his long forays in search of sustenance was given over to the attempt to understand the life of the dusty uncertain streets and his own relationship to this world. But it was very confusing, and also it seemed his mind was slowing down. Every day he felt weaker, moved slower, was less aware of or interested in the novelties and wonders he encountered. More and more he found himself sitting in a kind of stupor, in whatever shade he could find, not thinking of anything special and dozing with his eyes open. . . . *Sitting there in limbo.* . . .

Sometimes he heard rumors of work. At first, dependably, the adrenaline would flow and he would walk to the place, full of hope and confidence, only to founder on the rocks of no skills, no political affiliation, no sponsors. And the rich neighborhoods? Those he grew to hate deeply and rancorously, seeing them as hostile and dangerous places full of humiliation and insult and, possibly, danger. He spent much time hanging around the market because of the hustle and bustle there. There he could make a few coins carrying a shopper's basket, or beg or steal a piece of sugar cane, a mango or an orange. He spent the stultifying afternoons sitting under the tree talking desultorily with Sparky, the snow-ball man, or Miss Mary, the mango lady. He never slept in the tree, though it once occurred to him that it would be cleaner and healthier than the cardboard on the market's concrete floor.

One day as he was leaving the lavatory, he came upon a group of market women just entering the market. His eyes met those of a tall, black woman walking effortlessly under two heavy baskets of renta yams—a special variety for which his district was famous. Ivan stopped in confusion and ducked back into the toilet, recognizing Miss Pearl, Joe Beck's wife. Surely she had seen him. But she had looked right at him and then away without seeming to know him. He was relieved. Then it occurred to him that she had recognized him but didn't wish to be seen talking to anyone of his vagrant appearance. He went to the mirror and looked at himself. His hair was matted and uncombed and his skin had an ashy tone that appeared not only soiled but somehow unhealthy. He discovered that it was difficult to look into his own eyes, that it took a real effort. He forced himself, and a stranger's eyes met his briefly. They were evasive, lifeless, and haunted-looking, and he couldn't bear to look at them. His shoes were falling apart and his clothes were dirty. After that, he came into the lavatory each night and morning and washed himself at the cistern. Sometimes he washed his clothes, put them on, and sat in the sun until they were dry. But he felt uncomfortable in the market after that. Every day he saw someone else that reminded him of someone from home and he came to dread the prospect of such a meeting. He stayed away as much as he could.

Miss 'Mando would have said it was the hand of God and Miss Daisy would have shouted Ahmen, but it was simply hunger that brought him back to Coronation Market that morning.

He entered in flight from the meaty smell of hot patties baking in the tin cart under the tree. The familiar weakness was in his knees. A light veneer of sweat misted his skin like an icy shirt. He didn't know which he dreaded more, the hunger that kept a dull ache in the back of his throat, or the weakness of limb and the light-headedness that were its attendants. In this state he felt vulnerable, at the mercy of even the smallest child. He avoided people's eyes, fearing any word or challenge, and was extremely careful how he walked so as not to give offense by inadvertently stepping on a toe or brushing against someone who might resent it. In this state he strived to efface his presence in the world and to tread very lightly, indeed. He barely existed.

The shapes, colors, and odors of fruit teased the edge of his hunger. But it was meat that he craved, the smell and juice of burnt flesh, the crisp, fatty meat which it seemed, from his craving, was the only thing that could fill the emptiness in him and restore his strength. The sight of someone eating a patty was unendurable. The smell of fish frying. At times, without warning, the smell of roasting pig would be so strong in his nose that he could feel the heat of the pit and see the skin browning and crinkling in its red glow. He couldn't take his eyes from a large basket of sweetsops in front of a fat lady who seemed to be dozing. It seemed easy, at least possible. He ambled past, his face averted and tight with preoccupation, the hand snaking smoothly into the basket. He had one, big and very ripe from the feel. Then there was a faint pressure on his hand like a thin line of fire. He looked. The woman's market knife, a huge razor-edged instrument—for the purpose of slicing yams—lay lightly but firmly across his wrist.

"You see how you coulda draw back a nub, bwai?" she asked conversationally.

He felt that everyone in the area must be watching his embarrassment.

"Answer me, bwai?" Her voice was mercifully quiet. He looked at his feet.

"Is hungry Ah hungry, Mah."

"Look on me, son." She was a fat, black lady. Under her red plaid bandanna her face seemed inclined to lines of laughter and fun. Though she didn't seem angry, she wasn't laughing now. In fact the look she gave him made him feel worse. He felt the edge of the knife lift.

"Ask! You mus' ask, mi son. Cho, you can tek it—it won't bruk me. But you doan look like no ol' criminal to me. Bwai, listen me. Ol' time people have a word; dem say 'because a man sleep ina fowl-nest, it doan mean say fowl-nes' is 'im bed.' Eh? You understan' dat?" You no ha' nobody? Here, tek it—an' go see 'bout yourself, man. Ah can see say is not here you belong."

Silently he took the fruit. The unexpected kindness choked him up. He had expected loud abuse, even blows from the vendors, who showed thieves—the few they were able to catch—little mercy. He wanted to tell this lady something, but when he looked at her she was smiling professionally at a group of shoppers. "Yes, mi good Missis, buy you sweetsop, lovely sweetsop. See dem here . . ." And for that too he was grateful.

Like a bucket of icy water on a sleeping drunk, the incident shocked him out of his daze. He sat devouring the sweetsop with his eyes blurred by tears he couldn't control. But there was a new clarity. He seemed able to step back and see what was happening to him. He was like a man waking from a long and drugged sleep. In this new light he went over everything that had happened to him since his arrival, and remembered something. His clothes had been new to him, unfamilar. He jumped to his feet and reached into the watch pocket of his pants. Yes! In his hand was a frayed and water-hardened wedge of paper—the card Miss Daisy had given him, faded but still legible, barely:

PENTECOSTAL BAPTIST CHURCH OF CHRIST THE REDEEMER
(SANCTIFIED & INTERNATIONAL)
VERY REVEREND CYRUS MORDECAI RAMSEY, PASTOR
(DEFENDER OF THE FAITH)

BOOK THREE

By the Waters of Babylon

7

In the Habitation of the Righteous

By the rivers of Babylon, where we sat down
And dearly wept, when we remembered Zion.
The wicked carry us away, captivity,
Require from us a song . . .
How can we sing King Alpha song,
In a strange land . . .

—Rastaman Lament

The Very Reverend Cyrus Mordecai Ramsey (SJ), Defender of the Faith, was meditating in his little office behind the Tabernacle of the Faithful, as the towering, triangular cement-block hall which was the main building of his church was known. His mind ranged over the labors of his hand and, as the saying went, "was well pleased." He had reason: despite his relative youth—he was only thirty-five—he could look, as he was fond of saying, "forward and backward" without regret or anxiety. That is, justifiably backward to a life of solid Christian example and forward to even higher accomplishments and rewards in the faith.

'Course, he warned himself, one could not be too careful; there were always the snares and pitfalls of the world, the flesh and the devil. No one knew better than he how easily and swiftly are the mighty fallen. Love vaunteth not itself, is not puffed up. Humility. That was the word. In his circumstance, one had to fight even harder to avoid the sin of pride, to walk humbly with one's God. The thought was resonant in his heart and he couldn't help repeating it softly aloud, "to walk humbly with one's God, Ahmen."

No one could say he was puffed up. But still and all, tell the truth and shame the devil, they couldn't deny that his mission here in West Kingston was a powerful force for godliness, as His

Worship the Mayor had said at the dedication of the Tabernacle last year. And, while the ultimate credit was His, surely some small measure was owing to his faithful steward here in the thick of the battle.

The chair groaned as he leaned back and allowed his gaze to run over the front of the Tabernacle, visible through the open window. A massive grey triangle in the sunlight, its concrete frame rose to a dramatic point. He hadn't been at all sure when the group from Tennessee had approached him, but it certainly had proved a blessed union. The SJ had bothered them somewhat, until he had explained to his friend, Dr. James Earl Culpepper— Dr. Jimmie—that the flock would feel cheated if their leader didn't have the right kind of descriptive title and that in fact it was the flock who had bestowed the designation on him. The confusion was cleared up when he explained that it meant "Servant of Jesus." Dr. Jimmie's troubled blue eyes lit up then: "Well, Cy, whatever works, whatever works for Jesus." Dr. Jimmie was secretary of the Board of Overseas Missions to the pragmatic fundamentalist sect of Southern Baptists, which had adopted the Preacher's mission as something they called a "foreign witness."

But at first Preacher had his doubts. The shape of the structure seemed foreign, not at all like a church, or in fact any building he had ever seen. The doubts eroded, though, when Dr. Jimmie explained that it was an exact, though of course smaller, replica of the parent church in Memphis, and that to be invited to build on that model was an honor not granted to just any congregation, expecially a congregation of associate overseas brethren. It would be, Dr. Jimmie said, gesturing expansively, his childlike clear blue eyes glowing, "a showpiece for Christ." And it was, Preacher reflected, it was that. Eroding misgivings were washed away completely when Preacher heard about the generous program of fraternal Christian assistance that the Board of Missions was prepared to extend for the erection of the Tabernacle: "The visible and tangible symbol of their commitment to the fight for the hearts and minds of the people of West Kingston, Ahmen."

Yes, it had been a blessed union. And despite the gibes and sneers of certain envious "balmyard cultists," small-timers without vision, who were said to murmur about "Preacher Ramsey concrete dunce cap whe' de Yankee man dem buil'," that "favor something want to fly," the rapid growth in the size and devotion of the membership and in the influence of the Preacher was the best possible sign of His approval and blessing. What was it the

Bishop in Memphis had written in the mission society newsletter—"an outpost"? No, that was not it. Ah, yes—an "oasis," "an oasis of righteousness in the desert of the devil." The Bishop had a way with words. Praise the Lord, Preacher thought with pious satisfaction, let the ungodly scoff all they wanted.

His reverie was interrupted by a girl with a quietly serious manner that made her appear much older than she was.

"Preacha . . . Preacha?"

"Huh—yes, Elsa, what is it?"

"Dat bwai, y'know, sah—'im is still here, Preacha."

"Boy, which boy again?"

" 'Member, Preacha? 'Im say 'im is Sister Martin pickney?"

"Ah yes, yes—from the country. It took him long enough to get here. Tell Sister Saphira to bring in the effects, eh?"

"Effects, sah?"

"You know—Sister Martin's belongings. An' tell the boy to come in. Thank you, my dear. What would I do without you, eh?" Preacher smiled indulgently at her retreating back as she departed with an air of serious concentration.

For a minute he leaned back, a bemused smile bringing a kind of gentleness to his face. Then from force of habit he drew himself up, passed his hands over his close cropped skull, gave an unnecessary tug to his clerical collar, assumed an expression of spiritual authority, and cleared his throat like a man getting ready to utter profundities.

Country people . . . It was almost three weeks since he had sent the telegram and the boy was only now arriving. Who could say why they did things the way they did—no sense of time. Maybe they only checked the post office once a month, or had to finish the planting . . . More likely it was some old superstition that had to be observed, something that had the local obeahman shining with ignorance in the middle of it. What was the boy's name again? Ivanhoe. Funny how popular that name was among the poorer classes. You could always tell these boys from the country, starched and well-scrubbed in their country clothes, gawking at everything. He'd be visibly grieving, mouth all set to wail and holler at the first mention of the mother's name—definitely not a stoic people, no sir. When he heard footsteps Preacher arranged his face into a mask of dignified sympathy.

"Come in, my boy: so you got my message at last, eh?"

"Message, sah? Nobody don't tell me nothin, sah—only me maddah say you could help me wid a little work, sah." The boy was smiling with a forced brightness and talking very quickly as if afraid he would be cut off. And, from the birdlike glitter of his eyes, he seemed nervous, his restless gaze flickering about the room as if seaching for concealed enemies. Only one thing was as Preacher had anticipated: he didn't seem far from tears.

"Work? What work . . . What's your name, boy?"

"Ivanhoe Martin, sah, Miss Daisy Martin pickney, sah."

"Ah, right, right." The lines of sympathy came back. "She was a good woman and a true Christian, son. It must be hard, but we can take comfort in the knowledge that her place in the Kingdom is secure, secure."

Preacher repeated the last word and paused, waiting for the outburst. It was not forthcoming. Did the boy understand a word he was saying? He seemed quite hardened; in fact there was a funny smile on his face.

"So you wi' help me, sah? God wi' bless you."

"Arumph, well I certainly hope so, hem," he said, coughing. Speaking for the Lord now eh? But . . . the boy was presumptuous, though. "Yes," he went on in the deep, booming tones that could turn the Tabernacle out, "a good Christian woman and a loyal member of this Tabernacle."

"Ah can do anyt'ing, sah, *anyt'ing.*"

"Well, that's good," Preacher began, temporarily sidetracked. He wished the young fellow wouldn't interrupt. There was something strange about him, as ragged as a beggar and not a tear, not even a word about his mother. He drummed his fingers on the desk and looked at the boy who was smiling brightly. The thought occurred to Preacher that perhaps the boy was not quite right in the head.

"Now—you say you never received the telegram?"

"Telegram, sah?"

"Yes, telegram, sah—about your mother."

"No, sah."

"Then how did you find out?"

"Me maddah tell me, sah; she say you would help me wid a little work, sah."

"You playing with me, boy?" He immediately regretted the testiness in his voice; after all the boy had suffered a loss.

"Playing wid you, sah? How you mean?"

"Oh, never mind. I understand how hard it must be for you. The death of a parent is—"

"Oh, Ah see." Ivan was beaming as he began to understand.

"No sah, dass me granny who dead. Me maddah, Miss Daisy, *she* the one who tell me say you would help me—wid some work," he finished helpfully.

Preacher Ramsey glared at Ivan and prayed for patience, he wasn't one to suffer fools gladly. It certainly wasn't an auspicious beginning. Preacher liked to think of himself as a hard man but a fair one. It was true that his spirit didn't take immediately to the boy, but he too was a child of God. And if not for God, then at least for that simple loyal soul who was his mother . . . No, his duty was clear enough.

But even after the misunderstanding had been cleared up, the boy's response seemed lacking in feeling. True he was almost delirious with hunger and had been living like an animal in the streets, subject to God knows what kinds of degradation. Why had it taken him so long to come? What sinful influences had he been exposed to? Stubbornness and pride ruled him. It was probably hunger and desperation more than grace that had finally brought him, tail between his legs, into the flock. But what mattered was that he was there. Though he'd have to be watched closely; vigilance, that was the word. And discipline, discipline and the word of God. He'd come around—it wouldn't be the first time Preacher had wrestled hand-to-hand with the devil for some poor sinner's soul. Yes, it was the hand of God that brought master Ivan to him, and he was up to the task. But in fairness, the boy was respectful enough, seemed to learn quickly and was doing what he was bid. Firmness and a Christian example—that's what the boy needed. And Preacher was just the man for the job too.

In addition to the Tabernacle there were two other buildings associated with Preacher Ramsey's mission: a sprawling wooden house, one wing of which had been turned into a kind of dormitory, where Preacher lived, and a workshop to which were attached two small rooms for sleeping. The mission stood on a slight rise, separated only by a zinc fence and a gulley from the vast sea of tin and wood shacks known as Trench Town, because of the open gulleys that set it off from the rest of the city. A few blocks down the street and around the corner was an open air theater, where every evening the young people of Trench Town who could scrape together the admission found escape of sorts from the squalid monotony of their lives.

To Preacher the proximity and popularity of the movie house, "the devil's workshop" as he called it, was a constant challenge and irritation, a festering thorn in the meat of his content. He regularly wrote letters to the newspapers decrying the influence of such places and urging that they be prohibited from operating on the Sabbath. He denounced them from the pulpit. It was no coincidence, he felt, that the management scheduled triple bills at half price for those weeks when he was having revivals. Sometimes he felt that it was a test, a cross that the Lord had sent to assure his faith and character. At any rate the theater was a constant reminder of the presence and power of the enemy. That, and the sound systems that blasted their throbbing, sinful music which, when the wind was right, floated up to the Tabernacle on warm night breezes smoky with the smell of ganja, troubling Preacher's spirit, afflicting his flesh, and driving him onto his knees in the hot darkness.

Yea, who seeth the travail of the righteous? It was hard indeed, but he had never faltered. And though the enemy was everywhere, and was represented not only by the traffickers in sin, who at least were visible and unmistakable, but by false prophets like those the Bible warned about, those dressed in the skins of lambs, but who inwardly were ravening wolves, his feet had not missed a step, not a step. Praise Jesus, the Lord strengthened his hand daily and touched the hearts of the sponsors in faraway Memphis; the flock grew in numbers and devotion, and the shepherd went from strength to strength, Ahmen. But there was a price: he grew, increasingly as the years passed, less and less inclined to humor and increasingly distrustful of fun or levity. And there was, as is always the case in the Lord's work, the occasional disappointment—the backsliding of a prized convert, the defection and betrayal of a brother. But these only served to toughen him, even as the Lord hardened the forehead of Ezekiel, the Priest, Son of Buzi, who too had to wrestle with the sins of a rebellious people who were stiff-necked. When those deluded Rastas talked about Babylon, they were in their foolish way righter than they knew. He saw himself as a modern day Ezekiel struggling in a Babylon of his own. He felt a kinship to the tough unbending old prophet, hardened in the service of God, whose hardness saved the remnant of God's people. Oasis, he thought, was not the right word for his Tabernacle and household. It was more like fortress—the *Lord's fortress*—a citadel and a beacon beaming a witness for righteousness in a sinful place. But as for me and my house, *we shall* serve the Lord, Ahmen.

And the victories were known, visible for all to see, and all the more rewarding because the struggle was so fierce. Was there not more joy in Heaven over one sinner that repenteth, than in ninety and nine that need no repentance? And had he not brought many a hardened sinner trembling in sorrow and repentance before the throne of grace? And he had brought them not in ones and twos but in *numbers*, Ahmen.

Degradation, that was the visible face of the enemy. And in his unending war against degradation, Preacher maintained a place-of-refuge. This was a small dormitory for young girls, usually the orphans or wayward daughters of church members. They were sent to school and made to contribute by their labor, in return for which they were given a place to live and the necessities—the necessities, for the church could not afford nor did the Preacher allow frills and vanities. Everyone received a Christian education and the opportunity to make something of herself. The only requirement was piety and obedience. The only authority was God, whose word was the Bible and whose messenger, the Preacher. It was a mission heavily freighted with the possibility of failure, but these were rarer than one had any reason to expect. An occasional pregnancy, yes, or a willful daughter abandoning the teachings for a life of sin in the streets. And, despite the malicious innuendo of the envious, the Preacher's reputation for rectitude was so unchallengeable that no hint of any scandal from these failures ever attached to him personally.

Few men were admitted to this select community, Ivan being only the second. This was not really, as some suggested, that "two bulls can't rule in the same pen," but because Preacher saw and correctly so, that the life of the streets was more merciless and destructive to young girls. The snares were more glittering and insidious, and the fall longer and more crushing.

The first man represented a great success, all the more because it was so unlikely, involving as it did a junior grade knife-fighter and bad-man. This man, according to the people, had staggered into the Church yard one night, choking on his own blood while managing to call loudly for assistance. Where a lesser man might have called for an ambulance and the police, Preacher put first things first. He made the sinner as comfortable as his wounds would permit and most of the night wrestled with the devil for his soul. He first saved his soul and also, almost incidentally, his life, securing by that act a general handyman whose very presence around the yard was visible and continuous testimony to Preacher's power in the eyes of the Lord.

It was clear to everyone that it was the Hand of God that brought the bloody and half-dead "Longah" to Preacher's yard, for after his salvation—both spiritual and physical—the reputation and influence of the young revivalist grew. So it was no accident that Ivan was taken on as an assistant to this man. Preacher believed implicitly in the efficacy of example and proximity.

Less spectacular, because it was yet unfulfilled, but just as dear to him because of its clear promise of spiritual victory, was the case of the girl Elsa. She was the orphaned daughter of one of the earliest and most militantly devout of the flock. It was expected, therefore, that Preacher would take her into his refuge. What was not expected at all, was the manner in which the young girl seemed to leaven the spirit and soften the adamantine nature of the driven young preacher. She was a cheerful presence, as diligent at her school books as she was devout in her study of the Bible. In matters of faith she showed a precocious interest and understanding, evincing what Preacher referred to as "a spirit of grace," which was evident to any who cared to look. As she grew older, this attribute, instead of diminishing as was so often the case, seemed to deepen and mature, flourishing, Preacher often thought, like the seed that had fallen on good ground.

Seeing this, he took the unprecedented step of instituting proceedings to become her guardian in law as well as in fact and faith. Also unprecedented was the way in which the girl was able to coax and tease Preacher, if not into a state of joviality which would have been too much to expect, at least into a kind of peace, a relaxing of his stern and unceasing vigilance. Often when he looked at her his eyes grew warm and the hard lines of his face softened. In that mood, when he thought about his household, he would allow himself a certain indulgent rhetoric and he would think, looking into the girl's clear eyes, "the dearest jewel in my crown." He looked forward with an unspecified anticipation to the mature flowering of her spiritual promise.

• • •

Elsa leaned her chin into her cupped hands and watched Ivan shovel huge spoonfuls of stewed peas and rice into his mouth.

"When las' you eat?" Her eyes widened. "You mus' tek time chew—min' you choke. You want some more?"

Ivan watched her as she took the plate to the cook, fussing as she went, "I don't see how a meager bwai like that can eat so much." She brought back the plate full. "Dis time chew slowly. Preacha say you mus' masticate each mouthful twenty times." She sat, propped her chin on her arms, and watched his every move.

She put him in mind of someone, Ivan thought, a long time ago.

"Whass you name?"

"Ivan."

"Ivan what?"

"Ivanhoe, Ivanhoe Martin."

"You are a true Christian?"

"Why you ask?"

She scowled as if to say, I'm asking the questions here. "Because only born-again, washed-in-the-blood Christians can stay here," she explained in a tone that made Ivan know that this question was hardly worth an answer.

"Well Ah guess so," he said.

"Nothin' name guess," she said. "You better be sure."

"Elsa—Elsaaaa!"

"Yes, Preacha?"

"What you doing in the kitchen? You best come and do your homework."

"Ah do it already, Preacha."

"Well, then—come and read your Bible."

"Yes, sah." Silently she waved to Ivan, giving him a quick smile as she hurried out.

Chewing steadily, he watched her leave. Although she didn't physically resemble Mirriam, there was something in her manner that brought a painful longing to his chest. It seemed very long ago when they had been that age in the lamplight beside Maas' Nattie's barbecue. His belly felt heavy and uncomfortably tight. He could not stop belching and nausea was spreading through him.

"How you feeling?"

Preacher stood in the doorway where Elsa had vanished. Ivan had no idea how long he had been standing there watching him eat.

"Ah say, are you alright, boy?"

"Doan feel so good, sah."

"No wonder, the way you stuff the food down. We must remember that gluttony is a sin too, y'know," he said with his stiff little smile.

"Yes, sah."

"You say you want work? Well, I'll talk to you about that tomorrow. Go out to the workshop. There's a man there. Tell him I say to give you a cot out in the empty room behind the shop. Mek him show you where the shower is—wash yourself, eh? An you come see me in the morning."

"Yes, sah. Thank you, sah."

"Don't thank me, boy, praise the Lord."

"Yes, sah."

Longah was planing a piece of lumber when Ivan gave him the message. He grunted and didn't look up from his work, and Ivan couldn't tell whether his frown was one of concentration or hostility. The man was of medium height but so squat and heavily muscled as to appear short. He seemed quite uninterested in Ivan's presence.

Feeling sick and drowsy, Ivan squatted down and watched pale slivers of wood curl away from the blade. He thought he should try to talk with the man and make friends but something about the way Longah ignored him suggested that he wouldn't welcome conversation. He had small eyes, flecked with red and angry-looking, and a funny beard. Well, not a beard so much, Ivan thought, more like a thick matting of short hair which covered most of his face and neck and ran down into his open collar. He wished the man would hurry up and show him the cot. The idea of lying down somewhere and sleeping had become, now that it was so near, a kind of torture. The man continued planing the board, squinting his little eyes to check the work, and ignoring him.

Monkey-man, Ivan thought and smiled. Is mus' be him in de song "hugging up a big monkey man." He began to hum the tune. He was sure Longah heard him but he didn't care.

"Arright, you can come," Longah said, getting up and brushing wood shavings from his shirt. "Follow me."

Ivan walked behind him through the workshop. "Dere, you can bring dat cot—and dere," he pointed to a door, "you can sleep in dereso." He turned on his heel and walked away. Then he stopped and without looking at Ivan asked: " 'Ow long Preacha say you to stay yah?"

" 'Im didn't say," Ivan said, struggling with the cot. "Preacher 'im say fe show me de shower too."

"Well, don't plan on a long stay," Longah said.

The room was tiny and windowless, having been constructed as a large storage closet. When he closed the door behind him, it was dark and the air hot and motionless. But Ivan didn't mind. In fact the encircling darkness had a solid reassuring feel and the close wood walls gave him a sense of privacy and security. He lay in the darkness with his eyes open, staring at blackness and listening to the distant muffled drone from the streets outside. It seemed very far away and harmless. As he stretched full length on the little army cot he felt safe, as though nothing, even if the door to that dark airless room were to be sealed shut, could disturb the feeling of peace which he felt. His last thought as he fell asleep was that he wouldn't really care if he were never to leave that room.

At first he was a little afraid of the huge unsmiling man they called Preacher. He was so big and stiff—and one could hardly call that tight wrinkle that sometimes passed across his mouth a real smile. Besides, everyone, except maybe Elsa and Longah, seemed to quail and stammer in his presence. But the memory of the streets was still raw inside Ivan; he was happy to huddle in the shadow of Preacher and his Tabernacle.

Whether or not the youth Rhygin was ever a bona fide, born-again washed-in-the-blood Christian Baptist is something that people argued over later. Some maintained that during the first months, even years, his devotion was pure and indisputable. Others, like Longah, swore that from the first it was all a pose, that the influence of the devil was evident in the boy's face and eyes from the first, no matter how he tried to hide it, and that his faith began with the hot food regularly available in the kitchen and ended with the amplified organ that the Missionary Board had placed in the Tabernacle for the use of the choir and the Greater Glory of God.

But as they said, "after a t'ing happen every tom-fool did ben know." Hindsight required no genius, and surely there was nothing to be seen in the behavior of the quiet, frightened boy whom Preacher took on as Longah's apprentice and helper that suggested what was to happen.

He attended morning and evening praise with everyone else in the household, went to Bible-study three times a week and to at least two sessions of church on Sundays. Even Preacher who watched everyone in the flock closely could find no fault with him.

What with the luxury of hot meals, a room of his own, and an outdoor shower which Ivan could use as long and as often as he wished, the spiritual observances were a small price to pay. He would have been, if not happy, then at least content were it not for Longah. Happiness was not a condition to which anyone was encouraged to aspire in that sin-conscious household.

In the presence of Preacher or other Christians, Longah's mouth dripped piety, dropping "Allelulahs" and "Praise His Holy Names" like a sick bird on a branch. His manner, especially in the Preacher's presence, was one of gentle, almost transcendent, holiness. But when he was alone with his new assistant, which was most of the time, he gave full vent to a capacity for petty tyranny and a most unchristian, small-time sadism.

Ivan at first felt that his own slowness and ineptitude were the cause of Longah's behavior, and that his surliness and faultfinding would disappear as Ivan became more efficient in his work. So he went about his duties with a dogged, uncomplaining attention to even the most exacting and unnecessary detail. But he soon learned that, so far as Longah was concerned, nothing would satisfy unless it was his departure. Longah was sufficiently oppressive that Ivan thought seriously about leaving, but again, his memories of the streets kept him there.

His sorrowful countenance didn't escape the Preacher's notice, who welcomed it as evidence of repentance and spiritual growth. He happened to mention his pleasure in the signs of Ivan's spiritual awakening to Longah, who saw immediately the error of his tactics. After that he changed his policy toward the boy from one of active harassment to one of studied neglect and muted hostility. A kind of passive but armed neutrality settled between them.

Ivan's spirits improved slightly. He became stronger, healthier, and certainly more clean in his person. But until the day the trucks came he was still casting about for some alternative, short of sleeping again in the streets.

When he saw the workmen installing the speakers and amplifiers that were a gift of the Mother Church in Memphis, he felt the Lord call him to stay. Like all good Baptists, the Missionary Board believed in "making a joyful noise unto the Lord," and as Ivan stood and watched the control panel, electric guitars, and the keyboard, the call could not be resisted or denied. He knew he would stay. He was the first volunteer for the new expanded choir that was formed.

"Boy, you own a Bible?"

"No, y'know Preacha—" Wondering if he was to be given one.

"Hmm. You don't have Bible, but you buy pretty clothes though?"

"Well, sah—" Ivan squirmed under the forbidding stare. "Ah nevah have none, y'know, sah . . ." he trailed off lamely, feeling the explanation to be lacking. After all consider the lilies of the field . . . "An, an Ah need somet'ing decent fe wear to church, y'know, sah," he finished in a burst of inspiration.

Preacher glowered down, only partly mollified by Ivan's explanation. "Hmm boy, we will see."

Ivan slipped into the yard, holding his box carefully, half hidden against his chest. Quickly he entered his room, closed the door, and placed his burden gently on the cot. His new shirt and jeans hung on the wall but today he hardly looked at them. Slowly he opened the BATA shoe box and drew out a pair of blue socks. They were of a fuzzy material that stretched endlessly. The color was deep and rich with an electric glow in the half-light. They were soft and warm to the touch and smelled luxuriously new. Ivan spent a few minutes glorying in the rich color and feel of the incandescent socks, the latest craze among young people. Then he carefully folded them up and dug into the crinkly white paper in the box to reveal the real prize, a pair of imitation suede, ankle-high boots, the toes of which tapered to beautifully sharp points. First he admired them with his eyes, then he stroked them, running his hand with the grain to feel the incredible softness, then back against the grain to see the fuzzy white currents that formed against the blue. He filled his lungs with the new smell; it was hard to accept that they were finally his. So sharp. He looked at the clothes hanging on the wall and wished he had a mirror so he could see himself in the complete outfit. But that wasn't really necessary; he knew how he would look. The day he had been waiting on for ten weeks had finally come. The saving had been worth it. Many times over. He lay back on his cot and looked at the new clothes and grinned and grinned. The slim jeans and western-cut shirt with billowy sleeves, the incandescent socks and the boots, all in shades of blue—midnight blue, sky blue, powder blue, all blue to death. He couldn't stop grinning.

"Star-bwai," he whispered, "star-bwai to raas."

Then impulsively he jumped up and went to the shower where he scrubbed himself repeatedly, even though he had washed before going to the shoe store. Back in his room, he slowly dressed himself in the new clothes. The process, which he dragged out as long as possible, was very satisfying. He examined the feel and fit of each item as he put it on, but when finally dressed he felt vaguely dissatisfied, somehow let down. If only it were Sunday morning, he could go to church. He sat on the cot, carefully so as not to crease the clothes, and fretted. "Cho," he muttered, "let you light so shine before men. No so Preacha say." And walked out the door.

He had not consciously planned it. But when he arrived in front of the theater and saw the crowds of young people and the giant posters, all the pumping excitement of that first night with Jose came rushing into his chest. His concern for Preacher's warnings and certain wrath vanished. It was a Friday night double bill: *Bad Man's Territory,* starring Randolph Scott, and *The Streets of Laredo,* with William Holden. Such riches.

Oh Lawd, he thought, ah can' stan' it . . . Ah can' stan' it.

Keeping his mounting excitement admirably in check he bought a ninepence ticket and sauntered into the theater, a cool mysterious figure in blue. He was sure that a couple of young girls flashed quick, curious looks in his direction as he passed. The ninepence section was directly under the screen. It was filling rapidly with rowdy gangs of youths his own age, full of noisy greeting and excited anticipation, everybody styling in his own way. The show was even better than he remembered, the action swifter and more dramatic, the lines tougher, taut with understated menace, and all the fights—with gun, knife, or fist—were more bloody and satisfying. Again, there was no such thing as watching in silence; the identification was high and a contagious excitement spilled down from the screen and rolled in waves through the theater.

Afterward the show moved into the streets. The boys reenacted the good scenes. With amazing facility of memory and mimicry they drawled the best lines through their noses, walked the walks with hands hanging like claws above imaginary holsters, and made the moves. Wistfully, Ivan passed through the crowd and went back to the Tabernacle.

After that night, his life divided neatly into two separate and incompatible spheres. He became a regular at the theater, rarely missing an "action show," by which was meant a western or detective movie as distinct from a musical or love story which sometimes interrupted the serious fare. During the day he followed Longah's instructions, and went to choir practice or Bible study.

None of that spiritual stimulation elevated his spirit or captured his imagination in any way comparable to what he felt before the altar of the silver screen. Time for Ivan was measured by the changing of the bill.

It wasn't long before his judgment matured and his taste became more selective. Gangster movies didn't appeal to him much, they seemed to lack the clean-cut heroism of the westerns. Of course there were certain names: Humphrey Bogart, Edward G. Robinson, Richard Widmark, Sidney Greenstreet, or George Raft, which evoked a certain style, a cynical tight-lipped toughness which he liked. But in his innermost heart Rhygin was a cowboy. To miss a western, almost any western, brought sadness and deprivation to his spirit.

Now that he was a regular presence in the theater pit he came to understand the territorial protocol that obtained there. Groups of his peers sat in separate territories designated by custom, conquest, or some other mysterious process. He moved in the neutral areas that divided these territories and where independents were tolerated. He was regarded at first with a guarded indifference which changed gradually to an acceptance of the kind that is accorded to some familar object in the landscape. Inhibited by a certain natural reticence, he made no overtures. Soon the acceptance went deeper, being based on shared experience: after all they saw the same shows, honored the same heroes, and had the same references. Perhaps it was simply the recognition of mutual good taste, but the relationship between Ivan and the gangs became warmer.

He came to know the names of many of them, mostly the leaders. The rangy, rough, knock-kneed youth who led one group was known as "Bogart"; another was headed by an aggressive albino named "George Raft" whose mottled face bore the scars of a life devoted to war. To the right of the screen, five rows back, the legions of a youth known as "Hitler" held sway. The leaders ruled on the strength of their personalities and reputations—a mixture of wit and style, and a demonstrated willingness to beat down any challenge at whatever price. But actual violence was not nearly so frequent as the ritualistic gestures of challenge and confrontation would suggest. So long as territorial imperatives and reputations were respected a tense, prickly, but surprisingly durable peace prevailed, most of the time. Against outside threats like the management, the police, or a gang from some other area, internal rivalries disappeared completely.

Now when Ivan entered greetings were exchanged. Studiedly

cool, noncommital, but carrying nonetheless a certain understated respect.

"Wha'a go on, Color Blue?"

"Peace an' love, Hitler."

The first time this happened he was excited by the recognition and wanted more. But the cool greeting did not warm into intimacy. Then, he began to be comfortable with the distance and the identity which in his imagination he saw as a mysterious one: the lone, taciturn stranger riding into town, maintaining a certain distance and keeping his own counsel, on properly formal terms with everyone, seen but not known, until that day when some unsuspecting fool stepped over the invisible line.

The image pleased him greatly; he relished it and cultivated an even more remote and mysterious manner.

"Color Blue to rahtid. Cool blue, yes, dah name de alright."

Ivan's nod became a barely perceptible inclination of the chin; his smile a frosty, understated tensing and relaxing of the muscles of the face. When he spoke it was a slow drawl through lips that scarcely moved, reluctantly separating just enough to allow the words to escape. And he used few words.

The new persona worked well. The greetings became more frequent, warmer, and in a subtle way more respectful. One night Bogart offered him a cigarette. He took it even though he didn't smoke cigarettes. After that he kept a pack of Four Aces in his shirt pocket. Now when he entered the theater it was with a cigarette dangling Cagney-like from the corner of his mouth, the smoke stinging his eyes and justifying the hard squint through which he viewed the world. Occasionally he would offer a smoke to those who seemed to merit such intimacy from the mysterious stranger. . . .

8

Dodge City and Boot Hill

"Death before Dishonor"

Having sat through two showings of *Gunfight At O.K. Corral,* Ivan walked out of the theater in something approaching a state of grace. He was pacing along the sidewalk like Wyatt Earp, with the slow, measured stride of a gunfighter, when Bogart walked up to him at the head of his gang which silently fanned out in a half circle behind him like *Blackboard Jungle.* Ivan felt a slight current of menace, but he was easy. Bogart was smiling. It was a mission of peace.

"Aye, Color Blue?"

"Dem call me Rhygin."

They faced each other under the streetlight. Shoulders hunched, thumbs hooked into his belt with elbows straight, Ivan squinted through the smoke at Bogart and the semicircle.

"Well—Rhygin den. Good show?"

"Truly."

Suddenly Bogart bent over wheezing for breath. A fit of hollow, consumptive and explosive coughs rattled in his chest. He made an effort to control the coughing, failed, and was thrown to one knee by the vehemence of the fit. He didn't seem to have long for this world. Then he stood, gasping uneven gusts of air into his tortured chest, with an open rachet knife dangling ever so casually from his hand. The expression on his face was one of pure malevolence.

"Oowee!" Ivan shouted, laughing with delight and unfeigned admiration. "Doc Holliday to raas!"

He recognized the scene: Kirk Douglas as the consumptive and deadly Doctor. In that single performance Douglas nearly ruined the lungs and throats of a whole generation of West Kingston youth. With his, Bogart made a friend and a recruit.

"We a go down de ranch. Walk wid we."

"Arright den," Ivan accepted. He walked beside Bogart through the dark streets. Around them the gang swirled in constant motion, laughing, shouting, coughing, and discussing the movie. Ivan, at ease and happy in the boisterous rough camaraderie, offered around his pack of Four Aces. His only touch of tension came when they passed the dark and gloomy shape of the Tabernacle thrusting up into the sky.

One of the boys rattled the zinc fence with a tree limb and shouted, "Preacha Ramgoat, you ol' pussy watchman you, wake up. Me say wake up Ramgoat, you damn Sunday ginnal ° you."

The group hooted and jeered at the silent Tabernacle. Ivan was stunned. Until that moment it had been inconceivable to him that everyone did not think of the Preacher with the same respect and fear that the members of the congregation did. He half expected Longah to come charging out to avenge the insult to the Shepherd. But . . . dese youth yah doan 'fraid nutten, he thought, quickening his steps as they passed. Maybe he should have defended Preacher? It was only when he was safely past that he could allow himself to appreciate the humor of the jibe. Preacha Ramgoat, the pussy watchman, eh? He savored the phrase and laughed out loud. Never again would Preacha's moral presence be so totally intimidating. "Pussy watchman. Damn."

Yelling and laughing they ran on until they came to the gulley that separated Trench Town from the rest of the city. They moved along the zinc fence until they reached a hole. Ivan found himself on the wall of a gulley, across from which sprawled the mazelike shantytown, a formless, teeming city within a city. They ran along the wall of the concrete watercourse until they came to a footbridge. Here they crossed and followed a narrow track leading into a grove of scrubby underbrush. In a hidden clearing stood a small shack. In front of it, by the light of a lamp, three boys were playing cards. A sign with letters burnt western-style into wood, was nailed to a stunted tree under which the boys were playing. It said:

SALT LAKE CITY RANCH
Death before Dishonor
BOOT HILL 5 YARDS

"Is our ranch dis," Bogart explained. "We control on yah, is yahso we groun'."

_____

° Ginnal: trickster, con man, fraud.

"It arright." Ivan nodded approvingly.

"Dis here is breddah Rhygin—'im a go groun' wid we." That was his introduction. There were a few appraising glances, some nods and murmurs of welcome, that was all it took and Ivan was a member. They produced a *cutchie* pipe and sat around the fire on worn seats scavenged from old cars.

In the light of the fire Ivan recognized most of the faces and, as talk flowed easily back and forth, soon had names to associate with them. There were about ten, all about his own age. None—with the exception of Black LeRoy, to differentiate him from Coolie LeRoy who ran with the Dodge City Ranch—seemed to answer to the names their mommas gave them. They answered to the tough-sounding two syllable surnames that were the stock in trade of Hollywood press agents—names of consequence and with the right resonances that could be spat out with sharp, dangerous inflections: Bendix, Cagney, Bogart, Widmark. In those cases where the bearer of the name was *bad* enough, but the surname by itself was too common or in some way lacking in poetic and dramatic menace, then the full name was used for emphasis, so that Ivan also met that first night Edward G. Robinson, Sidney Greenstreet and Peter Lorre. It was a heady experience around that smoky fire on the edge of the gulley—to walk with kings . . .

Their identification was with the actors, not with the characters they played who were obviously ephemeral and transitory. It was the ability of the actors that made the characters *bad* and which endured, so that arguments took place over whether Bogart was *badder* than Widmark. A standing joke was about two country boys who had taken the names Jesse James and General Custer, failing to see the distinction between the real and the imaginary. These choices provoked so much scorn and derision that the boys quickly abandoned the "dead man name dem."

It was here that Ivan's education truly began. They lounged around the fire and talked knowingly and with a casual toughness and machismo of language that matched their *noms de guerre*. Their style was aggressive, their wit cynical, their bravado endless. With capricious dexterity they flashed their *okapis*, the ubiquitous, cheap German-made clasp knives known in the press as rachet knives, the weapon of choice of the gulleys and slums. Honor demanded that even the slightest gesture of challenge, the faintest nuance of disrespect had to be met. But if you were fast enough with the humpbacked evil-looking blade, if you could flourish it with the stylish grace of a gunslinger twirling his six gun, that was frequently enough and the actual *cutting* was unnecessary, was even regarded as a sign of oafishness. But that was before the legendary, dazzlingly fast Peter Lorre was cut down in the middle of his amazingly intricate two-handed Mexican attack, was sliced from cheek to jowl by a *crufty*, awkward country boy with a half machete, who called himself William Bendix and didn't know the difference between style and brute force—between art and murder.

It was all very exciting to Ivan. But that first night he was doubly nervous. Preacher's wrath weighed him down like a giant black vulture sitting on his shoulder. Every sound coming out of the darkness became for him a party of police getting ready to pounce. This was one of those "gangs of lawless youth and evil-doers" that Preacher was always denouncing. As he listened to their casual boasting of deeds they had seen, done, and would do, he was sure that Preacher must be right.

So when Widmark stood up, his hand cradling his crotch to indicate the nature of his business, and swaggered off announcing that he had a "mission," Ivan seized the chance.

"Bwai, I all have a mission too, y'know," he drawled.

"Alright, two a unu walk de breddah through den," Bogart ordered. "Since is all him first time on yah wid we and him don't know de gulley."

Safely back in his cubicle in the shadow of the Tabernacle Ivan's fears seemed foolish. He longed for the excitement of the ranch and wished he were back in front of the fire with the others. One thing he knew, before he went back he would have to buy himself an *okapi*, a good one, something pretty and dangerous-looking, maybe a pearl handled one with a gun-blue sheen on the blade.

His world had expanded enormously. Now he had a place to hang out while waiting for the show to change. Late at night he could sneak out and be sure that there would be someone at the ranch, walking partners to hang out with, to go to dances, prowl the streets, to check out the fast young girls with the eager eyes, quick tongues, and easy ways. He learned the political geography of shantytown, the territories of the various ranches through which the concrete highway of the gulley turned and twisted.

Ivan had dreaded the time when his new friends would have to find out where he lived since they regarded Preacher and his work with such scant respect. But he was surprised at how little reaction his confession evoked. Underneath their fierce rhetoric and warlike gestures their lives were not much different from his and they understood the demands of survival. Like him, many of these slick, streetwise urbanites were not long from the country either. Bogart the cool, the unchallenged leader, the man of respect, was by day Ezekiel Smith, a mechanic's apprentice. Some were apprentice carpenters, masons, or apprentice criminals like Cagney, scuffling to live any way they could. They sold newspapers, polished cars, did "day work" or when necessary begged or stole in the streets. Some were by day garden "boys" at the mansions and would-be mansions in the foothills, which Ivan remembered as a place of insult and fear.

But by night when the employers huddled behind iron gates and high walls, their garden boys in the little rooms out behind the servants' quarters dressed in their night finery. They pocketed their *okapis*, answered only to their war names, and headed for the ranches in search of companionship, adventure, and reputation.

These ranches surrounded the lower city. On the hills to the east, in the gulleys of the shantytowns of the center, and in the swampy mangrove wastes of the west, young men and boys sat around flickering fires in places called Dodge City, Hell's Kitchen, Boot Hill, El Paso, Durango, and even Nikosia. (There was terrorism in Cyprus at the time.) They smoked ganja, dreamed valiant dreams, and cursed the rich, the "high-ups" of society, and the police, especially the elite "Flying Saucer Squad," their sworn enemies. Periodically, almost at predictable intervals, pulpits rang with denunciations of lawless youth and wrongdoers, and editorials would call attention to the dangers represented by gangs lurking in the cracks and crevices of the social fabric. The Flying Saucer Squad would stage their well-publicized "lightning raids" and for a while the ranches would be deserted and the gangs scattered. Until society forgot.

On the ranch Ivan served his second apprenticeship in the streets, but not as an outsider this time. He learned about madmen and badmen, dead and living, men of great reputation and short careers. He boasted and dreamed of deeds he would do. Even as they cursed the rich, they cherished fantasies of "big money," sudden wealth of their own. Everyone knew a boy, just like them, who had won sweepstakes, made a killing at the Chinese-run lotteries, "Drop Pan" or "Picka Peow," or pulled off a "big job." Or a face man who lucked into the bed and fortune of a wealthy old white woman and earned his money "doing night work" by the inches. Or else it was the giant *samfie*, the great hustle, which they knew came at least once in his life to every man—you only needed the wit to recognize it and the nerve and luck to hold it. And failing any of those—well it was only something Bogart liked to say because it sounded good: "Live fast, die young, have a good-looking corpse." Which, every time he heard it, reminded Ivan of Cagney.

Cagney. The olympic-class grab-and-flee specialist who had revolutionized the profession and brought it into conformity with a mechanized age. Cagney, the short, muscular, quiet boy who stuttered when he was excited and consequently said little. He was incredibly strong, with the balance and timing of an acrobat and no nerves at all, when ripping through the streets hunched over the low handles of the stripped down fix-wheel he called his "bronc." On sultry days when all car windows were open and traffic crawled through the baking streets, Cagney bopped his bronc through the traffic, eyes alert for the carelessly placed wallet or purse lying on a lap or on a seat. More than one driver, they said, reaching out to signal a turn had seen his watch disappear in a blur of motion, a rush of wind, and the chip of racing tires grabbing the pavement. It was all done so fast that no one ever had a clear description, and the boys said that if the driver was wearing a ring that was slightly loose, Cagney would claim that too without even breaking rhythm.

Cagney, the quiet artist-athlete, in his own way a genius, who had taken an outmoded form and modernized it, finding the perfect medium for his particular gifts of speed, timing, and balance. Lacking speech he substituted an idiom of motion and grace. After him grab-and-flee was never the same, and the mounted army of imitators who came later, however good—and some like "Easy Boat" and "Copperhead" were very good—were only shadows of the master. Cagney who was never equaled and never caught, and who was spared the ravages of age. He never lived to see the reflexes slow, the legs begin to go, the timing off, the will and confidence falter, the shining beacon of genius dimmed by age. At the height of his power, Cagney was executing his ninety-degree swoop against three lanes of oncoming traffic and a changing light, and would have made it too, as he had so many times, but not for a panicky American in a sports car who closed the lane on him at fifty miles an hour. The purse lying in the wreckage of the bicycle contained two dollars. The weeping driver said he had never even seen Cagney . . . which could have been true.

By day Ivan did his work, went to prayer meeting and choir practice and learned all he could about music from Mr. Brown, the willing, somewhat abstracted, choirmaster. Then night transformed him, into a desperado of the imagination. He prowled the streets with Bogart and the boys, went to blues dances where highly amplified black-American music dominated, faced down other gangs, fled the clutches of Babylon, and rode with John Wayne, Gary Cooper, and Wild Bill Elliott out of places with names like Fort Apache and Rio Lobo.

9

Change and Decay

If you are a big, big tree
I am a small axe . . .

Ivan and Bogart were alone at the ranch. The full moon had crested Warieka Hill and they hadn't bothered to make a fire.

"Ay, Rhygin?" Bogart looked up from the Red Stripe beer he was idly sipping. "Is how long me an' you groun' now?"

"Bwai I doan know exactly—but is a while now, doh. Why?"

Bogart did not answer immediately. He seemed deep in thought. Ivan paid close attention to the expression on the battle-scarred face. Bogart was not given to introspection and abstract analysis, though he was extraordinarily quick at sizing up a situation and coming up with inspired, precisely correct, and effective responses. For all his apparently thoughtless quickness, he was never known to make a foolish move or to fail to find almost instinctively the appropriate gesture for any situation. But now he seemed uncharacteristically thoughtful and worried.

"You no see say things deh change breddah? Next to me you is de oldes' breddah on dis ranch y'know."

"To raas yes. Is bare yout' on yah now."

"Ah true. An it seem like say every day dem more desperate too—no have no cool an' no style neider, jus' want fight-fight an cut-cut up dem one another all de while too. You no see it?"

It was true and Ivan must have seen it too but the change had been so gradual that he hadn't been conscious of it. He thought of Peter Lorre and Cagney and others gone. "Yes, y'know . . . Now you talk, ah see it."

"An' not only dat," Bogart continued. "Look yah! Jes' the other day I all have fe box down a semi-Rasta bwai, on Parade, y'know." He seemed aggrieved. "Yes guy, Ah had was to box 'im down."

"Why, wha' 'im do you?"

"Wha' 'im do me? Wha' 'im do me?" Bogart repeated, the outrage in his voice increasing.

"Hear what de bwai come tell me? An' 'im say it loud too, so everybody hear 'im. 'Im say 'im is a black power rude-bwai an' 'im name Ras Chaka. An, 'im say 'im hear say me name *Bogart* and derefore 'im want to know if white man is me faddah?"

"What you tell him?" Ivan asked, laughing.

"Look 'pon me too? How white man is to be *my* faddah? What Ah tell him? Ah don't tell him nothin—Ah jus' box 'im down. So him spring up an' wan' draw him rachet knife. So me tek it 'way from 'im an box 'im down again an' when 'im shape to get up Ah kick 'im ina him head—not too hard, jus' enough to teach 'im respeck. You can imagine such a rudeness, sah?" Bogart's face was a study in outraged dignity and puzzlement.

"De bwai well faastie, an' fool-fool too," Ivan soothed. But Bogart was onto something. First time it was impossible even to conceive of any youth daring enough to openly make fun of the name of a star-bwai and warrior of Bogart's standing. But that was only the tip, what was happening went far deeper. It was a time of great but gradual change, mysterious processes almost imperceptible until one day you noticed that things were different, and only when you looked back could you see just how a thing had happened.

He looked over at Bogart's troubled face, its every honorable scar shining black in the moonlight. His aggrieved expression was funny but Ivan didn't laugh. He knew what was bothering him. It was not just the insolence, the faastieness of the Rasta youth—after all Bogart had handled that with his usual decisiveness and flair. It went deeper. Most of the youth coming up were growing the locks and taking African names, Ras Dis and Bongo Dat, talking about I-man dis an' I-man de other, everything was "dread" and it was bare "Jah dis an' Jah de next." The movies were still a great part of their scene, but now they shouted for the Indians and never took the white man's side, much less his name. But to ask Bogart such a rude question doh? If white man was 'im faddah? No first time dat *nevah* could tek place. Who these Rastas anyway? It look like it was just one Rasta one day; and the next day everywhere you look is nothing but Dreadlocks. Whe' dem come from anyway?"

Funny—he'd seen but he hadn't really noticed eh? One day you look up and everything just different? Ivan began to look back. He realized with surprise that some six years had slipped by since he had first stepped down from Coolie Man's bus. Six years to raas. Whe' dem go? Bogart was definitely right, it was not the same city, if anything it was worse. But how? Worse how?

He remembered how big, crowded, and frightening it had been. Now he was accustomed to it and had it all figured out. So how could it be worse? Well, some things worse an' some better. What better? Maybe it was only him. He knew more now, could take care of himself in the street and he ate regularly and slept dry—that was a lot. But what did he really have, what to look forward to? Thanks to Mr. Brown and the choir he knew music, at least something about it, and Mr. Brown agreed that he could sing. He was only waiting for a chance, the big break. But yet an' still what did he really have? No. Ah better go back to de first question—what was worse? Why had he said worse? Could anything be worse than what he come and seen? He remembered his first weeks in the streets, hungry 'til he was weak, dumb, frightened, sleeping on the concrete floor of the market; he felt a familiar tremor in his belly. "Bwai, Ah better res' it. Dem kinda thinking deh *bittah*. Rest it, Ivan, res' it. But yet it seemed to him that people were poorer, hard-pressed. Their nerves were bad, they were quick to anger and even violent in a way they had not been before. They had always been loud and contentious, demonstrative, but before it had been tempered and cooled by humor and forbearance. Now what humor there was was bitter and very angry . . . and everybody was irritable . . .

"An' de police, dat was worse. Definitely. When I come town most a dem ride bicycle an walk dem foot. Mos' dem do is box you up or lick you wid baton. But now? Now dem drive car an' carry gun an machine gun too. An' some of de youth too, ah hear dem a carry gun too. You say 'feh' dem wan' blow out you tripe wid gun shot. . . .

Something was happening. That was clear. . . . But it was just beginning, just beginning . . . where it would end? What it would be, this thing that was coming? He could not tell, but it goin' be dread. . . . As Rastaman would say: "It a go dread." So. . .

"Ay Bogart . . . you sleeping?"

"No guy, jus' a think y'know."

"Ah, you 'member when dem say dem capture de city?"

Bogart didn't ask who. He laughed. "Who coulda feget dat? De mad raasclat dem?"

"But check me . . . what you t'ink woulda happen if dem try dat all like today?"

"How you mean what woulda happen? Nothing but bloodshed breddah, pure bloodshed."

"Dass what Ah mean, t'ings deh change . . ."

That had been a while ago, not long after Ivan joined the gang. Everyone in Trench Town was talking about an unprecedented event, a Ras Tafarian "convention" being held on the open lands to the west of the city. Drawn by incredible accounts of strange and mysterious happenings, Bogart, Rhygin, Widmark, Peter Lorre, Cagney—all the old gang—had gone to see.

Smoky fires burned in drums set at intervals to mark off the huge field. The gaps were paced by sentries, serious in their robes and dreadlocks and carrying swords and staffs. At the center a bonfire blazed in front of a platform, over which fluttered red, green, and black banners with holy and mystic inscriptions. Robed cultists, smoking their *chalice*, a sacred water pipe full of ganja, danced to an orchestra of drums chanting, *"You cannot go to Zion with a carnal mind"* and

> *Dry up you eyes*
> *to go meet Ras Tafari*
> *Dry up you eyes an'*
> > *come.*
> > and
>
> *So long Ras Tafari call you*
> *So long . . .*
> *So long Ras Tafari call you*
> *So long . . .*
> *For de wicked is around you*
> *Seeking to devour you,*
> *So long Ras Tafari call you*
> *So long . . .*

A huge crowd, buzzing with speculation and amazement, surrounded the camp. Nothing like this had ever been seen in Kingston. The boys looked on in wonder. "Bwai," Widmark whispered, "it only want Charlton Heston fe come down wid de commandments now?"

Rumors swept the crowd. A young bull was to be sacrificed—no, that had happened already. It was a man who was to be the burnt offering tonight. No, dem couldn' mad . . . Yes, a bearded man in a state of high agitation had reported to the police that he had gone to the campsite to see what was happening and after being kindly received was invited to stay for that evening's ceremonies. He had been resting in a hut when he overheard conversation indicating that *he* was to be the evening's sacrifice. It was in the *Star* newspaper that afternoon.

"You lie."

"No, de man say is the grace of God alone save 'im."

"Who him? Whe' 'im name?"

" 'Im name Bullock, Missa Bullock."

"Cho, you too damn lie."

"No, see it yah, you can read it you'self."

Others claimed that it was the leader's son who had offered himself as sacrifice. Others that it was to be three virgins.

"Ah wish dem luck, oo. Whe' dem a go fin' dem?"

Toward midnight three figures appeared on the platform. The chanting stopped. The three were magnificently robed, and even from a distance gave an unmistakable appearance of authority.

"Is de Rasta King dem dat?"

"Is who dem?"

"De tall one in purple is Emmanuel David de Prince. The little mauger one wid de grayhead is Raccoon de High Priest, and de one-foot one wid de sword and shield is Little David de Armor Bearer."

"Cho, what a way him boasie, eh?"

"Bwai, look pon de one-foot Rasta stan' at attention?"

"You see it? Cho!"

Emmanuel David raised his staff over the crowd like Moses over the Red Sea, and immediately all was silent. The crowd was impressed despite themselves, for such obedience to authority was not common. Emmanuel David's kingly voice rang out in the silence. He announced that through the wickedness of Babylon and the schemes of the down-pressors of the righteous, there had had to be a change in the evening's ceremonies. The sacrifice planned for that evening was postponed.

"You shoulda did hol' on to Bullock," someone shouted, and there was a ripple of laughter from the crowd.

But Emmanuel David went on, unfazed by the laughter. The Holy Raccoon, loved by God, had been sent a new vision. A new vision from God Almighty, Jehu Jah Ras Tafari. Jah-God had commanded that the city be captured and purged from sin and wickedness that very night.

"The amount of sin in dis yah city can't purge ina one night," the same skeptic said. "Ah doan care how you holy."

This very night, Emmanuel David declared, would the city be delivered into the hands of the righteous even as Jericho was delivered unto Joshua, the son of Nun; even as the iron gates of Gaza fell before the might of Sampson, yes, and the Five kings of the Amorites before the Israelites: Adonezek, King of Jerusalem; Hoham, King of Hebron; Piram, King of Jarmuth, and all other high-ups of the ungodly.

The Prince's eloquence was incendiary. Hearing his words his followers danced and shouted with joy, waving their swords and staffs. "Deliverance, deliverance!" they roared, their swart and hirsute countenances bright with the ectasy of power and liberation long awaited, and now at hand. "Raas Ta FARiii," they intoned. "Let de powah from Zion fall on I."

So great was the passion and fervor that greeted the Prince's announcement that it seemed as though the capture and purgation of the city were already an accomplished fact. The spontaneous joy of the brethren generated an infectious excitement in the watching crowd.

"Wha' you t'ink Rhygin? You believe dem can do it?" Widmark whispered dubiously.

"I doan know, y'know?" Ivan admitted. He remembered Maas' Nattie's stories of black wars and heroes and wanted to believe. But there was something about this—this strange army, that didn't seem to be exactly what Maas' Nattie had talked about. Still . . .

They watched with mounting excitement as Prince Emmanuel David, flanked by the High Priest and the one-legged Armor Bearer, set out at the head of a procession. Over their heads fluttered an enormous banner and behind them came robed acolytes "of the ancient and mystical order of *Melchizedek*" reverently bearing a cloth-shrouded burden said to be the "Ark of the Covenant." Then came the drummers followed by the troops, the *dread* warriors of *Nyabhingi*, fairly dancing in their zeal, and who oddly enough showed no weapons save for wooden staffs and a few makeshift spears and swords. They were armed, apparently, mainly with their faith. As they marched on the sleeping city followed by crowds of the curious and skeptical they beat their drums, sounded their tambourines and chanted the praise names of God:

> *de word of de Lawd our*
> *God,*
> *Jehujah Ras Tafari*
> *is*

> *Mercy and truth*
> > *to those*
> *Who keep his Covenant*
> > *and*
> *His Commandments.*
> *So Haile dat man,*
> > *Selassieii*
> *Jehujah Ras Tafari,*
> *Negus Negusti,*
> *King of Kings,*
> *Lord of Lords,*
> *Conquering Lion of the Tribe*
> > *of Judah,*
> *De elect of heaven and*
> *De Light of Dis Worl'.*
> > *Selah.*

"The Lion of Judah," they proclaimed, "shall break every chain and give us de victory, again and again." They left little room for doubt as they raised a joyful noise unto their God and danced in ecstasy behind his Ark.

At first the line of march meandered somewhat as though Raccoon's vision were fitful, but it seemed to gain in clarity once they entered the city and he led them directly to Victoria Park. The Parish Church stood at the northern end and the celerity and certainty with which he headed for the official church of the establishment should have answered any questions as to whether the insurrection were political or theological in its inspiration. On the door, Raccoon posted a declaration denouncing the Anglican Bishop and all his works. It summoned him to confess his error, to renounce the white man's false religion, to proclaim the divinity of Ras Tafari and the primacy of the true faith and the Church Triumphant. Raccoon then performed a *Bhingi*, a ceremony of exorcism for the evil influences in the building.

The brethren then divided into two lines and marched around the park in opposite directions, playing drums and tambourines. They did this seven times before they entered the park and raised their banner on Queen Victoria's flagpole where only the Union Jack flew on ceremonial occasions. They made what seemed to some a less than wholehearted attempt to pull the Queen's statue down. This structure proved every bit as massive and unyielding as the portly, popeyed white lady whose figure it represented, so they contented themselves with draping it in dark cloth.

The High Priest then exorcised the spirit of colonialism and Emmanuel David declared the city captured. Emissaries were dispatched to inform the Governor and the Prime Minister of the change in their status and to summon them to formally hand over the reins of government and "bend the knee" to the new authority. The warriors took up defensive positions and were inspected by the Prince and his Armor Bearer, who seemed quite satisfied with the preparedness of the troops. The three leaders then took positions on a bandstand where the military band customarily performed concerts of imperial music, and composed themselves to await the arrival of the representatives of Babylon.

To the spectators there was something distinctly anticlimactic about the proceedings thus far. From the tree in which they had positioned themselves, Bogart and his boys begun to hear loud criticisms of the leadership. The onlookers were particularly dissatisfied with Emmanuel David as a military and political strategist and with Raccoon as a visionary, but they seemed to like the military bearing of the Armor Bearer.

"Cho raas—is dis me walk so far to see?" a man complained.

"Wait? Dem t'ink a so man capture city nuh? Is mus' joke dem man yah, a joke."

The invading force, particularly the leadership, loftily ignored the jeers and fired up their chalice while confidently awaiting the submission of the rulers of Babylon. Nothing happened. The crowd grew more restive and their comments louder and more insulting.

At that moment two sleepy constables on foot patrol appeared, blinking their eyes in drowsy astonishment.

"Babylon, Babylon!" the crowd shouted in warning.

When he saw that there were only two policemen, Raccoon the priest received a new vision. He announced that Ras Tafari would not be deprived of his sacrifice a second time. He now demanded the heads of the two Babylons for tribute. With cries of "fire fe Babylon" and "Babylon mus' fall," a group of warriors gave chase.

"Run Babylon!" the crowd shouted, hooting and laughing. "Rastaman after you!"

"Whaiiee, watch de Babylon dem a run! Haw, haw. Me say run Babylon!" The sight of the police in headlong flight pleased them mightily and their good spirits were immediately restored, especially at the prospect of seeing something really unusual like a sacrifice. But the expeditionary force returned with nothing more substantial to show for their efforts than the helmets and nightsticks that had been abandoned in flight.

When the police returned, however, it was in force. Six buses roared up to the park. Riot-ready troopers carrying long clubs and wooden shields poured out of the buses, their iron heels ringing ominously on the pavement. They formed a solid line behind the unbroken wall of their shields and peered out from beneath spiked helmets. With military precision they stomped their heels on the concrete and rattled clubs against shields, raising a fearful clatter.

Opposite the Rastas formed a ragged line, Emmanuel David attended by Little David, at the center. No one could recall seeing Raccoon from this point on, but then, his role was spiritual rather than military. The two armies glared at each other.

The Prince shook his staff and made a forward gesture. "Dere is no retreat here—advance," he bellowed. "Tek no prisoners!"

There was a pause as his troops gathered their courage.

"Raas!" Widmark observed. "Spartacus to blood claat."

And indeed, with the Biblical robes of the Rastas and the lines of shields and spiked helmets, the scene resembled nothing so much as the Roman legions against the slaves.

"True, but me no see Victor Mature," Ivan said.

Then as the brethren chanted "Fire fe Babylon!" "Jah Kingdom come!" "Black man fe Rule!" Little David led his troops against the foe.

The police held their position and allowed the charge to break against them like a wave swirling onto a reef. Then they advanced methodically, swinging their clubs like reapers in a grainfield. A club bounced off Prince Emmanuel's head with a resonant thonk, knocking him to his royal knees. Stalwart Little David dragged the monarch to his feet and teetered on his one good leg while flailing mightily around him with his sword. The Prince shook his head clear and bellowed:

"Too late! Too late to advance! Retreat! Retreat in good order!" and lost no time obeying his own command. Little David sounded the retreat on his *abeng* ° and the brethren, deserting their flag, streamed out of the park in all directions, robes billow-

° Abeng: Cow's horn used as a trumpet.

ing and dreadlocks flapping in the wind of their furious passage.

The only determined resistance came from a towering cultist who alone did not obey the signal to retreat. Downed by a blow to the knee in the initial charge, he staggered to his feet and limped into the middle of the police swinging a tree limb. His eyes were red and glaring, his mouth wide open, his neck tense and swollen with the force of a roar that was lost in the general clamor. He was surrounded and his scalp split open by a club. He was still cursing Babylon and struggling, with blood streaming into his matted locks, when they dragged him to the bus.

"Ah know dah breddah deh!" Ivan shouted. Poor Ras Sufferah had been right, he thought. He had said that sooner or later Babylon would bus' 'im head. Who ago feed him pickney dem now?

The police gave only token pursuit, some of them seemed to be laughing.

"Bwai," Bogart remarked, "even Victor Mature couldn't did help dem."

That was the end of the capture of the city. A few heads were broken and a few legs fractured, but no more serious injuries were reported by either side. The next morning's papers carried banner headlines: INVADERS REPELLED: THE CITY IS DELIVERED and treated the incident as low comedy. Certain inveterate letter writers and viewers-with-alarm, Preacher Ramsay foremost among them, took issue with that attitude, pointing out that several major crimes had clearly been committed, to wit: mayhem, insurrection, sedition, *lese majesty*, treason, and quite probably heresy and blasphemy. They demanded that charges be preferred. No one paid much attention.

The most serious damage seemed to be to the political careers of Prince Emmanuel David and Raccoon, neither of whom appeared to enjoy any further influence with their brethren. For weeks afterward gangs of small boys could be seen shouting "Advance! Tek no prisoners," then, "It's too late to advance, retreat," and racing away, their laughter pealing mockingly behind them. The only principal of the affair who was not diminished was Little David the Armor Bearer, who was believed to have been the beneficiary of divine intervention. It was said that after the rout, when the youngest and fleetest of the defeated army reached the campsite, some five miles from the scene of the battle, they found the Armor Bearer sitting on the platform in front of the embers of the fire. He seemed calm, was unsweated, and had a beatific expression on his usually militant features. He was strumming an instrument, they said, and singing sweetly in a calm and peaceful voice:

> *Oh if you only knew*
> *De blessed Ras Tafari, O,*
> *You could not stay away.*

No satisfactory explanation was ever offered as to how a man with one leg, last seen in the thick of the fray, could have beaten everybody back to the camp. But there were those who devoutly believed that only the hand of Ras Tafari could have reached down to pluck the valiant warrior out of the hands of Babylon. Selah!

"No," Bogart repeated, "if dem evah try dat today is certain death y'know."

"Dead toll in de hundreds," Ivan agreed. "And to t'ink all dat happen since I come town too? De police not into anymore stick an shiel' business y'know, now dem have gas mask favor Flash Gordon, and antiriot tank, whe' government buy from de German man dem, what spray out tear gas an' paint man red so dem can pick you up later."

"Dass wha' ah mean," Bogart said. "It different now. Flying Saucer Squad was a joke to what dem have now."

"Not only police, de yout' too. Look how Peter Lorre, and Bendix an' Widmark cut up, an over what? Bare foolishness. Fe nutten at all."

"Aye breddah, it dread so. It seem like de yout' dem jus' gettin' desperate, an' quick to shed man blood."

"An' look whe' happen down at Majestic las' month. Now *dat* is wha' I call *alias.*" °

"Bwai, me no ever wan' talk 'bout dat. My nerve dem no even recover yet. It *alias* no raas."

"Dah man deh, de one dem call Maas' Ray, is who him?"

"I doan know y'know, but him different, different bad."

"Listen no maastah, something a go happen. Hear whe' I tell you! Somet'ing *serious* a go happen." Bogart lapsed into a thoughtful silence.

"Bwai, I know say I poor an I black y'know. But dat night is the first I know say this government don't place *no value* at all fe me life." Ivan fell silent too, thinking about the incident. It was

° Alias: evil, alien, desperate.

then they had first seen that the thing that was coming was not ordinary, not ordinary at all.

They had taken a chance and gone into central Kingston to see a triple bill. It was alien territory contested by the Skull gang and the Mau Mau. They knew both by reputation but had no real contact or trouble with either. It had seemed to Ivan that there was an extra tension in the theater that night, though he thought it was just the natural insecurity of their being outside their area. But even after the first show his uneasiness persisted, a sense that something was going on, something sinister about which he knew nothing. Instead of dissipating this feeling grew stronger, and he would have suggested to Bogart that they leave after the first show had he been able to think of a tangible excuse. He had been on the verge of saying "Bogart, mek we leff de place, man!" That he hadn't said it may have been a good thing, because if anyone had recounted it later, they would probably not have believed the story.

The second feature had just begun when the screen went dark. The crowd had automatically begun to clap and stomp their feet when a voice cut through the noise.

"Stop unu noise. Show done."

The audience fell into a startled silence. "How show to done and only one film show yet?" The noise started again. Then a spotlight flashed on and revealed a figure standing on the wall *above* the screen. A slender, young black man in military khakis was silhouetted against the sky.

"Ah say," he announced into the surprised silence, *"show done!"* He wore a Sam Browne belt and a pistol in a clasped holster at his waist and he had a swagger stick tucked casually under his arm.

A mutter ran through the crowd. "Dis raas man mad?"

"Who him to come talk 'bout show *done?*"

"Don't is three show we pay to see?" People started groping under their seats for beer bottles and anything that could be thrown. They would show the little faastie bwai if "show done."

"Ah say show done *now,*" the fellow repeated, an icy sneer on his sharp features. He gestured with his stick and a cold metallic clicking ran around the walls. The lights went on.

"Jeesas Chris'," Bogart whispered. Their eyes widened in disbelief at the sight of the automatic weapons in the hands of the ten or so men posted on the walls. They were aimed into the theater.

"Ah bet you say you believe me now dat show cut," the young

officer jeered. There was a collective, muted sigh from the crowd and then total silence. Every eye was fixed on the menacing guns in a hypnotic mixture of fear and disbelief. Ivan sat tensed in his chair, afraid even to breathe loud. A clammy chill bathed his skin. He couldn't tear his eyes away from the silent, dangerous figures that ringed the theater. The hollow clatter of the bolts rang in his head with unspeakable menace. An acrid, musky odor filled his nostrils, a nauseous smell he had never encountered before, the stink of fear, of collective and infectious terror. As if from a distance he heard sobbing, and then a gentle clatter as bottles, knives and even he suspected some guns were surreptitiously deposited on the concrete floor. The officer stood rocking gently on his spread legs as though on parade.

"Keep your seats," he ordered somewhat unnecessarily. "This is a police weapon check. Get accustomed to dem for you going see more, as long as the bad-man dem amongst you think dem can walk wid gun and knife. Who belong to de Skull gang? Where de Mau Mau deh? Since unu bad, test me. Go on, *test me, nuh?*" He paused and waited. Then he laughed mirthlessly.

"Ah hear say gang war supposed to tek place tonight. Well, mek Ah tell all a unu something. Unu can feget about gang war de same way bullfrog feget 'bout tail. You hear? Now—one row at a time get up an' leave. Use de front entrance."

The crowd, as commanded, filed out sullenly. A detachment of police wearing military uniforms searched everyone who came out—man and woman alike. They were thorough, quick, and very rough. Occasionally they would shine a flashlight into someone's face and check some pictures they had. A few men were seized and detained.

Ivan, Bogart, and the rest slunk silently back to the ranch. The dark, familiar streets seemed threatening now. No one had anything to say for a long time. It was impossible for Ivan to express exactly the many things he was feeling. He wanted to curse and he wanted to cry. There was a deep, cold, sick, leaden weight in his chest and belly that went beyond mere anger or fear or shame, though all were present. He knew, they all knew, that they had just witnessed the end of something and the beginning of something else.

"After man is not bird," Bogart blustered without conviction.

"You believe say dem would *really* shoot we?" someone asked in a voice that was still shaky.

"All dem wanted was a raas excuse. Don't you see dem face?"

They didn't know it then but they had encountered the first graduates of the modern school of counterinsurgency and riot control that the United States had established in Panama for the benefit of its good neighbors to the south. It was also their first exposure to Detective Superintendent Ray Jones, the first local officer to graduate from that school, who was to become a legend and a symbol. They called him "Maas' Ray."

10

You Cannot Go to Zion

You cannot go to Zion
wid a carnal mind . . .

—Rasta Chant

Preacher Ramsay was having difficulty concentrating on the report in front of him. His friend Dr. Jimmie and the Board of Missions in Memphis would be waiting on the witness and Preacher prided himself on his punctuality. But the words and phrases eluded him. He shifted in his seat and gazed restlessly around the study. Faint laughter came from the next room where the girls of the place-of-refuge were supposed to be studying and meditating on the Scriptures. He looked sternly through the open door and his expression softened. Elsa was sitting in a corner just visible from his desk. A Bible was open in her lap but she was staring through the open window with a bemused expression on her face. Her deep set eyes seemed to shine out of pools of shadow. Well at least she wasn't involved in the skylarking, he said to himself. She always had been different, more thoughtful. Ah wonder what she can be thinking on so serious? She really wasn't a child any more. In fact she was just at that troublesome age. The thought disturbed and excited him, but he had seen no sign of any trouble as yet. He bent over the report, then pushed the papers away petulantly and stole another glance at her. She was now looking down into the open book, a picture of concentration. Her chin rested on her crossed arms and as she read she moved her head from side to side, gently, and he was sure unconsciously, caressing her cheeks and lips against the cradle of her arms. Preacher reached for his Bible.

He leafed idly through the pages. The Book of Job. Not at all one of his favorites, Job complained too much. What he needed was a psalm, a good psalm of David to calm and reassure him even as they had laid to rest the devils that plagued Saul the King.

But as he was turning, some lines from Job:16 seemed to reach out and seize his attention. He paused and read, "Oh, what is man that he should be clean? And he that is born of woman that he should be righteous?" This was not what Preacher wanted, but his eyes continued down the page. ". . . how filthy and abominable is man who drinketh iniquity like water." He closed the book angrily. Even the Good Book seemed to mock him tonight. Or was it a warning? God do not slumber nor do he sleep. Why did he feel . . . *How* did he feel? Not guilty? What had he to be guilty of? Troubled, he looked into the next room. All he could see was Elsa. She was gazing into the darkness, her head still moving in that unconscious motion.

He swiveled his chair around and looked through the window behind him. A light was burning in the workshop. Why would Longah be working so late? He sat upright.

"Elsa. Elsaa." His voice sounded loud in the quiet house. "Please step this way," he continued in a more normal tone.

"Yes, Preacher?" She was there too quickly, before he could collect his thoughts. She stood respectfully before him, her head tilted inquiringly.

"Uh . . . oh." He looked up. God, how rapidly she was developing. "Yes . . . I see a light in the workshop and—I wonder if you happen to know what Longah is working on?"

"Longah, Preacher? Oh is not Longah, sah. It must be Ivan working on his cycle." Her voice was light, informative, guileless.

"Hm, I see."

She waited looking at him expectantly. He felt awkward. The silence was getting too long.

"Anything else, sah?"

"Like what?" He looked at her quickly. She suddenly seemed embarassed. Why?

"Oh—ah jus' thought maybe you wanted to see him, sah."

"If I want to see him I'll go to him, eh? What do you and that boy find to talk about so much anyway?" No, that was wrong. He wanted it to be light and teasing but it sounded accusatory, much sharper than he had intended. "Elsa . . ."

"Ye, yessah. Preacher?" Her voice barely audible.

"Elsa, I know you don't think of these things. But you're getting to be quite a young lady, my dear." He paused, looking at her but really congratulating himself on the properly paternal tone.

"You see, it doesn't look, well right, for you to spend so much time with that boy. Not that I think anything wrong or anything

like that, but even appearances y'know—can't be too careful. . . .
After all trouble never sets like rain." He hadn't meant to say
that. He saw her flinch, her eyes widen.

"Is that you think of me Preacher? *That?*"

"No no no, nothing like that Elsa . . . Just be more careful,
appearances and all that, eh?"

He was a man who prided himself that everything he did was
carefully worked out beforehand. But he had neither planned nor
intended that conversation and didn't like the way it had gone.
He sat fuming and listening to the distant hum of conversation
and girlish giggles as his charges prepared for bed. Could they be
laughing at him? Impossible, but his irritation grew. They
wouldn't dare. It was all that boy's fault. The moon was full,
maybe a nice quiet drive in the hills, that'd calm him down.

As soon as he stepped into the yard he heard the music. At
first he thought it was just unusually loud and near sounding, then
he realized it was coming from the workshop.

Ivan was bent over some pieces of metal in a pail. A small
radio was set on the bench. He was so engrossed in his work and
in shaking his behind to the music that he didn't hear Preacher's
approach.

Preacher watched Ivan, his anger growing. What did Elsa see
in this boy anyway? He reached across and turned the music off.

"Who turn—oh, evening Preacha!"

"You know I don't allow this music in the place! What you
doing here so late?"

"Just fixing my bicycle, sah."

The damn boy look so pleased with himself. There was something almost impudent about that too bright smile of his. "You
know my rules. Are you going to let the Lord come back and find
you doing this? Eh? Eh?"

"Doing what, sah?"

"Doing what? Boogie-woogieing and shaking up yourself in
my yard."

"Nothing no name boogie-woogie again, y'know Preacha. Dat
done long time."

"I don't care. I don't care what you call it, it's the devil's
work, y'hear. The devil's work and I don't want it in my yard."

"Yessah." There it was, that insufferable meekness over his
damn insolence.

"You should be reading your Bible. You hear I tell you! Reading your Bible, three times a day!"

That boy was a little too smart for his own good. "Yessah" like butter wouldn't melt in his mouth. Who did he think was fooled? Preacher slammed the door of his Cortina and drove off with a most unchristian clashing of gears.

The rumble of his shouting floated into the girls' room.

"Hmm, Preacha on the warpath tonight," someone muttered sleepily.

"Yes, him mus' be see what we notice?"

"And what's that?" Elsa demanded.

"Not a thing mi dear, not a thing," the first purred. "But all de same I sorry fe Ivan."

"You can all stop you giggling and signifying. Unu too have bad mind for you own good," Elsa said. She closed her eyes. Preacher was just in a bad mood, that's all. He was her guardian and worried about her more than the other girls, that was only natural. . . .

Wonder why Preacha so vex doh eh? Ivan thought. Is who trouble 'im? What a way 'im look like 'im did wan' lick me down—and fe what? Jus' sake of little music? Boogie-woogie! Imagine dat! Him never hear 'bout blues an' Ska an' Rock Steady an' dah new thing dem call *reggae?* Cho, Preacha too backward, even fe a big Christian man like him. Talkin' 'bout de devil work when is almost de same music play every Sunday inna him church! Even Missa Brown admit say de roots is de same but de purpose is different. Me no see it doh, de way dem sister inna de church shake up demself an feel good is no different from a good blues dance—same jump-up rocking beat an' heavy heavy soul wha' mek dem sister dem shake an' tremble an holler one time. But dat is de Lawd's work, doh? See how life funny? Still, is why Preacha so vex tonight after is not me eat him white fowl, eh? Boogie-woogie to raas! Cho. Preacha deh joke.

The new music was something else that had just seemed to creep into the scene. When Ivan looked back he could see how it came, but this was a change that excited him. It seemed to him a sign and a promise, a development he had been waiting for without knowing it. This reggae business—it was the first thing he'd seen that belonged to the youth and to the sufferahs. It was roots music, dread music, their own. It talked about no work, no money, no food, about war an' strife in Babylon, about oppression, depression, and lootin' an' shootin', things that were real to him. Even Mr. Brown, scared as he was of Preacher, had to admit that whether or not it was sinful or sacreligious it was at least their own music—and he guessed that had to be an improvement. Ivan had no such doubt. He had heard stories of poor boys who were singing this new music, cutting records and becoming star-boys. That excited him as much as the music did.

When he had first come to town, at the dances nothing was played but rhythm and blues from America. And the local song-sters patterned themselves after Americans, singing their hits and mimicking the voice, the style, the slightest intonation so well that you could hardly tell the difference. They would be billed as the island's own "Satchmo" or Roy Hamilton or Billy Eckstine. But now that was over and the music was being made right here. All he wanted was a chance, and he would show everybody. The people back in the country probably thought he was dead, but one little chance and he'd show them that Ivan don't dead.

"One chance, jus' one. Thass all an' *all* I need." He even had a couple of songs he'd been working on, writing out some words and roughing out the music. He'd asked Mr. Brown to look at the music. Maybe he'd help—Mr. Brown was all right. Sometimes after choir practice he'd look the other way and Ivan would try out the songs with Rufus on the keyboard and Sonny's guitar behind him. One chance and he was ready. . . .

Then it would be time to leave Preacha an' the Tabernacle and all the blasted rules. Except Elsa, he'd miss her. She under-stood kind of. She was the only one who knew anything about his night life. She kept his secrets too, all about the ranch and Bogart and Widmark and the rest. He told her about the movies, all the stories, and the things he saw in the streets. He could trust her, his little friend. An' not so little all the same, y'know.

It was she who gave him the old rusty bicycle frame that he was fixing up. Well, at least she said it was no use to anyone. It was shaping up real nice too, in a week or so it would be finished. Over a month now he was working on that bicycle. Took all his money too, every penny he could scrape up, new tires, silver fenders, secondhand wheels from the boy that worked in the China-man shop on the corner, it was shaping up nice. If he could just raise a light and a seat and everything tune up, bicycle ready. He'd take her for a ride first thing. Show her some of the places he was always talking about. If only Preacha wasn't so strict with her he could take her to a show. . . . How come his min' seem to set so much on Elsa lately? There was a lot on his mind these days but somehow even with the bicycle which took up all his spare time and the record he dreamed of making, she stayed in his thoughts.

It seemed like weeks he hadn't been to see a show, or even down to the ranch. He was always cleaning and scraping and painting and oiling. But the bicycle was almost finished. It hung in the back of the workshop where he could look up from his work and see it shining up there. Longah said nothing but every now and then Ivan would catch him looking at it with a strange look in his little pig eyes. Look 'til you eye dem drop out, Ivan would think, it make me no difference.

After Preacher's explosion about boogie-woogie he didn't get much of a chance to talk to Elsa. She seemed always to be busy with duties that kept her in places where Ivan had no excuse to be. But at choir practice or in church he noticed a new quality in her manner, a timidity and self-consciousness that hadn't been there before. She was always looking at him, puzzled, questioning, surreptitious glances heavy with unvoiced meanings. It became a game: he trying to catch her looking and to meet his eyes and then to make her smile or break her composure. But he never saw her alone and the less he saw of her, the more she was on his mind.

From where they were working in the shop they saw Preacher drive away. Then they saw her come out and walk across the yard to the shower, apparently oblivious to their presence. She didn't raise her eyes from the ground in front of her and walked slowly as though deep in thought. In her loose robe her hips made a sinuous, womanly, motion. Ivan pretended not to hear Longah's suggestive grunt. He wanted to talk to her, had in fact been waiting for such a chance with Preacher gone. But Longah's pig eyes missed nothing and everyone said he was Preacher's spy.

Still when he saw her making her slow way back he walked up to her openly. "Elsa, what happen?"

"How you mean what happen?"

"Ah can't see you, how come?"

"You don't want to see me." A faint smile played around her lips. "What happen to you at choir practice last night?"

"Oh, so you miss me?"

"Personally no. But crusade is nex' week an' Preacha was there and asked for you."

"I was working on the bicycle—it almost finish, y'know. Come see it, nuh." She looked doubtfully toward the shop where Longah kept his head bent ostentatiously over his work. Ivan made a gesture of dismissal and his voice became cajoling, "Cho, come look 'pon it, nuh man."

"Alright, le'me see this great bicycle den."

Slowly she strolled up to the shop and looked at the bicycle hanging in the back. Ivan tried to appear nonchalant as he waited for her to speak.

"Oh Ivan, it look so nice. You really do a good job."

"I always do good work, y'know," Ivan said.

"Truly? I wouldn't know about that." Her voice was soft. "It finish?" she asked

"Almost finish," Ivan said, as they went outside again, away from Longah's ears. "It only want a seat—"

"Oh?"

"—an' the other day I fin' one," he finished, looking at her.

She looked away, the same faint smile around her mouth. "You fin' one? What a way you lucky."

"Yes, I fin' it on me bed."

"Somebody mus' be like you."

"Ah hope so, for I like dem."

"You don't say—but that's nice, eh?" Her smile was broader, her eyes challenging.

"Anyway," he said smiling back, "nex' week when it finish you mus' come for a ride."

"I don't think so, y'know," she said softly, her voice wistful, half regret, half flirtation.

"Cho, you mus' come, man. Is you Ah fix it for, y'know."

She shook her head dubiously.

"Jus' a ride," he coaxed, turning the full brilliance of his eyes on her.

She looked away. "Well—perhaps. It depends . . ."

"On what?"

"Whether or not you are a true Christian. You young boys are too rude."

"Some Christian rude too," he said.

Her smile disappeared. She turned to him frowning. "What you say?"

"Just dat some Christians rude too?"

"Just what you mean by that? Ivan, who you talking about?" Her voice was sharp and anxious.

"No one, just a joke."

"You sure it was just a joke? Tell me what you mean?"

"Really nutten'. Ah never mean nutten'." But she had turned and was hurrying away, apparently deeply agitated.

"But anyway I grateful for the seat," he called.

He was filled with excitement as he returned to the shop. Something had passed between them that left him with a warmth that even Longah's inquisitive stare couldn't dampen.

"Ahrumph."

Ivan glanced quickly at the older man, who was staring after Elsa with a look of openly lascivious speculation in his eyes. It was meant to be noticed, and succeeded in cutting into Ivan's warm feeling.

"Aharumph," Longah rumbled again.

"Wha' happen you have chest cold?"

"No, but you better watch how you play inna Preacha garden, y'know."

"Ah doan wan' hear you nastiness dis mawnin', y'know Longah."

"You may not wan' hear but you better listen. Is a long time Preacha tend dah little cherry tree, y'know. An' when fruit ripe is Preacha to pick it. An' if him doan pick it I figure say I will pick it meself—an' it look like it soon ripe too," he finished with a suggestive chuckle. Angrily Ivan looked at the malice in Longah's eyes. the leer on his face. There was something obscene and cheap about the way Longah talked about women. But he'd never put his dirty mouth on Elsa before.

"Why you t'ink Elsa would want a monkey-royal raas like you? You t'ink is Thalia dis an' you goin' get Coolie-Roy to help you?" He kept his voice as even as he could, grinned into Longah's open-mouthed surprise and walked away, seething.

That oily voice had spoiled his feeling. "Fucking maggot," Ivan cursed. It outraged him that the shaggy ol' ape would bring that kinda talk about Elsa to him. And that shit about Preacha couldn't be true. Preacha was her guardian and an old man. Longah lie. That's all. Him damn lie. But suppose not? That would explain a lot. Especially why she was keeping herself so scarce, and her funny response when he said some Christians were rude. The thought of Preacha and the young girl brought a sick feeling to his belly. No it couldn't be true; Longah was trying to make trouble as usual. He had a lot of bitch in him for a big man. But suppose is not lie? Preacha tek care of Elsa since she small an' him have control . . . That was too serious to think about so he focused his anger on Longah. But he'd been paid back. What a way 'im jaw drop down when Ah mention Coolie-Roy an' Thalia. Fucker, 'im didn't know I know dat. It shock 'im. 'Im don't shock yet. Mek 'im keep on mess wid me.

Ivan had found out—the night he'd admitted he worked at Preacher's—that Bogart and the boys knew Longah and held him in contempt.

"De pussy bully," Widmark had said.

"Preacha Ram-goat pussy watchman," Bogart had added, laughing.

According to them Longah spied on all the young girls in the church and reported to the preacher any contact between them and young men. He was not above trying to blackmail the girls into his bed, they said, because which gal woulda want dat monkey-man otherwise.

" 'Im is a no-good, low-down rascal man who tell lie pon pussy," Bogart summarized. "You know how him get de name Longah?"

Everyone chuckled expectantly when Ivan shook his head, as though in anticipation of a familiar story which his ignorance presented an excuse for repeating. There seemed to be no one in West Kingston that they did not have some outrageous story about.

Bogart settled himself in front of the fire and took a long drag on the cutchie pipe. His eyes shone with malicious glee. "Well Longah, 'im really name Rufus," he said laughing. "You see how 'im ugly and crufty-looking? Well, dem say 'im was even worse looking when 'im firs' come town.

According to the story Rufus worked as a garden boy for some high-up people. The man was a merchant or something like that. Also working there was an extremely pretty black girl named Thalia, who was a nursemaid for the children. According to Bogart, Rufus was quite taken with the young woman, but not nearly as much as she was taken with herself. She would have nothing to do with him, but the more she repulsed him the more ardent he became. One afternoon Rufus was talking to some of the other garden boys in the neighborhood when Thalia appeared, taking her charges for their afternoon walk. She strolled by, most desirable in her starched white uniform with her nose and her ass in the air.

Conversation died away as the girl became the object of all eyes. She was clearly pleased with the admiring glances because her walk became saucier, and her expression more haughty. Rufus, wishing to impress the other young men, called out with great and ill-advised recklessness,

"Wha's happening, Thalia mi love?"

Thalia stopped the baby carriage, put her hands on her hips, curled her lip scornfully, and surveyed Rufus from head to toe with an expression rich in loathing. Rufus, regreting his impulse, stared back imploringly. But it was too late.

"Since when me and you is frien'?" she demanded. "Me is you *love?* What I would want wid all like you? What you have dat I want? You have money? You have looks? You have color? You have education? No! You doan have nothing in you favor. You ugly, you poor, you ignorant and you black. When you see me a street don't talk to me, y'hear?" She sucked her teeth, tossed her head, and started off, her proud batti rolling with indignation.

"After you is nothing but a damn *garden bwai,*" she called over her shoulder. "You think garden bwai money can get me?"

Had she not added that, and omitted the part about being poor and black, the boys might have relished Rufus's humiliation, feeling it to be heavy-handed but not totally undeserved. But with those remarks she had included them all in her scorn. No man, she well *faastie,* they agreed. She should be taught a lesson. But how? Clearly she wasn't about to have anything to do with any of them. The knowledge that she was desirable enough to get a more affluent lover, perhaps even one with a *car,* rankled deeply. The rumor that she was carrying on with her rich white employer was also cause for resentment. But the suggestion of a letter to his wife to get her fired was rejected as too low-down. Also rejected as being too crude was the suggestion that she be grabbed, stripped, and made to run home naked. Other ideas were considered but none seemed suitable, and without Longah's persistence, the entire matter might have been forgotten. As one young man said philosophically, "Well, if me can't get her, mi brother bound to."

"What you mean? Who is you breddah?"

"Everyman."

But Rufus, who even then displayed a certain low and devious cunning, devised a scheme calculated to exploit Thalia's weakness. He secured the services of Coolie Roy, an inordinately handsome coolie-royal boy with a very sweet mouth and impeccable manners, who also had an elegant Raleigh sports bicycle with a little motor. Rufus had a gold watch. Another boy had a new pair of John White shoes. Someone else contributed a handsome windbreaker that his brother had sent him from America. Attired in the collective finery, Coolie Roy was impressive to behold.

Thalia began to notice this polite handsome fellow on her afternoon strolls. He never stopped to talk, however, beyond flashing a smile and "Good evening Miss, how lovely you look today," as he put-putted by on his bicycle. As was intended, she became intrigued, as much by his obvious prosperity as by his dashing good looks and polite indifference. Clearly, this was no garden bwai. It was arranged for her to learn via the grapevine that he was a clerk in a downtown store, who was studying accounting in night school and was assured of a big job when he finished his studies.

Coolie Roy played her like a fish, with just the right mixture of flattery and indifference. Soon they were going to the movies together, where he was both generous and attentive. He reported his progress regularly to the syndicate. But Rufus, mean-spirited as always, accused Coolie Roy of deliberately taking too long in order to enjoy "sporting out" the girl with the syndicate's hard earned cash.

Feeling his talents to be insufficiently appreciated, Coolie Roy was greatly aggrieved and threatened to withdraw. "Listen nah maastah, if it was so easy why you never do it yourself? When you sick you go doctor, well me is a professional too, a specialist, a fucking specialis'. You must have proper respect, man. Cho, Ah soon jus' finish wid the whole damn business too, y'know."

Rufus apologized but demanded quicker results. Mollified, Coolie Roy continued on the case and finally Thalia agreed to come visit him in his room. What she didn't know was that Rufus and the other members of the syndicate were concealed outside the door.

"Dis a true?" Ivan demanded.

"Yes, man," Bogart said impatiently. "But wait it doan done yet."

"But how you know is true?" he insisted.

"So everybody say. You can ask anybody in Trench Town. Ah true man. Listen! So Roy an de gal ina de room. De rest a dem outside. When Rufus him hear de moanin' an' groanin' coming outta dem room 'im almos' couldn' control 'imself. 'Im somethin' stan' up stiff-stiff and jus' a jump ina him pants. 'Im have to tek it out mek night breeze cool it. 'Im hear when Thalia say, 'Ooh Roy, honey, you do it so nice . . .'

But Roy, him don't say nothin', him just a grunt and jam. Uhuh . . . jam, Uhuh . . . jam. And every time him jam, the bedspring them bawl out and the gal moan. "Ooh so nice, ooh so nice." Poor Rufus him couldn't contain himself, every time Thalia moan him moan too an' mutter to himself, "Hmm you moan? You don't know what moan is yet." Him was so *hot* y'know that the other bwai dem say dem almost have fe run out of the yard to keep from laugh out and give 'way the game.

Anyway, them hear when the gal bawl out "Ooiee Jesus, Jesus, Jesus" and everything get quiet. Then him hear Roy say according to de plan, "I'll be right back darlin', don't move." Hear her nuh, "Not a inch honey, Ah can't move a inch."

Hear me nuh! Ah say, when Rufus him hear that, him strip off him clothes to raas, and just a dance up an' down, up an' down, from one foot to the other, wid him long cod hang almost to him *knee.* Roy come out an piss 'gainst the door loud so Thalia would figure thass why him get up. When him done, him say, "I'm comin' darlin'," but is Rufus who jump inside an' grapple wid the gal on the bed.

Them outside quiet to see if it would work. At firs' all them hear is little rustle, rustle and some creakin' as Rufus position himself. Then dem hear Thalia grunt an' den whisper wid her voice hoarse an' tense like she under pressure, "Lawd, *wait* man. Wait, me say. *Wait.*"

Den she kinda squeal two times y'know, den she wail out, *"WAIEE, Lawd Jesus—it longah dan first time."*

Then, she must be grab it wid her hand, because dem hear her start fe cuss. "What happen how it so big now? But after me no have not a damn place fe put something like dis!" You out fe kill somebady, nuh?"

Hear the damn fool Rufus him nuh, "Please honey, don't stop me now. Let me jus' finish, nuh."

All them hear is a hell of a crash when de gal fling Rufus off her belly an' him lan' pon de floor. She scream and jump up to turn on de light. "But you is not Roy? Who dis raas?"

But Rufus push her back on the bed an' bolt out the room wid 'im somethin' flashing 'gainst 'im leg and spittin'.

Next afternoon Thalia, prim and prissy in her uniform, walked her charges down the avenue past the hedges hiding the smooth lawns, but her walk turned out to be a gauntlet. At that time of the afternoon the garden boys she had scorned were busy watering their lawns, and from behind every hedge she was greeted with cries of, "Lawd Jesus, me no have nowhere fe put all that! Waiee Roy, *it longah dan first time!*"

She endured it for a week, then left her job with very little explanation. Rufus became known as Longah-dan-first-time, and then simply Longah. But he didn't escape unscathed either, because boys who didn't like him, of which there were a few, lost no opportunity to pant imploringly, "Lawd Miss Thalia, beg you mek Ah finish, nuh" whenever he came in sight.

It must be Preacha only one who don't know what Longah name really mean, Ivan thought. And is this man want come put him dirty mouth on Elsa? Him must be forget what happen to him. Him shoulda did dead.

According to the story the night he staggered, choking on his own blood, into Preacher's yard, he had been left for dead by Wappi King, a notorious bad-man and knife fighter with whom Thalia had taken up for exactly that reason. As dem say, what go roun' come roun'.

WATCH-MAN VERSHANN

Me see it long time, y'know. Clear as day, so me doan know how Preacha never see it. Even a blin' man coulda did see it. But all the same from the very firs' me spirit never tek to de dyam little mauger bwai. I don't know why Preacha have him on de place so long too. Is a long time now I suspec' dat him a go down Trench Town gulley go smoke ganja, drink rum an' wrap up himself with dem little rude-bwai dem. I suspec', an' I all know fe sure when him drop dat word bout Coolie Roy an' dat little faastie gal Thalia. How else him coulda know dat eh?

But I cool it. I just lap me tail, bide me time and watch how de play develop. I notice too how Miss Elsa she fin' plenty excuse to come on by the workshop whenever Preacha not dere. I see dat long time, and how she just light up whenever de Maas Ivan him come by where she deh. Is a proper little woman dat now too y'know, well ripe up in herself. Ah believe she t'ink she nice too, jus' like Thalia. Me *know* dat de *bwai* is trouble, from de very firs' I know it. Member how 'im hungry and dirty when 'im first come? Now 'im no wan' do nothin' but listen radio and dress up ina pretty clothes like 'im nice. Especially since 'im start fix-up the bicycle 'im hardly want do any work on de place. An' who know what else on here him fix up too?

Look de other mornin'! De bwai stroll into de shop bout ten o'clock dress up in pretty hat an' pretty shirt. Playing radio an' poppin' 'im finger like 'im is a star-bwai. Not a move to do any work you know? No sah, jus' a sing to 'imself an' look pon de bicycle an' skin 'im teeth in a big smile. So hear me no,

"So—you have on pretty hat dis mornin' doh."

Him doan answer me, jus' suck him teeth an' go on listen to dat rude-bwai reggae song 'bout Johnny-Too-Bad, y'know: "Walkin' down de road wid you pistol in you waist, Johnny you too bad."

So hear me again no,

"Hey pretty bwai, pretty hat—yes, you man—Johnny-too-bad, bring me de hammer."

Hear de raas bwai, nuh?

"What happen, you can't get it youself?"

Now, you wouldn't believe dat Preacha place dat bwai under my charge eh. So Ah jus' tell 'im, Ah say, "No, is *you* mus' get it—you is a bwai." So 'im bring it but you could see dat 'im wasn't pleased at all. But I never done wid 'im. See, I know 'im never have de hat yesterday, and I figure say is somebody knit it fe 'im, y' see. So hear me,

"Yes, Ah see you have on pretty hat dis morning?"

"Wha' happen, you like it?"

Ah doan answer 'im direckly.

"Yes you really look like Johnny-too-bad, all you want is a gun fe look like Johnny." Him kinda smile at dat, you could see say him really think 'im is a star-bwai. So Ah lick him wid,

"Well, before you get de gun, you better go get a broom an' sweep out de shop. You is still a little bwai."

"Cho, you go on go look 'bout Preacha work, 'im say like 'im too good to do dat, and jump on de bicycle an' ride off.

'Im think say I vex, but not so. I glad to see 'im do it, because I goin' make sure say Preacha see who is on de job. Plus somethin' was in it, and I must find out what. So I a do my work an' try to puzzle out wha' goin' on. Den it come to me. Some a cook pickney dem was a play in de yard an' Ah call dem.

"Look yah, unu know whe' Elsa is?"

"No, y'know, Missa Longah, we doan see Miss Elsa."

"How you mean you doan see her?"

"Since mornin' sah, we no see her."

"Ahoo, since morning eh?"

"Yes, Missa Longah, why you smiling so, sah?"

Tell the truth I me tryin' not to laugh out loud. Is me chance this. At last Ah have that bwai where I want him. All I ha' fe do now is make sure Preacha find out without it look like me have anythin' fe do with *how* him find out. So I just serious up me face and bend over de work so dat when Preacha return him goin' find at least one man whe' him suppose to be and doin' what him suppose to be doin'. Of course, I was just a pray dat dem don't return before Preacha come back an' miss dem, so when I see de car drive up Ah say to meself, "Tenk you Jesus." Little bit later I see Preacha comin', and no matter how 'im try to keep 'im face smooth and 'im voice easy, I could see dat somethin' was a trouble 'im.

"Oh Longah, do you know where that boy is?"

Now me know dat is not Ivan him really lookin', but I playin' fool to catch wise y'know. Hear me:

"Hi don't know Preacha. Maybe he's gone for a cruise on his bike, sah. Gone ride out and sport himself."

"Sport himself eh? And what about his work?"

"Oh sah, I can manage, never you worry sah."

Preacha don't say nothin'. 'Im go back inside but fifteen minutes later 'im back again prowlin' up and down de yard.

"No sign of him yet eh?"

"No sir, not a sign. I hope nothin' don't happen to him." An' I look up and try to look worried. Hear him,

"Yes yes. Of course." And him walk off.

About his fourth trip I guess him t'ink it kinda lookin' funny so him say,

"It's the crusade Longah, the crusade. The record masters are here from America and if they don't get to Hilton's studio this afternoon we'll have no records."

"Oo, I see Sir." Nodding me head to show say I understand 'im problem. Course, Ah look dead at de car park up under de mango tree but Ah don't say nothin', just keep shakin' me head like Ah believe is dat troublin' him. Preacha really take me fe a fool. But Ah notice all the same, that him don't say, "Longah, you take them," and Ah careful not to offer. First because I see that 'im want an excuse to be vex, an' because I was takin' no chance to miss it when Preacha an' Ivan an Elsa buck up dat day deh.

If I did plan it meself it couldn't did happen better. 'Bout four o'clock, the bwai him ride into the yard like nutten don't happen wid Miss Elsa she siddown on the bar as bold as you could want. The bwai was leanin' down, smilin' and whisperin' into her ear and she just a smile so soft. Dem say "chicken merry, hawk near?" Well is it now, eh?

Well, I don't know where Preacha was but him reach de yard before she even have time to jump down off de cycle. Preacha him vex till him stammer. "An'-an'-an'-and where have you been!" him bawl out.

Elsa face freeze. The smile leave it and she jump down.

Hear the bwai him: "Just for a ride Preacha."

"For a ride, and I can't find you? You, get into the house, I'll talk to you later."

Elsa lap her tail and slide off like when you beat puppy, she don't say a word in English.

Preacha waving the master. "You know how long we've been waiting on this eh—eh? If it doesn't get to the studio we won't have any records for the rally."

"Ah can tek it down right now sah."

"By the time you get there it will be closed."

"No sah, I gone right now." And him jump on the bicycle and tek off, glad fe an excuse to get 'way from Preacha.

I sorry it done so quick. Ivan might think 'im get 'way easy, but Ah figure say it doan done a raas. An' if 'im did see Preacha face as 'im stan' there puffin' and blowin' and starin' after him, Ivan woulda know it was only beginning too.

As Ah watch Preacha stomp off into de house Ah marvel. Is the second time Ah see him act like 'im need excuse to vex. Since when Preacha need excuse to vex and punish sin? I wonder if 'im really know what 'im vex 'bout? I only hear when 'im slam de door and holler, "Elsa, Elsa!"

Ah woulda did pay money to hear what 'im say to her dat day, but Ah sure of one thing, that bwai don't have long to stay.

YOUNG GAL VERSHANN

And y'know, I told Ivan to let me off down the road. But him just laugh in that way him have an' say we don't have nothing to hide, and like a fool I listen to him. Now everything crash. Ah wonder what Preacher goin' do? Feel me heart, how I frighten. I never see Preacher so vex yet. Why him don't come get it over, eh?

That Ivan—him is really somet'ing. When I wid him is like him can get me do anything. Everything seem so easy, and him have answer fe everything. Is nothing that we can't do, and when you listen to him talk you believe it too. Like the bicycle—who would believe that him could fix up that ol' frame? But him do it. Take all him money, buy the parts, an' work every evening till it fix up.

Wonder if Preacha going beat me? I don't know if I going to take any beating, y'know. I too big for that now. And besides, even if is me say so, I never been a sinful chile. Is a long time now I take Jesus as my savior, and Preacha never yet have to question me faith or chastise me behavior. So why I go wid Ivan today? When I done know already say Preacha not going to like it or understan'? How come the boy just on me mind all the time? But still, what I do wrong?

I couldn't say when it happen. Yes, and it frighten me an' make me tremble too. You think is one time I pray over it? I pray and pray and pray again until me knee them burn me, but everytime I gone to bed Ivan face full up me eyes. The style him walk and the way him smile, an' that, that something inside him—you see it in him eye them sometimes burning, burning like fire . . .

As God is me judge, I *never* mean to go off with Ivan the whole day. But when I turn the corner and see him riding up, looking so nice an' handsome in the tam. An' him whole face light up when him see me an' me knee them just get weak, y'know. Him didn't seem surprise to see me at all.

"Hi, how you like me hat?"

"It look nice."

"You like it?"

"Is a nice hat, yes."

Then all of a sudden him eye them get real soft and shy like, and him say,

"You know, is somebody give me, y'know."

"Hmm, you lucky."

"I believe so, at leas' I hope so."

"Why?"

"Because I like somebody—a lot, and I hope . . ."

My face turn hot and I don't know what to say or do, but inside I saying, "Ah glad, Ah so glad." Cause I know that he knew that is me leave the tam and Ah wanted him to know it too.

"So come for a ride, nuh?"

"Oh Ivan, Ah really can't, y'know."

"You want to?"

"Well—yes."

"So just a little ride Elsa, what's the harm?"

What's the harm? Ask Preacha what's the harm. But him look at me so pleading an' so hopeful in 'im eye like that's all him could ever want . . . And besides dammit, 'scuse me Jesus, I *wanted* to go.

"Alright then, just a short ride."

Short ride? It wasn't what you could call comfortable on that crossbar but—it was so, so warm. Leaning back on 'im chest and 'im reaching round me to hold on to the handle with his face against mine . . . Some kind of feeling that I never feel before reach me. I forget time, forget Preacha and almos' forget sin. But, swear before God, nothing that happen today is sin, *nothing*.

All I do is go ride out with Ivan. Look how much sea this country have an' I never go yet, until today. Ivan say him use to swim in sea everyday when him was in country, but Preacha don't defend that kind of t'ing. And after the skirt wet up it had to dry out, don't it? Nothing wrong happen and what happen *couldn't* be wrong. Oh Lord, I wish Preacha would come on, anything better dan waiting. Oh God, what him going say?

What I going to do? Lord ha' mercy, I can't give up Ivan you know, I can't. When him hol' me in the sand, the feelings, oh Jesus, the feelings . . . I woulda give him anything, anything. Is nothing I could keep from him, if that is sin—but Ivan prove him love, because I couldn't did stop him at all. . . . Better go wash me face and fix up me hair, after I don't do nothing to cry for? Lord, hear Preacha coming—an' him walking like him vex too.

She fixed her eyes on the door as the footsteps came closer.

"But I don't do nothing," she whispered. "Nothing."

He filled the doorway, a stiff, stern figure. She tried to meet his eyes but couldn't, and it wasn't his anger that caused her to lower her eyes.

"I never do—" she began timidly, when she could no longer stand the silence.

"Be quiet." His voice was hoarse. "You betrayed me."

"No Preacha."

"Obedience is better than sacrifice." His mouth quivered and he rasped out each word as though he were in pain. Jerkily, like a man in a trance, he advanced one step at a time. "I had such hopes for you, such hopes."

"But Preacha—"

"*Git down*. Git on yo *knees* and pray. *Pray* for repentance."

"But Preacha—"

"On your knees *sinnah*, y'hear me. And pray that the evil in your heart be put from you as far as the east is from the west. Pray, I said *pray*, on your knees. . . ."

Under his glare she sank, unwilling and resistant, to her knees.

"Pray and repent. Pray that the burning in your flesh does not lead to the burning of your *soul* in hell's *fire*."

When he heard her sob it released a frenzied eloquence in

him. He fell to his knees on the cold concrete and prayed aloud. In a voice that shook and cracked and quivered and roared he prayed over the sobbing girl. He prayed until sweat beaded on his forehead and dripped onto the floor, until white foam caked his lips. And still the words poured out in a demented stream.

Her knees were on fire. Her legs trembled. Her head swam. And still he went on preaching until his voice was a whisper, a hoarse croaking whisper. After that his caked lips moved without sound. Elsa collapsed sobbing.

"Oh Jesus, Preacha mad . . . Oh Jesus, Ivan, Ivan what Ah going to do! Oh Lord, Ah can't take it . . . Preacha mad!"

11

You Can Get It if You Really Want

The young woman yawned and stretched, arching her back kittenishly in the bed. She came awake clear-eyed and alert with an unmarked freshness of face, a brand new, unused quality like something just unwrapped from the store. Then she sat up and looked expectantly around the sunken bedroom that was dominated by the bed. Against its cocoa colored silk sheets, her shaggy blond hair and sun-browned skin made a nice contrast. Some of the eagerness left her eyes when she saw that the room was empty.

Still she felt good—mellow but lucid and with that afterglow of fatigue that came after great sex, fine liquor, and good smoke. She yawned and stretched again, voluptuously this time, catching the flash of her limbs in the angled mirror on the wall. The room was dim and cool, with a faint but exciting smell that combined sweet smoke, sex, and a musky man's cologne. Her clothes were nowhere in sight. Strange. She remembered a wild progress from the living room that left a trail of garments leading to the bed. He hadn't seemed like the kind of man to tidy up, but the room was now immaculate. Distant domestic sounds came to her faintly. She half-remembered the house being very large. She wondered how many people were out there. She didn't think he had any family. Where was he? She began to wish she had her clothes.

The room impressed her. A couple of huge paintings against one wall, rough-textured semi-abstract native scenes in warm greens, browns, and reds evoked jungle, mountains, and sunshine. The most elaborate stereo component system she had seen anywhere outside the movies was against the other wall, its metallic surfaces and hard lines at odds with the native scenes and the rich mahogany of the headboard. She looked again at her reflection. A nice picture, she thought, *Playboy* centerfold. The idea mildly shocked and greatly pleased her. In the mirror she saw something hanging from the headboard. She turned and found herself looking up close at a holstered handgun. She hadn't remembered that, but then the entire evening after they left the hotel bar was a pleasant, exciting blur. She felt adventurous and thought of a funny postcard she wished she could send to the girls back home. But a handgun? And obviously he carried it around with him. A faint, warning, fear-tinged thrill nudged the edge of her consciousness. She didn't like guns and until a minute ago would have sworn that nobody she knew owned one, much less carried one around and slept with it on the bed. Well, hey! Different culture—different strokes. She wished she could remember more about him. The insides of her thighs throbbed pleasantly with a memory of their own. He was very strong, *that* much she remembered, and forceful and tireless, and—large. She stretched and smiled widely.

A toilet flushed close by and then there were footsteps. She lay back and closed her eyes, liking the clean lines of her limbs against the sheets.

His heavily muscled body was running to fat. As he padded into the room, she had an impression of solidness and power in the thickening frame. He had only a towel draped around massive loins that evoked some ponderous male animal. She watched him cross to the dresser, disappointed with his rather cursory glance toward the bed. Neither young nor old, he was olive-skinned and wore a goatee. His face too had begun to thicken, showing heavily lidded eyes and a fleshy, sensuous mouth—the face of a man who lived perhaps a little too well. There was something powerfully self-assured about the face, his body, the way he moved, a male arrogance so natural that at first she didn't even see it as that.

He busied himself patting aftershave onto his jowls, and oiling and brushing his wiry slightly nappy hair. She saw the thick hairs on his chest and crotch whiten under a puff of talcum. He inspected himself in the mirror with the seriousness of a man buying a racehorse. She wondered if he would be quite as self-absorbed if he knew he was being observed. She yawned prettily and stretched, arching her back so her young breasts stood out.

"Ah, you wake up, mornin'," he said, still looking in the mirror.

"Hi." She smiled warmly. He glanced at her.

"I have business, didn't want to wake you."

"Oh you should've . . . been nice to wake up together."

"Another time. You going back to the hotel? I can drop you off."

"Where are we?"

"Stony Hill, right above the city."

"I like your house, it's lovely."

"Thanks."

"In fact I *love* your island."

"Woulden live anywhere else."

"I *know*, don't blame you. It's *so* beautiful. The most erotic place I've ever been." For the first time he looked directly at her and smiled faintly.

"You sure is the island?"

"Oh yes, all of it, that means rum, grass, mountains, moon and you, especially."

"Well, we treat our women good," he said. "Famous for it."

"Where are my clothes?"

He rang a bell and before she could cover up a young black woman appeared at the door.

"Yes sah?"

"The lady's clothes, dem ready?"

"Yes sah."

"Bring dem nuh."

The girl disappeared and then returned with a neatly folded bundle. The clothes seemed to have been brushed and ironed.

"Thank you." She turned an especially warm smile at the girl, who was already leaving. "Who's that, she's so lovely."

"Yes, an' only sixteen too, y'know." His voice seemed to take not only pride, but credit.

"Really, she's well-developed, isn't she?"

"On this island, everything ripe early," he said, and selected a lightweight bush jacket suit from the closet.

"Um, nice."

"You like it? I have a little tailor downtown make them up for me. Don't believe in flying up to Miami to buy clothes. Support local industry. Good for the country." There was a strong echo of civic virtue in his voice, "You want some music?" Without waiting for an answer he crossed over the the stereo and turned it on.

"You always sleep with a gun?"

"Always—it's for your protection too."

"But why?"

"Better to have it an' not need it, than to need it and not have it." He seemed inordinately pleased with this formulation.

"Why would you expect to need it?"

"Listen baby"—his voice became just a shade truculent—"this island full a people who don't wan' work. Want everything but don' wan' do nutten. You get me? Some like animals—break into your house, kill you, take anything you have. What I have is mine—I work hard for it an' no nigger going come and take it so."

"That bad, huh?"

"You damn right, worse in fact."

"What time is it?" she asked, thinking it prudent to change the subject.

"Going on twelve, you hungry?"

"Yeah, in fact starved."

"Good, good, Ah like a woman who eat hearty."

"What's for breakfast?"

"Anything you like."

"You decide."

"It probably ready. Ah going to show you real Jamaican hospitality."

"You already have." Her smile was radiant.

"You ain't seen nothing yet, baby, we going have a traditional Jamaican breakfast, the kind you won't get in that hotel. What you looking at, eh?"

"You," she said softly, allowing her eyes to glow warm and seductive.

"What about me?" he asked, carefully combing his beard and mustache.

"Your face—it's strong, masculine but sensual too, very attractive." She could see he was pleased, "What do you consider yourself, black or white?"

"Jamaican."

"But—what kind of Jamaican?"

"You Americans." He shook his head. "Always thinking about race. We don't, y'know."

"*What?*" she exclaimed.

He reached over and turned the music up. "You're a beautiful woman. Get dressed an' le's eat. I have meetings."

The room pulsed with the catchy, erotic beat of the music they called *reggae*. The D.J., sounding like a Jamaican trying without much success to sound like a black American, babbled something about "a hotter platter from the Hilton empire."

"Hey, that's your name."

"I'm in the music business—is me."

"In the business? He said empire, are you an emperor?"

"Disk jockey foolishness," he replied modestly. "A emperor, cho."

"You're a funny, funny, nice man," she said to the emperor. "Are you rich?"

He laughed loud. "No but I do all right. An' I don't believe in leaving nothin' for relatives to fight over. Only live once. Live good." There was that air of profundity and originality in his tone again.

"You have a family then?"

"If you mean wife an' children no. Nothin' like that."

"*Never* been married?" There was a kind of flattering disbelief in her voice.

"I always say, why buy cow if milk free," he said, and laughed heartily. "What's the matter?" he asked, noticing her preoccupied look.

"I was thinking that I'm going to feel very self-conscious walking through the hotel lobby in a black formal."

"No problem," he said, pointing to a closet. "Look in there an' see if you find something."

It was full. "Oh my God! You sure you've never had a wife?"

"Nothing like that. Friends leave them, y'know."

She riffled through and selected a playsuit. It fit perfectly.

"Very nice, he said. "It suit you, keep it, nuh. To remember me by."

"I couldn't."

"Not to worry, le's go eat." He was strapping on the gun. The loose shirt covered it.

"You can *do* that?"

"I'm a businessman. The country needs me. I provide jobs an' investment. I gotta protect my property and life, eh?"

She followed him through the house to a patio shaded by a large mango tree.

"My God," she breathed. "Paradise."

Enclosed by potted ferns and exotic tropical plants with broad richly colored leaves of interesting shape, the patio was cool and shadowy, but outside a vibrant yellow sunlight seemed to crackle off sprays of white and red bougainvillea and hibiscus. In the distance a royal blue ocean stretched into the horizon.

"My God, I must still be stoned. You eat here every morning and see this?"

There must have been something faintly accusatory in her tone, though she certainly hadn't meant anything of the kind, for he said shortly, "I've earned it." Then his smile became proprietary and self-satisfied as if he were personally responsible for the natural splendor. "Food getting cold." He held her chair for her.

The table was set for two but there seemed to be food for ten. The food was strange to her, very colorful and presented in exotic eye-catching arrangements. "You will have to tell me what everything is," she said. "It's beautiful."

"The girl is good. I trained her myself. When she came to me fresh from her mountain she barely knew a knife from a fork." He seemed proud.

"It's almost a shame to spoil it," she said.

"Food is to eat," he said. "Dig in."

He ate a lot, and with gusto, his jaws sawing up and down with the methodical frenzy of some greedy marine carnivore. The steady rhythm of his chomping stopped only when he explained something about a dish.

"For an American woman you have good appetite, good." He nodded approvingly.

"Everything's delicious—besides good sex makes me ravenous."

"Ah know," he said. "I have a good buddy run a hotel. He say if you watch a couple eating breakfast you can tell what kind of a fucking they did the night before. Especially the woman." He laughed loudly, rubbed his belly comfortably and winked at the girl who was standing inconspicuously where she would see his face. She giggled obediently. He leaned back, looked approvingly at the wreckage of the meal and gave a slight gesture, part of which was a snapping of his fingers. The girl began to clear the table with silent efficiency.

"Ah feel for something else," he mused. The girl watched his face intently. "Zelda, any more herring roe out dere? Good! Fry up one for me nuh?"

The girl brought the fish eggs, a big brown mound that looked like a steak. He took the plate before she put it down and passed it under his nose. "Aaah," he signed and his eyes glowed with something close to ardor. "Good stuff. Good stuff. Nex' to Spanish Fly is the best thing in the world. Put lead in you pencil. Compared to this oysters is foolishness." He speared off a chunk, chewed with his eyes closed, swallowed, and beamed.

"I like a man who enjoys his food," she said.

He swallowed, then asked, "Where you say you from again?"

"Utica—Utica, New York. It's twenty degrees and icy there this morning."

"I have a cousin in Brooklyn," he said. "An' you say you're a teacher?"

"I told you that? Yes, third grade."

"You don't look like a third-grade teacher to me. More like a first-grade model or film star."

"Why thank you, sir. Is that why you were looking at me in that assertive and hypnotic way that I couldn't resist."

"No," he said, "that was because you have the best batti I ever see on a white woman." His smile was both complimentary and mocking.

"Oh," she said uncertainly.

"Come—Ah drop you off. You staying at the Sheraton?"

"Thank you Zelda, it was delicious," she called, and was rewarded with a shy smile.

In front of the house, a man gave one last finishing lick to the shine of a long, very white convertible, then held the door for them.

"Down or up," he said.

"Down."

The top slipped noiselessly out of sight and sunlight filled the car. At the end of a sloping lawn the land dropped away and the ocean lay before them.

"Far out," she said, blinking. "Far fucking out."

He was busy with his shades. "Y'know," he said, "a man was here one time—said he was some kind a writer. He sat right here, an' he look at the house and the view. You know what he said? Him say, that if he lived here, he'd hire a man to come in once a month and beat him with a stick."

"You're kidding. Why?"

"Thass what I ask him, figuring I was with some kinda freak. We get a lot of them from up your way y'know. But now I think on it, he was probably jus' a damn communis'."

"But why'd he want to get beaten?"

"Because him say, anybody who live here, and look out on this every morning, need to be reminded once a month that he is not God." His belly jiggled with the force of his laugh.

"You like that, huh?"

"Except the beating part."

The car was powerful and silent. He used the gears like a

Formula I racer, aggressively downshifting into the tight hairpin turns and taking them with a flawless timing and machismo, signaling ahead with loud impatient blasts of the horn. Despite the sharp corners and yawning drops she felt quite secure; the big car growled, snarled, and held the road well. She leaned back into the seat and turned her face up to the caresses of the sun and wind. White hilltop villas flashed by, perched on little pinnacles of land.

"Great day!" she shouted. "Great car!"

"Cho, I tired a this one, he said carelessly. "Ah order a new one—a Mercedes—vomit green."

"Umm," she murmured, trying to look suitably impressed, and was silent the rest of the way, feeling a rush of warmth for this vulgar, powerful man with the pistol in his shirt.

He watched her walk into the hotel with the long legged swinging walk that he had noticed American women affected when they thought they were being watched. "Fine bitch. What a batti. Boy, these tourist women will do anay-thang. Nothing them won't do."

Once he left the hotel, the city proper began—hot, congested, and with roads like minefields. If the damn government didn't do something about the roads he'd soon have to stop bringing his car into the city! With the top down he was very much a part of the life of the street and the big car was conspicuous, shining almost mirrorlike in the sun. He enjoyed the attention. There were some approving whistles. Young men rolled their eyes and called out, "Baas car, sah, how fas' it go?"

"Fas' fas'!" he'd shout, revving the motor to impress them. That was, he thought approvingly, the old Jamaica, the lower class taking a kind of vicarious pride in the elegance of the more highly placed. But that was less common than it used to be, now it was more like class warfare. Pedestrians and cyclists refusing to clear the road. And you better not brush one with your car. There had been stories of motorists being pulled from cars after accidents and mauled by the crowds. But duppi know who to frighten as dem say. *Quashie* ° know better than to mess with him! The three-fifty-seven magnum on his waist was not there for fun. Look that boy! You'd think say the street belong to him. He touched the horn and revved the motor. The boy didn't seem to hear. "Wha' happen? You pay more taxes than everybody else, man?" he called.

° Quashie: pejorative term for poor blacks dating to slavery.

"G'way Pharoah, down-pressor," the boy said, making a derisive gesture toward the car.

"You raas you. Ah bet you doan touch it," he challenged.

But he was accustomed to both responses, and both had become in a strange way a necessary part of his being, his identity. Damn, it was almost two. He shouldn't have spent so much time with that tourist woman. But why not? Hell, don't he was a healthy and natural man who loved women and was good at what he did? All this new talk about "social obligation," *that* was what he called a patriotic obligation. All these white women rushing down here like ants take them bed, and acting like them shit made Bruce's patties. *And,* on top of that: at the same time they acting so condescending and superior, they out there rubbing up with every little black waiter an' doorman dem can find. Somebody had to show them that not everyone on the island ignorant and poor, that some of us have culture and breeding and understand, what's the term, gracious living. And could lay the rod too. Say this for them, they knew quality—it hard to say which impress them more, the house or the rudeness. He wondered what it was about American white women made them holler so loud. Something was going on up there, the men couldn't be doing their job. Nuh, madness man. Madness! Last night at the bar, he'd never laugh so much in his life. "Baba" talking as usual about him is a cocksman. Hear the tourist woman nuh, "Surely you mean cocksperson." Ah think Baba going choke on de rum. Is that them up to up there you know—the man dem up there confuse, not sure what them supposed to do. Then the women dem run down here and want to kill off the male population wid pussy. But we up to the task man, more than up to it too.

Pity though, he'd have to give the meeting a pass today, because the last one was damn interesting. That wonder boy Ray Jones, now that was a case to watch.

At first he had thought it was just to be some more of that yaba-yaba university bullshit about "high intensity crime incidence," "predictable patterns of antisocial pathology"—now what the raas that mean? And "sophisticated methods of peer group infiltration and control" or "maximum acceptable crime incidence ratios." He had the feeling that very few members of the Lower Kingston Businessmen's Association had been able to cut through it either. But they certainly responded when Jones came out and said that it wasn't a case of "police and thief" anymore, the children's game where cops chased robbers. It was socially naive, Jones said, to expect the police to stamp out crime in a place like West Kingston where damn few people had any "socially acceptable" way to survive. That wasn't a police problem but a social one. And it was silly to expect police to arrest everyone they saw breaking a law. The old fuddy duddies exploded and wanted to know if he was saying that crime was inevitable. Jones was smooth though, and had the guts of a burglar, he merely grinned. When you boil it down to gravy that was exactly what he was saying. Not only that, but since it could not be stopped, then it was the job of the police to control and direct it. The man stan' up there and tell these respectable, Christian businessmen, that the most modern approach was to allow certain kinds of crime. In effect to give a police license to some criminals—the "victimless" kinds, ganja trade, gambling and so on, in exchange for the kinds of information (Jones called it "prior intelligence") that would enable them to grab up the killers, gunmen, burglars, and other dangerous types who threatened the lives or property of decent citizens. That was a hell of a trade-off, cops and crooks in partnership! A hell of a state the country was in when a police officer was standing up and admitting that?

Hell, everyone know that police always had informers and took a little rakeoff from rackets! But Jones was out to make this official policy and seemed to be getting away with it too. Hilton had only one question, who was going keep an eye on the police now? His name wasn't Marcus Garvey but he could prophesy too, and he prophesied some very rich police soon soon. Yes, he would keep an eye on Mr. Ray Jones. Already he was hearing about him. The riff-raff that hung around his studio talked about "Maas' Ray" in whispers. And the young man had a sense of drama too, y'know. Two separate cases last month: a store and a warehouse. When the boys dem cut through the roof and drop into the place what dem find? Maas' Ray and a squad of police.

"What take unu so long? Remember this nex' time, Maas' Ray don't like no damn waiting, hear?"

It seemed to be working too. He'd bet Jones was using the ganja trade. For three reasons. First there was a direct relationship between the availability of ganja and the level of violence. And exactly opposite to what those ignorant preachers and teachers said, it didn't cause violence, it prevented it. Damn, tranquilizer to raas. When no ganja was available they drink up the white rum and that's when man get chop up. Didn't just the other day "Feathermop," the gunman and enforcer, tell him: "Listen no maastah, when I have to fuck up a man, I doan smoke no weed that day, y'know, I drink some white rum. Cause anyhow I smoke up the weed, I jus' a go *reason* wid him."

And the second reason Jones must be using the trade: ganja was everywhere, everywhere. Ganja traders dealt with everyone—rude-boys, gunmen, Rastas, pimps, everybody, so they knew what was doing. And last but not least, plenty money changed hands. In fact, that was something else he would have to watch: no point in Ray Jones one, raking off all that money. Hell, he'd bet his life and live forever, that that was where Ray Jones's control was—the ganja trade.

Hilton turned onto the road leading to his studio. Hell, he didn't need no new strategy. He had seven outlet stores *and* the studio an' everyone of them in a high crime area. When is the last time anybody even so much as break a window? He had the best strategy right under his shirt and every little dirty criminal in the city knew it. There wasn't another man in his position who could feel as secure down here. He not only felt perfectly secure, he liked it. None of the so-called middle class people he knew either understood or believed that. They were snobs, that was why they couldn't understand when he said he actually liked it down here with the quashie. Hell he ate with them, drank with them, smoked ganja with them, and when he was younger and more rhygin, fucked their women too. He liked them or rather his position with them, but he wan't no fool. It was a jungle down here and he was the baddest cat in that jungle. One tiger to a hill, and he was that tiger. It was a matter of respect and what they respected was brute force and ignorance. Why you supposed he didn't have to hire guards for his shops? The faintest scent of weakness and you're finished Dad, done. Kaput. Sure life was brutal and hard for them down here. But he come and find it that way, and what was his was his. He was no local charity. They'd gobble up everything he had and nothing would change, except him. Yeah, he liked the people but he sure as hell wasn't going to share their poverty. For what?

The do-gooders could sit up at the university and talk damn foolishness. Not only was his conscience clear, he slept good, ate good, fucked good, and was happy. Life hard but it sweet.

There was the usual crowd at the gate. All of a sudden every niggah in Kingston was a musician. Hell, not only a musician but a goddamn *star* too. The lot of them be better off looking work—or something to thief.

"Missa Hilton. Missa Hilton."

"What?"

"From eleven o'clock we been waiting, sah. We been waiting on you, sah."

"Come man, about what?"

"Missa Kenton, sah, him sen' us."

"Oh, you have a song?"

"Yes, sah."

He put the car in neutral and sat back. The group of men stood uncertainly.

"Well? Lemme hear it nuh."

"Out here, sah? You mean right here so?"

Oh, dem want a studio appointment now. He reached over and put the car in gear.

"You want me hear it or not?"

"Yes sah, wait sah."

About five of the men came forward. They looked embarassed and resentful and tried as best they could to organize themselves. There was something distinctly hopeless about their mood. After a few bars, Hilton raised his hand.

"Dass alright," he said curtly. "I can't use it—too slow." As he drove off the group was still singing. The driveway *was* dusty and the breeze was wrong, but he didn't tell them to stand there with dem mouth open.

Had the youth been ten minutes earlier they would have been recording, and he would have been in trouble for knocking so insistently on the glass door. But sweaty and wild-eyed though he was, he had the look. Unmistakably the look. Never mind the package he waved so urgently, or the sense of haste that he projected, his hungry eyes were all over the studio. Missing nothing.

"What you want?" Hilton barked, making his voice even more brusque than was usual.

"Ah bring the masters, Missa Hilton, for the crusade, y'know, sah."

"You know you nearly spoil a session boy? What's the blasted hurry?"

"Is next week, y'know, sah, an' Preacha say—"

"Arright, tell Preacher him get the records nex' week. An' don't you come running in here again." He took the package and turned on his heel, certain that the boy wasn't finished. He wasn't. He ran around him, holding out a crumpled music sheet.

"Look nuh Missa Hilton, jus' look, sah. *Please.*"

"What is it now?"

"Ah have a song, sah—"

"Cho, you an' half a Kingston."

"No sah look, words, music everyt'ing, look sah. Is a sure hit y'know, sah."

"Oh, so you not jus' a singer, you a composer and arranger too?" he said mockingly.

"In a way, sah. I have training an' experience y'know, sah." The words tumbled out in a burst of earnestness.

"Experience? Wha' kin' experience you have? Show me you clippings man." Hilton's mocking grin broadened with the kind of amused tolerance one directs toward a precocious child.

"Me's de soloist, tenor soloist in de choir sah, an' I study music wid Mr. Brown. Gimme a chance, sah. I'll show you, sah. A sure hit, sah."

"Wait," Hilton drawled. "Duppi fool you? Who tell you say I buy any church music down here."

"Is not church music dis, sah, look nuh! Is de living reggae. Good beat, lively tune, dread, dread reggae, sah, a hit. Ah dead, sah, if is lie Ah die."

"Well ol' man, I doan want you dead. Mek Ah see it," he said, laughing and taking the paper. "Oh so you is a *Christian* rude-bwai? 'De harder Dey Come' eh? You know what? Come back nex' week." He would have turned away except the boy was wringing his hand and babbling something hardly coherent. Profuse and extravagant thanks, tears of joy and gratitude. Hilton understood that God would bless him, that he'd not be sorry, that it was a certain hit. "Look," he warned, "I never say nothing about a recording session, y'know. Is jus' a audition. You know the difference?"

"No matter, sah, jus' the chance, once you hears . . . business *mus'* tune."

"Nex' Friday, same time," Hilton said.

And the youth was gone with a gait somewhere between a run and a swagger.

"A star is born to raas," Hilton said. "Anybody know that yout' deh?"

"No sah, never see him yet."

RHYGIN VERSHANN

"Him say nex' week. Nex' week. Friday to raas. Him say nex' week. Him say nex' week."

It was all uphill back to the Tabernacle, but Ivan didn't notice. He never touched the seat. Standing on the pedals and leaning over the handles he sprinted the entire way, his legs churning to the intoxicating rhythm of "Him say nex' week. Him say nex' week."

"Ivanhoe Raas Martin, Recording Artis' to blood. Him say nex' week. *Dis bwai is moovin' on.* Him say nex' week. *You can get it,* nex' week, *if you really want.* Him say nex' week. *But you mus' try, try, try an' try.* . . . Next week."

Nothing name fail now. Is this bring him all the way from Blue Bay so long ago. Why else had he ended up in the Tabernacle with Mr. Brown? All for a reason and this was it—couldn't be anything else. Sweating and out of breath he skidded into the yard, dropped the bicycle and started toward the buildings at a run, almost colliding with a figure that loomed up out of the darkness.

"Ivan! Wait!"

"Wha'? Who?"

"It's me, Preacher Ramsay."

"Oh yessah?"

"When you came here after your mother's death I took you in."

Oh Jesus, Ivan thought, me did forget—what a hell of a time for one of Preacha sermon dem?

"True Preacha," he said, "an' I grateful, y'know sir."

"You were starving and dirty and confused in mind. No, be quiet. But your physical condition was as nothing to the state of your soul. And I took you in. You say you are grateful but those are words. Look at your conduct man, your conduct. You out to bring sin and dishonor to me and my house. You better leave this place. See two weeks' pay. I don't want to see you here tomorrow."

"But Preacha—"

"No, no! It is better for the Lord's work that I am trying to do here that you find someplace else. Better for all concerned. I will continue to pray that the Lord turn you from the path you seem hell-bent on taking. But I want you off. Understand?"

"Sure Preacha."

Ivan's smile was happy and there was a visible excitement in his face that puzzled Preacher. It wasn't exactly the response he had been expecting. Not at all. The boy was so steeped in sin and ensnared by the flesh that his mind wasn't right.

"O.K. sah. Thanks for everything sah. Me really thank you. Tell Elsa she'll hear from me."

Without question the boy was not right in his head, Preacher thought. And he'd see about Elsa. Right now as a matter of fact. But the boy actually seemed *pleased*. Well good riddance—things would be much easier in the household without him.

DAUGHTAH VERSHANN

The skin over her knees felt as if it had been rubbed with a grater. In the small of her back was a ball of pain and constant numbness. But her physical ills were as nothing when set against the turmoil and confusion, the conflicts of obligation and desire that plagued her. For two days she had not seen Ivan and the girls said that Preacher had run him off the place because of her. That was so unfair. Poor Ivan! Where would he go now? What would become of him? All because of her, when they hadn't done anything really wrong either.

An' Preacher, now something about him frightened her. He had always been an exact man and severe. But now he was like a man mad with righteousness and the spirit of chastisement. Wonder if him forget the Pharisee dem? He kept her on her knees, raving and praying over her, until they both were exhausted. She could take that, the long, hot nights of exhortation and forced penitence, the burning knees and aching back, the repetition until her head swam: sinner, sinner, *sin, sin, sin*. But never to see Ivan again? Ah can't tek it. Ah can't tek it. Me belly bottom feel like it wan' drop out. Wherever 'im is, Ah going to him. I goin' fin 'im. But how I do that? Me never live anywhere else but in Preacha house, can't even remember nowhere else. But . . . how me to stay, when Ivan out there somewhere. God know what happen to 'im? But . . . Preacha is a true Christian. If Ah really beg 'im, really really beg 'im, don't him will take Ivan back into the church? Give him another chance? Yes Ah goin' beg Preacha. . . .

Clinging to that fragile comfort she managed to drift into a shallow and fitful sleep. She was dreaming, or was it the voice that came to the boy Samuel as he slept in the Temple?

"Elsa," it said. "Elsa."

"Uh, who dat?"

"Shh. Is me, Ivan."

Oh me God, Ivan! Ivan come back! Him is here, thank you

Jesus. Hardly thinking of consequences she stumbled out of bed, opened the door and was clinging to him.

"Ivan, Ivan, you mad. Suppose Preacha catch you?" But she didn't let go. She stepped back and studied his face as if to see what scars the events of the last few days might have left. Ivan seemed neither penitent nor worried. In fact he stepped boldly into the room exuding confidence and happiness. She had never seen him so radiant.

"I have fantastic news, great, fantastic news."

"Where you been? I been so worried Ivan but I goin' beg Preacha take you back."

"Cho." He gave an impatient gesture of dismissal. "Listen me, I been looking for you to tell you, everything different now. Great news, baby." He lowered one shoulder and shuffled into a jubilant reggae step.

"What? What news?" she whispered.

"Missa Hilton? The man I been trying to see. Ah saw him."

"An' what?"

"Him say, him say, I can record on Friday."

"Ooh Ivan, you lie! Really! Oh God, great." She could feel the excitement and triumph pulsing in him. "Is true, you really mean it? Oh Ivan."

"Look Elsa, I'm goin' need you help."

"What? Anything, Ivan."

"Well, I have fe rehearse. You have fe len' me a key to the church."

"Ivan, you mad? How I to do that?" Her eyes filled with doubt. Deflated and crestfallen she stepped back and looked at the floor. "Them kind of music can't play in the church? Preacha will kill me. Oh Ivan."

"Elsa is me big chance this, y'know. It change everyt'ing. Is this I come town fe do, born to do. When the song hit—you don't see what it mean for us? Me and you? You have fe give me this chance, you have to."

"But if Preacha catch me, me life done," she wailed.

"Hey, done with him and start with me."

"What you mean?" she whispered, her eyes big and luminous.

"You nah go live in Preacha house all you life," he told her, whispering, with rising intensity and conviction as he drew a picture of a new life for them. Did she plan to marry Preacher. No? Well then it had to happen sometime. Somebody, the Lord even, had sent them a way out. They had to take it. It might not come again. He felt her hold him and shiver. "You a woman now. You have to choose between me an' Preacha."

She stepped back and looked into his eyes. "I'm trusting you, you know Ivan." She left to find the key.

"Don't worry," he said when she returned with it. "Preacha'll never know. I'll turn the amp down real low."

"Do," she said, "or Preacha will kill me."

"Nobody can do that. You have me now."

She crept trembling back to bed, her mind racing. Next morning she was surprised at how peacefully she 'd slept.

SHEPHERD VERSION

Something, he didn't know just what, was wrong. He was sure of it. At first Elsa had been suitably penitent—frightened and a little confused—but that was to be expected and in her favor. It showed she wasn't hardened and defiant in sin. But for the last couple of days she had been different, less troubled and with a secret calm that worried him. A comfortable sinner was a doomed sinner. Where had the tears gone? He hadn't forgiven her. He wondered if that boy were still hanging around: "Tell Elsa I'll be in touch." But he wouldn't dare. Longah had been told to chase him away and to report any sight of him. No, he hadn't been around. Besides even if he had, Elsa wouldn't have the nerve to encourage him. Still, a walk around the yard might be in order. Vigilance! Watch and Pray as the good book said.

He found the bicycle hidden under a bush, and fought his rising fury in order to think things out. The police? The boy *was* trespassing after he'd been warned. No, best to catch him himself. But first the bicycle. He locked it in the workshop and checked Elsa's room. She was sleeping peacefully. Well, the boy had simply found that life was not easy in the streets. He had probably sneaked back into his old room for a safe night's sleep. Better to check though, that boy would do but anything.

Was that a dim light in the church? Maybe the choir had left something on? Ivan couldn't be there unless—His preacher's instinct was titillated. Allelulah, the boy had seen the error of his ways! Ridden by the spirit of repentance he was in the church trying to square himself with God. That was the source of Elsa's peace. The girl should have told him! After all, more joy in Heaven over one sinner who repenteth . . .

But it was not the sound of penitence he heard as he approached the Tabernacle, no indeed. It sounded like a guitar plugged into his, no, the Lord's amplifier and Ivan's voice. . . .

> *For the harder they coome . . .*
> *Is the harder they faalll.*
> *One an' aawll . . .*°

Far from trembling on his knees before the throne of Grace, the miscreant boy was rocking on his feet to the beat of that brothel and barroom music—and *in his church!* There was no abomination too vile, too unthinkable for this boy. Preacher gloried. For the first time in weeks he had a clear, unambiguous, righteous source of anger, one not clouded by uncertainty. He watched for a second, feeling his rage and urge for vindication grow. No, the boy was mad. But he had him now. No one, not even Elsa, could defend this, this trespassing, breaking and entering and desecrating a holy place. *His* holy place! And another even more rascally-looking boy was playing the guitar as Ivan sang:

> *The oppressor is trying to keep me down*
> *making me feel like a clown,*
> *Just when he thinks he' got the battle won*
> *Ah say, 'forgive them Lord, they know not what*
>   *they done . . .*
> *Because, the harder they come . . .*

Preacher had seen and heard enough. More than enough! What a liberating, righteous anger! "What are you *doing!* Playing that—that filth in my church!" he roared.

Both of them froze. Ivan with his mouth open, the accomplice in surprise and fear.

"Preacha, look nuh, sah, I have a chance y'know—"

"A chance, you want a *chance?* You're going to jail. I'm having you both arrested. Y'hear, arrested!"

"Fe what, sah?"

"Breaking into my church, that's what."

The other one was edging toward the door but Ivan seemed quite composed. "But we didn't break in, sah."

He was reaching into his pocket. For what? A knife? He was capable of anything. But it was only a key he was holding.

"We have a key, sah, we nevah break in."

"A key, where did—" He lapsed into silence, realizing. So apparently had the boy. "No Preacha—" he began.

Preacher snatched the key and ran out of the church. The boy was shouting something he didn't hear.

Sleepy and surprised she still admitted it. Firmly and without remorse. "Yes. I gave him the key, I had to do it."

She *had* to do it. Not a hint of regret. Without knowing when it happened he was shaking and slapping her. "Why? Why? What else did you give him?"

"Nothing. Nothing else."

With each denial his frenzy increased. Her cheeks were puffy and her head rocked back and forth under the blows. She was lying. A lying slut. A whore. Desecrating his church and house. "Liar. Liar! You gave him your lips, your body. You were fornicating. Liar, whore! Slut!"

"No. *No.* Preacha I gave him nothing." The blows brought tears to her eyes but her voice was strong and determined. He flung her on the bed and left her bruised but still defiant.

"I—gave—him—nothing—*yet.*"

RHYGIN VERSHANN

He was very worried about Elsa. She had told him how Preacher had been acting funny lately. He wouldn't have left her last night, or his bicycle either, but Mack had convinced him that it was best. He didn't really think Preacher would actually hurt Elsa, at least not physically. After tomorrow they'd be together, or if necessary they could even leave today. But he was quite tense as he turned into the Tabernacle gate. Is the last time, he thought, after tomorrow I finish wid this damn place.

Longah was almost cordial. He looked up from polishing Ivan's bicycle and grinned cheerfully.

Why would Longah be polishing his cycle?

"Hey, Ah hear you resign you post man. What you doin' here?"

"Ah come for me bicycle," Ivan told him.

The grin widened. "Oh, which one?"

"Cho, Longah, doan joke. You know which bicycle—dat same one you have dere."

"Dis bicycle is yours? Where you buy it?"

Longah's pretense at innocent surprise was beginning to vex Ivan. He was in no mood for that shit this morning. "Don't fuck y'hear Longah. You know is mine.

The pig eyes glinted with malicious triumph. "Dis a no joke. Dis bicycle belong to Preacher. Where you buy this bicycle dat you claiming?"

So that was the game. No, Longah couldn't be serious at all. He was just being his usual annoying self. "I don't have to prove nutten Longah. You know is me fix it up. Is me buy the parts. The wheels alone cost me six dollars. Don't joke. You fucking with you life."

"I grateful to you all the same, 'cause Preacha give me the bicycle. Preacha premises; Preacha goods."

He *wasn't* joking at all. He meant, with Preacha's help, to steal the bicycle that had taken so long to fix. "Den . . . you not giving me it?" Ivan was surprised at how calm and slow his voice was.

"If is yours, take it den, nuh?" Longah sneered, carefully lifting the bicycle and placing it behind him. Then turned to face Ivan, rolling his heavy shoulders into a crouch. "Preacha say if you come on yah, you trespassin' an' I mus' put you off de place. Him say to use any means necessary. Ah goin' beat your blood-claat."

"I leaving. Just gimme me bicycle an' I gone." He tried to step around Longah and found himself rolling in the dust with his head ringing and one side of his face growing numb.

Longah was grinning widely. "You know how long I wait fe dis?" he challenged. "Git up man. Git up mek we see how you can take lick. You raas you."

Ivan shook his head to clear it and spat blood. Why did Longah hate him so? He looked at the triumphant grin, and it seemed that all the daily harassment, all the provocation, all the unfairness and abuse were concentrated there. He got his feet under him and started up, but another jolt against his jaw and sent him rolling in the dust again. This time his vision blurred; a red haze fogged out everything.

Then suddenly a strange thing happened. His head cleared and he was there but not there. In one way he seemed detached and floating above it all, seeing himself lying on the ground with a burly figure crouched above him. He saw himself rolling quickly out of Longah's reach, jumping to his feet and whipping out his *okapi*. He saw Longah stop, look alarmed and break off a bottle. It was just like watching the scene in *From Here to Eternity* where Lancaster and Borgnine are in the bar. He heard himself say, "If it's a killing you want Fatso, it's a killing you get." From a distance he saw himself balancing on the balls of his feet, knees bent, switching the *okapi* from hand to hand as Peter Lorre used to do.

But the same time he was actually standing in front of Longah watching his eyes and hands, the *okapi* balanced and darting. He felt alert but not alarmed. Everything had slowed down and he seemed to have all the time in the world to dodge and slash. His face hurt and he was angry but it was a cold, controlled anger. He seemed to know Longah's moves before they were made and methodically he danced away from the lunges and slashed. The fight assumed a weird rhythm like a dance: dodge, slash; dodge, slash. Each time he cut he felt the point rip through the shirt and stop against something satisfyingly solid but soft. Each time Longah grunted but kept charging, and Ivan kept dancing and slashing, dancing and slashing, all apparently in exquisite slow motion.

Until Longah trapped him against the workbench and he felt a burning in his ribs where the jagged edges of the bottle tore his flesh. Then he was on top of Longah who no longer had the bottle and was screaming in fear and trying to protect his face.

"Don't—fuck—wid—me," Ivan said, punctuating each word with a slash, scoring long shallow furrows across the cheeks and nose. Blood bubbled up between Longah's fingers and he screamed like a baby. Then hands were pulling on Ivan, lifting him off the bigger man. He heard Preacher shouting, "The criminal kill Longah! Call the police! Excited people were running around, and he was kneeling in the dust, holding his bleeding belly and puking violently. He thought he saw Elsa's shocked face coming toward him through the crowd.

"Elsa," he panted, "tell Hilton—" Then everything rocked crazily and he knew nothing until he awoke in the police station with his ribs bandaged.

12

The Rod of Correction

JOSE VERSHANN

The grass was raggedy, brown and worn. A few tired-looking almond trees with whitewashed trunks provided the only shade in the exercise yard. Jose rose high in the air, trapped the ball with his belly and in the same fluid motion eased it onto his feet as he landed. He feinted right to draw "Big Tree" over, then cut sharply left leaving "Tree" stumbling and swearing as Jose raced over the courtyard, his bare feet flashing around the ball.

"Jesas, you see move, Jose baad," one of the men exclaimed.

"Is so we stay in Trench Town," Dillinger bragged.

Jose lofted a floating pass into the center of the goal, made a disdainful gesture to the other players, and then strutted toward a group of men who were watching the game from the shade of one of the almond trees.

"Cho, unu no ready fe me," Jose said. "See it deh, skill to raas, y'know." His teeth flashed in a wide grin. Even the loose prison shirt and baggy off-white shorts could not disguise the feline grace of his movements. But before he could reach his friends under the tree a shrill whistle split the air.

A guard beckoned. "Jose, come yah!"

Jose turned toward the guard, his expression wary.

"Come Seemit, you have visitor."

"But, is not visitin' period dis?"

"Dis come on and shet up," the guard said.

Jose gave an elaborate shrug in the direction of his friends and followed the guard, parodying his self-important marching gait and bow legs. The men under the tree laughed. The guard looked at Jose suspiciously.

Jose grinned and shrugged again. "Cho, dem fool-fool," he said, dismissing the laughter.

The guard turned down a gravel walk that led to the administration building, not to the visiting area. That was funny—what kind of visitor? His first in five years. And why in the administration building, out of visitors' hours? With six months to go Jose wanted no trouble of any sort.

"Aye, Capral, is administration building we a go?"

The bowed legs kept marching beneath the wide khaki shorts. The black boots crunched the gravel. "Jus' come on." The guard was not about to admit his ignorance to a prisoner, especially one like Jose who was famous for his insubordination.

Shit, Jose swore to himself. Ah bet you is some little raas-hole runnin' dem mouth to de warden. I know is mus' dat. An' is six month I have to do too, y'know. Me a deny *everyt'ing*. Doan know nutten about nutten, y'know. You see trouble doh, sah? Ah bet you is dat little gal-bwai. Dirty little sodomite, is must him. Him dyam mouth run like sick niggah *batti*. Me will kill him raas too, y'know. Ah wonder is what, de ganja or de lottery? But dem can't trace nutten to me. Me sure of dat, an' me nah admit nutten. An' me nah serve no more time neider, before dat Ah go over de raas wall. Ah swear. Ah dead before Ah serve no more time, dead first.

But it wasn't the warden who awaited them in the office. It was a lanky black man whom Jose had never seen before, with a lean shrewd face and eyes hidden behind aviator shades.

"Hose Seemit, sah," the corporal said, saluting sharply and slamming his heel into the concrete.

The man lounged against the warden's desk and riffled through the file. "Thank-you-corporal-that-will-be-all," he drawled in a supercilious school prefect's monotone without looking up.

So is a police, Jose thought, studying the bony face and nicely tailored clothes. Is can who him? Him look fit an' hard too. Instinct told him to be very careful so he stood saying nothing and pretended to be gazing stolidly at the wall, while covertly studying the man, acutely aware that he was also being watched from behind those shades. Him have time? Me have time too—six months, Jose thought. Is who him doh? Definitely a police, a police star-bwai. What him want wid me?

The only sound in the room was the whine of a large overhead fan, its blades lazily pushing the stale air.

"You know me?" The sudden question startled Jose.

"No," he grunted.

"No *what?*"

"No, sir. No, SIR."

"Well, I know you. I make it me business to know you! Jose Smith, number 07116, small-time criminal from West Kingston. Trench Town to be precise."

Jose said nothing. Mek him go on insult me, he thought. He looked at the man and smiled sweetly.

"How much time you serve here?"

Jose looked at the file, raised his eyebrows as if to say, you can't read? Waited just long enough so that to wait any longer would become insolence, and said humbly: "Five years, sah, five year an' five month."

"Fe what?"

Jose was silent.

"Fe what?" the man barked, curling his lip.

"Dem say me t'eif a motor bike, sah."

The man grinned. "Dem say, dem *say?* You were picked up dead drunk and riding the vehicle, not true?"

Jose kept his face straight.

"Not true?"

"True, sah," Jose mumbled. "But—"

"Nex' time you t'eif a bike," the man said, an undertone of laughter in his voice, "try don't t'eif one what belong to the Police Commissioner son, eh?"

"Yes, sah."

"You were sentenced, as a habitual criminal and trouble-maker, to six years at hard labor. You will be released in six months with exactly no time off for good behavior. True or not?"

"True, sah." So tell me something I don't know, Jose thought. Is what dis "guess me dis riddle"?

"Well Jose, mek Ah ask you dis." The man's voice became conversational, almost intimate. "Mek Ah ask you, what you learn from dis? Anything?"

"Yessah," said Jose, looking straight ahead. "Ah learn a trade, sah."

The man smiled bleakly and looked thoughtful and amused.

"You learn trade, hmm? I tell you what you learn—not a damn t'ing, not a damn t'ing. You control all de ganja selling in de yard. You an' you boys run a lottery. A *lottery* in the general peniten-tiary, and coerce inmates to pay in their money too. Dass the trade you learn?"

"No, sah," Jose said, more than a little shaken. He watched the man apprehensively. What really did he want? It was then Jose knew that before he left this room, something of importance would be taken from him. He couldn't think what or how much, but he knew he would lose something.

"Both these activities, Smith, are against the law and in direct contravention of prison regulations. But, I see here that you have applied for six months *off* for good behavior? Now Smith—" He raised his eyebrows and frowned at Jose over the top of his shades.

A damn comedian, Jose thought, what him want? What him really want eh?

"Time *off* for good behavior? We have enough to keep you here for another six years, and it would probably be good for the society at large too."

"No, sah—" Jose's voice cracked with genuine alarm.

"Don't interrupt me Smith. Yes we could, y'know. But instead I'm here to tell you that your application will be granted. That's funny, isn't it, Smith? Six months off for *good* behavior. You know why this seeming miscarriage of justice is taking place? Not because you have fooled the authorities, but because I need you. I need you on the street, in Trench Town, and not here getting fat at government expense.

"T'ank you, sah—"

"Interrupt again and you're in trouble. Don't thank me either. Listen. Now if you have the sense God gave a bedbug, which is debatable, you will be back in Trench Town, drunk as a lord, by nex' week. Eh?"

"Ah really doan understan' sah." It was not just puzzlement in Jose's manner and voice, it was alarm.

"I thought I had good news, Smith. You don't understand, huh? But use your head, eh. Left to your own devices, you will be strutting, fighting, and fucking across Trench Town for a month or two and be back here in under a year. At the most! But it doesn't have to be like that, if you smart. I have an offer for you, one that you are in no position to refuse."

The man paused and looked at Jose. Jose was silent, wary. Overhead the wide blades of the fan droned in the stuffy air.

"Interested, Smith? Of course you are. You're no fool, you only act like one sometimes. I think I can use you—

"Wait, sah. Wait, wait before you say anyt'ing else. One t'ing, sah." Jose's voice was pleading.

"Yes?" The man seemed amused.

"Me is not no informer, sah. You better know dat. Dass one t'ing nobody can say."

"How I know that was what you was goin' say?" The man

laughed. "But you may be a fool? I would say that." Here the voice crackled, it was cold and no longer amused. "You are *damn well whatever I say you are*. But you will be no use to me if anyone know our arrangement. And I promise you, one word, one whisper out of you, and I see to it that you dead a jail. But, on the other hand—" The voice became gentle and purring again. "I can promise you freedom to operate in West Kingston, within limits of course. You'll have money, you'll have protection, and you'll have an organization. In return you'll take instructions from me."

There was another silence; the man seemed preoccupied but didn't appear to expect any answer. A part of Jose couldn't help being intrigued, but mostly he was worried. Every instinct, every alarm developed in a life spent from the age of ten outside the law, was signaling caution.

Abruptly, the man arose, like somebody remembering an appointment. He crossed to the door and there he stopped. His tone was neutral and businesslike, free from either cajolery or threat. "On Monday you'll be released. On Wednesday you will come to Central, ask for Special Services and Detective-Inspector Ray Jones." Halfway through the door he stopped and leaned his head back inside the office. "Fail to be there," he said with a smile, "and I promise you that you will be back here before the month is over—whether you do anything or not." And he was gone.

Raas claat! *Maas' Ray* to blood. Numbly Jose followed the guard back to the courtyard. It was a real struggle to compose himself and get a story together for the boys, but by the time he was back under the tree his buoyant swagger had returned.

"Is who, Jose? Wha' happen?" Dillinger asked.

"Oh," he said, lighting a cigarette and grinning, "de warden a let me out Monday."

"You lie!"

"If Ah lying, Ah flying. Time off fe good behavior to blood claat. Him say him have a decen' job fe me in a brick factory. 'Im say Ah *resourceful* and should go far."

"Rahtid," Al Capone said. "So you a go straight den, Jose?"

"Rehabilitashan, man." Jose laughed. "Rehabilitashan to raas." And he looked over the wall at the sun on the distant mountains and laughed softly and long.

Just look at the trouble and disgrace that boy bring into my church, though, eh? But thank God, it was over now and not any worse than it had turned out. Longah had taken a lot of stitches and some blood but he would live. The gate had to be locked against the horde of idlers and sensation-seekers congregating out-side, hoping for a sight of the blood. But maybe that same curi-osity would fill the church on Sunday. One had to look on the bright side. And Elsa, at last she seemed to have recognized the real nature of that boy. Nobody had seen her since the fight. She was in her room too ashamed to show her face. As a matter of fact those seemed to be her steps he heard right now. They seemed to be approaching the door, too.

"Preacha?"

"Who is it?"

"Elsa."

"Is it important?"

"Very . . . sah."

"Come in then." He bent over some papers on his desk as he heard her enter. Oh, he'd forgive her, but not immediately. He pretended to pore over the papers and heard her stop in front of his desk. "Yes?" he said.

"I just want you to know that I am not going to stay in the house of a hypocrite, Preacha."

He looked up, disbelief on his face. "What did you say?"

"That I cannot stay in the house of a whited sepulchre." She looked frightened but determined and was wearing her best clothes. She carried a small suitcase and a cardboard box.

"And—I suppose you've come to say goodbye?" He tried to smile, to make his voice express an amused tolerance for someone who was overwrought. He thought he saw her mouth tremble but then she pulled it into a firm line.

She spoke slowly, pronouncing each word distinctly. "No Sir. I came for whatever little money is in that bank book that you said my mother left for me. That's all." She was holding out her hand stiffly.

"Elsa, you're upset—but this is silly. . . .

"Preacha, either you give me the bank book or I'll go without it."

"Elsa—think what you doing. Where you going to?"

"To Ivan."

"But he's in jail."

"Where you an' that dirty brute Longah put 'im. Call yourself Christian—after how you do that poor boy?"

"That's enough. I won't be spoken to that way—and another thing, leave now and you can't plan to come back, ever."

"Come back! Come back, Preacha? Fe you tear me outta me bed and rip off me clothes and box-box me up again?"

"Be sensible," he said quickly. "You're a minor and my ward."

"Las' night I was a whore an' a slut though. Well is the firs' and las' time anybody goin' call me that or put dem hand ina me face. Don't worry, Preacha Ramsay, you not seeing me here again, in life."

"Elsa, I didn't mean—"

"Just give me the bank book—and I'm taking Ivan's bicycle too. You know it's his own, him pay fe it twice."

"You're bound to regret this, y'know. Mark my words. An' mark them well. But I not going even try to stop you. You make your bed hard, you will lie in it. It's the devil in you. Look in that second drawer you will see the bank book. It may look like a lot, but you'll find it isn't. . . . But he was talking to an empty room, and her footsteps were echoing in the hall.

Elsa left on Thursday night. Preacher secluded himself in his bedroom and was not seen by anyone until Sunday.

On Sunday the overflow crowd at the Tabernacle stood in the yard where dirt had been swept over the bloodstains. Those who couldn't get in the yard stood outside the gates. Aside from the faithful, most were there out of curiosity and love of gossip. Even committed nonbelievers like Bogart and the Salt Lake City Ranch boys mingled with the crowd, pointing proudly to where "Rhygin slice up Longah like bacon." But it was hard to tell just what kind of collective premonition had brought out such a large crowd. There had been much speculation about what text the Preacher would take for his sermon on that day, and even if he would appear at all. Most thought that if he did show up, he would preach Ivan and Elsa out of the church.

Elder Sampson conducted the service as he sometimes did, but as the time for the sermon drew near without Preacher's appearance the restlessness and disappointment of the crowd became palpable. Not that Elder Sampson was any lightweight as an exhorter. There were many who felt that he was the most dynamic Preacher since the famous Bedward the Prophet. But another of his pulpit-thumping, sin-healing performances was not what they had come to see. That is why such a profound hush fell on the congregation after the whisper rippled in from the crowd outside: "Preacha coming, Preacha coming . . ."

He strode silent and unsmiling through the Tabernacle and ascended the pulpit without greeting or in any way acknowledging the Elder. He turned to the waiting church with eyes that stared fixedly at nothing, and so they said, were red as bloody fire. Without greeting or preamble he began to preach.

"Dust to dust, ashes to ashes. Let the dead bury the dead." At first they thought that Longah had died and Ivan was to be hung. The silence intensified and, people said, the whole church seemed to hold its collective breath. Preacher's voice rose and railed in words that cut and thundered. Then, gradually, understanding dawned and with it a sense of horror.

"*Lawd Jesus Chris' Almighty God!*" A woman broke the silence in an involuntary outburst of fear and disbelief. "Oh me God," she whimpered, "him preachin' her death. Him preachin' Elsa death."

It would have been awful enough if it had been a normal funeral sermon on the fate of "those blessed dead who die in the Lord." But it was the reverse, a vengeful exorcism, the damnation of a soul "dying in filth and abomination far beyond the reach of God's grace." By any standard, it was the most horrifying performance that anyone could remember, and the awful words were made more so by the fearful contortions that twisted Preacher's countenance. Before he finished, children too young to understand the words began shrieking and had to be taken out, people wept openly in pity and fear, and the crowded church was almost emptied. The word spread across West Kingston that "Preacha Ramsay mad. Him up deh doin' the devil's work, preachin' the soul of a poor girl *living* into hell."

Someone—people suspected a rival in the church—wrote to inform Memphis about this diabolical abuse of the pulpit. The debate that ensued on the Board of Missions was long and impassioned, with some rather shameful references to "primitive African diabolism." But steadfastly defended by Dr. Jimmie, Preacher and the Mission ultimately prevailed. As a compromise he was found the victim of a "spiritual collapse and excess of zeal," and summoned to Memphis for a period of prayer, guidance, and rest.

They brought him in manacled and forlorn, a small, almost frail figure between the two hulking constables. He felt all eyes on him and his spirit quailed. Old Maas' Nattie's advice had been ringing in his head for the past week: "Bwai, me say Courthouse is not a nice place, no go deh. *Me say nuh go deh, yaah.*" But how could they convict him of anything? Look at the size of Longah and look at him. An' Elsa would testify about the bicycle. They could not fail to see the injustice of the whole business. No way they could find him guilty. It wasn't until he heard a slight commotion at the door and looked up to see Bogart and the youths from the ranch that his spirits improved. The younger boys were looking at him with big eyes and pointing up in his direction. He bared his teeth in a hard grin and brought his manacled fists up in a short salute. Powah. Then at a sudden murmur from the crowd he looked up to see a strange figure walking in.

The Honorable Justice Mr. Josephus V. O. Allen with his dull black robes rustling officially, the powdered curls of his wig encasing a somewhat narrow head and nestling on prominent ears, was authority personified as he glided to the bench, took his seat, and turned a cold eye on the gallery. Mr. Justice Allen was a man of elegant, even fastidious manner, acutely aware of his own dignity, and just beginning to be plagued with the uneasy thought that his considerable abilities were being overlooked. Surely after all his time on the bench, he ought by now to have been called to the Upper Bench as one of Her Majesty's High Court Judges? It was really nothing short of disgraceful, the level of political favoritism and careerism in the Service. Quite, quite unfortunate.

Deftly he extricated a scented hankerchief from his sleeve, dabbed daintily at his pursed mouth, and checked the docket. Another stabbing, Merciful Heavens, these people! Really, always at each other's throats and then coming before the bench lying and crying and literally *filling* the Court with their mothers, grandmothers, and concubines, all just waiting for sentence to be pronounced to begin their Godawful keening and hollering like some kind of a wake. Really quite distressing. His nerves surely could not stand the circuit court much longer. But at least none of those dreadful Ras Tafarians were in court this afternoon. Mr. Justice Allen nodded crisply t!oward the door, controlled an impulse to stop his ears, and braced himself.

"OYEZ, OYEZ, OYEZ!" the portly Sergeant-at-Arms bawled

at the top of his lungs, "de 'onorable resident Magistrate's Court of Kingston is now in sesshann, before the 'onorable Justice Mr. J.V.O. Allen, presiding. The case of 'Er Majesty versus Ivanhoe Martin, defendant, will be 'eard. All manner of persons soever, 'aving aught to do, or knowledge dereof, come forward an' ye shall be 'eard."

They came forward. Preacher in a voice redolent with good works and charity repudiated, related his untiring effort to provide Ivan with Christian guidance and example. Longah, bandaged like a mummy, speaking in a voice so faint and tremulous as to excite snickers from those in the court who knew him, presented himself meekly enough to be mistaken for the last of the Christian martyrs. Elsa, remarkably lively considering the perdition to which she had been so finally consigned by Preacher, testified firmly, if tearfully, about the matter of the bicycle, staring defiance at Preacher as she did so. Ivan, no remorse evident in voice or manner, maintained stoutly that he had merely been defending his person and property.

"And in doing so, you found it necessary to, Ah, *cut* the victim some, hem, *thirteen* times?" Mr. Justice Allen drawled, peering at the accused as though much hinged on his answer.

"Yes, sah," Ivan said. "But Ah never cut him to kill him, y'know, sah."

There was a muted cheer from Bogart and his colleagues.

"Hmm," said the Justice, "Hmm."

He was not in the best of spirits. In the morning session he had occasion to sentence a Ras Tafarian, one "Ras Stimulus," to six months at hard labor for creating a public nuisance and six more for smoking ganja as he did so. The fellow had created a monumental traffic jam at rush hour by parading down the center of the city's busiest thoroughfare declaring that he had "come to claim his father's property." Mr. Justice Allen had been mildly amused, and had thought his sentence indeed lenient.

Not so, however, a group of the man's supporters. On hearing the sentence, a number of women, later identified as the "wives" of the accused, set up a loud wailing, shouting, "Whaaiioo, what a wicked ugly brute," and similar references to his person. And, before enough police could be found to clear the courts, some twenty or thirty of the fellow's coreligionists, pointing their staffs threateningly at the bench, roundly denounced him. Now, Justice Allen was not a superstitious man, nor even a particularly religious one, but to be *cursed* in unison, and in rather frightening terms, by some thirty chanting zealots, and in his own court! Most unsettling. The call to the High Court could not come too soon. The demented chanting still echoed in his mind—one, one, what was the word? Ah, one bloody *malediction* after the other— "because that he remembered not to show mercy, but persecuted de poor an' needy . . .

Set thou a wicked man over him, an' Satan at his right han' . . .
When he shall be judged, let him be condemned
An his prayer become sin,
Let his days be few, let another take his office . . .
Let his children be fatherless and his wife a widow . . .
Let them seek their bread in desolate places . . .
Let his widow become a harlot, an' his mother's sin never be forgotten . . . ."

It was disgraceful and if the truth be told, quite unnerving. What was the country coming to, when one of her Majesty's justices could be treated with such scant respect and by his own people too? And now this Ivanhoe Martin, who seemed to see nothing wrong in taking violence to the very threshold of the church. These people really had to be taught to respect the institutions of society.

"Ivanhoe Martin, rise and face the bench," the clerk of Courts intoned in his best Gray's Inn accent. The Magistrate dabbed his cheeks and mouth and fixed the defendant with a baleful look.

"*Hem*, young man, you have been given every chance to make something of yourself," he chided. "*Hem*, you have been taken into the church and given every opportunity to lead a good Christian life."

Here Longah and Preacher nodded vigorously.

"And *hem*, instead of which, you have gone and filled your head with foolishness, and—violence." This was greeted with much self-righteous nodding on the part of the witness for the prosecution. "But, *hem*—since this is your first offense, *hem*, I am not—going to send you to jail." The Resident Magistrate paused, nodded as though applauding his own restraint, and dabbed his lips. Preacher and Longah looked dismayed. Elsa smiled hopefully. Ivan looked worried.

"I, *hem*, am going to give you a chance to come to your senses. I hope this will bring you down to earth once and for all. You will receive eight lashes of the tamarind switch."

"Lawd Jesas," Elsa cried.

"Silence in the Court!" the clerk roared.

The Resident Magistrate pursed his lips, frowned, and rapped sharply with his gavel.

Mostly he was afraid as he followed the guard. Not the fear of danger, the sudden adrenalin charge that quickened the reflexes and strengthened the limbs. This was the fear of pain, the nauseous, gut-loosening fear that weakened the body, sapped the will, and made him want to cry. This belly-sickness had been his dominant feeling since the sentencing, and he hated it. But it was not the only one. Another feeling lay buried, almost smothered by the nausea, a clean, clear, gem-sharp nugget of hate, hate for Preacha and Longah and the smug smiles they exchanged when they heard the sentence, for the judge perched up there in his wig like a head-man jancrow, black but talking like a white man, and for the police with their hard, ready hands and sadistic grins. He had felt warm and good when Elsa took the stand. But that was remote now, as was the flush of triumph when he saw the respectful looks of Bogart's boys, looks that told him his reputation was now big in the streets. All long gone, pride, hate, anger, defiance—all that was left was fear.

"G'wan inside," the guard said, pushing him into the cell. "Never min', you doan have long to stay there," he added, grinning.

Ivan staggered and grabbed the edge of a bunk to support his weak knees. Two hard-bitten men sitting there looked at him impassively. He heard muffled sobs and whimpers coming from somewhere.

"What you get?" one of the men asked.

"Tambran' switch, eight strokes," Ivan said.

"You lucky, dem a go cat me." The man grunted.

"Tambran' switch worse," the other said, "me know."

Ivan felt his belly quiver and for a moment thought he was about to puke.

"Is black dog an' monkey," the first said. "Both a dem wicked."

"Aaiiee." The wailing increased in intensity, startling Ivan.

"Shettup you damn bawlin', after you doan get lick yet," the first man growled, making a gesture of disdain toward an upper bunk.

"Ah can' tek it. Ah can' tek it, Lawd Jesas, Ah can' tek it," the voice whined, and then subsided into a muffled sobbing.

"From mornin' him a bawl," the man explained. "It gettin' on me nerves."

Ivan's too. It was mostly an inarticulate anguished sound of pure animal terror, as though whoever was crying had completely lost control, and it made the waiting infinitely worse. Ivan looked at the two men. He could see the signs of pressure under the oily sheen of sweat on their tense faces.

"How soon?" he could not help asking, but dreaded the answer.

"Damn soon," one said.

"*Whaaiiee,* Ah gwine dead, Ah gwine dead. Lawd, Ah gwine deado!"

"Shet up!" one of the men shouted. The wailing turned to sobs again.

"What you do?" the man asked Ivan.

"Cut up a man who fuck wid me," Ivan said matter-of-factly, and felt a little better at the man's expression of respect. A low wail of anguish came anew from the bunk.

"Me soon lick him me-self, y'know," the second man said.

"You ever get cat yet?" the first asked Ivan.

He shook his head no.

"You eat any'ting since morning?"

No again.

"Good," the man said.

"You goin' shit up youself," the second explained. "Boun' to. Everybody do it." The top bunk started up again.

"What him do?" Ivan asked, nodding toward the upper bunk.

"Carnal knowledge, Ah hear," the first said. "A ten year ol' gal-pickney."

"And you?" Ivan asked.

"Atrocious assault, dem call it," the man said, and smiled faintly.

The second man didn't say anything.

Footsteps echoed through the cell block. Two policemen appeared, along with a brown-skinned man wearing a white gown with reddish brown stains on it and a stethoscope around his neck. He read from a piece of paper in his hand,

"Eustace Golding."

The first man got up, a little unsteadily at first then caught himself. As he passed Ivan he handed him his unfinished cigarette. Fine beads of sweat stood out on his face.

"Good luck, breddah," Ivan whispered. The man grunted. Ivan heard the footsteps recede. The sound from the top bunk was steady, soft, and very high pitched. It reminded him of the squeaking of a newborn animal or the broken sound the doomed parrakeet had made before the hawk took him that long ago day on the mountain.

"Try doan listen," the second man said, pressing his hands over his ears. Even so, Ivan heard a loud crack immediately followed by a sound more terrible than anything he had ever heard. It was a sudden, loud, piercing scream, with nothing remotely human about it, that rang through the prison and then cut off sharply.

"Nine to go," the second man said.

Ivan felt what strength he had remaining leave him. "Me nah bawl so," he told himself fiercely. After the second scream, the man with his hands over his ears began to shake violently and sing in a wavering voice, "Rock of Ages cleft for me."

"How much this one have?" the doctor asked, listening to Ivan's heart. There was a strong smell of rum on the doctor's breath.

"Eight sah, tambran switch."

"Hmm," the doctor said, " 'im well frighten, but is a good, strong beat. Execute the sentence."

Ivan couldn't control his shaking as they stripped him down to his underpants. Some irrational voice kept telling him that it was all a nightmare, that he would awake and it would all be gone, that nothing like this could be happening to him. They led him into a walled courtyard which was empty save for a wooden barrel set on low blocks. As they approached Ivan saw a hole on one side of the barrel and straps on either side.

"Approach the barrel," the sergeant said. They pulled his underpants down.

"Better tek them off," the doctor said. "No point messing them up."

Ivan stepped out of his underpants and approached the barrel.

"Lie across and place your genitals in the hole," the sergeant said.

Ivan looked at him in astonishment.

"Come, you wouldn't want dem damaged."

The sun had warmed the barrel that was against his belly. A rank smell of stale urine arose from the inside. He felt the straps being tightened around his ankles and wrists. He opened his eyes and then shut them quickly. On the earth about a foot from his eyes was a pool of vomit carelessly covered with dirt. Huge flies buzzed about in it. Someone, he thought the doctor, came up and probed under his groin where his genitals hung into the hole. He felt a hand pass lightly over his back, which despite the hot sun overhead, felt chilly and damp.

"O.K. sergeant, try avoid the kidneys, eh?" the doctor said.

Ivan bit his lips hard. He heard a whistling sound, the crunch of the sergeant's boots, a sharp hiss, and then everything happened at the same time: Jagged currents of pain tore along his nerves and exploded in his brain. A piercing scream filled his ears. His throat burned raw as the intensity of the scream seared it. His entire body reared up, bucking convulsively against the straps, then thudded back onto the barrel. A hot rush as his bladder emptied and he lost control of his bowels. As from a distance a voice counting,

"One."

Then an aftershock of pain from his ravaged nerves, so intense that he at first thought he had been hit again, and felt his heart stop briefly.

Whiiss . . . *Whack* . . . four.

The sergeant looked at the limp body and sucked his teeth in irritation.

"You wan' check him, sah? Him faint 'way."

"Finish the sentence," the doctor said. "He's young and strong."

"But, sah—you doan wan' me dash some water on 'im?" the sergeant persisted.

"No, dammit," the doctor said. "Get it over with."

BOOK FOUR

Presshah Drop

AH SAY,
    Presshah drop!
     Oho,
    Presshah drop,
    Oyeah,
    Presshah
    Uhhumm,
    Presshah,
    Presshah gonna drop on you. . . .
                  —Toots Hibbert, *"Pressure Drop"*

13

But you must try,
try, try and try . . .

DAUGHTAH VERSHANN

She had the door bolted and the single window shut tight, as much to keep out the raw life of the teeming tenement as to conceal the trouble and shame inside. Even so, she couldn't block out the laughter or curses or the shrill yelps and whinnies that came through the wall, from the next room where a brown-skin girl with dull eyes received a stream of guests.

"What a way dis life stay doh, eh? Imagine—me firs' night wid Ivan . . . Who coulda have dream is so we was to spend it?"

The room was hot and with the window closed, the air quickly grew stuffy. She couldn't bear to look at his back. She closed her eyes but they were drawn to him every time he shifted or moaned. Finally, because there was nowhere else to look, she turned out the light and sat through the night in darkness.

His sleep was shallow and troubled and he muttered constantly but nothing he said made any sense to her. Occasionally there were only moans and whimpers. At times she heard names: Miss 'Mando, Maas' Nattie, Mirriam, Preacha, Hilton, and her own. Who was Mirriam? He moaned and she thought he must have come awake for she felt his warm, wet head settle in her lap and his arms go around her waist.

"Nevah min', Ivan," she comforted, stroking his damp face. "Nevah min,' darlin,' it done now. It finish."

"No, noo—no done. It *nah* done so—*it no done a raas*. . . ." He shook his head in violent denial.

Her dress clung to her thigh where his head rested. When his body moved in the pool of sweat there was a squish so that at first she had thought he was wetting the bed like some troubled child. Indeed, there was something primal about the broken whimpers that issued from his lips. She wished there were something she could do. But he hollered at the slightest touch, whenever she tried to wipe the puddled sweat out of the channels that looked like something mangled by a big cat. When she mopped his face and limbs she felt the sweat spring back as soon as the rag passed. The fever burned and trembled like something alive beneath his skin. She was certain that the sweat must sting the puckered flesh of his back and she debated whether she should try to let some warm coconut oil drip gently over it to keep the salt off.

He wouldn't die, of that she was sure, though at times during the first night even that did not seem so certain. What fretted her was the effects that the beating might have. Where he was right now was unclear and troubling. His babbling was incoherent and from time to time he started up moaning as if frightened.

"Hush Ivan, it done, it all over." She soothed him and wondered just what changes she might find in the Ivan who came back to himself, and to her.

She knew only one other person who had been officially beaten. But Maas' 'Zekel Jackson had been old when it happened, so it did not, she encouraged herself, mean anything. Still he had been a vigorous old man—well strong, as people said. An old soldier, he was called by everyone Hol'-de-fort-for-I-am-coming Jackson, and he would parade for the children, shouting loud commands and obeying them smartly, shouldering imaginary arms and stomping his bare heels against the asphalt while snapping fervent salutes to the queen. He sold cane juice and coconuts from a cart which he parked under a big divi-divi tree in front of the school. She couldn't remember, or had not ever known, just what his offense was; but she remembered that his sentence was only four strokes, and people said it was wickedness to beat an old man like that. Maas' 'Zekel was never himself afterward. He seemed to get feeble and he babbled, grinned to himself, and could no longer control his bladder. People said the beating had turned him fool-fool and 'wu'tless. Him mus' be dead by now, she thought.

But Ivan was young and had plans, surely nothing like that would happen to him. Yet when she heard him muttering and moaning in the darkness she fretted. "Watch and pray," she told herself. "Watch and pray, 'im is not de firs' an' 'im sure won' be de las'."

Toward morning he seemed to turn cooler, then began to shudder violently. She was alarmed, but he sat up and in a normal voice complained of being thirsty. He drank some bush tea with rum and fell into a deep sleep.

"Tenk God fe Jesus," she said, listening to his regular breathing, "Ivan arright—'im goin' to arright." She felt a rush of joy and relief which was quickly followed by exhaustion. Now, she thought, now, we new life can mek a start.

But would he be the same? How would they live? She tried to force herself not to worry about money or how she felt stifled by the cramped little room. So far nothing good had happened there. The landlord was a fat, brown man with foul breath and a grin that revealed carious teeth. There were always circles of sweat under his arms and around the crotch of his trousers. He always grinned at her.

"Is you one a go stay yah?" he had asked, running his eyes over her bosom, when she had first inquired about the room.

"Me brother coming from country soon."

"Aho, you breddah? Ah see." He named a figure just about double what she had expected.

"But, dat soun' high, sah?"

"Well, me dear, it *might* could go down y'know," he said, his eyes gleaming with a moist good will. "Is up to you." He counted the notes carefully and stuffed them into his pockets. "Ah really hate to tek money from a nice young gal like you." His grin peeled his lips back from blackened stubs. "You know?"

She knew and shut the door firmly and pressed her back against it.

And at the jail when finally the sergeant, sick of her tearful presence, had let her in to see Ivan, all he could talk about was the appointment with Mr. Hilton.

"Tell 'im say me mother dead a country—or say me sick ina hospital. Anyt'ing, but mek him know say me coming back wid two baas song."

Her heart had sunk as she stood among the crowd watching Hilton move around the studio, barking orders to his assistants, curtly dismissing pleas, and making coarse jokes at which everyone dutifully laughed.

"Lawd, but Missa Hilton no stop yah, he heew!"

He was what Preacha would call a man of the world. He was rich and was always in the papers, described there as a "sportsman," "socialite," or "leading businessman." Even though he was swearing and joking in the broad accent and slang of the people, it was unmistakably clear he was the boss. Everyone grinned in his face, and when he mentioned someone by name, if only to insult him familiarly, people beamed as though great distinction had been conferred. He reminded Elsa of someone she couldn't immediately identify but the comparison nonetheless disturbed her. He laughingly brushed off a number of hangers-on and stopped in front of her, bearded mouth grinning and dark glasses glinting.

"An' wha' 'bout you, mi love? What you want? Bet you wan' make a record—fe me." His voice was soft and insinuating, especially the pause before the "fe me," which set the hangers-on to laughing and nudging each other.

"Missa Hilton nah miss *nutten!*" they crowed admiringly.

"Yes, him is a nachral man."

"No, Mr. Hilton," she said formally, "is only a message I have for you, sir—from Ivan."

"Ivan? Which Ivan dat?" He seemed puzzled but before she could speak his assistant whispered something to him.

"Ah yes—de star-bwai. So you's a messenger eh? What's de message den?" He stroked his beard and smiled.

She felt that behind his glasses his eyes were looking her up and down. She hesitated, unable at the last minute to tell her carefully rehearsed lie. "Ivan *say* to tell you, sah, that 'im mother dead in the country and he had to go. But he said he will have two good tunes for you when he return."

"But," Hilton boomed, "I like the messenger better dan de message? What a way she nice eh?" he appealed to the gallery.

"Yes, Missa H. Is a nice little daughtah, sah."

"Missa H. 'ave good eye man, I like 'er meself too, y'know."

Her face grew hot under the stares of the men.

Hilton stood watching her with an amused expression on his face. "You sure you doan wan' mek—record?" To the onlookers the joke must have been even funnier the second time.

"You mus' be de firs' one walk through that door who doan wan' mek record. If you change you min' honey, jus' come see me . . . mek a firs' you up."

"What about Ivan, sir?"

"Oh yes—tell 'im to check me when 'im come back."

She had rushed out with her cheeks burning, the comments and laughter following her.

The remembered embarrassment became anger when she thought about it. "Is only because of Ivan," she fumed, "why I didn' run outta de place, or better yet, tell 'im about 'imself. 'Im damn liberty after all. . ." And it was something more than his condescending familiarity that upset her. She had a funny feeling about the man and his studio, both. Him—in the studio surrounded by his henchmen. She sensed something like a memory which kept teasing and eluding her. Could it be from hearing Ivan speak of him? She didn't think so. But other than that she didn't know anyone like him, rich, powerful and so people said, a lover of women and worldliness. What was that to her? She growing up in Preacher's house could never have known anyone like that. He was going to give Ivan his big chance, that was all.

Ivan stirred and moaned and she was afraid he would start ranting and muttering again. But he was quiet for the rest of the night and she must have slept because the next thing she knew it was morning and she was slumped against the wall. Ivan's head was still in her lap but he was awake now, weeping and embracing her.

"It arright Ivan, it arright—it done now."

"Oh Elsa," he sobbed. "Jesas Elsa, Jesas Elsa . . ." and then he slept again.

In the daylight she could not avoid seeing the angry-looking ridges on his back, with pockets of yellow pus forming along the edges. The room was full of the salty-sweet smell of flesh exposed to tropical heat.

But when he awoke again he seemed more himself, his voice weak but calm, and his speech coherent. "Elsa, is what day dis?"

"Wednesday. You feel bad?"

"Not so bad. Wednesday . . . Jesas, you mean I doan remember nothin' since Monday?"

"I believe so," she said.

"How me back stay?"

"Ivan, Ah can' even bear look pon it. How it feel?"

"Like dat, y'know. Elsa, you see Hilton?"

"Yes, yes Ah see 'im. No worry. 'Im say to check 'im when you come back from country." Remembering her lie, she giggled.

"Great," he whispered, excitement creeping back into his eyes. "Great, if dat is arright den everyt'ing cool. De res' no matter."

"Ah have something else fe you too," she said with an air of great mystery. "Guess what?"

"What?" He studied her with puzzled anticipation.

"Look!" she reached down to tug at something under the bed.

He leaned over to see and gave a shout of pain.

"Look," she said again, and beaming, pulled out the bicycle. "Ah get it fe you."

"Wha' Preacha say?"

"After Ah never ask 'im nutten, is tek I tek it." She could not keep the pride from her voice.

"Elsa, you is a lion." He looked thoughtful. "Where we deh?"

"Is our room dis."

"An' is t'ree day I been here? I bettah start work on de second song. Oiiee!" He started up, gasping with pain.

"You have wait 'til the back healup little. What dis song about anyway?"

"Success," he said grinning. "What else?" Though weak his smile was that of the old Ivan.

> *Persecushan you must bear*
> *Win or lose you gotta get your share,*

"How dat soun'?"

"It soun' *irie,*° go on, nuh."

"Arright listen:

> *"You can get it if you really want.*
> *But you mus' try, try an' try, try-an'-try . . ."*

BABYLON VERSION

"You see it?" Hilton laughed. "Ah tell you the bwai feel 'im is star already."

"Is a direck star-bwai jersey dat, yes," his assistant Chin agreed, smiling at the huge yellow star that Elsa had sewn in the middle of Ivan's shirt.

"But you know sah, 'im damn good too y'know."

Not so much "good," Hilton thought, but possessed. He watched Ivan strutting and dancing, the jersey clinging to his thin torso, his eyes and teeth flashing in a face shining with sweat and exultation. The boy might have begun by wailing in the church as so many of them did, but this had little to do with any church music. It was something felt, deeper and more primal than any training he may have tapped into. He rode the music hard, just a shade off the beat, threatening and caressing the mike, writhing

° *Irie:* Stimulating, powerful, good, awesome, in either a religious or sexual sense.

and lashing around the hot center of the music, defiantly strutting across the floor.

"Dis one really feel it," Chin said. "Spirit tek 'im."

The second song had an assertive and rebellious spirit heightened by the up-beat semireggae rhythm Hilton put around it. The words were only one element—the voice was good, rich toned and flexible, easy with the music—but the total effect was a combination, a fusion of words, melody, and rhythm into a passionate affirmation of a vision as hard, resistant, stubbornly desperate and macho as shantytown itself.

> *uumhuh. Ah say . . .*
> *De harder dey come . . .*
> *Is de harder dey fall*
> *One an aall . . .*

There was no way these songs could fail to appeal to shantytown youth, Hilton thought, and make some money. It was the kind of music he was always being criticized for publishing; that the government was always threatening to ban from the air as being subversive, putting ideas in the sufferahs heads.

> *Ohyeh, De harder dey coome*
> *Is de harder dey fall . . .*

He could hear the question already. Tell me something Hilton, jus' who the raas is the "Dey" whose fall you celebratin'?" You know what you really doing? Hell, he knew. Music never kill nobody yet. On the contrary he was providing a service.

See, look at the quashie dem. The boy had their attention to raas. And they were a hard audience, but 'im 'ave dem! Every hard-bitten one a dem swaying, believing, triumphant. . . . While the music played. While Ivan whirled, strutted, and wailed on the crest of the beat, lashing the air with an upraised fist, triumph shining from his eyes, a pained intensity in his face. Having made a believer of himself, he was his own truest convert:

> *But I'd raddah be a free man in mah grave*
> *dan living as a puppet or a slave*
> *so, as sure as the sun will shine*
> *I'm gonna get mine . . .*

In that moment he was a star; he knew it and the boys listening knew it too. Hilton let him sing himself out long after he had more than he needed.

"Alright cut. Dass enough." He had to shout twice before the musicians stopped and left an echoing silence to hang over the studio.

Ivan was stranded. He stood open mouthed, abandoned by the music like a creature suddenly plucked out of a sustaining environment and left exposed and vulnerable in a strange place. He blinked and shook his head as though awakening from sleep while he visibly tried to collect himself. Then he rushed over dripping sweat and shining with eagerness.

"*Yea*—it alright," Hilton anticipated the question. "We can use it."

"*Great,* sah, *great.* Den when it to release, sah?"

"Release? Slow down man, business firs'. You better read dis." Hilton handed him a standard release and watched his face closely as he studied it. The boy was so charged up there was no way he could hide his feelings. It was almost a shame to bring him down. But he had promise, and the sooner he came to terms with reality the better for everyone. He had yet to see one that didn't think that just because they cut a few sides they should be millionaires, or who later didn't claim to have been robbed. The boy was peering at the paper as if he were nearsighted or illiterate.

"Wha . . . What's de meaning of dis, sah?"

"You can read. Just what it says. You get fifty dollars for the record. Twenty-five for each side."

"You mean dass—all?"

Hilton had seen that expression before. Actually it was a range of moods quickly passing across the face. First, the quickly disappearing look of joy; then shock and disbelief; then the tenacious confusion, the self-deprecating smile of someone apologizing for a foolish error, followed by hardening suspicion that it was no mistake, and then last, the unsuccessful effort to mask anger and disappointment. Hell, business is business and life hard, Hilton thought. He'd seen the process before, and he had never known one of them at that point to successfully resist the desire to see his name on a record.

"Well, young bwai?"

"Twenty-five dollah a side, sah? That no seem right."

"Oh—den what seem right to you?"

"Well, I doan rightly know but . . ."

"Come on." His voice showed impatience. "You mus' have some idea or you couldn't say it doan seem right? Talk up, man."

The boy bit his lip and an expression of appeal crossed his face.

"Well, some kina percentage if it hit, sah—or, or at leas' two hundred dollars?"

Hilton laughed.

"No, sah. I doan think I'm signing dis for any fifty dollars y'know Missa Hilton." Ivan turned his stubborn and angry face away.

"Well, it look like say we have a new producer now, Chin. Ah wish him luck."

Chin didn't say anything.

"Look," Hilton said to Ivan, "come yah. I'm a fair man. You doan like the terms? Is a pity we didn't discuss dem before. But . . . jug no bruk; milk no dash way. You doan like the terms doan sign. Produce it yourself den. You can buy the tapes an mix dem yourself, eh. Let's say fifty dollars an hour for studio time, fifteen an hour for the sidemen eh? You soun' like a businessman— you can raise that easy, right? Den I'll even press dem fe you. Flat rate per thousand, say dollar fifty each. Over a thousand, a dollar each. What could fairer dan dat? You think you can sell a thousand—two, three? Jus' decide and place your order, O.K.? Place your order man. Cash in advance . . . Oh, you don't want to order a run? Cho man, you disappoint me. But think it over all de same—you know where to find me."

Ivan let the release paper flutter from his hand and walked to the door. The swagger was gone, instead he seemed to be walking blindly with the rubber-legged automatic motions of a fighter who has been hit and is operating on pure reflex.

"You wan' mix it and press some, sah?" Chin asked, looking at his shoes.

"Damn right, but jus' a small run. An' don't release it til I tell you."

"Yes, Mr. Hilton," Chin said quietly.

Hell, he'd be back—in day or two at the most, Hilton thought. Maybe resentful and defiant, but most likely apologetic and anxious for more work. Well, he'd have to see about that—maybe in six months, after he'd had a chance to learn manners. There was no damn shortage of would-be singers. But he'd have to listen to the tapes again. This fellow seemed to have a little something extra—a spirit and a feeling, hard to put into words exactly. But, whatever—if he was to be any good to anybody he'd have to be brought into line. He'd have to gentle him the way you do with a young horse, or a young gal.

But a week passed and Ivan didn't come back. Still, Hilton trusted his instinct. That boy wanted to hear his name on the radio and his voice in the juke joints so bad you could smell it. Could be, he was so vex when he left that he had done something dumb and involved up himself with the police. What was his name, Ivan what? He'd have to check. Hell, he'd not even asked. So. . . Give him a month, and if he didn't show they would put the record out anyway. Then, if Ivan showed up he'd buy him out. Wouldn't be the first time.

The month still had a few days to run when Hilton saw him standing in the crowd at the gates. From the sullen expression on his face he didn't seem to have learned anything much.

"So. . . What you want sonny? To mek another record?"

"No."

"Then what you want?"

"I'll tek the money." His voice was little more than a mutter.

"What you say? Speak up, man, I can' hear you."

"Ah say, I'll tek the money for the record."

"Which money? Which money, man? Talk quick! You mean the forty dollars?"

Ivan looked at him. Something flickered in his eyes and was quickly replaced with a look of dogged resignation. "I'll settle for dat," he said dully.

"Damn right you'll settle." Hilton peeled off some bills. "An' damn lucky too. I'm not particular to do anymore business with you, y'know. Now what you say your name is?

"Ivanhoe Martin."

"Ivanhoe what?"

"Martin."

"O.K. Sign here an', sport, nex' time you make a record re-member that is me control the recording business in this town. An somet'ing else too—I mek hits. Not the public, not the DJ's. *I* make hits, O.K.?"

Ivan didn't seem to be listening. His face was turned away and he snatched the bills and shoved them into his pocket without even looking at them.

"No Sonny, count them! Dass better. You see that extra ten dollars? I didn't have to do it y'know—but I wouldn't want it said that Boysie Hilton is not a kind man." He drove off chuckling loudly.

At lunch time every day Chin smoked a single spliff, which he insisted was for his asthma. He looked up without expression when Hilton came in.

"You remember that fellow who wouldn't sign? Well, you can release the record."

" 'Im sign now?" Chin's voice was neutral.

"Yeh, but tell the DJ's not to push it."

"But is a good record you know, sah." Chin looked as if his response had surprised him and he regretted having let it slip.

"Even so, I don't want it on the charts. No point building up that bwai. 'Im too damn faastie. A damn troublemekah."

14

Whosoever Digget' a Pit

'osoever digget' a pit
Shall fall in it,
Shall fall in it
Shall fall in it . . .
For if you is a big big tree,
I am a small axe . . .

BEARD MAN VERSHANN

An unbroken wall of bushy shrubs bordered the railroad tracks and screened out everything except the sky and empty tracks stretching into the distance. It was a place spectacular in its emptiness and confinement, offering no reason for anyone to come there except in search of total solitude. The small boy huddled motionless beside the tracks made no impression except perhaps to deepen the sense of desolation. He was painfully thin and very young. His face appeared pinched and aged under the crown of dreadlocks which framed it.

The man, when he appeared, made more of an impression on the empty, isolated place. He was a larger replica of the boy. Brooding eyes and dramatically towering locks gave him the look of a slightly demented ascetic. He was slender but not thin like the boy, and his face, though tense and intelligent, did not have the wizened, aged appearance that the boy's did. As he walked up behind the boy his deepset eyes seemed to soften and grow dark, as though with suppressed pain.

The boy gave no sign that he heard the slow footsteps even when the man's shadow fell over him.

The man placed his hand gently on the boy's thin shoulder. "Come Man-I, mek we go home."

The boy tilted his head to look up at his father and his cheek rested on the man's hand.

"Come," the man said, gently squeezing the shoulder, "Is jus' me an' you now. Mek we go home."

Quick tears filled the boy's eyes and his face became very young. He stood up, and took his father's hand and they walked slowly and silently together down empty tracks.

BABYLON VERSHANN

Jose's Hondo wove through the traffic, narrowly missing a number of vehicles including a green Cortina. The driver swore and darted after him, cutting on a siren as he did so. He pulled up even with the Hondo and crowded him toward the sidewalk.

"Police," the driver said. "Pull over and keep your hands in sight."

Jose got off the bike and spread his legs, placing his palms flat on the roof of the car. The driver patted him down. He did not seem to see the bag of ganja on the back of the Hondo.

"Dis damn well better be important, Jose."

"Trouble Maas' Ray, bad trouble, sah." Jose was sweating and his look of distress was genuine.

"Trouble? What kin' a trouble?"

"Dem shoot Pedro wife a country dis mornin', sah."

"How you mean dem shoot? Who shoot her?"

"Army, Maas' Ray."

The policeman swore again. "She dead?"

"Yes, so dem say."

"She had ganja on her?"

"Pedro get way wid dat, sah."

"Alright, leave it to me." He started toward his car.

"But, Missa Ray—what Ah mus' tell the trader dem, sah?"

"To hold off until you hear from me."

"But, sah—" From his tone Jose was still uneasy. The policeman stopped and looked at him coldly. "But look nuh, sah—" Jose went on, "dem pay protection, y'know, sah, an' now one a dem dead up. Now, how that a go look, sah?"

"O.K. it's a problem, I admit. But leave it to me. Just tell dem to hold off 'til I get back to you. Not to worry."

"So how Pedro wife, sah?"

"What you mean? Dass up to you. Find someone reliable to replace her, nuh. And get in touch with me the usual way."

Maas' Ray was quite peeved when he got back into his car.

Yes it was a problem, but how much of one wasn't clear. Could those fucken military intelligence cowboys be trying to destroy his intelligence channels? Not a damned thing to do but charge around setting ambushes and shooting off their toys. Or else zooming over the mountains in helicopters, doing their best to destroy the peasant economy. They should be restricted to their damned barracks and parade grounds. That was their business, beating the retreat and trooping the fucken colors. Why the blasted government thought a country this size needed an army was beyond him. If it was a matter of national pride and the damn fools wanted to fight so bad, why not send dem to Rhodesia or better yet South Africa where de Boers could light up dem ass? What they should on no account be permitted was to continue farting around with law enforcement. What the hell did that say about the police force? When he had attained a measure of calm he signaled headquarters.

"Jones here. Put me through to the Commissioner." The old fart would grumble and mumble and do exactly nothing. He was an old-fashioned civil service type and the first black to hold that position. He was, therefore, inordinately sensitive to any hint of criticism or any suggestion that the prestige of the force was slipping. He also wallowed in the delusion that the relationship between the two services was one of hearty cooperation sharpened by jolly competition in the pursuit of national security.

"Oh yes, Mr. Commissioner. Jones here, sir. I was just informed that the army went in again today and shot one of my people."

"Yes, I was just informed myself. But one of your people? No one indicated—"

"No sir, not an officer. One of my informants in the ganja trade."

"Oh." The voice at the other end seemed relieved and a little impatient. "Oh, I see. Well we've been over that ground. I can't exactly raise a fuss, now can I? They'll simply say that they can't be concerned with which particular law breaker may or may not be a police informer."

Detective Superintendent Jones took a long breath. As usual, no fucking support. The old dummy, and as long as he had been in police work, too . . .

"I quite understand sir. Your position is ticklish. But if and when my information dries up and the crime rate soars, no one is going to blame the army—sir."

Jones heard, as he was obviously intended to, a clearly audible, peevish hiss. He didn't care. The Commissioner's voice took on a tone of icy formality:

"Mr. Superintendent, what do I understand you to be saying?"

"Just this, sah. Though we may not like it particularly, the enforcement of the law in West Kingston depends on the availability of dependable intelligence which inevitably places the men in the field in close contact with—uh—undesirables. If my operation keeps being disrupted by interference from the military, which may or may *not* be accidental, then the effectiveness of the entire police presence in West Kingston is going to be—doubtful. Already—" Jones thought better of the rest.

"Yes, Jones? Already—?" the Commissioner's voice challenged very softly.

"Truly sorry to have to say this sir, but you ought to know. In the last two weeks our boys have picked up three very wanted criminals. And sir, each time, before we even had a chance to interrogate them, officers from MI were at the scene waving authorization from the Minister and babbling about national security." (Eat *that,* Mr. Fucken Commissioner.)

"The *Minister?* Are you sure . . ."

" 'Fraid so, *sir.* A network of *known* criminals with some kind of immunity from the army. And we never had a chance to find out just what the game is. Already the rank and file are asking whether the police are still in charge of criminal investigation." (How's that Mr. Commissioner, Sir? The goddamn soldier boys running an intelligence ring in my goddamn area with the connivance of your old school tie buddy, the Minister.)

"Well Superintendent, I'll see the Minister on this. But one can hardly explain that ganja traders enjoy our ah—protection?"

"I quite understand sir. But it would be terribly helpful if it could be established that the CID Special Task Force controls what comes into this area, and that it is a touchy, terribly delicate situation and that there should be no interference or encroachment. Yes, sir. Thank you, sir."

He hung up, scowling. "You damn right, 'yessir-thank-you-sir!' " he muttered. "Or else it going to be fucken war out here. Every time MI take off one of ours it going to be two of theirs. Dem could have letters from the Prime Minister. . . . CID special task force not preaching beatitudes to any little dutty criminal."

He sat thinking and scowling and drumming his fingers on the dashboard. Maas' Ray didn't take frustration well. On such occasions a petulance crept over his face, giving him the appearance of a sulking school boy. He picked up the radio phone again with the motion of a man who had made a decision.

"Is me again, get me Sgt. Philpotts in special services. Aye Foggy? How that surveillance going, eh? Good. Four? Who de other one? Well it no matter. Listen, get a tactical squad from Harmon Barracks an' tek dem. No, better mek it a ten-man force, full firepower, no use tek no chance. Ah want you to tek dem raas, *now.* Today! Don't worry, I will deal wid dat. An' look, dem have some question to answer but—if not, so life stay. Dat doan matter neider, so long as you tek dem. O.K.? No, no. Not the station, the safe house. Arright, lick dem, raas."

STAR-BWAI VERSHANN

Eheh, but dis *irie*—fifteen dollar—Elsa goin' vex but it wort' it. He stepped back from the small mirror and danced a few jubilant steps just to see the gold threads shimmer with the movement. *Irie, irie, irie!* Star-bwai to raas. Tonight a fe me night, yes. Cho raas, it late already, where Elsa deh? Why she so late? He put on the black, fake buckskin vest over the gold shirt. Tonight a fe me night an' I *ready. Yes, dis bwai is moovin''on.* Between the bed and the dresser there was hardly space to move much less dance, but he couldn't sit still.

Cho, if only Elsa would act right tonight. Me have surprise fe her too! If she woulda jus' get up offa her sanctify holy rolly foolishness. Bwai, dat damn Preacha sure full up her head wid plenty shit doh. Everyt'ing frighten her an' everyt'ing is sin. . . .

But still, is a lion gal doh—look how she tek care of everyt'ing when me back did tear up, an' I never even know where I deh. An', after I all get de blow from dat t'eifing yellow dawg Hilton, I good fe mad y'know, when everyt'ing crash-up so. Mad to raas, everyt'ing crash. Is bed I tek y'know—coulden move fe days. She did shock too, but she try hide it an' go on like nothin'' much happen. An' not another word again 'bout married firs'. No, sah. She jus' come lie down next to me, an' hol' me, and whisper, "No matter what Ivan, we always have each other." An' she just come 'gainst me soft an' naked so—is a good good gal, yes. Anyway all that done wid now. Today de record release and nobody can stop I now. Nobody, not Hilton, not Preacha, nobody can stop I now.

Sure as the sun's gonna shine
I'm gonna get it, what's mine

He heard her footsteps approach the door and waited with impatience as the door opened.

"Hey Elsa, guess what?"

"What Ivan?" She crossed wearily to the bed, sank down, and removed her shoes. "Me foot dem a kill me." She was so intent on her feet that she didn't see his new clothes, or notice his excitement. But . . . what a way she look tired ina her face an' even ina her eye dem, Ivan thought. But wait til she hear de news. She mus' feel better. An' after tonight t'ings must be better. Better mus' come.

"Elsa, de record! It release." He waited for interest and animation to come into her face.

"Oh? Truly?" she said.

"Look here Elsa, to celebrate—y'know? Is fe you."

"Fe me?" She looked up wearily, almost uncomprehendingly at the box he was thrusting towards her. "What you tek you money buy now? You buy the food I ask you?"

He would not allow himself to be irritated by the note of censure in her voice or the way she prodded the box listlessly with her finger. "Cho forget food man! Open it. Is a big night tonight."

She managed a faint smile and tugged uncertainly at the wrapping.

"Cho! Open it nuh, man, tonight we goin' celebrate." He tore the box open and held up a piece of boldly colored print. "Mini, man, de lates' t'ing. Sexy, eh?"

She stared at the skirt, half infected by his enthusiasm, then her face went dead again. "Ivan, you know me nah wear nutten like dis? How you could expect me to wear something like dat?"

"Why not, is the lates' t'ing. Wear it man, you be de sexies' daughtah in Kingston tonight when we go celebrate de record."

"Celebrate what? You sell de record to Hilton for fifty dollars, you doan have no more money to get y'know. You have any money leave at all?"

"Yes but—when the other producers dem hear it, an' when it hit, I can make more, even make me own too. Bwai, we drive way from dis place tomorrow. Get dressed man."

"Ivan, I'm tired. I been walking and looking work all day."

"Cho, come on wid me man—look, you don't' even have fe dance . . ."

"We don't have any money fe that. I still have fe buy some food and look work, an' I want to go to church Sunday."

"So . . . that's it, eh? You want me to go walk and beg rich people work? You really doan understan' eh? I have a *record* now. I done wid all dat y' know."

"Well, I doan done wid it though. My foot dem killing me an' you talkin' 'bout dance."

"So . . . what you walking for—you tek me fe joke? You doan believe I'm gonna make it? You don't."

"No y'know, all I'm saying is dat—I'm tired."

"No, you want me fe go beg rich people yard-bwai work fe ten dollars a week, fe de *res' a my life?* Well understan' dis—Ah dead firs'. And anyway, I don't have to. I'm gonna make it, hear? I'm gonna make it, baby."

"Ivan, Ivan you such a dreamah."

"Dreamah? *Dreamah?*" He was almost shrieking with disappointment and outrage. "Me? Dreamah? Is who go to church an' talk about milk an' honey in de sky? An' wan' call *me* dreamah? Well me nah look fe no milk an' honey in de sky, is right down *yahso* I deh look mine. Fe me an' you. You know what? I better lef' dis rahtid place, y'know, sah."

> Talk about the pie up in the sky,
> Waiting for me when I die . . .
> But sure as the sun will shine,
> I'm gonna get mine, what's mine . . .

The joint was gummy wid presshah, yaah, an' rocking under a steady, steady reggae roots beat. And crowded! Yea, thick and deep, a glittering and colorful mass bobbing and pulsing, stomping it out. Shantytown Friday night, yea. Ivan had added a small black tam. Neat, not voluminous like the Dreadlocks wore when they wanted to cover their locks. With the shades and the shirt and vest, he was easily the baddest looking rude-bwai in the place. Totally appropriate for the newest star shooting to his orbit in the entertainment firmament.

In the motion and excitement his anger and disappointment began to lighten. But it wouldn't go away. He was hurt yes, and angry with Elsa for not coming, for refusing even to try on the mini that he had so carefully selected and dearly bought, but mainly for her hopelessness, tiredness, and fear that told him more eloquently than words that she could not share his excitement—or his faith.

He had chosen the spot carefully. There were newer places than Paradise Tile Gardens. Spots that had come into fashion and gone out since that first night. But this was *de* place. It had a tough, sophisticated crowd and it played mainly Hilton's records. Besides that, the first time he had been an anonymous slack-jawed country boy playing cool. Tonight he was citywise, slicker than grease, badder than yaws, and cooler than first time, standing on the verge of destiny. . . . *Oh yeh, dis little boy is mooovin' on . . . .*

A hard-driving excitement lifted him and would not let him be still. Restless, he slid into the crowd and worked his way toward the jukebox. He could barely hold down his excitement as he ran his eyes down the columns looking for the new label that would have his name. He looked again and again, certain that he had overlooked it in his haste. Surely Hilton would have it in the jukeboxes by now! The record was out. He'd heard it on the radio this morning. Well, Speedy, the operator, would surely have it. Yeah, he had it. He was just waiting for the right time, a full house, the right psychological moment, to present Hilton's latest offering.

But the waiting wasn't easy. The crowd, flexing, stylin' and jammin' like it was just another Friday night, was frustratingly oblivious to the importance of the occasion. It took an effort for Ivan to keep from approaching people and announcing himself and the coming of the greatest offering in reggae history. But he was cool behind his shades, his fortune on his back and five *deggeh* dollars in his pocket. Maybe he should have asked Bogart and dem to come with him? But suppose the record didn't play? Impossible! But suppose? Maybe he should go reveal his presence to Speedy and make something happen? Then without warning or introduction his voice was blasting out of the speakers, filling the space and riding easy over the rhythm. *Aaiee it dread so!*

> Well they tell me of a pie up in the sky
> Waiting for me when I die . . .
> But between the day you born and when you die,
> They never seem to hear you when you cry . . .
> But the harder they come . . .

Yes, sah! Is it! And it had their attention too. Even the most blasé dancer seemed to move it on up and to be listening to the message too. *Lively up you self yes!* He heard murmurs of approval and even cries of *"Irie!"* and *"Gummy!"* But it was hardly enough. Hell: recognition, wealth, fame, the love of women, the respect of men, the adoration of multitudes would scarcely suffice. His amplified voice resonated around him. Goose bumps crawled over his skin. Shit, dis a all? The record was over and he felt empty. Dis a all?

"Baas song dat jus' play, eh?" he asked the man next to him.

"Eh?"

"Ah say, great song man, a sure hit."

"Is arright." The man shrugged offhand. "No bad." He clearly had no notion of how close he had come to a violent end.

Ivan stomped off. "Aye, don't I know you?" He felt a hand on his shoulder. He turned eagerly, sure that the hand belonged to someone who recognized the greatness of the song he had just heard, and who associated him with it. He looked into Jose's glinting shades and easy grin.

"Raas, but you looking good, breddah," Jose said as if they had parted just last week. He seemed hardly to have changed and was flanked on either side by a high styling daughtah, dressed, as they said, 'to puss foot.'

"Is my song that jus' play, y'know," Ivan said.

"You lie!"

"No man, to God, a my song dat—just' release today. What you t'ink?"

"*Irie* man, is a good song, man. Good, good song. You movin' up alright den?"

"Movin' up, yes," Ivan agreed modestly.

Jose's appreciation seemed totally genuine and spontaneous and his women's faces mirrored it. Jose threw his arm around Ivan's shoulder. "Is me show 'im aroun' when "im firs' come town y'know. Is *lie?*"

With that easy gesture Jose took complete credit for everything, but Ivan didn't care.

"We have fe drink a beer to celebrate," Jose said, beaming at Ivan as though at a favorite nephew as he took in Ivan's outfit. "Yes yes, is me bwai dis. So—de record jus' release? How much time it play, jus' once?"

Ivan nodded.

"Wait," Jose directed, and swaggered off into the crowd.

"So you is Jose frien'," one of the women said in a voice that promised much. Ivan nodded, watching as Jose's tall figure weaved imperiously through the dancers and approached the operator. The same self-assured Jose, arrogant walk and all, dispensing greetings as he went.

"So . . . you a Jose frien' an' you mek record—nice," the same woman purred again. Ivan acknowledged with a casual wave. What was Jose up to? He was pointing toward them. Speedy shook his head no. Jose leaned down and reasoned with him. The music stopped. The unexpected silence was almost tangible. Then Jose's voice filled it.

"Hear I now—dis a Jose speaking. Jose who is known to you." He held up his hands for attention. "Tonight de management of Paradise Tile Gardens, bettah known as *De Gardens,* is happy to present to you de latest and de hottest reggae disk to come out of de world famous Hilton Empire, Ahuh. Rocking reggae music, yeah. Jus' release today—a song what boun' to be number one in dis year festival. Listen it good, an' 'member whe' you hear it firs'—De Garden. A tune dey call "De Hardah Dey Come" by the baad, bad yout' dem call Rhygin-Ivan—up an' coming recordin' artis', returning from a triumphant tour of Lucia and St. James, de man—Rhygin-Ivan. Come on up, man." He beckoned Ivan up and raised his hand high.

"Ladies and gentlemen, de yout' dem call Ivaan."

Ivan waved and grinned, quite ready to believe every word. Though he noticed that Speedy didn't look too happy as Jose bowed, grinned and waved like a politician. As he led Ivan back to the bar, the record started again. Jose bowed and waved and accepted congratulations and reveled in the self-generated attention like it was his moment. Which to a great extent it was. Ivan didn't mind. When they got back to the women Jose winked at him. "Is so new record mus' introduce," he said, in the righteous tones of an upholder of standards, *"aftah all."*

When the song was over they became the center of an eddy of folks offering congratulations and just wanting to bask in the celebrity. Ivan took it all calmly, but on the inside his blood was high. He felt an undeniable gratitude toward Jose, who, in a festive mood, kept offering drinks to all comers. Ivan grew uneasy as he made no move to pay. Did Jose think that, as a man with a record just released, he was in a position to buy drinks for the crowd? There was no way that he could think of to clarify that situation without a certain embarrassment.

"Ah have fe go check a guy, Jose. Be right back," he said as casually as he could, and sauntered off. He didn't really want to leave yet, but the situation tricky bad.

Jose caught up to him by the gate. "Wait, whe' you a go so quick breddah?"

"What's de big idea, man? Who a go pay fe all dem drinks, eh?"

"Cho, chicken feed dat, me pay already. Look yah." Jose flashed a hefty roll. "But still I like de way you slide out—you learn a lot. But nevah try fool Jose doh." There was a brief eyeglass to eyeglass confrontation in the darkness.

"Who a try fool you?" Ivan blustered. "By de way, don't you all have some money fe me from time?"

They glared at each other again, then surprisingly Jose's charming smile flashed easily across his hard face.

"Yes, you a learn." He threw his arm across Ivan's shoulder. Ivan watched warily. He'd seen William Holden make a move like that in *Streets of Laredo*.

But Jose was cool. "Yes, you movin' up. Real nice. Mek big record—tu'n bad-man—slice up Longah like ham. Yes, from de firs' Ah like you style. Me spirit tek you." He drawled this praise in a tone of wonder and pride. Ivan was astonished at how much he knew, and naturally flattered too.

Then Jose turned businesslike. "But . . . about dah record deh tell me something? Ah bet you doan have twenty dollah ina you pocket. You lucky if Hilton pay you fifty fe it."

"Well—" Ivan started to lie, but he was impressed.

"Cho, no bother lie man, me know de scene an' dah brownskin fuckah too. . . Moreover it reach me say you nah go see even one more cent."

"How you know dat?"

"Connection man, connec*shan*. But not to worry, Ah goin' fix you up wid somet'ing. Ah lookin' a good man, a bright bwai. You can handle big money?"

"Sure," Ivan drawled. "Certainly."

"An' keep you mout' shut too."

"Sure man, but what you talkin' 'bout?"

"Ah say I can work up a letgo fe you man, big money, no sweat."

Despite a rising interest, Ivan held back. He couldn't help but remember the last time Jose had volunteered to make his fortune. "Well—mek Ah hear how it go, man," he persisted.

"Cho, come den," Jose commanded and started off. Ivan hung back. "Wha' happen, sah? Is 'fraid you 'fraid prosperity? Wha' happen to you?"

"I'da like all hol' down right yah fe a while, guy." He knew it sounded lame but was embarrassed to admit that he wanted to hear his record and see people dancing to it for a while longer. An' besides, the last time Jose took him anywhere. . .

"Cho, is you name you wan' hear, don't it?" Jose's voice was sympathetic.

"Yeah, well, sort of, y'know."

Jose shook his head. "Bwai, you really no understan' how dis t'ing go. You nah hear it again tonight, y'know. It done play, *done.*"

"How you mean?" Ivan protested. "You yourself say is a good record an' it jus' release."

"Yeah it good." Jose laughed. "But Hilton no like you at all. 'Im put out word say de record not to push. It nah even get near de top twenty, so Speedy tell me. It not suppose to mek de charts at all, *atall.* You bettah come wid I."

He followed Jose into the darkness, thinking about what he had just heard. You mean to say, Hilton was rich enough to keep money outta 'im own pocket, jus' fe keep one poor black bwai inna 'im place? Dat mek any sense doh? So 'im wasn't jus' a talk. 'Im really did burn me, but I feel say once de record come out, it woulda set me up to mek a move. Him t'ief de record, dat hurt, but it no kill. But dis a wickedness, man. De raas man, even doh 'im mek record, 'im have no respeck or feelin' fe de music—or else 'im coulden do dis so. Is jus' business wid 'im. Bullfrog say 'what is joke to you, is death to me.' Well is that now. Kill me record, might as cheap 'im kill me too. But Ivan wasn't even angry, there was only shock and bitterness starting in his chest that left him numb and unfeeling—at first.

Jose stopped in front of a Honda that looked new. Whatever he was into must be good, Ivan thought. Whatever it was, he was ready too. Why not? "Den, Jose," he murmured, surprised at how steady his voice was, "Ah hope say dah one yah really belong to you dis time."

"So you hear 'bout dat." Jose laughed. "Is arright man. Dem time deh me was still a yout'. But now I put away childish things. Everyt'ing cool breddah, enjoy de ride."

15

An' Dere We Wept...

An' dere we wept,
When we remember Zion
How can you sing King Alpha song
In a strange lan'. . .

"Me name Ras Petah," the slender Dreadlocks said, "but some call me Pedro." He extended his hand formally to Ivan, bowing slightly as they shook.

"De bes' raas cutter in Kingston," Jose said. The Dreadlocks inclined his head slightly, as though accepting that designation were no more than his due, and sat down at the table where mounds of tightly wrapped cylinders of ganja were stacked.

"You hear dah tune 'De Harder Dey Come'?" Jose asked.

Ras Peter nodded slightly. His medusa head bent over the weed as he examined each wrap, sniffed and felt it before slicing expertly into it with his razor sharp cutting knife.

"Well is Ivan dat—'im sing it, y'know," Jose said.

The Dreadlocks seemed distracted and he appeared to carry with him an air of deep melancholy. "Truly," he murmured, and managed a fleeting smile. "Ah hear it one time—could be a great song." He looked at Ivan and nodded and again Ivan sensed the lurking sadness.

"Is all de herb dis?" Jose nodded at the table.

"De laas' truly," Peter said.

"Well, we can mek a run soon, Ah get de word," Jose said, watching the Rasta closely. "Tomorrow if you want. How you stay?"

The knife stopped. Slowly Peter raised his head and Ivan saw a gentle face in which huge eyes rimmed with dark shadows of pain seemed to glow out at them.

"Bwai, Jose, Ah miss de queen y'know, sah—an' de bwai. . ." His voice became muffled and he shook his head. "De bwai, 'im miss 'im maddah bad. . . ."

The three men were silent, surrounded by a brooding stillness. There was only the steady hiss of the blade through the herb.

> *An' dere we wept, when we remember Zion . . .*
> *'Ow can we sing King Alpha song*
> *in a strange lan' . . . ?*

"Bettah mus' come," Jose said akwardly. "Anyway, I bring dis breddah yah fe work wid you—is a good breddah—if you agree to it.

"So . . . is jus' business you come 'pon," Ras Pedro said in a dull voice and without looking up, as though he were talking to himself.

Ivan felt that they shouldn't be there.

"Well, me nah even a consider dat y'know. My bwai sickly as y'know—from birth 'im chest weak. I not sure say 'im a go mek it widout 'im maddah y'know. . . ." The uninflected voice trailed off and Ras Peter stared in the direction of his visitors. Though Ivan was sure he didn't see them.

Jose shifted his feet and seemed about to say something, but he didn't and the silence hung on. His evident and uncharacteristic discomfort heightened Ivan's feelings of awkwardness and intrusion. He watched Jose, waiting for some signal, and trying to figure out what was going on behind his impassive expression and dark lenses. Finally Jose stood up silently and nodded toward the door. "Arright Pedro, later den. Come Ivan." His voice seemed loud in the room. Pedro neither moved nor answered.

Once they were out under the stars Ivan felt a great release.

"Whew," Jose breathed. "Bwai, it heavy in deh, eh? Breddah Pedro under heavy heavy presshah."

"Wha' happen?" Ivan asked, thinking of the tense and anguished face.

"Army shoot 'im baby maddah, say is mistake. But is two week now—so I figure Pedro ready fe trade again." He shook his head, "Well, mek we leff yah den."

Ivan didn't move. "Wha' happen?" Jose urged.

"You g'wan," Ivan said. "Me will stay."

He had spoken impulsively and wasn't really sure that he wanted to return to the grief-heavy atmosphere of the little house. But he was sure that De Gardens had no further attraction for him tonight. And, besides there was something in the quiet, open manner of the young Dreadlocks that affected him deeply.

Jose looked at him in surprise. Then he smiled. "Good idea

breddah—it might work out. Pedro a de bes' cutter I ever see. 'Im have a feeling fe herb."

Ivan waited until the noise of the Honda had faded, then he knocked timidly on the door. There was no answer. He tried it and the door swung open with a loud creak. Ras Peter sat immobile before the musty-smelling piles of ganja.

"Ah—well—Ah come back," Ivan stammered.

"One love, man," Ras Peter said, and nodded. Then his lips moved but the words were inaudible.

"Wha' you say?" Ivan asked. Ras Peter turned a gentle ironic smile on him and intoned louder: " 'Ow sweet an' pleasant it is for brothahs to dwell together in unity.' "

"Oh," said Ivan.

"It is as de precious ointment dat flowet' over de head an' into de beard, *Selah.*" He nodded and smiled. "Welcome, kindred."

Ivan was embarrassed. "Well—one heart, man," he said.

"Tell me somet'in'," Ras Pedro said, looking at him intently. "is Jose sen' you back?"

"No," Ivan said, surprised. "No one sen' I nowhere, y'know. Is jus' me wan' come back."

"Is Love breddah, come sit wid I an' smoke Jah blessed herb too."

They sat and smoked in silence, but Ivan felt that in some subtle way the atmosphere had changed. The silence between them was easier. Ras Peter handled the herb with meticulous and respectful care. He passed the *chalice* with a ritual formality that reminded Ivan strangely of Maas' Nattie. The smoke was resinous, rich-tasting and very strong, lifting him swiftly to a region where thoughts floated lazily like clouds, to be carved into strange shapes and patterns as by a sharp, lucid blade of light. Across the table, as if at a distance, the tangled pillars of hair framed the dread-man's face in serpentine frenzy, making sharp contrast with its rather delicate features and sorrowful calm. Suddenly Ivan's recent blows and present problem seemed less urgent, in fact almost comic. Ras Peter, across the table, seemed lost in sorrowful reflections of his own. He seemed, Ivan thought dreamily, to have the entire Bible in his head, and to take a peculiar comfort in its doleful verse which he kept intoning to himself with a hypnotic monotony.

"Even today," Ras Peter said, "is I complaint bittah. . . . I stroke is heavier that I groaning, yeah." Nodding his shaggy head, he seemed to be contemplating the words behind his half-closed eyes. Then abruptly he stood, indicating with a nod that Ivan should follow. "De firs' born," he said.

Looking into the bedroom, Ivan had the illusion that he was much too high and seeing double and across time. A diminuitive, younger version of the Dreadman lay there, sleeping but betraying by his labored breathing and the fever shine on the taut skin of his face that all was not well in him. Ivan watched the Rastaman looking at his son with eyes that glowed with pride and fear. His lips were moving again, as though by strewing incantations into the still air around the boy, he could hold off whatever it was that he feared.

"Dey dat sowet' iniquity an' ploughet' wickedness, reapet' de same," he promised, "an' 'hosoever digget' a pit, shall fall derein."

They returned to the other room. From time to time Ras Peter arose and wiped the sweat off the boy. At other times he merely stood, with worried eyes and lips moving soundlessly, looking down on the sleeping face that mirrored so exactly the features of his own.

Ivan found himself talking, at first to distract Ras Peter. But somehow he kept seeing Elsa's face and talking about how she had lifted him out of the madness and pain. . . . By the time the sun came up it was all settled.

DAUGHTAH VERSHANN

"Lawd Ivan man, cho! You can' done man? Forget dat, nuh? Ignorance is not sin after all y'know." Elsa's voice was pitched to a low whisper but her exasperation was evident.

Ivan's expression was a parody of insult and outrage. He placed the palms of his hands on the top of his head in an exaggerated gesture of female distress. His voice was shrill and distraught: "But Ivan you must be *mad*. How you coulda go *expeck me* fe do such a t'ing. Lawd, Ivan madoo . . . Me's a *true Christian*—you coulden expeck me fe go mix meself up wid all like dem? So . . . is dis me leave Preacha house fe come see? Lawd Jesas."

"Hush your damn mout'," she hissed. "You want dem hear you? I'da jus' dead if dem hear you."

If Ras Peter and Man-I, asleep in the adjoining rooms, were ever to hear how ignorant and foolish she had been, shame would probably kill her. And she wouldn't be able to blame them for being hurt. That's one more thing she had to thank Preacha for. In his house Ras Tafarians were the ungodly, the very servants of the anti-Christ, deniers of God, spreaders of heresy. They were worse even than obeah men and balmyard cultists, for their doctrinal error and spiritual degradation was aggressive, willful, and defiant. Their hostility to decent society and devotion to ganja compounded their perversity and added to it the real possibility of madness. As with everything else Preacher said, she had accepted that too, unquestioningly.

Imagine doh, eh? What a t'ing like ignorance? It was hard to believe she had ever held those views. Look how the solemn-faced little bwai Prince Man-I tek to her—it touch her heartstring dem, the way 'im perk up an' seem to recover strength since she started looking after him.

Ras Petah see it too, an' you could tell 'im grateful. 'Im show it in every way. To think how she did 'fraid for Rasta an' scorn dem. Now, she couldn't wait for evening to come, when Ras Petah stayed in the house reading Jah-word and reasoning with her an' the bwai in that deep slow voice of his. An never had she detected anything more than a brotherly love an' respect in him. Not in his voice, not in his eyes, not in his manner. Is a good t'ing too, cause it look like nearly every night Ivan 'im find someplace to go. Most of the time him say 'im gone to moving picture show, but plenty morning rooster crowing long time before she hear the Honda pull into the yard. Funny doh, it didn't really trouble her much when he stayed out. She wasn't sure why—it seem like it should vex her more for she really love 'im. She guessed she always would an' she knew he had deep feelings for her too. But her bwai, that was somethin' else. Little Man-I needed her, and because of that, so did the father. She felt something in herself open up before that need, blossom and flourish. Preacha woulda dead, she sometimes laughed, to see me livin' not wid jus' one man but wid t'ree—an' two a dem is Dreadlocks.

The cramped tenement room was a bad memory: the hot eyes and moist looks of the fat landlord, the rummy voices of the girl next door an' her visitors; the hot futile pilgrimages looking for a day's work, door to door—all that was behind her. Now she had for the first time in her life what she could call a family and rich contentment in a life she could never have imagined. An' look how I never even want come at firs'?

In the beginning she had thought that Ivan was helping Peter with his fishing canoe, but it soon became clear that something else was going on. Now she knew it was ganja money that paid the rent on the little house she presided over with such satisfaction. And bought the tonics, special foods, and medicine that the boy had to have. Once already, Man-I, failing fast and needing blood transfusions, had to be rushed to the hospital. If it weren't for the ganja money what kind of life would he have? Painful and probably short—she didn't even want to think about it.

Once she would have been deeply troubled at the thought that Ivan made his living outside the law—some would say as a criminal. And with ganja too, "the devil's weed," as the members of the Tabernacle maintained. Yes, but that was before the tenement and the record and the footsore days under the scorching sun, begging work from rich women taking their ease on their verandahs and looking at her like she was a thief or worse. And maybe too it was because of Ras Peter. There was just something about him that she trusted. He would not, could not she felt, do anything to harm his people. He said that the herb was something Jah gave to the black man to comfort him in his period of oppression. It was, he said, the only good thing that black man had that white man didn't try to take for himself—an' now they were starting to turn their greedy gaze in that direction too. Not that she had the same feeling about all of them. The tall black one dem call Jose for example . . . Something about him her spirit didn't tek to—too boasie. Something about him definitely troubled her. Between him and Ras Peter, Ivan was in the middle. She wished he didn't seem to style himself after the one Jose so much. That, and the police, was all that bothered her about the trade. Whenever she see a police, now, her heart jumped and she felt guilty.

If it were a question of plenty money and big living, maybe she'd feel sinful. But it was nothing like that. In fact after the rent and house money and medicine, and the payments on the Honda that Peter and Ivan had paid down on, hardly anything leave. Ivan wouldn't save at all, and maybe he didn't need all them flashy star-bwai clothes that him like so much—following Jose again, she felt. Not that him didn't look good when him dress himself up. But that was the only little extravagance and, as Ras Peter said, "De breddah young, daughtah, 'im boun' to want test de world. Being 'im young an' 'im spirit *hot*, Babylon de Great look good to 'im. Mek 'im run 'im course, 'im will soon settle, daughtah." He looked at her and smiled slyly. "Maybe if you give him all a son, 'im spirit will cool down."

All the same doh, forget the motor bike and the clothes, just to have roof over head and food a belly was not too common in shantytown. She felt very lucky.

She heard someone stirring about the house. She slipped out of bed and went to start the fire.

"Petah. Mornin'. How Man-I."

"Praises daughtah, 'im sleep all night—nevah even need no medicine."

"Maybe, dis time him goin' alright. I pray so."

He flashed her a quick, grateful smile and nodded toward the room she had just left. "De breddah still asleep?"

"Yes, y'know—is little before day 'im come in," she said.

"No min' Elsa, is jus' yout' a drive 'im spirit—it nah go las' long. Before I get Man-I, an' hair-on unto Jah love, is same way I did stay. Is only fe a season."

"I was thinkin'," Elsa said, changing the subject. "If you bring some mesh wire I coulda fence off piece a de yard an' run some fowl, y'know. Man-I could have de eggs. . . ."

RHYGIN VERSHANN

Dah Jose deh, look like 'im know everyt'ing. 'Im sure did right 'bout de song. Yeah, 'im read it like a book. Fe 'bout two weeks, no more than dat, the song big up on radio, man. The firs' day on Parade when Ah hear it a play outta de record shop? My song an' my voice fullup the road, an' some small bwai dancing on the sidewalk an' point my way when dem see me. Yes, fe a short while you could hear it everywhere. People a sing it. It play on radio in de club dem. Den silence. Even the request shows where you could hear when de people call in dem reques'. No more reques'. Silence . . .

One night he and Bogart had walked all over West Kingston looking for a telephone that worked. They dialed the DJ who called himself "Numero Uno, the cool fool with the live jive," and asked for "De Harder Dey Come" that "irie irie tune by the baad yout' name Ivan." Even though the furry voice hastened to agree that it was a heavy, heavy song for which he had many requests and purred that they should keep listening for it was coming right up, neither the song or any of the requests came over the air. And the record suddenly was unavailable in the shops. But Hilton never bothered to remove it from the jukeboxes around town, so occasionally it came back like a mocking echo to haunt Ivan when he and Jose were making their rounds. It wasn't that he was brooding over it. Not at all, but coming up unexpectedly like that, it was like a tongue probing a broken tooth and refusing to stop despite the sharp stabs of pain it produced. He even played it himself sometimes.

But he rarely thought about that anymore because it was a boss hustle that Jose had fixed him up with. Elsa was happy taking care of Man-I and he was happier and freer than he had ever been. They were making it way better than most. So whenever he heard the song in a bar, it came as a surprise, something out of the distant past, more like the pain dem say people who had a hand or leg chop off sometimes felt in the missing limb. Nothing more than that. He was making it. The joke was on Hilton and Preacher and all who tried to down-press him.

Yeah, dem should see 'im now. Cruising along on Honda, charged with mellow mellow mountaintop, goat shit ganja, money in de pocket an' the open road before 'im. "Ah mekking it to blast," he hollered, swerving the bike back and forth across the road. "De bwai survivin' yes. Movin' up too."

An' his name was up deh too. People pointed him out, the yout' wid the bad song dat Babylon suppress. A friend of Bad Jose an' the man whe' slice up Longah like ham. Not a yout' to fuck wid at all. Always dress soft soft and wid money in his pocket. Even if Jose had carried him down for his money that first night, and he was by no means certain that he had, he'd made it up—completely.

Behind him he had a crocus bag of good herb. At least he thought it was good but he was anxious to hear what Pedro said. None of the traders had Pedro's feel for good weed. He could look at the color, smell it, roll it between his fingers and taste it, then tell you where it grow, how long it cure, whether it reap too early or too late and predict exactly how it would smoke and how it should be cut. That's why they did so well. Serious smokers, and who in shantytown wasn't a serious smoker, knew that if Ras Pedro chose and cut herb the quality would not vary. "Pedro nah sell no bush."

The Water Works was up ahead. That was where the motorcycle cop usually hung out. On the first run, the sight of the cop had petrified him. He still wasn't too easy about sailing past a Babylon with a crocus bag of herb like breadfruit going to market. But Pedro hadn't blinked.

"Raas Pedro man, you no see de Babylon up ahead?"

"Relax man, enjoy de ride," Pedro drawled with amusement in his voice.

"But, 'im no mus' stop we, breddah?"

"De guilty fleet' where no man pursuet'." Pedro laughed and waved to the officer.

"Wait, 'im in de organizashan?"

"Ask me no question, I tell you no lie," Pedro explained. "All you wan' know is say if 'im not dere, or if him no wave back, den is trouble."

"Wha' kind a trouble?"

"Army road block or somet'in' so. In dat case you either tek back road, turn back, or else hide de weed ina canefield. Only t'ing . . . you ha' fe mark de place good where you hide it. One mornin' me an' de queen hide a whole bag. *Bwai*, total loss you know. I mus' be search every canefield from Caymanas to town. Up to today no *collie* don't fin'."

But it still made him uneasy. Suppose a different Babylon was there? One that didn't groun' with the plan? He waved and the cop smiled and waved a casual salute. It was part of the excitement all the same. So far they hadn't even come close to being stopped. Still, he remembered Pedro's baby's mother and his knowledge of the many things that could go wrong sharpened his appetite for the life.

Ras Pedro recognized that and cautioned Ivan constantly about taking needless risks. He himself seemed almost incapable of anger and there seemed to be no challenge that could move him to recklessness. "Leff it," he was always saying. "Walk away from it, breddah. For like a dog returneth to 'is vomit, so returnet' a fool to 'is folly. A wise man fearet' and departet' from angah; but de heart of de fool *rageth*." For some reason, the traders listened to him with a respect that was almost loving. They accepted his rebukes and instruction with a grace that they showed to no one else, not even Jose. Arrogant and sharp tongued as he was, even Jose seemed to walk gently around the ascetic Dreadlocks with the gentle voice.

Ivan turned into the yard and revved the engine. Elsa and Man-I came running from behind the house. "What you bring fe us," she called.

"Us?" he said. "Who name us? Dis is fe Pedro and dis is fe Man-I, if 'im tek 'im medicine like a good bwai. What I have fe Elsa, have to wait 'til later."

"Cho, stop you rudeness, Ivan."

"Bwai, you min' Miss Elsa today?" he asked sternly. The boy nodded solemnly, the broke into that sweet, slow smile that made him look so much like his father. "An' you tek you medicine?"

"Even doh it bittah and burnet' de tongue," Man-I intoned seriously, in such perfect imitation of his father that they all laughed as Ivan gave him the candy.

Pedro arrived on the scene walking slowly and attempting to hide his relief behind an impassive face. "So—you reach. Praises. An' what you bring fe I? Ah hope you don't tek we money buy no bush, y' know."

"Bush jah? Nutten name so. Dis weed prime!" Ivan boasted.

"Well we no will see? Man-I, go get daddy cuttin' knife." He opened the bag and dug his hand into the herb, feeling the leaf. "Hmm," he muttered as though thinking aloud, "it look like we have fe go sell dis bush to de tourist dem."

Ivan hoped he was joking, but his look was very grave as he sniffed a bud. He crumbled it and tasted a fragment. Nothing showed on his face. Scowling either with concentration or distress, he extracted a seed, examined its size, fullness and color before cracking it between his teeth. His expression grew downright mournful.

"So . . . is dis me partner tek we money buy?" he mused, shaking his head as he looked into the bag.

"Dis a prime herb," Ivan insisted. "Good price too. I tes' some before I mek de purchase. Wha' wrong wid it?" he finished anxiously.

Ras Pedro didn't answer. He seized the knife and looked up slowly. The melancholy expression turned into a wide smile. "You hear I-man say anyt'ing wrong wid it?" He laughed.

Pedro sorted and spread the weed, skillfully mixing buds and leaves as he cut. Ivan wrapped the piles into little brown cones. These were to be distributed to the bars, clubs, and cafés in their area, they would collect last week's receipts as they did so. As usual Pedro took Jose's cut off the top. Then he took out the money for next week's buy and slipped it into the hollow handle of the bike. The balance he split evenly.

"Not bad," he said, "not bad at all."

"Hey Pedro?"

"Haile up, man."

"All de other traders, dem pay Jose dat much?"

"Some pay more still y'know."

"Why Jose not rich den?"

"Wait, you no understan' how dis t'ing go? Dis money no stop wid Jose, y'know."

"So who it go to?"

"Why you askin' so much question, man? Don't we meking it arright?"

"Sure, y'know, but . . ."

"But res' it den." His voice was curt.

"But," Ivan persisted. "I figah Babylon mus' get some, but still . . ."

"Look breddah, I know nutten an' Ah don't *wan'* know more dan nutten. In fack you coulden pay I fe know more. An' if you want dis partnership to continue doan ask me no damn question."

Ivan was surprised and hurt at his tone. Ras Pedro never raised his voice or swore, and always seemed careful of others' feelings. "Arright," Ivan mumbled sullenly.

"Well, mek we go sample you good herb," Pedro said in a more conciliatory tone.

The Lone Star café and lounge was where Jose made his weekly collections. All the traders passed through. The line of new Hondas outside was a dead giveaway, if anyone cared. These machines were the badge of the trade and a sign of the prosperity of this elite group of grass-roots entrepreneurs. In the back of the café there was a private room to which only traders were admitted. When they entered there were only three men there: Sidney, a wizened little fellow with very shifty eyes, a big, raucous youth called Midnight Cowboy, and his partner, Duffus.

They greeted Ras Pedro warmly, Ivan politely, but with reserve. Ras Pedro bared his head, unleashing his spectacular locks, before handling the herb. As he loaded a bamboo water pipe he explained "Is me partner choice dis, brederin. So we welcome you opinion still." He took a few deep pulls to get the fire going and said, "An' Jah said, 'behold de earth bring fort' *grass*, an' I have given dee every herb bearing seed, which is on de face of the eart'."

"Selah," the group chorused.

" 'Ow sweet an' pleasant it is for brederin to dwell together in unity."

"It is as de precious ointment," the men replied, "dat floweth over de locks an' into de beard."

Ivan was warmed by their judicious praise of his blend as the chalice went around. Soon they were all floating along in a kind of warm camaraderie and the room was funky with smoke. Midnight Cowboy, who was sitting next to Ivan, kept looking at him speculatively.

"Speak, breddahman," Ivan invited.

"Is you dem call Rhygin?"

"Truly."

"So, you new to dis den."

"In a way."

"You need some protection den."

"Like what?"

Midnight Cowboy sat up and reached into his bag. He came out with a cloth wrapped bundle which he slowly and reverently unwrapped. "Like dis," he said softly.

Ivan felt his breath catch in his throat.

"Is a match pair," Midnight Cowboy whispered. "T'irty-eight caliber."

The pistols lay on a soft cloth like an offering on an altar, gleaming in the half-light. The handles were of creamy, elaborately embossed mother-of-pearl, wickedly curved. The metal seemed to glow with blue life. Ivan swallowed and touched them tentatively. The sight of the guns uncovered a need that he had not previously recognized.

"Go on Rhygin," Cowboy urged. "Feel de balance, man. Dese can't miss y'know."

"Ah so?" Ivan muttered, hefting them. "Me no even sure dem work."

"Jus' doan pull de trigger," Cowboy said. Someone laughed.

What a way dem jus' fit into me han' dem, Ivan thought. Comfortably as though some distant gunsmith had measured them to his grip. They filled his hands, seemed to complete them as though his hands had been empty, unfilled before they came into them.

" 'Ow much," he asked out of a suddenly very dry mouth.

"Fifty dollars fe de pair—wid bullets."

"Expensive," Ivan muttered. But how could they not be? Such masterpieces.

"Cheaper dan you life," Cowboy murmured. Duffus laughed assent.

"What you t'ink Pedro?" Ivan appealed.

"Who you out to kill, me breddah?" Pedro asked. "You truly out to shed man blood?"

"Nobody. I doan out to kill anyone," Ivan said, a little defensive and half ashamed of the desire that was making him dizzy.

"Den leff it. Leff it, Ivan. Wisdom is bettah dan weapons an' war," Pedro said. "But one fool destroyet' a city," he finished, glaring at Midnight Cowboy.

"Hey breddah man—dem cheaper dan you life," Cowboy repeated.

Ivan hefted the guns again, feeling the balance and marveling again at the natural, steady way they nestled into his grip. He held them together and turned his wrists over to see the play of light on the barrels. He twirled them backward western style by the trigger guards, pleased at the easy graceful way they settled back against the heel of his hand.

"Rahtid," Cowboy breathed. "Gunslingah to raas. Is a starbwai dis!"

"Ignorance. Brute force an' ignorance," Ras Pedro snapped.

Carefully, reluctantly, Ivan replaced the weapons on their cloth. He couldn't take his gaze away from the hypnotic shimmer of the metal.

Midnight Cowboy let them lay there. "Dem really fit you," he said. "Nevah see a pair of gun fit a man so."

"Put dem up," Pedro said. "Dem t'ing deh shouldn't even bring aroun' Jah holy herb."

Cowboy shook his head wonderingly. "Dem really fit 'im," he said again.

"Ivan, envy you not de oppressah," Ras Pedro advised sternly, "an' follow not in any of 'is ways. Dat a Babylon business, brute force an' destrucshan. Come on y'hear, sah." He stood up suddenly. "You coming, Ivan?"

"Dem cheaper dan you life," Midnight Cowboy said.

They were halfway home before Pedro spoke, a thoughtful, sad note in his voice. "Tell me somet'ing," he said. "You really did wan' buy dem?"

"Well," Ivan evaded, "kinda, I doan know—maybe." But he knew he was lying. How could he explain to Ras Pedro the fierce desire that he had felt when he saw them. The sense of finding something he was meant to find. They maintained an uncomfortable silence the rest of the way.

16

Double Back

He dat increaset' knowledge, increaset' sorrow.
—Ras Petah

"Is now . . . a now yes." The words buzzed around in his head and
he nodded in emphasis. He had the feeling. "Yes, now a de time."
It was exactly the time, he felt that very strongly. Recently, the
idea had been edging its unbidden way into his consciousness. He
hadn't received it warmly at first. Instead, in a sporadic and aimless way, he had made some preparations without acknowledging
what they really were. Then, before day this morning, he sat up in
bed and knew that it was time. He left the bed and set out, just so.

Well, not quite just so—in his collie bag was the evidence of
intent: a blue satin cowboy shirt identical to the one on his back,
a pair of mirrored aviator shades of the kind they called "cool-
too-bad" or simply "McAtahs," after the American general, a
woman's wrist watch, bright gold with (so Cowboy swore) thirty-
six jewels, hot off the wharf and worth every cent of the fifteen
dollars he'd asked. And a book, for Maas' Nattie, *The Philosophy
and Opinions of Marcus Garvey*, which Ivan had gotten from a
customer; a "very conscious" young breddah from the university.
The one thing he had forgotten was the last copy of the record.
And he had been saving it for this trip too. . . .

So in an offhand way he had been planning it, all but the date.
That final step he had avoided until this morning when he sat up
in the bed and listened to the night sounds. And now the sun had
risen and here he was, halfway up Mount Diablo.

The engine snarled and spat and the tires clawed their way up
the steep road. The air was crisp and, as soon as the mists burned
away, would be very clear. The rains were just over, the renewed
foliage bright and shiny. The freshly scrubbed countryside sparkled in the early morning sun. He was very high and not from
ganja. The wind in his face brought that rich damp-earth-after-

rain smell that reminded him so forcefully of his grandmother's yam ground on the valley floor. Now, after all the elapsed time, all the evasions and postponements, his sudden eagerness to be there made him tremble with an impatient yearning that made him even higher.

It was an excitement that was hard to control. He kept speeding up dangerously. His impulse was to shout into the valley just to hear the echoes come back, "Rhygin a go home to raas. Raas claat to raas, de bwai a go hoooome." The sunlight on the lush leaves was almost too intense. As if under ganja, he saw the foliage vibrating in sharp rich shades of greens, blues, and even purples. It made him drunk. Energy rose in him. He had money in his pocket and was riding a new bike. Behind him he had gifts, on his back fine clothes. He was a genuine recording artist even though he had forgotten the proof. He saw it clearly in his mind. Maas' Nattie's house, the café. Maybe Dudus would be working on his father's boat in the cove and they could go out to the reefs. *Aiie*, but the district would talk about the homecoming for a long time. Maybe he could spend a few days, come down the big river beneath the silent green mountains again.

Reckless with excitement, he hitched his rear backward and stretched for the handlebars so that he lay flat over the gas tank. He gunned the engine and the Honda leapt forward, throwing itself toward a steep curve. Then a loud, peremptory blast drowned out the whine of his engine. Jesas, if is evah Coolie Man, Ah mus' dead, he thought, and searched the narrow road for some margin. Inside, a voice said, go inside. He jerked the handlebars, aiming the front wheel for the narrow strip of grass between the asphalt and the mountainside. Belching greasy black smoke and skittering gravel from beneath its wheels the truck brushed by with a rush of air as Ivan struggled to control the bike.

"If you born to heng, you can' drown," he said rejoicing, and tried to ride slower. He thought he had felt the side of the truck brush his shoulder. He knew he had to calm down and take it easy. What, after all, was the hurry now? Nothing ever changed much in the district and who was expecting him? Slow down, man. Enjoy de ride. Discover how sweet an' pleasant is dy fathers' lan'. The voice in his head sounded like Ras Pedro's. The road ran along a ridge beside a deep valley, narrow with steep, densely wooded sides. There was a car stopped by the roadside and a man was taking pictures. Ivan stopped too and looked down. He couldn't see the bottom of the ravine. Instead there was a sluggish lake of viscous ooze; some oily substance that was pale red, an unnatural chemical-looking color, seemed to be slowly crawling up the sides of the valley.

Ivan thought he was hallucinating. But it was real enough. A discordant, unnatural presence, stark against the green hillsides.

"You know is what, sah?" Ivan asked the man.

"Yes, I know is what."

Ivan waited. The man paid no further attention to him. "Please sah, if you could tell me?" He asked humbly, trying to hide his annoyance.

"Progress," the man said, not looking at him. "Industrial waste—from de bauxite plant." The way the man grunted his answers discouraged further questions.

Ivan went on thoughtfully. Whenever possible he glanced into the valley. The deadly stream followed the road. He wondered how far it stretched, this stream of blood from the heart of his country. Finally he stopped and smoked a spliff, staring down at the oily, red surface and wondering what the fuck it really was and what it meant.

In what seemed like a very short time he reached the mountaintop. The same vast plain stretched before him, bringing sharply back the memory of that other time he had seen it from Coolie Man's bus. Now the scars of raw red earth seemed ominous. The journey that had seemed interminable then, now seemed so short. He couldn't be much more than an hour out of Blue Bay. All this time he hadn't been so far away—except in his mind? That was hard to believe. But the prospect of home excited him again. Long suppressed memories streamed back without order or control. Faces, places, sounds, people's voices, smells, all in crazy intoxicating sequences: the hill in front of Miss Mando's house, Mad Izaac's tree bending in the moonlight, Miss Ida's golden toothed smile, Mirriam's maroon eyes, the coral reef—all clear and exactly as he knew them.

He had been on the coast road for some time now and felt that he must be getting close to the turnoff into the hills. First, he'd go give Maas' Nattie the book and sit with him. Now that *he* had some stories to tell. From the old man he'd find out about Dudus and Mirriam. Then he'd go find Dudus, most likely on the beach. After that he didn't know. . . .

"Hol' down! But . . . dat a Blue Bay town roun' de corner? Dat can' right. How me coulda miss de turnoff? Not possible, man. But it was the town. Den, right yah is where de fishin' beach is.

Where dah wall deh come from, an' all dem big rooftop? No, dat suppose to be de fishing beach. Maybe is not Blue Bay. I doan reach yet, dis mus' another town? Bwai, is coulden laas' I laas? See a gate coming up. Whe' de sign say?

Private Property
SUNSET COVE CONDOMINIUMS
soliciting forbidden

The gate was closed but he could see a white gravel driveway, mowed lawns and whitewashed villas behind hedges of flowering shrubs. His disorientation was complete. Nothing fit into his memory. Dat a de fisherman dem beach. Wha' kin' a raas private? he thought. He was both angry and frightened, and still not really sure he was in the right town. He kept going slowly, looking around trying to recognize something and to collect his scattered thoughts. He was quite dazed. Alright, he'd go to the café. That was around the next corner. Already he could catch glimpses of the trunks of the coconut trees. Alright, he'd find people he knew there. They would explain what that wall meant. He speeded up and turned the corner.

The little café was still nestled in the grove of tall trees on the narrow headland. Raas. Wha' happen to de tree dem—an' de beach who pave it? *Bumbo!* It was as if a huge machete from the sky had taken the tops of the trees, leaving the slender trunks standing like futile, mocking sentinels. The café was unchanged except that where there had been sandy beach there was now a tiled floor enclosed by a low wall. In this area, a group of white people reclined in long chairs. They had tall glasses at their elbows, wore swimsuits, and were turning red in the sun. He sat staring slack-jawed and uncomprehending at the scene. The only black face he saw belonged to a white jacketed waiter who emerged from the café with a tray. Alright, he'd go ask for Miss Ida. But somehow he knew he wouldn't find her there.

Heads turned toward the sound of the bike. The waiter nodded his head vigorously at something the man he was serving said, and went inside. He emerged on the road side of the café and waited as Ivan rode up. He seemed about Ivan's age but Ivan didn't recognize him, and though their eyes locked the waiter made no sign of greeting. Ivan slowly approached the building and then stopped.

"Whaddya say, fellah," the waiter said, running his words together and speaking through his nose. "This is a private club, main."

It was the "main" that did it. Ivan realized that the nasal, barely comprehensible sound coming at him was the waiter's version of a yankee accent—his master's voice, so to speak.

"Whe' you jus' say?" Ivan demanded.

"Private club fellah, members only, you dig?"

"Ah diig." Ivan drawled and sat looking at the youth with rising anger. "Tell me somet'ing, you know a lady name Miss Ida?"

"Ida? Nope, Dadio. Sure don't." The waiter turned away, "Ah got 'ta make it main, you dig?"

"Dig, me raas," Ivan said. "Have manners bwai, I talking to you."

Something in the tone of his voice stopped the waiter. "What else you want?" he asked ungraciously.

"Daas bettah, maastah. You know a bwai name Dudus?" The waiter shook his head. "Dudus Thomas. 'Im daddy name Maas' Burt."

"Oh, you mean Butch?' Im is de waiter here at night."

"Whe' 'im live?"

"Blue Bay."

"Where in Blue Bay?"

"Nex' door to Public Works." The waiter started back into the building.

Ivan caught him in the doorway. He snatched him by the collar and swung him around, jamming him against the wall and staring into his startled eyes. "You raas, you! Is right yah me born an' grow, y' know. Talk 'bout private club? You know me?"

The boy shook his head vigorously.

Ivan jerked him for emphasis. "No, you doan know me a raas. Is you fucken life you tek ina you han', y' know, you little raas hole, you. Me wi' cut up you blood claat an' pay fe it, y'know. Next time a breddah ask you question you will have some manners, eh?"

He jerked him again. The boy nodded. "A de fucken' white man work you love so—bettah dan you life?" The boy shook his head no, and Ivan pushed him away.

He rode out slowly, his rage gradually turning to confusion and sadness. He knew that, as annoying as the waiter's faastiness had been, something far more had set him off. With his mind racing, he turned toward the town. Why had he not expected changes? But he had. He'd expected people to be older. Some dead, children grown up . . . But not this. Who coulda expec' dis?

When he found the house next door to the Public Works he

stopped and observed it for a long time. He had half decided to turn away, when the door opened and a stocky young man wearing black trousers and a white shirt emerged. He recognized Dudus-Butch immediately.

"Ah excuse—you seem like you lookin' somebody?" Dudus asked politely.

"Is true," Ivan said.

"Is only me an' me family live here. Wha' dem name?"

"Somebody I used to know," Ivan said.

A puzzled frown crossed Dudus' face and he took a few tentative steps toward the bike. "Wait?" He squinted at Ivan and took a few more steps. "Oh me Gawd? Is can't? But . . . wait?" He kept advancing.

"Yes," Ivan drawled. "Is me yes, Ivan." He removed his glasses.

"To Gawd!" Dudus shouted. "Is really you!"

They ran together whooping and swearing. The noise brought a slender young woman carrying an infant to the door.

"Raas Dudus, how you fat so?"

"Good life, man. Jesas, look Ivan! Ivan to bumbo!" Dudus babbled.

"So you is de Ivan Ah hear so much 'bout?" the woman demanded.

The infant made Ivan laugh out loud. He was fat, brown, round-faced, freckled, and good humored. "Cho, Dudus is no way you coulda did deny dis one," he said.

"Ivan dis, Ivan dat. Ivan 'til Ah tired," the wife said, studying Ivan as if to see how he measured up to his notices.

"Aye, run go get some beer," Dudus told her.

"On me," Ivan said, reaching into his pocket.

"Not a raas," Dudus said.

"Come, I give you a ride go shop," Ivan said.

The bike was admired and exclaimed over. He took each one for a ride. Yes, they'd heard the record on the radio. Everyone had. They were waiting on the next one. Then Ivan dutifully admired the house, furniture, and the baby all over again. They drank beer and talked while Dora fixed a meal.

He learned that Maas' Nattie had died the same year he left. He was a little annoyed when Dudus at first couldn't remember who he meant. Miss Ida had sold the café to a white man and left. He wasn't sure where she had gone. Nor was he certain where the old man was buried, or what had happened to his land. He didn't regret the fishing. Working at the café was easier and cleaner and the money better. He glanced at his wife, then winked at Ivan and mouthed something. Ivan could only make out something about "white woman." Maas' Burt, he said, was still going strong, but he did no more fishing. Now he took tourists out to see the reef. He had a boy who dived down and chipped off pieces of coral which they dried and sold.

"You mean 'im a *dig* up de reef?" Ivan asked.

"Is not 'im one," Dudus said. "Is good money."

Ivan shook his head, remembering Maas' Burt holding the glass and laughing, puffing on his pipe and saying *It wonderful to raas, man.*"

"Mirriam married. Ha' nuff pickney too," Dudus volunteered. "Guess to who?" He had a mysterious grin on his face. Ivan couldn't guess.

" Black Raphael."

"You lie! You mean her cousin?"

"Same one, de one we used to call River King."

"How? But 'im never ha' nutten fe tek support wife an' pickney?"

"You no go a river yet?"

"No, y'know."

"Go look," Dudus said with the same mysterious air. "Progress, man. Den, Ivan, you doan notice all de development?"

"Ah see it."

"You mus' be t'ink," he said beaming, "dat a Kingston one got progress."

"No," Ivan said, "I guess not."

Suddenly he was very restless. He gave Butch the shirt and shades, and to a quite surprised and somewhat overwhelmed Dora, gave the gold watch. Promising to come back for dinner, he headed straight for the river, wondering apprehensively what form progress would take there. He hoped to catch a glimpse of Mirriam. But he was more intrigued by Dudus's mysterious manner. What possible transformation could have happened there? And how could it have transformed the brooding, solitary Raphael into a breadwinner? Maybe, if Raphael still grew that legendary mountain top ganja, they could hook up a business arrangement.

Nothing, it seemed, was as he remembered it. But the river? What could they possibly have done to the river? He couldn't think of anything, but from what he had seen so far, it wouldn't be anything good. And Dudus—no "Butch"—seemed so proud about it all. He hadn't been present, so it was all sudden to him. Maybe he didn't have any right . . . Raas, he still wanted it all back just like it had been. But is so life go all the same, nothing was fe ever.

The bridge was unchanged from that day he had jumped off it. Didn't seem so high—but it was still a hell of a jump, especially fe a small-small pickney. And the river was just as green, mysterious and unhurried as it rolled down between the mountains. The only change was the little white house across the street near the beach. But that wasn't much. The mountains were just as tall, majestic, and beautiful as he remembered. Teng' gawd, at last a point of contact, something to say that it had not all been dreams and visions.

Ivan sat on the bridge, lifted his eyes and spirit up to the hills, allowed his memories free rein, and felt a certain peace steal over him. He couldn't see them, but he heard singing coming from around a bend in the river and knew that women were washing their clothes there. It was easy and pleasant to imagine that Miss' Mando and Mirriam were among them.

The sun had begun its dip toward the sea, washing the river valley and surrounding hills in the familiar reddish-gold radiance. A poignant silence, only intensified by the distant singing, evoked his childhood with such immediacy that he wanted to weep, not from anger or grief, or even pain so much, but because of the iron tyranny of time. He had gone from what he now could see was the thoughtless expectation that everything would be exactly as he had kept it preserved in memory, to the humble gratitude that something, one thing, was as it used to be. There were even rafts yet, gliding their unhurried way to the sea. Two, no three, had rounded the distant bend, dark specks against the green, imperceptibly growing larger. They were still too distant for him to make out details but their shapes seemed in some subtle way different, bulkier than he remembered, higher too. Ivan looked at the current into which he had jumped so recklessly, so long ago. He doubted he would do it now. But there was something reassuring, almost hypnotic about the silently swirling eddies.

When he looked up the rafts were much closer. They *were* more substantial and heavily loaded. No not a load, those were people. Raphael bringing his family for a Sunday ride down the river he held in such personal reverence? Then one of those heads would be Mirriam, who might look up and see him. Should he move? Would she recognize him? An idea struck him and filled him with shock and ambivalence. He would look carefully at the oldest child. . . . That day on the river before he had found Miss Mando's corpse . . . Could that explain the sudden marriage? His palms began to sweat.

Soon he was able to see that, with the exception of the rafts-men, the people were all white or, more truthfully, a roseate pink. Wearing bright colored, sporty clothes, they had cameras slung from their necks and their voices, carrying over the water, reached him in snatches as the wind allowed. It was a jarring sound that splintered the silence and his mood. These people sat on raised platforms while behind them the black guides bent sweating backs to their poles. If Johnny Weissmuller had sud-denly dropped whooping out of one of the overhanging trees and grappled with an alligator in the water, it wouldn't have surprised him.

The river brought them to him. They approached the bridge not forty feet from where he sat. He studied them silently, with-out returning the jovial hails from a fat couple sprawled on the raised seat. He was certain that the man behind them steering the raft was Raphael. Those gargantuan, rippling shoulders of such surpassing blackness could belong to no one else. Just as they were passing beneath him, the fat woman leaned back and said some-thing to the raftsman. Ivan saw her hand brush casually over his leg as she spoke. But it was not an intimate or sexual gesture, there was something absentminded, offhand about it, reminding him of the way one stroked a favorite horse. The raftsman leaned down and peered into her face as if trying to understand. She laughed and only then did the man's face collapse into a great simpering grin. He nodded vigorously and his white teeth flashed in the sunlight. Then, still grinning, he retreated to the end of the raft, flexed his muscles, and struck a pose. It seemed practiced. His powerful muscles bunched and stood out but the posture was distorted, one of servility, the power leashed, controlled, dis-played, and his face was a mask of ingratiating, slightly stupid amiability.

"Beautiful," the woman said, laughing, and aimed her camera. Then the current swept them under the bridge.

So the change was not in the river. What had happed to the solitary, reserved giant they had called River King, and of what lineage and family was the grinning buffoon who had his place? *Ayeh—win or lose I'm gonna get my share . . . what's mine.*

No wonder he had missed the turnoff on his way in: it seemed no more than a stony track steep and rutted, running up the gut of the mountain. The bike bucked and twisted beneath him. Nothing was familiar. Even the shapes of trees, once so intimately known to him, had changed. He had been sure that he'd recognize every tree and every turn. Now he had to remind himself: Granny house is four mile, jus' a chain or two after the first stan'pipe. Look for a big hog plum tree. But he was almost past the stand-pipe before he recognized it. Now fe the hog plum tree where he used to shoot so many pecharies. No, not that one—a big big one. Wait, a it yes, but how it so small—an' whe' happen to the path. Bush-bush full up everywhere. But . . . dis coulden the right place after all? Right down dere should be the tin roof. You mean say bush-bush grow up, cover it?

He looked in vain for some landmark by which to orient himself, then panicking, thrust himself blindly into the shrubbery in the direction in which memory told him the homestead lay. Vines tangled his feet and slapped his face. Thorns raked his skin and hooked his clothes. He made slow, sweaty progress. He tried looking over the dense thickets for the breadfruit tree that shaded his people's graves. In vain. Whe' de kitchen? The pig sty? De coffee patch? The goat pen? *Lawd Jesas, a whe' me deh?*

In great agitation and bleeding from countless scratches, he retraced his steps to the road. He was breathing hard and felt hot and sticky with sweat. The scratches itched. He wiped the sweat from his eyes and climbed the hog plum tree. The little basin was unbroken bush. But it was the place, for he recognized the view of the valley and the opposite hill. There, he could see roofs shining through the trees, the smoke of cooking fires. People still lived there. There was mad Izaac's tree. This was the place. . . . Desolation.

He saw the breadfruit tree, but the stone wall was invisible. No, the little plateau where the house, kitchen, animal pens, fruit trees had once stood had been reclaimed by vegetation. All signs of human presence, industry, organization, order, were gone without visible trace, and he would have needed a machete to hack his way to the graves. There was no evidence of the passage of his generations, the ancestors whose intelligence, industry and skill had created a self-sufficient homestead there. None—at all . . .

Jesas Chris' Almighty Gawd . . . Me no believe dis. . . . Me *can'* believe dis. . . . He shook his head dazedly. . . . *Nutten,* not a gawd t'ing no lef'. *Nutten* no deh yah now, me can' even get down deh. Lawd Jesas, me people dem . . . Me people dem. Me people dem! Lawd Jesas, me *people*.

He sat under the tree numbly. The smell of its rotting fruit filled his nose and his head was full of the humming of the flies that buzzed around the sweetness. It was not easy to come to grips with the shock and desolation he felt. Ah shoulda did stay. Ah shoulda did stay an' tek care of de place, he thought. The worst insult that people had was the sneering "Cho, you no come from nowhe'." For the first time he was feeling what that really meant. Now he realized just how important this sense of place was to his most fundamental sense of himself. He had the same urge that he had had the day his grandmother died, to put his hands on his head and bawl and holler. He wanted to go get a machete, to cut a path to the graves and clear the bush away. But . . . what de raas is de use . . . What's de fucken use? He felt empty, and frightened, futile, miserable, and very alone. He would never, he swore, come back ever.

Mechanically, like a sleepwalker, he stumbled over to the bike and started it up. Since Ah deh yah, he thought, me might as cheap go check 'pon Maas' Nattie place. . . . Might as well jus' done wid everyt'ing one time.

He rode over the narrow ribbon of rock that he had galloped over behind the old man that night so long ago. He passed groups of people, families dressed for church and, as he guessed, bound for the river for a baptism. They looked at him with mannered curiosity and greeted him with the reserved politeness of the hills. He knew that if he stopped and identified himself they would fall on him, exclaim loudly over his return, and press small gifts of produce on him. That had indeed been part of his vision when he set out, but now he returned the greetings curtly, dreading those squinting expressions of semirecognition and the words, "Wait, but don't you is a Martin?" So he averted his face and kept going.

He recognized Maas' Nattie's gate and slowed. Voices came over the wall so he rode past and walked back, hoping to look down into the yard without being seen. He wanted, if possible, to avoid any more shocks. At first he saw no one. A pair of goats were tethered to a tree. The brilliantly colored house still stood. The barbecue was cracked and tufts of grass sprouted from the cracks. The shrubs and fruit trees were still there, though not as well-tended as he remembered, and the grass was high. But clearly people still lived there. A hammock, he noticed, hung between two guava trees and was occupied. All he could see of the person was a mane of long, sun-streaked hair. A woman? A *white* woman in Maas' Nattie's house? *Bumbo!* Raas, me min' mash up. Ah mad to raas. White people no live all like hereso. Dem stay a hotel an' dem big house over de city. What is dis I live to see?

He blinked his eyes but the hair still swung down, brushing the ground. Then the creature in the hammock spoke and he got a second shock, for the voice was clearly that of a man. The door opened and two more apparitions emerged. *"Bumbo,"* Ivan muttered, snatching off his glasses. *"Bumbo.* You mean to say dem have 'merican nyaman?" Because that was all they could be, white Dreadlocks. The man's hair hung around his shoulders in a tousled mop. He wore only jeans cut off above the knees and a full beard as unkempt as his hair. The woman with him was blond, very brown of skin, and wore nothing at all. Nutten a raas 'tall. He could see her streaked pubic hairs like a fluffy cloud at the base of her plump belly. The two people seemed happy, at least they were wearing wide, strangely rigid grins. The woman had a tin pail and the man a pipe which he handed to the figure in the hammock. The woman went over to the goats and squatted down in a most immodest way. The goats edged away. She seized the rope and hauled in the larger one. Then, setting the pail, she reached into the hairy underbelly in search, apparently, of udders.

"G'wan milk dah one deh nuh? Ah bet you?" Ivan muttered, and almost laughed aloud when her questing hand closed around the ram goat's balls.

"Dem say white people can do anyt'ing—milk him mek me see."

The woman swore and closed in on the other goat. He knew he had to be seeing visions. The collie he had smoked must be the baddes' weed ever grown on the island. But what could these creatures be? They had obviously been there for some time, for their skins were deep brown except for clusters of angry-looking red welts and inflamed pustules left by insects.

"Oh gross—what a bummer," said a clear girlish voice, and the woman snatched the pail away just as the nanny-goat squatted and let fly with a disdainful stream of piss. Clouds of smoke drifted up from the hammock and sniffing it, Ivan knew that he had before him, in the presence of these barefoot, naked, raggedy, insect-bitten and none too clean-looking apparitions, the only white Dreadlocks in the whole world. They seemed so charged that they could hardly move and the men giggled incessantly and spoke slowly and with great effort.

"I—am—so—fucked—up," one giggled.

"True wud," grunted Ivan. "Ah can' stan' it."

The men stood and started slowly and unsteadily toward the barbecue.

"Great," complained the woman. "Take the fucken pipe."

"So come on, already," one of the men said.

"Oh, all right." She got up and flounced after them. Her flat batti was a network of fiery red pimples. The men took off their shorts and the three lay on the warm barbecue, reminding Ivan of pig carcasses drying on a jerky rack.

Wait 'til sun go down! Mosquito goin' mek unu fart. Bwai, who a go believe dis doh? But, nutten coulden name duppi? Maas' Nathaniel Francis whe' you deh? You no see what a go on ina you place, sah? Mek I leff' dis place, y'hear. As he was passing the gate he noticed a sign. Now, what dat coulda mean? he wondered. WOODSTOCK, SOUTH?

He slammed the bike into curves at high speed on his way back to the city, riding as if demons were on his tail. Twice he was almost killed, but he didn't slow down. He gave himself over to the rhythm of the curves and slopes, the rush of wind, the dark roads, trying to empty his mind of thought. But a spirit of desolation and sorrow rode with him. The only other time he had made the trip it had seemed long. He had been leaving one country and going to another, so the length was appropriate. Now he saw to his sorrow that it was really quite short a journey. And, absolutely the same country.

He felt rootless and adrift in a world without rules or boundaries. "Ivanhoe Martin, you no come from nowhe'," he told himself bitterly, and knew the pain of losing something important, but unexamined and taken totally for granted, so that the first awareness of its importance came only with its loss. " 'E dat increaset' knowledge, increaset' sorrow." As Ras Pedro would say.

Instead of the joyous and triumphant homecoming of the mind, he had learned, abruptly and with no preparation, that he had no home to come to. *"G'way bwai, you no come from nowhe'."*

Ras Pedro and Elsa were sitting at the table with a Coptic Bible between them when he walked in. They looked up. Ras Pedro was the first to break the silence.

"Haile up breddah, one heart, man."

Elsa rose to meet him and stopped. "Ivan, somethin' happen? How you look like you see duppi so?"

"Maybe 'im see one, yes," Pedro said laughing.

"Ivan, where you bin, you hungry?"

Absently Ivan kissed her and started toward the bedroom. "Not hungry, only tired," he said.

"Den, is where you gone so long?"

"Ah doan go nowhe'—an' I wish to God Ah never go, too," he said and threw himself on the bed. She stood in the doorway and watched him, worry and apprehension on her face.

"Is arright," Pedro murmured gently. "You can leff 'im. De breddah get a blow, daughtah. Ah feel say 'im get a blow today—but 'im will arright."

"Den Ivan, what you eat since morning. Eat somet'ing, nuh?"

"Nuh hungry, only tired," he muttered, and remembered that "Butch" was expecting him for dinner.

Apparently he had been very tired for it was three days before he emerged from the bedroom.

"Yea," Ras Pedro said mournfully, "Ah feel me breddah get a blow."

17

Presshah Buil'

Walkin' down de road
Wid a pistol in you waist,
Johnny you too bad . . .

TRIBAL VERSHANN

Far, far back in his mind, lying dormant and unused but nevertheless very present and comforting, had been the notion that the
mountains and the river would always be there, unchanged and
waiting. Not that he had any plans to go back, except maybe for
an occasional visit to show off any success that might come his
way. And to feel the presence of his generations. To renew himself with the splendors of his childhood. Or else, at the other pole,
worn down and broken like Mad Izaac he could creep back and
lose himself in the warm untroubled waters of his beginnings and
await the end. He had never articulated this, had had no reason
to, not even to Elsa. But all these years this certainty had walked
with him, an invisible anchor, a silent comfort.

And not him alone either. The same certainty was a part of
the psyche of all the city's dispossessed. One heard it often. So
often in fact that it had become almost a cliche, words that no one
really heard, or took too seriously, any more. But, serious or not,
illusion or not, empty phrase or not, there was a reason why it
came so often to the lips.

"Bwai, me no have fe take dis shit, y'know—me can jus' go
back a me bush."

"Not because you see me so, y'know—me come from somewhere, y'know."

"No bother t'ink say me have fe stay yah, y'know—fe me people land deh a country, await."

But there were times now when Ivan wasn't sure of anything.
Even his memories were tarnished, suspect. Maybe like Mad

Izaac, who saw what no one else could, he too was the victim of false history, memories of realities that had seemed so solid and permanent but were really ephemeral things, shared by no one. All that was real was what he had now. The past had deserted him and the future . . . raas, what name so?

Midnight Cowboy was charged with ganja and a vision of fatalistic inevitability. He smiled a long, slow smile. "Me breddah," he cried expansively, "what is fe you, is fe you! Me know long time say you boun' to come to I. Is keep a keep dem fe you."

Ivan passed the money. Cowboy didn't count it.

"Dese," he said, "is fe you. Dese is you fuchah.° You can depen' 'pon dem."

Ivan went into the canefields and acquainted himself with them. He practiced until his ammunition and his excitement were spent. When he came out he was exhausted but felt as though something had been replaced. Not restored, for what was gone could not be restored, but there was something in its place.

Even so, it come an' it go. Some days a heaviness take set on him. Seal 'im off in silence far far inside where a dark and empty place was. Never for long doh, because right after that strength and nature come back wid a rush, stronger dan first time. Dass when people start call him Rhygin an' everyt'ing else. Is desso it begin. De yout' see him, pointed an' whispered, eyes big with awe. Women smiled boldly and made offers—offers which, mostly, he accepted.

"You know Rhygin? Which Rhygin? Rhygin de singer man . . . Rhygin whose reggae did so dread dat Babylon had was to kill it. Rhygin de rudie . . . Rhygin de face man, de dancer man who no woman could refuse . . . Rhygin de mouth man, de word man . . . Rhygin de planner, de dreamer . . . Which Rhygin? Rhygin de mysterious, none know whe' him come from . . . Rhygin de dangerous . . . Rhygin de man cutter . . . Rhygin, de bull bucker de duppi conqueror . . . Rhygin who tek de Preacha woman . . . Rhygin, who Babylon bust two tambran' switch over him back an' him doan grunt yet . . . Rhygin, who doan spare nothin' in skirt . . . Rhygin, who mek pussy fart. Oh dah Rhygin deh? Ohyea, dah Rhygin deh . . . Rhygin, who tight wid bad Jose an' walk wid a slim Dreadlocks wid holy eyes? Same one—you no wan' mess wid him. Him alias."

° Fuchah: future.

"Is so dis Rhygin alias?" "Wait, unu must be doan know? Dis Rhygin carry thunder inna him hand dem. Rhygin carry lightning inna him fist. Me say Rhygin alias, Rhygin badder dan cancer, worse dan a heart attack. Rhygin stormy. Him hot hot. Oyo, Oyo, Oyo, me say Rhygin stormy. . . . Rhygin who no know him fad-dah . . ."

He heard the whispers and smiled. And as the youth pointed and whispered the women grew bolder and more insistent. Ras Pedro saw it all and smiled wearily. "A woman did a wicked dance, an' cause a man to lose his head. Aaiie, me young breddah, you can' done de worl' y'know, nor escape de flesh. You can not go to Zion wid a carnal min'. You can' done Babylon wid you cod. Res' you spirit breddah. Res' it."

"Is me train dah breddah deh!" Bad Jose as usual took full credit: "All you see deh, is I do it." Why not take credit? Times was always hard, but de herb was always a comfort. Business was good. The traders made a good living. Babylon was no trouble. There was space for everybody. "But all de same," Jose mused, "dem say bird whe' fly too fas' always fly pas' him nes'."

"It doan done yet," Midnight Cowboy insisted. "It only a begin. Is who recognize dat de yout' have a mission? An' who supply de tool?"

DAUGHTAH VERSHANN

Ras Pedro right as usual, y'know. Wherever it was Ivan go dah Sunday deh, something happen to 'im—'im get a blow. It no leave no mark but still it show. An' 'im won't tell me whe' 'im go neider. De mos' 'im do is laugh funny an' say, "To God, I meet up wid some American nyaman dem, down to de dreadlocks an' all. Dem was a smoke ganja an' nevah have on no clothes." An' every time 'im say it poor little Man-I laugh 'til 'im cough.

An Man-I ask every time "tell me again what de 'merican nyaman dem was a do?" Ivan look real serious, not a hint of a smile. "Bwai," he say, "dem was a milk a ram-goat, y'know." Even Ras Peter laugh then too.

But fe true Ivan change—some ways good and some she didn't care for. One thing was that he spent a lot of time with Man-I now. In fact the boy wouldn't give her any rest, pestering her all day long when Ivan was away, which was now most of the time. Man-I seemed to love the time Ivan spent with him under the mango tree, Ivan keeping him from his schoolwork with stories, strange stories about Ras Menelik, Osu Tutu, King Prempeh, Quaco, Cudjo an' Granny Nanny the maroon queen mother, myal men ° and obeah men with even stranger names like Bamchicolachi and powers stranger still. She had never heard anything like that in Preacher's house, but Ras Pedro sometimes listened and seemed to approve. And Man-I drove her crazy with "Whe' Uncle Ivan gone? When Uncle Ivan coming back?" And anyway, that was the only time that Ivan seemed truly at peace these days. Funny too, cause the business was very good and the boy stayed healthy. They almost forgot what it was to be hungry. But there was no peace in Ivan except then, when lost in his tales, his eyes grew soft and dreamy and his voice calm. He seemed very content in the boy's pleasure.

But apart from then, his eyes glittered and he seemed like a duppi was riding him, allowing him no rest. He was up and down, always on the move. He made extra trips for herb, was always urging Pedro to show him the secrets of cutting and mixing so they could double the business. But he never saved anything. So the money come in; so it go out. He spent a lot of time in the clubs and at the film shows. She was sure he was taking up with some of the good-time gal dem in their miniskirts an' short shorts. He had stopped pushing her to dressup herself like that and come out with him. She wasn't into that kind of life at all. But she didn't have no argument over it neither. She jus' tell him, "Ivan, you know I not inna dat kin' a life deh. If you laas' somet'ing out deh, you go seek it. Me will be right yasso when you come home—dass if you come at all." There it rested.

'Im mussa not fin' it either, cause 'im was still out dere, every night de good Lord sen'. One t'ing puzzle her doh—if is woman 'im have out dere, den how come 'im was so rhygin when 'im come in? No matter how late, 'im would always wake her up, no matter how late, ready long time—always ready. Hot, urgent, an' nevah tired. Not that she was complaining, but sometimes, a morning time, when Ras Pedro would smile a sly smile an' say "Morning Miss Elsa, morning *Rhygin*," she would feel her face turn hot. Because no matter how she try, seems that sometimes, when her nature come down, she jus' had to holler one time. Loud too, y'know. No, if is woman 'im out deh looking, den either 'im

° Myal men were practioners of benign magic, obeah men of witchcraft which was not benign.

doan fin' none, which she didn't for a minute believe, or else him have more nature than everybody else.

"Ivan . . ."

"What?"

"Cho . . . uhh, tell me somet'ing?"

"Eh?"

" 'Ow come you . . . oh . . . so . . . How come you so . . ."

"Sexy?"

". . . yes?"

"Rhygin a me name, so me nature rhygin too . . . Open you leg, nuh."

And his moods were unpredictable. Sometimes, except for Man-I, he would spend long periods in silence. At other times he talked nonstop, firing out fast, intense bursts of words as though he couldn't help himself. Big plans, bwai! They should stop buying herb. Instead he and Pedro should capture some hilltop land in country and grow some. They could supply the other traders. Then he'd make records again, but this time as an independent producer of his own songs.

"Since when you turn farmer, breddah?" Pedro laughed.

"All de while, y'know," Ivan said seriously.

"Not only dat, you wan' tu'n capitalis' too?"

And all the time the words, plans, and dreams were tumbling out as if there were someone else inside him talking, and not really to her, or Pedro, or even to himself. She had never known him to be without great hopes and dreams, but she sensed that this was in some way very different. And it was all since that Sunday. . . . Maybe not though, but she was sure about one thing.

The day he got up from the bed—that first day. He asked her for any money she had in the house.

"But is only Man-I school fee an' de house money you know, Ivan."

"No matter, you get it back Friday."

"What you need it for?"

"Ah have to fin' a bwai, it can' wait." That she could see. When he came back he was lit up, glowing, and seemed tense and excited as if he could not quite control or hide the nervous energy that flowed through him. She was sure that he carried something under his shirt.

"You fin' 'im den?"

"Yes y'know, Ah fin' 'im." He avoided further questions by going into their room and closing the door. She would never forget that closed door, for he had never closed her out of their room before.

He was in there for what seemed like a long time and when he finally emerged she could see that he was trying to act too normal. She had to know, and it didn't take her long to find them in his private box under the bed. She had listened guiltily for the sound of the Honda, would have died of shame if he found her prying into something which he clearly wanted to keep from her. And when she found them she wished she hadn't.

What a distress doh eh? Ah know Pedro doan know say Ivan bring gun into de house. What if Man-I ever fin' dem? Lawd Jesas, no talk so . . . But what Ivan could want wid something like dat, an' two a dem too? Ah can' tell Pedro an' Ah can' doan tell 'im neider. What a distress! It wan' look like Ivan tu'n gunman. No, 'im jus' a keep dem fe somebody. Is mus' dat. An' at leas' everytime I peep, both a dem still in de box. Or, maybe is only one wrap up? Ivan walkin' roun' town wid pistol in 'im waist? Jesas me God . . .

But what really happenin' to Ivan doh, eh? Look dis mornin'. Pedro gone wid Man-I fe 'im regular checkup. Ivan sleep late as usual. Soon as she see de headline she run go wake 'im since it concern ganja.

"Look, Ivan!"

"Umm wha'?" Whe' you a wake me up for?"

"Paper say police in Miami hol' a plane load down wid ganja. Dem say is here it come from too."

Is like ants tek de bed y'know, de way Ivan leap up an' snatch de paper.

"Look yah, street value seven 'unred t'ousan' dollah!" That wake 'im up fully. He stared at her like a madman. "You hear ah say, seven 'undred t'ousan' dollah to raas? A soon come. Whe' me pants?"

"Don't you see where dem say U.S. government goin' sen' down helicopter to help de defense force clamp down on de trade?"

"Cho," he scoffed. "Dat a propagandah, pure propagandah. Arright, a soon come."

'Im did'n even wait fe Pedro and the bike but set out on foot, more like 'im runnin' dan walkin' an' stuffing 'im shirt tail inna him trousers.

Why I jus' feel say Jose know somet'ing 'bout dah plane deh? 'Im tek me fe fool? When I see him an' de man dem a level off de hilltop up at Pinnacle 'im laugh an' say dem a mek cricket pitch. Cricket pitch? Well, 'im shoulda did tell we. Seven hundred t'ousan' dollah! Who a go get dat eh? An' we a run from soldier an' gunshot every day? Fe what? Small change. Look Pedro Queen, dead instantly. No man, Jose shoulda did tell we. Suppose de yankee man come down yah come "clamp down." Viet Nam to raas. What a go happen to de acre me an' Pedro an' de Coolie man put in? Is my raas future dat, y'know. I bettah find dah Jose now.

He decided on the unusual extravagance of a taxi. The driver was full of secret information, which given his eagerness to share, could not possibly be secret much longer.

"Fuck bauxite," he declared passionately. The single greatest resource the island had was ganja. Didn't Ivan know that the Prime Minister and the entire cabinet each had their own secret plantation? "Big business to raas. Look, you see John Connally come down talk 'bout him inna de cattle business?" He laughed out loud. "Who Big John t'ink is idiot? Who woulda leff Texas so come a Jamaica fe run cow? He, he, heaw . . . Especially when everybody know say the bes' ganja in the worl' come from right yah." He laughed again.

Ivan did not know who Big John Connally was. What movie was he in, the name sounded familiar, it had to be a cowboy star? But for once, his mind wasn't on Texas. "I doan business wid all dat," he said virtuously, "I'm a Christian."

The driver gave him an aggrieved look and was silent for a while. "You know what wrong wid dis country?" he asked rhetorically and did not wait for an answer. "Too much damn fly-by-night Christianity whe' come down from de U.S.," he began, eyes glinting maliciously.

"Praise de Lawd, brother," Ivan said. "Praise his holy name."

Rhygin left the cab down the corner, since his arrival by such means would indicate that something urgent was on his mind. Jose and his current inamorata, a lady known as Pinky, were lounging at a table. A few traders sat around sipping beer. Rhygin had expected, especially after the taxi driver, that the central topic of conversation would be the plane. Not so. Business as usual. He brought a beer over to Jose's table.

"Play a game a skittles, Jah?"

"Why not? One cent a point?"

Ivan knocked over a skittle. "Your play, man. You read de newspaper?" He kept his voice low and casual.

Jose missed an easy shot. "Uh huh. Your play."

"Dem catch a plane in Miami. Say it come from here."

"Ah read dat."

"Well?"

"Well—what? Dem say two get t'rough. Your play."

"Dem—who say?"

"Dem, man. You know 'dem say.' My play."

"But Jose, suppose dem come bu'n down de fields, whe' we deh?"

"Dat a propagandah fe quiet down de Christian dem. Nutten in it."

"But still, if dem kin' a risk deh in it, we suppose to get somet'ing."

"Your play," Jose growled.

"Cricket pitch, eh?" Ivan said.

"Some cricket jump high." Jose giggled.

"Seven 'undred tousan' dollah, Jose? Is joke dat?"

"Propaganda, man. Your play."

"Still somebody making big money. Who?"

"Ask anybody. Everybody know who."

"But is you I asking, Jose." Their eyes locked.

Jose laughed. "De prime Minister, Agriculture Minister, de Bishop of Kingston. Everybody know dat."

"It look like I jokin', Jose?"

"Your play."

"If dem selling dis t'ing fe export, me an' Pedro have a acre an a half y'know. Why de t'ree a we can' sell it direck an' mek some real money? Eh, wha' you say?"

"I feel I better done dis game, y'hear?" Jose laid down his stick deliberately. Ivan couldn't see his face as he bent over the table. "Pinky, you better go bring a beer." He straightened up and watched the woman walk away. His voice was low and tense. "Ivan listen me. I doan know nutten 'bout any export, *nutten*. Get dat raas straight. If you no like our deal, is a tousan' man ina Wes' Kingston alone, whe' jus' a dead fe trade wid I. If you no like it, leff it man, split. Dass all. Jus' leff it." He looked at Ivan and turned away.

"Wait—"

"What?" He half turned.

"You know say I doan wan' split, ol' man. But which law say dat all like we so can' mek big money too, eh?"

It was either that Jose had been under more pressure than he had shown, or else something—and Ivan couldn't imagine what—that he had just said set Jose off. Shouting, he spun to face Ivan. Veins bulged in his neck, and there was an edge of hysteria in his anger.

"Look yah, you little raas. When I pick you up, you deh 'pon you ass! Half starvin'. Now you got Honda park up outside. Every night you deh a club a sport woman. Wha' do you? You is idiot? Real money? How much money you an' Pedro split every Friday, eh? Dat no money? You bettah raas glad you mekkin' a livin' at all. You know dem say, 'when man know say 'im chairback weak 'im no lean back!' You know what, mek I leff dis place, y'know."

He seemed in a blind fury as he stomped out, kicking a chair out of his path. The people in the café were looking pointedly everywhere but at the little scene. But they had missed nothing. Feeling very foolish, Rhygin went after Jose. In a way he was right, he and Pedro were doing pretty good.

"Hey Jose. Jose. Hol' down breddah . . ." He broke into a run. "Hol' down man, is still one love, y'know. . . ."

Jose didn't stop. Rhygin didn't know whether he had heard him over the roar of the bike. Something strange was going on. Both Jose and Pedro seemed almost frightened whenever he asked about the upper levels of the trade. The idea that Jose might have been simply acting occurred to him. Part of Jose's cool was never to raise his voice or show any kind of pressure. He'd been shouting and raving, stumbling into chairs, why? Still, they were making it. Play it cool an' check the action—for now . . .

· · ·

"Wait, dem coulden burning cane already? After is not crop time now, eh?" Ras Pedro said, squinting into the sun. "You no smell smoke?"

"Truly," Rhygin said, "is long time I smell it. You hear 'bout any strike or trouble 'bout yah? Mus' be accident if the cane burning, man."

"Ivan, look 'pon de mountain up by Pinnacle."

Beyond the flat cane-filled plains the full range of the mountain was punctuated by dense pillars of black smoke billowing into the clear blue of the sky.

"Blood claat," Ivan whispered. "Propaganda no? Tu'n back

Pedro." They stopped and looked in silence at the burning mountain. Six, seven, no, ten columns spewed into the air and mingled into a single dark cloud hanging like a pall over the peaks. Four helicopters, angry dragonflies, hovered and darted through the smoke like giant prehistoric insects routed from their nests by fire.

"Ah bet you, not a root a ganja doan leff up deh," Pedro said. "De whole harves' fe dis year."

The rumble of heavy trucks drove them into the canefield just before four army trucks lumbered past. The soldiers wore full battle dress and seemed cheerful, even exuberant. Their camouflaged fatigues were decorated with sprigs of green flowering buds, which made a strangely gay appearance against the drab khaki green battle dress.

"Laugh man, unu feel good, eh?" Rhygin muttered.

"Retribushan," Ras Pedro said, "Retribushan mus' tek unu."

Rhygin looked at the brethren's face and knew what the sight of those grinning faces and casually held automatic weapons must be costing him. He thought of the lost fields and the first strange night he had spent in Pedro's presence. He heard the rumble of another approaching truck. His hand crept inside his shirt and settled around the pearl grip, already warmed by his body and through which he could feel the rhythm of his own heart. He had the soaring feeling again, as though he were outside himself, neither thinking nor counting odds or consequences, just watching the play develop. He saw, as in a film, a crack spread across the windshield, the driver's startled face and the truck crashing out of control into the canefield.

Ras Pedro's voice and hand brought him back. "No—*no* me brederin. Sometimes you worse enemy live inside you." He gently seized Ivan's hand and held it with a firm pressure. The calm slow voice continued. "But you coulden mad enough? Remember that is me one an' god Man-I have fe care 'im now, y'know. You mad, man?"

"It wan' look so," Ivan said, wondering how it was that Pedro's voice and manner always seemed so detached. "You know 'bout de pistol dem?"

"Long time," said the Dreadlocks. "An' it trouble I spirit too. I feel say I understan' whe' a go on wid you, but still an' all, I man no defen' blood shed. To Jah, I swear I doan wan' see it come to dat—black man a kill black man. . . ."

"But dat come an' gone, an' come again," Ivan muttered.

"Come we go fin' Jose an' ask 'im if all dat smoke over pinnacle a propagandah," Pedro counseled.

"Aye, you t'ink we coulda chance it an' go see wha' really happen up deh? De soldier dem gone."

"Bwai, you know how dem stay dem day yah. Dem good fe all have ambush set up on de mountaintop. Mek we tu'n back."

The helicopter strike force of "Operation Friendship" spent four weeks scanning remote hills in every area known to produce herb. Neither the aircraft nor the teams of soldiers which followed hard on their tails missed very much. Either by fortituous accident or design the operation came just as the crop had begun to mature. The press and clergy hailed this outstanding example of international cooperation and the forthright action of the army. Operation Friendship was an outstanding media and diplomatic success, everyone agreed.

The peasant growers were stoic. "Mek Babylon go on," they declared. "De 'copter dem have fe go back where dem come from, but de herb is fe *evah*—worl' widout end. Mek dem bu'n de field dem—little rain fall an' de herb spring up back, green and lovely. Herb can' done, y'know."

The traders and their urban customers were thrown into consternation. Panic buying and hoarding gobbled up whatever stores were already in the shantytowns. But for a while the supply held up to demand and the only immediate effect was a rise in the price. But soon special hoards from previous years—especially good herb that had lain in the earth "gaddering strent" were dug up. The musty, potent, earth-smelling herb was quickly sold, as folks prepared for a long drought. Whatever field ganja had escaped the army's flamethrowers was hurriedly cured and brought in, but scarcely mature and still green, it was rank and impotent. An abomination and a disgrace, Ras Pedro said.

He and Rhygin had been luckier than most. They had an extra crocus bag that Ras Pedro had insisted they invest in because of its unusual quality. "Real firs'-time-feel-good collie," as he had said. But they disagreed vehemently—at least Ivan was vehement and Ras Pedro calmly adamant. As long as it lasted, he felt, it should go to their regular customers and at the old price, which was what they had paid. Ivan saw such a course as madness. Things were bound to get worse. They should hold it. Before long, weed of such superlative quality would be worth its weight in gold, fuck gold, ten dollar bills. "Reap not where dou hast not sown," Ras Pedro admonished him calmly and frequently, "an' take dou not de path of de oppressah." The bag was sold in a day.

The traders met and counseled together, but meeting led nowhere since there was nowhere that it could lead. Some who had hoarded were very flush for a while. One youth named Fudgehead even made a down payment on an almost new Ford Cortina, a display of extravagance and poor judgement he was soon to regret, when he could not explain to the satisfaction of the police the source of his sudden affluence. "Imagine, a dutty little sufferah 'ave Cortina park up outside 'im hut?" Mostly the traders grumbled and cursed the captured plane that started the trouble, the pilot, and his mother. Jose was philosophical. When business was flush nobody bawled, so now "keep unu fucken mout' shet." Apart from that or similar expressions he said little and was rarely to be found.

When the trickle of weed into the shantytown became a mere dribble, the consumption of raw white rum increased. So did the incidence and level of irrational acts, and aggressive behavior as the hot rum delivered a jarring shock to nervous systems mellowed over the years by herb.

The entire grassroots economic system, embracing grower, curer, cutter, distributor, and a variety of ingenious middlemen who scratched precarious existences in the interstices of the trade, was completely disrupted. Officially "unemployed" folk became truly unemployed, without income of any sort. Burglaries increased. Predatory behavior—acts of robbery at gun point, knife point, machete point and even by sheer desperation and brute force, became common. Press and clergy loudly deplored this evidence of growing social depravity, by which they did not mean the reported increase in the incidents of wife-beatings in the hillside villas. The Prime Minister made a get tough speech which greatly comforted his constituency in the suburbs. It was so well received that every fifteen minutes his shrill, slightly hysterical voice could be heard over the radio delivering the most quotable lines.

"An' Ah want *evrahbody* to know that under this administration the police force not reciting beatitude *to anahbody.*" Behind their high walls, locked gates, and barred windows, the respectable element nodded agreement and made clucking noises. *Presshah drop.*

Ras Pedro had an emergency fund saved up. Elsa had put by a small amount each week from her house money. Ivan had no cash but sold his wristwatch and big German radio. Had Man-I not come down with an attack of greater virulence and duration than any previous, they would have weathered the crisis.

The doctor shook his head. He mumbled something to do with bone marrow, anemia and remission. Drugs and blood. Blood, drugs, and money. Gloom descended. Everything that was nonessential was sold. In such times, Ivan insisted, the pistols were a necessity, but if it came to that, he'd sell them. Ras Pedro didn't argue. They agreed the Honda was a necessity, and Rhygin burned a lot of scarce money out the exhaust scouring the countryside for herb. Soon even the purchase money was gone. Elsa's little flock of leghorns dwindled rapidly. Ivan came up with a small cut of good herb. He never explained its origin and no one pressed him. They distributed it to their outlets and this time Ras Pedro said nothing about the price Ivan quoted. It was when they went to collect that matters came to a head. Pedro separated out Jose's cut as usual.

"We doan know where any more coming from, y'know, Pedro. We caan' pay Jose dis week."

"I can' even pay de doctor Wednesday," Ras Pedro said.

"Mek Jose tek his share from de seven hundred tousan' dollah dem mek in Miami, man. Doan pay him."

"Even so we ha' fe go explain de situation to 'im," Pedro said.

"No tell 'im nutten, yah sah. Is cause a dem mek de army bu'n down de fields. I say no tell him raas."

"No breddah, we ha' fe tell 'im somet'ing. Maybe we jus' give 'im a portion to show say we mean to pay, when we can."

There were neither traders nor the women attracted by their high style and free spending in the Lone Star café when they arrived. Jose, his cool, inscrutable mask in place, was sipping a beer in solitary splendor at his usual table.

"Rhygin, Pedro, one love bredrin!"

"One heart!" Ras Pedro said.

"One destiny!" Jose replied. Rhygin nodded.

"Hail up man. I glad to see unu all de same. Unu trade dis week, but I can' see unu. But Ah see unu now, my heart glad."

"Cho," Pedro said seriously. "You know me nah scamp you, Jose. I evah do dat yet?"

"Firs' time fe everyt'ing," Jose said, and smiled to show it was a joke.

"About dat—" Ivan began, but Pedro hastened to cut him off.

"My bwai sick, sick bad . . ."

"Life hard," Jose said, "but somet'ings harder still."

"But it go like dis, I really can' pay you all dis week. You ha' fe see wid me 'til another time."

"If I see wid you, I ha' fe see wid everybody, an' my people nah go see wid me. Is only fifty dollah I a deal wid."

"Ah bring what I can, still, but de bwai *sick*, Jose."

Jose waved his hand as if to dissociate himself from that. Ivan, his face angry, started to speak, but Pedro shook his head emphatically. Jose looked at Ivan steadily as he spoke.

"Is not my concern dat, y'know. I all sorry fe de bwai—*truly*, but if you trade, you pay. Dass all."

"Jose, you mus' see wid me dis time breddah. I doan try dodge you, y'know, I come to you like a breddah. . . ."

"Doan beg him a raas," Ivan said. "You can' pay dis week dass all. No pay 'im, man."

Jose laughed softly. "Wait, Pedro—you no tell dis little bwai how it go? It doan look like 'im understan'? Duppi fool 'im."

"Forget dat Jose—I a ask you fe see wid me," Pedro said. "I *asking* you man."

"No soft story man, I can' deal wid dat. Is only fifty dollar I a deal wid." Jose kept his eyes on his beer bottle and held out his hand.

Pedro looked at the hand for a long time. "So . . . all you deal wid is money. Nutten else—jus' money?"

"Jus' money breddah." He reached over and slipped the money out of Pedro's limp grip. "One love, man."

Ivan stood clenching and unclenching his fist as he watched Jose count the money and slip it into his pocket. Jose knew Man-I personally and knew that he was sickly. An' Pedro—what did he know that caused him to seize up so? Why 'im let Jose take the money like dat? Fuck dat.

"Aye . . . I nah pay you till nex' week Jose. Tell you boss dem to tek my share outta de money from Miami. Is dem cause the fiel' dem to burn down."

"Tell 'im nuh, Pedro," Jose ordered.

"Tell me nutten—Ah pay you when I can."

"When you can? When you come out, you mean. Tell 'im nuh Pedro."

"Come out from whe'? Come out from whe'?" Stepping in front of Jose, Ivan reached into his shirt. "Yea—come out from whe'? I doan 'fraid you, y'know, Jose."

"I know. How you to 'fraid me? Rhygin a bad man, a gun man." Jose was smiling as if quite amused. "But is not me you to 'fraid, y'know, not I. Pedro you better talk to dis bwai."

Look what I do fe dat bwai too? From de firs' day 'im little
mauger raas come a town? Well, 'im way pass 'im nest dis time.
See it yah now. T'ings very thin. If it get out say Rhygin trade an'
no pay, de res' a dem boun' to try it. He had expected it sooner or
later and maybe it was good. Maybe he needed to demonstrate
what could happen to anyone who broke ranks. It wasn' that him
woulden give Pedro a break, but den everyone goin' want one
too. Maas' Ray hol' him direckly responsible an' dah man deh
would do but anyt'ing. When de trader dem was a mek big
money, dem glad to pay, was a beg to pay. Dem ungrateful, man.
The feeling of abandonment and ingratitude angered him. The
more he thought, the angrier he got. Especially at Rhygin. Look
how good he was to the bwai? And, in a funny way he really liked
his style too. But business is business, and he knew Maas' Ray
dreadful bad.

"Maas' Ray? Look nuh, sah, a little trouble. Is a funny time,
sah, an' t'ings thin ina de trade . . . Is one a de trader dem, sah—
yes sah, de one whe' work wid Ras Pedro . . . Dem call 'im Rhygin. But is not my fault, y'know, sah . . . What I wan' you do?
Well, 'im is a boasie bwai an' 'im mout' big—if i'm get 'way wid
it, everybody gwine know. . . . Dass right, sah. O.K. sah, dat
should do it." Jose started to hang up, then on a sudden impulse
didn't. He had had no intention of saying what he did next, but he
had been getting the impression that Maas' Ray was blaming him
for the entire situation. He wanted no further blame.

"Wait sah, one more t'ing." He stopped but it was too late.
"Well sah, it may not true, sah, but you should know—dem say de
bwai is a gunman. Arright den, sah." Even before he hung up on
the phone he was fully sorry that he had added that last. But sorry
doan mek it. It was up to Rhygin to tek care of 'imself. "If nanny
goat diden know how 'im batti hole stay 'im shoulden did swallow
pear seed," ° after all. . . .

RHYGIN VERSHANN

Ivan ran into the room where Ras Pedro and Elsa were keeping anxious watch over Man-I. Though he kept his voice down it
was evident that he was excited. "Ah track down some herb,
Pedro. Good herb, too."

° Traditional proverb.

"How much gas we waste 'pon bare rumor, Jah? Dis one ha' herb, dat one ha' herb . . . Come to fin' out, no herb no deh, none." Ras Pedro's voice was listless.

"But we ha' fe check it out. How Man-I?"

"Neider bettah, neider worse—same way."

"We have fe get some money . . . I a go check 'pon de herb."

"How you a go pay fe it, Ivan, even if—which Ah doan believe—dem ha' any?"

"Dem say is Bhyah 'ave it. 'I'm will trust we 'til later," Ivan said. "An' if not—"

"An' if not, what?" Ras Pedro asked, looking up for the first time.

"Well—Ah may ha' fe persuade 'im," Ivan said under his breath.

"So . . . is dat we come to? To Jah, Ivan, ol' Bhyah a me good frien'. We can' into dat at all."

"How you mean?" Ivan blustered. "Look Man-I! We ha' fe do *somet'ing,* whatevah necessary still."

"But not dat breddah, not dat. We is not animal! We 'ave consciousness, man."

"So—what den?"

"Is might bettah we sell de Honda, breddah. For, if anyone should go fe herb is me, an' I nah leff' Man-I so."

"So, me wi' go, what's de problem?"

"Oh Ivan—like how you doan pay Jose las' week . . . You no see de risk you running? Bettah we sell de Honda Ivan, no go man."

Elsa, who had been listening in silence, looking from face to face, said, "If any chance at all, *at all,* deh . . ." She bit her lip and looked down. "Pedro, Ivan right, y'know, if is any chance at all, we have fe try."

Pedro looked at the boy and was silent.

"Well—jus' reason wid Bhyah, Ivan. Jus' reason wid de ol' man, y'hear? Leff' de gun dem yah, an' jus' reason wid 'im. When 'im know de situashan, 'im wi' see wid we."

"An', me no know whe' Jose up to? You mad Pedro 'bout leff de gun dem—but I wi' only reason wid de ol' man, arright?"

"Praises man, one heart. An' tek care, nuh."

Head soaring from the first really good ganja he'd had in weeks and jubilant with success, Rhygin was gunning along Spanish Town road. Old Bhyah, whom the traders called "Coolie

Rasta," had really shown him something. Made him feel a little 'shamed too, even though he had not had to "bogart" the weed. When he heard about the boy, the old man had squatted in his hut smoking his clay pipe and saying nothing, studying Ivan deliberately through grayish eyes almost completely grown over with cataracts. His lank, gray hair framed his face and mingled with his sparse beard.

"Ayeh," he lamented, in a high querulous voice, "Ah feel fe Ras Pedro—to me heart." He puffed smoke. Ivan fidgeted.

"Res' yoself, young bwai. How you so . . . so nervous wid ol' Bhyah, eh?"

"I dey pon haste," Rhygin explained. "You can help we?"

"An' if Ah say no? What den? You a go bu'n gun inna me belly? Shoot ol' Bhyah like 'im was a peadove?" The cracked voice could have been asking whether Rhygin knew what time it was.

"Say what?" Ivan asked.

"Me see, long long time, what you have inna you shirt, young bwai. But is one t'ing I wan' know—is so Ras Petro sen' you to me? 'Im really know say is so you come? Me no believe so, y'know. Pedro nevah do such a t'ing. Some a dem other trader, yes. But not Ras Pedro, 'im is not a hog. 'Im is not dawg. 'Im is a conscious young man."

"Is true," Ivan mumbled.

"Me bwai, know somet'ing . . . Coolie man no 'fraid dead y'know. Him ol' now. What is dead to 'im? But Ah gwine give unu whatever ganja is here. Tell Pedro nex' time come 'imself, an' I will bu'n *kali* fe de little bwai recovah. Tell 'im Coolie Bhyah sen' a love."

He rose, a trifle unsteady on spindly legs, and walked away shrouded in a rickety dignity that shamed Rhygin.

"Maas' Bhyah. Maas' Bhyah." The old man turned. "Look no sah, de pickney sick bad an' times dem desperate, y'know. But me coulden did bring no vi'lence to you, y'know, sah. Me woulden did do it, sah.

The old man nodded and waved his hand either in dismissal or acceptance, Ivan didn't know which. But anyway now he had almost a full bag of rich, pungent weed on the back. The old man had said simply, "tell Pedro pay whenevah." At present prices they would be able to afford whatever Man-I needed and put some away. It was more than a help, it would save their lives. He wondered what there was between Ras Pedro and the half-blind

old Indian who saw so clearly and who reminded him so much of
someone . . .

In his hurry and excitement he had to remind himself about
the speed limit. It would not do at all to be stopped by a strange
Babylon for something stupid like that. He looked for the regular
Babylon under the mango tree where he usually sat on his big
black motor bike. But he wasn't there. Then Ivan saw him not in
his usual place but half hidden by the cane.

He waved casually, and with his hand still aloft saw that the
Babylon was talking into a walkie-talkie and kicking his engine to
life. He didn't seem like the usual cop. Ivan watched in his mirror
as the big bike swept onto the highway behind him. The huge,
black, police machine with the helmeted and goggled rider was a
menacing sight as it closed in. When he heard the wail of its siren,
fear ran through him. He opened up the little Honda but it was
no match. The black juggernaut approached rapidly. Ivan looked
over his shoulder and saw that the Babylon's gloved hand held a
gun. The fear left him and he saw the next few seconds clearly.
Gently he reached into his shirt and cocked the pistol, keeping it
against his belly where it would be hidden from the cop. As the
other machine drew abreast he turned in one smooth, unhurried,
Randolph Scott motion and fired. The pistol bucked against the
heel of his hand. The blast was loud and echoed over the plain.
That brought him back. The heavy bike, engine still roaring, hit
the pavement with the shriek of metal gouging concrete, skidding
and spitting sparks. The rider was plucked from his seat. He
seemed suspended over the road for an instant before hitting the
hot cement with a splat. For a second, the bike spun violently and
erratically alongside the Honda like an animal dying hard, then
siren still wailing, it scraped across the road and into the ditch.

Ivan was sweating and trembling. A wave of nausea filled his
belly. A burst of vomit shot from his mouth, burning his throat hot
and bitter, then it gracefully billowed out on the wind and hung
in silvery streamlets in the sunshine, before falling. Rhygin controlled the Honda and kept on, feeling very weak. He took the
first turnoff he came to and using back roads, he headed into some
scraggy low-lying hills. He had to plan a route back into the city.
Like a scout behind enemy lines, he would slip back home to
leave the herb that meant life to Man-I. Then he would slip away.
The image pleased him. He saw himself as a calm, cold-eyed and
very cunning desperado outsmarting posses and search parties.
First thing was to get home before the Babylons had a chance to
organize a real search.

Ras Pedro and Elsa were sitting on the steps when he rode up. He raised his fist over his head in a gesture of triumph.

"Ah get t'rough to raas," he cried, holding up the bag like a prize.

"Shhh," Elsa said. " 'Im sleeping."

"Here, dis will help a lot. Is all Bhyah did have." Pedro was looking intently at his excited face.

"Ivan, you nevah—"

"Nutten like dat . . . Is sen' Bhyah sen' dis fe you." He brushed past and went into the bedroom and started rummaging under the bed.

"What happen Ivan? Why you run into de place like a mad-man?"

"Where de raas bullets dem deh, eh?"

"Is what happen?" Elsa wailed. "Lawd Jesas, me know something happen, me know it."

"No time—I ha' fe fin' Jose now. Listen de news, you will hear all 'bout me, man." He straightened up and started out.

Pedro stopped him. "What you do, Ivan?" His eyes were troubled.

"Cho, is arright. . . . It will be on the news. If everyt'ing arright, you should see me later. If not check de ranch tomorrow—ask fe Bogart. Otherwise I contact you. One love, man." At the door he turned and gave a brief smile and a jaunty salute. Then he was gone.

Yes, he'd played that scene like a star-bwai. . . . Man on de run to raas. When it came over the radio, Pedro and Elsa would understand how cool he had been. He felt alert and invincible, capable of beating all odds. At the same time he felt both peaceful and intensely alive. His heart pounded and he could feel it driving the blood into his head. His first move was to find Jose. Clearly Jose must have set him up. Why else would that Babylon come after him at gunpoint? If that was so they knew he did it. They would have his name. A short-lived stab of fear brushed him. His name, address, and description would be on the radio. Hey, so what? Let them put it out. Mek everyone know is who drop the Babylon. Manhunt to raas . . . Unless Jose could prove he had nothing to do with it. Then the police would be looking for an unknown gunman. Jose better talk good, or else, as long as Babylon had his name—you can' heng but once. Raas, Jose—a informer to blood? What a worl'? But, give him de benefit firs'. . . . 'Im better talk damn good doh. . . .

He had expected the traders to be at the café discussing the shooting, and he was disappointed to find the place almost empty, the only patrons being a group of women at a table drinking "Baby Cham" and talking.

"Anybody see Jose?"

"No, y'know?" one said.

"Wha' 'bout de back room."

"Me no know." She shrugged. "Go look, nuh? We no go back deh, y'know."

The woman barely looked up from her conversation. Her answers were offhand. She certainly couldn't know who she was talking to so carelessly. He passed through and eased into the back room with his hand on the pistol. Empty to raas. Feeling somewhat cheated, he sat down to think. He knew he couldn't stay there too long. It was funny that none of the traders was there, only that bunch of women. Where de raas was Jose? Babylon would be watching the place—or on their way. Where was Duffus an' Midnight Cowboy an' Sidney an' Bulloh an' Stagecoach? No, he couldn't stay here. But where to go? What's de nex' move? All de same, Babylon couldn't move so fas', is hardly two hours since he dropped the cop . . .

> Ah say, de harder de come
> is de harder dey faall
> One an' aaall . . .

His song floated into the room. The beat and his own voice picked him up immediately. The tiredness and anticlimatic depression left him. He got up to leave. The music wasn't in his head. One of the women was playing the jukebox.

She was standing in one spot, head thrown back, eyes closed, her body swaying and moving in the funk of the beat with a sweet, vaguely familiar grind. From the expression on her face she was gone to a far far place. He stopped to watch and found himself moving with her in perfect and erotic harmony. A biting lust, insistent and not to be denied, filled his gut. He watched her jamming softly in the gummy gummy beat and knew that the daughtah was his. He knew it. He hoped she would recognize him. Power and confidence swelled up in him as he paced in a deliberate stalking half-dance over to where she stood. He felt like he was bounding across the floor in great graceful slow-motion leaps in time to the beat, like some movies when everything slow down.

"You like de tune den, daughtah?"

"Like it yes," she murmured without opening her eyes. "Like de singer too."

"You know 'im?"

"Who don't?"

"Me no know 'im." He grinned. "Is who him?"

She looked him dead in the eye and smiled dreamily. "A lickel mauger bwai who t'ink 'im nice." She moistened her lip with the pink tip of her tongue.

Ivan laughed out loud. He liked her style. "Maybe 'im is?" he drawled. "Nice?"

"Like you?" she asked.

"Who know?" he said.

She nodded agreement and went into a series of smooth spins, coming round each time on the beat. Each time she faced him she added a word: " 'Im . . . name . . . Rhygin . . ."

"Ah so? Den, I know 'im good," he said, as though surprised and delighted.

"Dem say 'im alias bad, y'know."

"Really?"

Her turn for surprise: "I hear say 'im *goood*. I woulda like *know* 'im."

"Why?"

"Because—I good too."

"It wan' look so."

"You t'ink so?" She smiled a pleased, coy smile.

"Ah t'ink so, yes."

"Well . . . ?"

"Come wid me, daughtah."

"It nice here, mek we stay." She wiggled in the music and pouted.

"You can come—but I can' stay." He turned away.

"Arright den," she said quickly and followed him. He knew she would.

On the Honda her arms came around him and he could feel her hand brush gently over the butt of the gun. She gave no sign, but he felt the hand nestle around it as she flattened herself against his back.

"Where to?" he shouted over the engine.

"We can' go my place," she breathed into his ear.

"Why not?" He was immediately suspicious. It had occured to him that the best place for him was the bed of a strange woman, one with whom he had no previous contact.

"Me have man, honey. Ah doan t'ink 'im goin' to like what I plan fe do wid you."

He could feel her warm lips moving against his ear. "So where, den? We can' go my place eider."

She seemed to consider for a while. "You have money, honey?"

"All de while, baby."

"Well mek we go to a hotel—a nice empty hotel where Ah can bawl out if ah want."

"So, you is a bawler?"

"When it nice me, yes."

"Bawl? You doan bawl yet!"

"Is so you, Rhygin?" she mocked. "Easy to say, hard to do."

"It hard to do it, yes," Rhygin said. "Feel it nuh, baby." He pushed her hand onto his crotch.

"Jesas Chris'," she breathed with great respect. "Like how you mauger, is must borrow you borrow dis." She grasped it firmly and issued an outrageous and unbroken string of sexual promises, threats and challenges.

"Him name High John de Conqueror," Ivan said. "You like him?"

"Oh honey," she moaned. "Ah fin' you at last."

A hotel was just as good, he thought. But he'd let her get the room, safer that way. He hadn't felt such desire since he was a young boy. There was, about this woman clinging so softly to him with her busy tongue and inventive mind, something that teased and challenged and promised. There was also a sense of famil-iarity, of fulfillment as at the successful completion of a long search. This feeling came on him with a rush of exhilaration and a kind of reckless joy. Nothing, he felt, could touch him now. The image of the cop flashed before him, rammed backward as if he had ridden into a steel cable. This time it was sanitized, distanced, purged of fear or guilt or any sickening sense of destruction. It was pure, abstract motion and power, like something on the screen. He wanted very much to tell her about it.

All the while, calling him honey, she kept talking. Even in his lust he recognized, in her startling and exciting vulgarity, some-thing practiced. He had known whores before. But if that was what she was, her act was out of control. Hanging on to a ram-pant High John, she talked and promised herself into a state of grace, her excitement answering his own. Without doubt, she was the girl in the red dress, the one from his first night in town. "If you live long enough, every t'ing will happen to you," Miss 'Mando used to say. He wanted to believe.

"Hey. What you name?" he shouted.

"Delores," she whispered. "Delores . . . Delores . . . Delores . . . You like it?"

"You know a guy name "Needle?"" he asked and was immediately sorry. "Nevah min'—it no matter."

"But . . . Ah use to know 'im good," she said. "But 'im dead now."

Like de Babylon, Rhygin thought. What a hell of a day. Everything jus' fit. A soaring feeling of utter well-being and power, a sense of fulfilled destiny, of invincibility, as if for the first time in his life he had stepped completely into his true self. . . . An' what a bad, *baad* self it was too?" Then he remembered. He had grown so accustomed to flush times and full pockets that he had quite forgotten he had very little money with him.

"Raas! Ah come out widout de money, y'know?" He waited to see what would happen. To this kind of woman, a man without money was hardly a man.

Her response was immediate. A long, scornful sucking of her teeth and a burst of mocking laughter. "Cho," she said disdainfully, "you t'ink *me* care 'bout dat? I know a place, honey." That was when he knew, beyond doubt, that this was indeed his day. . . .

It was impossible to say which bawled more, the woman or the bedsprings. After his first wave of desire was spent he felt vaguely dissatisfied. Something wasn't right. Delores lay beneath him still shuddering and uttering little whimpers in the aftershock of orgasm.

"Come, mek we move," he whispered. He felt her stiffen.

"What you mean? Where?" She was looking at him almost in fright.

He laughed reassuringly. "Nevah min', me doan done yet. We jus' a go nex' door. Dis yah bed too loud."

"How we to do dat? You mad?"

"De whole floor empty, come on." They argued but he insisted. Grudgingly and with much argument and noise she followed him. The bed across the hall was worse.

"See—Ah tell you. Mek we go back," she begged.

"Not a raas," he said, and threw the mattress on the floor. "Now," he said grinning, "you have no place to dodge to. You ha' fe give up."

She seemed angry, grumbled, sulked, tried to withhold herself. They grappled on the floor, locked together again and again. There were moments of immeasurable sweetness but mostly it was like primitive war, guttural, inarticulate, mindless. Shining with sweat, tired, sore but unsated, Rhygin pushed himself up on his hands, locking his elbows, and grinned down at her. Her eyes were glazed. Her lips drew back catlike from her teeth and her nostrils flared with each breath.

"Wait, tell me somet'ing?"

"Umh?"

"You know Jose?"

"Which Jose dat?"

"De one I ask you 'bout in de café. De one who sen' de Babylon after me, mek I had was to shoot 'im off de bike. Dat Jose."

He watched her face closely. Her eyes cleared and focused on his. Then she quickly closed them. She moaned deeply and her legs came up and locked around his back and she pulled him down into her.

"Oh-God, so-you-is-a-bad-man," she breathed. She seemed both frightened and excited by what she had just heard.

He felt himself harden again. "Ahuh," he grunted. "Ahuh. Ahuh, me a bad man—a baad man."

"Oh!" she said. "A bad man . . . A bad man . . . A bad man." Then: "Ooh, you a go kill me—ease up, nuh. Ooh."

They lay together exhausted. Rhygin couldn't feel her body apart from his. Through the thin mattress, his hands rested on the lumps over the two pistols. Then over the sound of their breathing, he heard the floor creak outside. Quiet movements. He rolled off the woman, pulled out the guns, and put a finger to his lips. There was a silence. Delores, round-eyed, lay trembling on the mattress. The door across the hall was kicked open. The blast of handguns was deafening in the confined space.

Naked and gleaming like a newborn baby, his turgid penis standing out woman-slick and reeking of carnality, a pistol in either hand, Rhygin stepped out the door and truly into legend.

The three bunched in the door went down with the first burst, their wild fire adding to the confusion. Rhygin didn't think, feel, or see. He leapt the railing, landing on the stairs behind the backups. His guns kept barking. There was nothing but noise, shouts, and confusion and he was running through a back door.

His ears were ringing, bright yellow flashes danced on his retinas and the smell of cordite and woman was in his nose. He raced into the night ducking into every dark alley and turn he came to. Then he leapt a zinc fence and went to earth under a car. Now, if only dem doan have no dawg, he thought. What really happen? He had only fleeting impressions. More like a dream than anything else. Certainly less real than any movie he had ever seen. The wail of sirens in the distance added to the cinematic effect. Every Babylon in de worl' down deh. The sound of gunfire in his ears grew louder. He saw the three cops shooting into the empty room, scattered as if by a hurricane. Then confusion. He tried to remember details, but couldn't. Noise and shouting. He remembered shouting himself and firing as fast as he could. But he couldn't remember what words he had said, or if there were words at all.

He became aware of his body, of the clammy sweat drying in the cool night air, of the pebbles pressing into his flesh, the dust sticking. He looked down and in his shoulder muscle saw a neat hole seeping a lazy trickle of blood. There was no pain and he hadn't seemed to have lost any strength in that arm. "Raas, how I get lick an' doan feel it? But listen out deh . . . Babylon ragin', but dem get shock tonight—is how much I drop, sah? For the first time he began to realize the enormity, the incredible reality of what had happened. It was history to raas. Wait until the breddah dem hear 'bout it. He wondered if the music men still sold songs in the villages. What a Nine Night song this would make!

The feeling of power and invincibility flooded him again. Starbwai can' dead. Star-bwai can' dead. Pedro, Maas' Nattie unu no see! Ras Sufferah look! Babylon get a blow. But how to move now? Here he was, naked, hiding under a car in a yard somewhere in West Kingston. If daylight found him here he was finished. He listened to the angry sirens and knew that nothing mattered. If people were about, they would all be moving toward the sounds as fast as they could. He listened. There was no sound in the alley beyond the fence. He crawled out and looked. It was empty and dark. He jumped the fence and started up the alley. It didn't matter. Nothing could touch him. Stark naked, dusty sweat coating the front of his body, an empty pistol dangling from each hand, he walked with unhurried steps and lofty dignity toward Trench Town gulley.

Dem a loot, dem a shoot, dem a wail—in Shantytown.

"But me can' tell nobody dis? How me fe go tell anybady?" The drunk blinked his red-rimmed eyes and stared into the darkness. Something *had* moved through the circle of light at the corner. He'd seen it pass briefly under the streetlight. It was coming through the darkness now. It coulda been a duppi or a gunman—but it couldn't be both. But, me nevah hear say duppi carry gun? His much abused, rum-raddled brain rejected the message from his eyes. His vision was blurred but he *had* seen something, and it was coming up the dark alley. A blurred, indistinct shape taking on some clarity as it approached the lamppost on which he was leaning. He shook his head in fear and confusion.

It loomed up noiselessly out of the shadows. A gray shape that looked like a man, unnaturally tall and stark naked, throwing a long shadow before it. Then it was under the light for an instant. It was gray in front and black in back and held a gun dangling in each hand. It passed right before his eyes, moving with ghostly silence and great and incongruous dignity. It turned fiery eyes in his direction, said in a sepulchral voice, "Tell de worl' you see I," and was gone into the darkness.

His unsteady legs gave out. Is true, he thought, I better leff de blasted rum before it kill me. Is mus' a warnin' dat. Me gran'-faddah sen' duppi to warn me. I ha' fe leff out de rum. It was an exceedingly bitter thought to a man who so loved his bottle.

"A naked duppi wid two guns, doh? Lawd Jesas save me! Not a drop again, I nah drink. Nah even *smell* a rum bottle again, no, sah!"

"Blood claat," Bogart said, pouring white rum into the wound. "So, is four Babylon you drop? I can' believe it."

"Or five or six," Rhygin drawled. "It could be more."

The younger members gathered around the shack of the Salt Lake City Ranch muttered exclamations of astonishment and awe. None of the four youths lucky enough to be there when Ivan walked up out of the gulley would ever forget it. The sharp sting of the overproof rum did nothing to reduce his euphoria. He had already given a dramatic reenactment of the shootout to the group. As he told the story, details came back to him with the dramatic, photographic clarity and sharpness of a remembered movie.

"It gone t'rough clean," Bogart said, inspecting the shoulder. "It shouldn' too bad. Jesas. Four Babylon!"

Ivan was writing on a piece of paper. "Bwai, what you name?"

"Dem call me Alan Ladd, sah." Alan Ladd was visibly proud to be so singled out.

"Tek dis to de editor, but you can' mek dem question you, y'know. You understan'?"

The boy nodded vigorously. "Drop it an' run, sah."

"You look like a bright bwai, go den," Rhygin said, and then reading from the paper:

I have made a record of crime history.

—*Sgd* Rhygin.

"Yessah, Missa Rhygin," Alan Ladd said, and set out at a run.

"Arright see some clothes yah," Bogart said. "An' you can tek de bronc too."

"You know Midnight Cowboy? Fin' 'im, man. Tell 'im say I need some more bullet. All 'im can get. Keep dem here at de ranch. I shall return. . . ."

"Cool man . . . But four Babylon—is a raas record dat."

"At leas'," Rhygin said.

"Jesas."

DAUGHTAH VERSHANN

She knew that she wouldn't sleep at all tonight, nor would anyone else in the house either. She turned the rediffusion box ° down low so as not to disturb the boy with any news that might come over. She was sure the police had left but every sound from outside caused her to sit up. The night sounds came to her ears as enemies.

"Oh Jesas," she muttered, and got up and went into the next room. "Come, me love," she said, opening her arms. "Ah know you not sleepin' neider."

Man-I looked at her solemnly. He wasn't crying but didn't seem far from tears. His face seemed ancient as he walked into her arms. "Wha' happen Miss Elsie? Whe' Uncle Ivan an' me daddy?"

"Hush," she said, "you daddy soon come. Hush. Go to sleep."

"Why all de Babylon dem lookin' fe Uncle Ivan?"

"I doan know—I really doan know, Man-I." She rocked him.

"How I to sleep, mam? Somet'ing bad happen. I know say Uncle Ivan ina trouble."

"Hush bwai, nevah min'. What kin' a trouble? Doan worry

° Rediffusion box: A speaker—usually rented—tuned to only one frequency; common in Third World countries before the availability of cheap transistor radios.

youself! Go to sleep!" She held him tightly and rocked back and forth. She felt some of the tautness leave his body and saw his eyes close.

"But I glad," he muttered sleepily. "I glad 'im shoot dem still."

"No, doan say dat, Man-I," she murmured, and looked at the young face. Poor motherless little t'ing, she thought. Why 'im always have to look so sad? She smoothed his locks back from his forehead and saw his eyes open drowsily, then turn defiant. "I glad," he whispered fiercely. "I well glad."

'Im doan know what 'im saying, she thought, how 'im to understan'? She watched him slip into a troubled sleep in her arms and was comforted by his gentle breathing, and his weight against her.

She must have dozed for when she started up Ivan was standing in front of her. "Ivan, de police—"

"Ivan dead," he said smiling. "Rhygin time now."

"Police was here lookin' fe you. Pedro gone fe warn you."

"Police was here? When?" He seemed interested but hardly worried. Just the reverse, there was a kind of tense, almost joyous excitement in his face.

"Jus' after you leave. Dem say you shoot one—is true?" Watching his face she felt a hopeless pain.

"You t'ink is one I drop?" His eyes lit up. "Is at leas' four I kill."

"Ivan no say . . . God forgive you. God forgive you, Ivan."

"Rhygin," he said. "Ivan dead. Keep on de rediffusion. . . . You soon hear a news flash 'bout me."

"What happen to you shouldah? Where you goin' to hide?"

"Hiding? Who hiding? I not hiding you know, Elsa. After me nuh no parrakeet?"

"But all de police dem lookin' fe you—all a dem!"

He looked up from where he was rummaging in his box. "You believe me now?"

" 'Bout what?"

"Dat I goin' to famous? Listen de radio, man, you wi' hear."

She looked at him through eyes that were suddenly blurred, fighting down a rush of hysterical, angry laughter. "You mad! Ivan you mad to blast."

"Why I ha' fe mad? No, I doan mad, I jus' vex. What I to do? Mek dem blow me way or tear up me back again? Nevah. Not so. Not a raas! De harder dey come yes—Rhygin deh 'pon dem. Deh pon dem to blood claat."

She looked at his wildly glittering eyes and knew for certain that he was mad. "So where de Honda?"

"Honda? Babylon mussa have dat."

"So what goin' happen to we? How Pedro to trade now?"

"Look—Ah gone. Babylon may return. Tell Pedro I need some more bullet. Tell 'im to check me, 'im wi' know where."

"Where you goin'?"

"To fin' Jose. Is 'im start dis whole business."

"So what you wan wid him?"

"Cho," he said, laughing, "read 'bout dat tomorrow." And he was gone.

She felt the boy's arms tighten around her and realized that this time he was comforting her. "Doan worry Miss Elsie, Babylon can' ketch Uncle Ivan," he whispered.

" 'Im name Rhygin now," she said, and felt her tears begin. 'Im mad, she thought, but we ha' fe stan' beside 'im—long as we can.

18

Manhunt

Rhygin was here
But 'im jus' disappear
Wid two pint a beer
An' a half-penny pear . . .

—Children's chant

TRIBAL VERSHANN

"No, no, no." The editor's voice was weary, a thread of exasperation showing through his cultivated calm. "It is *not* a question of
glorifying crime. It's the nature of the story, naturally dramatic . . ."

No! The Robin Hood element was not being overemphasized,
at least not by him or his editors. . . . The readers, that's who!
How could anyone expect them not to respond to the underdog
motif? One man against an army? What, the headlines? Well, the
headline writer may have been a little carried away, at first:

LONE GUNMAN BLASTS OUT OF POLICE TRAP
I have made a record of crime history, Rhygin boasts.

So it may have lacked some balance, but what about the editorials? Had they not deplored the violence? Saluted the brave
members of the force who made the supreme sacrifice? Called on
all sections of the public to assist the police? Called for his speedy
apprehension and the removal of the man Rhygin from society . . .

"Of course." It *was* true that he had five of his most experienced reporters digging into the background. Too much emphasis? Hardly, did you have any idea of the level of public interest?
The number of letters and telephone calls? Sure some callers were
only curious, but there were hundreds with theories, and inside
information to offer. One simply had to follow through, can't you
see?

"The picture? Ah yes that . . ." One would have thought that the police would *welcome* the wide dissemination of the man's picture? A little melodramatic? Of course, that's what made it so newsworthy. The two sixguns and the wild-west pose? So whatever happened to the public's right to know?

The conversation was beginning to sound distressingly like government interference with the freedom of the press, after all. Besides, without wishing to tread on any official toes, one might point out—respectfully—that if the elusive Rhygin were becoming some kind of folk hero, it was less a consequence of anything the press did. than of the quite inexplicable failure of the police and military to come up with one poor, powerless, semiliterate rude-bwai. But the line clicked in his ear and went dead.

"Chin, you doan fin' dat damn master yet?" Hilton bellowed.

"Not yet, Missa Hilton," Chin shouted. "Is a long time, y'know, sah, since it put back yah."

"Fin' it raas. Y'hear me. Fin' it or fin' another job. I want records in de store dem tomorrow, before dem catch 'im, y'hear me?"

"Yes sah, Missa Hilton. So, is now you wan' push de record, eh?"

"What you say?"

"Nutten sah, Ah lookin'."

One man? No man, nutten can' go so. That one man could escape, apparently unhurt, from what the press called a fusilade of police bullets? After killing three and wounding two? And leaving behind a whimpering sexually exhausted woman and all his clothes? It rang too many cultural metaphors and had too much of the quality of a movie, a definite star-bwai movie, too.

Opinion among the poor—in Trench Town, Ackee Walk, Concrete Jungle, Lizard City, Rema—was immediate and almost unanimous from the first day. Even the high-ups were intrigued by the dramatic and heroic elements. This kind of cinematic violence was new, and the citizenry not yet hardened by the plague of gunplay that later was to so distort and coarsen the quality of social life. This was the opening salvo, if only they had known it. That it was not greeted with the horror that would later descend, was due in large part to the fact that at first, Rhygin, single and unaided, had killed only armed men, themselves intent on his life.

Opinion swung significantly with the report that the wanted man had gone to the room of one Joseph "Bad Jose" Smith where he had shot and wounded a woman. "Shoot a woman? No man, but me can' defen' dat? After all." When it emerged that the woman in question was the mysterious Delores from the hotel, and that she had quite apparently lured him into the police trap, opinion swung again.

"Maybe she deserve it," people said wisely. "Some woman too treacherous, y'know."

It was held to be very significant that she had only been wounded. The man was obviously a marksman, judging from what had happened in the hotel. So clearly he must only have intended to warn and punish her slightly.

At first, confident of his sources and a quick arrest, Detective Superintendent Ray Jones cooperated fully with the press. He took personal charge of the manhunt and allowed reporters to accompany him on "lightning" raids on locations supplied by his informers.

After three well-publicized such operations which yielded nothing but mocking signs—RHYGIN WAS HERE/ BUT 'IM JUS' DISAPPEAR and BABYLON DE GRATE HAS FALLEN—the relationship between press and police became quite strained.

The phrase *Rhygin was here/ But 'im jus' disappear* was picked up and began appearing on walls all over the city. It became the opening lines for nonsense doggerel that children chanted to keep time playing bull-in-the-ring and jump rope. The mocking couplet even appeared in huge letters on the wall of the Central police station and the Embassy of the United States.

A rumor spread, to the effect that Rhygin had left the country. Other people had it on good authority that he hadn't really survived the hotel incident. His body had been quietly spirited away by confederates. The shooting of Delores seemed to dispel both those. In addition, authoritative sightings were reported in bars, cafés, night clubs and whorehouses in such widely separate parts of the country that the existence of at least five Rhygins would have been required.

A raft of armed robberies, not all of them minor, were reported. The perpetrators of these, though of widely differing ages and appearances, always announced mockingly as they left "Rhygin was here . . ." In most cases this was seen to be a transparent effort to muddy their trails. But there were cases when the description and the style seemed to fit.

Rhygin was positively identified by a number of elderly spinsters—and a few adolescent girls—in whose closets and beneath whose beds he sought overnight refuge. He always escaped, leaving remarkably little trace, before the police arrived.

Given the graffiti that sprang up: RHYGIN SIX: BABYLON ZERO, his many reported appearances, and the known facts, it was inevitable that supernatural explanations would be evoked.

The proprietor of a balmyard, one Shepherd Bedward II, accepted full responsibility. Not two weeks ago, he claimed, he had prepared and administered to the wanted man a special bath, the main ingredients of which were oil of *bullet-can'-touch-you* and oil of *police-can'-see-you*. As a consequence Rhygin was invincible. However, Bedward let it be known, for appropriate consideration he would administer ritual treatment that would render the recipient superior to the forces at Rhygin's command.

Malicious people maintained that Shepherd Bedward's business had improved remarkably. They also claimed that the strange thing was that these new customers, all of whom came furtively and by night, were young men, obviously in good health, and all above the five feet seven inches required by a certain agency of the government. When an enterprising journalist, one J. Maxwell, mentioned these coincidences to Maas' Ray and asked if the rank and file might not, out of misguided zeal, be resorting to nontraditional police practices, the place of business of Shepherd Bedward II was raided. A number of phials were seized, and the proprietor charged with practicing obeah. The same journalist was moved to wonder editorially why had not the good Shepherd foreseen such a development and immunized himself with at least the same treatment he had given Rhygin.

A rival shepherd, getting his cultural references a little confused, put out (a great deal more discreetly however) that he would treat any bullets brought to him with a "quicksilver process." The efficacy of silver bullets against supernatural presences being widely known.

Chin did not have to seek other employment. The record appeared in Hilton's stores and was an overnight smash. It immediately hit the charts and came incessantly over the airwaves. The juke boxes in clubs, cafés, bars, and lounges punched out little else. The powerful sound systems in music shops blared the songs into the streets. The lyrics were published in the newspapers. The request shows received, almost exclusively, calls for the songs—especially from young women in lower Kingston.

An English psychiatrist at the university developed and published a psychological profile based on the lyrics. He concluded that Rhygin was "obsessed with a 'wild west' image of himself, had delusions of destined greatness, a typically psycopathic obsession with heroic violence, and a paranoic and unjustified sense of being oppressed."

This reading was immediately engaged by a young political scientist of Marxist inclinations. His widely circulated analysis saw in such lines as "I'd rather be a freeman in my grave/ Than living as a puppet or a slave" an expression of the legitimate, historical anger of dispossed urban youth. The lines "The oppressor is trying to keep me down/drivin' me underground" were not only prophetic, but indisputable evidence of "a nascent crypto-revolutionary impulse." The flip side, "You Can Get It If You Really Want" was an explicit call for "redistribution of wealth and a clear expression of a primitive Marxist consciousness." That this was not an isolated radicalism at work, was made obvious by the failure of the police to find Rhygin. The masses clearly saw him as an embodiment of their latent revolutionary feelings, for who could believe that they were not hiding and protecting him?

Prior to the appearance of this document, the middle classes, as represented by the Chamber of Commerce and the Manufacturers' Association, had been silent and presumably ambivalent. Hard on the heels of the Marxist interpretation, however, the two groups, acting in concert, took out advertisements announcing the establishment of a fund to aid the families of the victims and generously to indemnify whoever could supply information leading to the capture of the "mad dog" killer.

These advertisements generated intense discussion since the amount of the reward was breathtaking. The speculation turned to laughter with the publication of the following news story:

CAR THEFT AT HOTEL NEW KINGSTON:
RHYGIN TAKES CADILLAC FOR JOY RIDE

A brand new convertible Cadillac, the property of Mr. Ian De Vaz, the President of the Manufacturers' Association, was recovered from the bottom of Salt Pond yesterday afternoon. According to witnesses, including the doorman at the hotel, a gunman identified as Rhygin . . .

"But . . . de bwai great, man? What a way 'im have style, eh? Mek Missa De Vaz tek him reward so go fix up de car, eh?

Then, there next developed a rather embarrassing contretemps, fully and somewhat gleefully reported in the press, between Detective Superintendent Ray Jones of the CID Special Services and one Major Marsher of Military Intelligence. Military Intelligence was understandably put out by a remark attributed to the Superintendent, to the effect that "We would have Rhygin long time—if only the military would stop obliterating the trail with their hobnailed boots and amateurish house-to-house searches." The Superintendent denied making the statement. But Major Marsher felt it necessary to point out that it was not men of his command who had laid so incompetent an ambush as to have five of their number mowed down by a single criminal. Could the distressing failure of the CID, he wondered, be in any way attributable to the wanted man's quite distressing familiarity with police procedures? Perhaps, he further suggested, the relationship, if any, between the extralegal operations of one Joseph "Bad Jose" Smith and certain officers of the CID might profitably be investigated?

The Superintendent and the Major were summoned to an extraordinary "summit" meeting in the offices of the Minister for National Security. The Commissioner was present as was the Commandant of the Defense Force. It was not reported what the agenda was, or exactly what was said, but the meeting was not a long one. Adjectives like "grim-faced" and "tight-lipped" were used to describe the demeanor of the participants as they emerged.

One consequence of the meeting was soon known, however. By order of the Minister and in the interest of the public welfare, the record "The Harder They Come" and its reverse side, "You Can Get It, If You Really Want" were proscribed and prohibited from broadcast over the public airwaves, sale in stores, or electronic amplification at any public gathering. Performance of the music or lyrics by any singer or group of musicians was similarly prohibited under penalty of a fine of up to two thousand dollars and/or six months at hard labor—mandatory.

Rhygin was, however, still at large. And with every passing day, larger than life.

JOSE VERSHANN

"So Jose—but how you not smiling too? How you not laughing eh? Everywhere I go, I see sign: RHYGIN WAS HERE. Every little dutty criminal I see—smiling. Unu doan smile yet! So how *you* not smilin', Jose?" Maas' Ray's eyes were bloodshot and tired looking. It was the first time Jose had ever seen his eyes. His face was flushed and veins pulsed in his temple.

"Every damn t'ing happen in Shantytown you traders know—but them doan know where Rhygin is? How come, eh?"

"But I doan know, y'know, sah. Some a de traders dem ungrateful, y'know, sah—but sah, Maas' Ray—"

"But nutten, Jose. Who bring dat damn bwai into the trade?"

"Me sah, but—"

"Shut up. I tell you to recruit dependable traders, to control them. I protect you. You mek money. Have power, women, respeck. An' what you do? Bring me dis damn bwai?"

"But Maas' Ray, I goin' fin' 'im, y'know, sah. If 'im inna shantytown at all, I *mus'* fin' 'im, y'hear, sah. Dat certain, sah. All I want is a clean gun, y'know, sah."

"I think, Smith," Maas' Ray said mildly, "that that would be best for everyone, eh?"

"Yes, sah."

"Especially for you, Jose. You know dem say 'cat no have cheese, him eat pear.' "

"You wan' him dead or alive, sah?"

"Him or you Smith, him or you. Either way . . ."

Nothing had changed in Trench Town. It was still the same hot, smelly, crowded, noisy, chaotic maze of shacks in, around, and between which children, adults, goats, pigs, dogs, and chickens milled. But few people greeted Jose as he moved through, grim-faced and with the police .38 hanging from his hand. Even if he didn't find Rhygin, at least the word would be out that he was looking, that he wasn't afraid.

"Aye, who see Rhygin?" he asked repeatedly.

"Rhygin was here/but 'im jus' disappear," children sang out and ran away. Adults shook their heads without meeting his eyes and remembered urgent business elsewhere. Young men either smiled stupidly or returned openly hostile looks. None of his traders were at home or in their usual haunts. He also began to get an uneasy feeling that wherever he went he was expected, but no one greeted him warmly. No one even pretended friendliness.

When he toured the ranches along the gully, the youth met him with a hostility and scorn that neither his reputation nor openly displayed gun could inhibit. When he walked up to Salt Lake City the members simply stared.

"I a look fe Rhygin," he said.

"So we hear," one said.

"Trousers too big fe Horse: Dawg say 'give me yah, I wi' wear it,' " Bogart said, looking innocently at the sky. They all laughed.

"I have fifty dollar fe anyone put me in touch," Jose continued stubbornly.

"Judas only get t'irty," the little faastie one they called Alan Ladd said.

"De businessman dem a offer more Jose, keep you money," Bogart advised. "Rhygin good fe fin' you an' den it won't cost yo·· nutten."

"At leas' not money," Alan Ladd added.

Mek dem go on laugh. Damn fool dem. Dem t'ink say Ivan can escape? Ignorant bitches dem, wid all dat talk 'bout obeah an' how bullet can' touch 'im? Backwardness dat. Well, when I fin' 'im today, we goin' see if Rhygin can' dead. But . . . what a way dat bwai ungrateful, eh? Raas man, you can cuss dawg, but you can' say 'im teeth not white? Look I give de bwai Honda. Give him place fe live. Give him money, steady, steady money. An' is so 'im pay me? Is arright doh, anyhow I meet him up today, him is a dead raas man. Is Trench Town dis. I control on yah from birth, y'know. Where dis little raas bwai come from? Yet, dem a laugh after me an' to me face too! Laugh after me? Me? Baad Jose? De raas king of Trench Town? De one dem call Bogart, faastie little shit. Talk 'bout Rhygin goin' fin' me? When I get Rhygin, is him nex' y'know. Bogart nex' to blood. Ah wonder if 'im t'ink say I 'fraid fe Rhygin? Rhygin doan badder dan me, is only lucky 'im lucky so far.

"Aye, Jose. You doan fin' 'im yet?" a boy asked mockingly. "You sure say you really lookin'?"

"Laugh," Jose invited. "Unu laugh, man. Go on. Hey, I may not fin' Rhygin, but I mark *your* face, y'know, breddah. Rhygin soon gone, but Jose is here fe evah . . . wait, why unu stop laugh?"

Y'know, it really look like de whole a dem t'ink say I 'fraid fe Rhygin. Is bare luck why 'im get outta de hotel. I still feel say de Babylon dem shoot up each other ina de dark.

But as his frustration and anger grew so did his doubts. Just who was dis Rhygin? Suppose it was more dan luck? Cho, nutten no name obeah—ignorance and superstition dat. When me fin' 'im today . . . But, maybe 'im not in Trench Town after all?

"Haile up, Jose. One love, man. I hear you looking fe me." The mocking voice was very close. Jose began to turn around but caught himself. He froze. His only chance was to dive to one side, turn and shoot. But his nerves would not obey him. He was suddenly cold all over, sweating and shaking.

"Aye, Jose?" The voice was nearer and very conversational. "You know say you dead?" He heard the loud, chilling, unmistakable click of the hammer being cocked. The sound released him and he was running. It was like a foot race for he moved with the sound of the shot. He heard the bullet whine past his head. Then he jumped over the gulley wall, landed on all fours some twenty-five feet down on the concrete floor, and still kept running. He heard the sound of shots and mocking laughter. He never saw or smelled the piles of dog feces and the animal carcasses that strewed the gulley floor. He never saw the crowds of children and young men drawn to the bridge by the gunfire.

"What, where unu bin? You no hear? Rhygin run Jose outta Trench Town."

"You lie?"

"Ah dead. Inna de broad daylight wid every Babylon in de world a look fe 'im too."

"De bwai dread, eh?"

"Wha' do you, man? Bold as you want. Dem say, Jose tek dawg shit mek road."

DREADLOCKS VERSHANN

Saturday Night: collection night and the traders drifted into the Lone Star Café. Jose had not been seen or heard from since his meeting with Rhygin in the full view of half of Trench Town. He had to see what would happen. He came early and watched the traders slide in one by one; Sidney, Duffus, Midnight Cowboy, Stagecoach, Easy Boat, Bulloh, Fudgehead. They casually checked faces and tried to be inconspicuous. They didn't greet each other as usual. They were guarded in their speech, seemed watchful, and an air of uncertainty went with them. Ras Pedro knew why. One reason was that the place was crowded. Ever since the newspapers had reported the café to be "a favorite haunt" of Rhygin's, all kinds of strangers had begun to frequent it. They were apparently drawn by a desire to brush shoulders with a celebrity for they craned their necks every time the door opened and made the traders generally uneasy. There were, they knew, certain to be police among them.

But even among the traders themselves there was a kind of

reserve. None of them knew for sure yet what the others' position was on the question of Jose and Rhygin. And the reward was a great temptation. Even after they had all managed to slip inconspicuously into the back room, Ras Pedro still had no real idea just how most of them felt. He knew that they feared Jose, or at least his mysterious connections. But still an' all, his protection held up, most of the time. They all grumbled about the size of the cut, but within the organization they had made a living. In the hardscrabble, desperate world of West Kingston, a very good living indeed . . . No, he would have to keep his own counsel, and watch everyone. But the faces gave nothing away, each man came in wrapped in a totally uncharacteristic impassivity. He looked at Sidney. Old habits of secrecy and caution curtained off his feelings. But . . . as he nodded to Pedro, was that a faint, amused glimmer showing through? He could not be sure until they were all present.

"Well," Midnight Cowboy asked loudly, "anybody see Jose? 'Im nah come fe money dis week?"

Then Pedro knew. He knew from the laughter that erupted, as if in the privacy of their room everyone had, at the same time, removed a constricting mask.

"Jose gone undergroun' man," Duffus said.

"Mus' be looking police protection." Stagecoach laughed.

"But 'im come fe money every Saturday?" Cowboy persisted.

"Come fe money? I hear say 'im gone Olympics," Bulloh said.

"Wha' do you, man? Dem say when Jose hear de pistol, not even Coco Brown fit ketch 'im!" Duffus said with tears in his eyes. "Dem say dawg shit fly like dus' dus' ina breeze blow."

"De bwai Rhygin is a lion," Cowboy declared when he could again be heard. "A nachral raas genius y'know. Me spot 'im from de firs' an' anyt'ing 'im need, Midnight Cowbwai is 'im man."

"Me too," Stagecoach said.

"An' I," Sidney said.

They all seemed to be watching Ras Pedro, but he remained silent behind a watchful and pensive look.

"Where 'im deh, anyway?" Duffus asked.

"Who?" Pedro asked. "Jose?"

"No man, Rhygin." They all watched him carefully.

Ras Pedro laughed. " 'Im deh 'bout, man. Where he goes, nobody knows. Truly, it not safe to know dat."

They agreed without further question. "What 'bout de trade?" someone asked.

"I feel dat we should go on," Ras Pedro said. "I feel say Babylon really doan have no time fe we. Dem main concern is wid Rhygin now."

"But what 'bout proteckshan?" Sidney asked.

"Who you a go pay—Jose?" Pedro asked. The meeting broke up laughing.

"I not sayin' dat you know whe' de man deh," Midnight Cowboy said as he passed, "but I know say 'im need dis." He dropped a cloth bag into Pedro's lap.

Pedro knew without looking what it contained. "My breddah, you know say I doan defen' bloodshed an' violence?"

"Everybody know dat Pedro," Cowboy said. "But is still you walkin' partner life you a talk 'bout now."

Pedro slipped the bag under his shirt. A number of the traders, as they left, silently slipped a few dollars into his hand. He heard Midnight Cowboy's loud voice outside, talking to the barmaid.

"Hey, sistah? Rhygin record still on the box? Fuck Babylon den, I a play it raas."

> *Ah say de hardah dey come*
> *Is de hardah dey fall—one an aall . . .*

DAUGHTAH VERSHANN

Prince Man-I was smiling. "Thank Gawd," she whispered and felt his forehead. It was cool and dry. There was no sign of the fever that had seemed to rage within the frail body, stripping the flesh so that the bones of the face showed through the taut skin. He opened his eyes and looked at her. The feverish glitter was gone. The eyes, enormous now in the drawn face, were clear, peaceful, and trusting.

"How you feeling, Man-I? He smiled and nodded. "You hungry?" The smile widened. She propped him up, feeling his ribs under her hands, in a body that was almost weightless. "Come drink dis, buil' up you strengt'." She spooned up the soup and watched the jerky movements in his throat. You can almos' see de little soup go all de way down, she thought. Drink it, me pickney, so streng'ten you ches'. When dis done—what? The last chicken from her flock was simmering in the pot. She heard Ras Peter come in and felt him looking over her shoulder. The boy's eyes looked past her with an anxious expression.

"Daddy, you see 'im?"

"Yes. Ivan arright, Man-I."

"Babylon can' never ketch 'im, don't it? Don't it? Daddy."

"You mad? Wha' dem fe tek ketch Ivan? Nevah happen, son."

"Praises," the boy said, and closed his eyes.

"All power to Jah," Ras Peter said. "Come wid me, Elsa." Ras Peter's face changed once he was out of sight of the bed. He lost the confident smile and Elsa could see haggard lines. "How 'im look to you?" he whispered.

"Fever gone, pain gone—'im really look bettah."

"Praise Jah. If only we doan ha' fe give 'im any more blood it will alright."

She wanted to scream at him, to drive the wistful dogged hope out of his voice. She kept her voice gentle. "Pedro," she said, "is de las' chicken dat." She said, "De doctor say 'im need good food, special diet . . ."

"See few dollahs yah," he said. "T'ings t'in ina de trade, but small-small money coming in. Since we nah pay Jose no more we will mek it." He dug out a handful of bills and a cloth bag from his pocket. He kept back some of the money.

"How 'bout de Honda?" she asked.

"Well, de lawyerman say we might can get it back. But, we goin' have fe sell it, it look like. Lawyer man no work fe nutten, y'know."

"Den how you to trade? An' de boat, dat sell already?"

"Long long time." He shook his head and tried to smile hopefully. "But, praise Jah, Man-I look like 'im getting bettah."

"All 'im ask 'bout is Ivan," she said, keeping the resentment out of her voice with difficulty. "How you feel 'bout dat?"

"How you mean, how I feel? Don't Ivan is me kindred? 'Im is your man too? Is all a we Ivan fightin' for, y'know." He looked at her.

She stared back defiantly. "You sure a dat?" she said.

"Certainly," he said.

"But Pedro—all dis killin', Pedro! T'ink say you no defen' bloodshed?"

He looked out the window. "Truly," he said. "Ah don't. I nevah hol' a weapon ina my han'—not since I get conscious of Jah love. You know dat. But it nevah stop de army from kill off Man-I maddah. Ivan is fe we. All de trader dem support 'im. You woulden expect *me* fe give him up?"

"No, not to say give him up. But look all de trouble. What good can come from it? Wha' price to pay? Eh?"

"Ivan pay more still," he said quietly. "Look, no worry. I put de rest a Bhyah ganja in de street. By week end we have medicine money. We a go mek it, man." He turned away.

Oh, me Jesas! I hope Pedro nevah t'ink say me was a talk 'bout de reward money. Him coulden t'ink dat of me? "Pedro—"

But he was already gone. Miserable and confused she turned to the boy. He was asleep with a serene smile on his face.

BABYLON VERSHANN

"Mr. Commissioner, with all due respect, sir. It sounds as if I'm being put in a position of having to deny that again sir. *Infra dig*, sir—for a man with my record . . . Absolutely, I guarantee it. No sir, no time frame, but it's assured. Beg pardon, sir? A bloody slander, sir—the boys in MI . . . That's right, sir, no basis in fact. Of course, there are rings of informers drawn, of necessity, from the criminal element, but this Rhygin was never among them. Absolutely never on any government payroll, sir. You can, sir. No risk of embarrassment."

"Oh, I see . . . Yes, sir. Mr. Commissioner, sir? That would be a disaster for everyone concerned, sir. Total and absolute. I can assure you, sir, you'd have my immediate resignation and that of all my officers. No alternative. Yes, sir? Then sir, I propose you say to the Minister that it'd be disastrous for the morale of the men and ultimately for law enforcement. Tell him that more house-to-house sweeps and roadblocks will simply make all authority look ridiculous. You can say, sir, that a new technique has been put into effect, that without committing yourself to a time frame you are confident that . . . What, sir? Definitely, within a week. Thank you, sir—and sir, my men need it badly, *badly*, sir. After all it was their brother officers who were killed. Very wise of you, sir, very astute. You won't regret it. And sir, ha ha, the peasants say 'is not the same day chicken eat cockroach that 'im get fat.' Ha ha, sir, quite."

"Bloody old fart," Maas' Ray muttered, hanging up the phone. "Sergeant?"

"Yassir?" The door popped open.

"Bring in Sidney."

While he waited he composed himself. He wiped his face, straightened his tie, and by the time the sergeant returned with his charge, Maas' Ray was wearing an expression of unruffled confidence and power. Imagine, even Sidney? Sidney whose soul I own, whose balls stay in my pocket? Even him. The sergeant left and closed the door. Maas' Ray studied Sidney silently from behind his shades. Blasted little criminal. A small time scuffler, cringing like a gulley dog even before the kick. Dartin', shifty eyes. Denials to unspoken accusations trembling already on his lips. He held his cap before him in both hands, stared at the floor, and managed, without movement or gesture, to radiate an obsequiousness so total as to be almost pitiful. The little shit.

"So Sidney, how you do?" he asked in a conversational, almost solicitous voice that startled Sidney so much he nearly looked up.

"Times hard, Missa Ray," Sidney whined.

"But you arright, eh?" Maas' Ray prompted.

"Oh yes, sah." Sidney nodded vigorously for emphasis. "Me arright, sah, tenk you Maas' Ray. Yes, sah." He kept bobbing his head as if his well-being had been immeasurably enhanced by his great good fortune to be in the officer's presence.

"Sidney—how much time I lock you up?" No answer. "Eh? Three, four, nuff times eh?"

"Yes sah, Missa Ray."

"An'—how much times Ah let you go? Plenty times eh?"

"Plenty times Missa Ray. Plenty time, sah." The furious bobbing again.

"An' when trouble reach you, an' you 'fraid fe go Station, where you fin' youself—my yard eh?" Sidney nodded humbly. "An' doan I help you? How much time I help you, Sidney?"

"Nuff time, sah." Sidney nodded, his eyes shining with humility and gratitude. He got carried away with the fervor of his gratitude. "Oh plenty time, Missa Ray. Sah, you is like a *faddah* to me."

Maas Ray's eyebrows raised slightly behind the shades. He smiled icily. "Good, Sidney, good. Den how de hell you know dat I lookin' Rhygin fe de las' two weeks an' you hidin' him in your swamp hut and don't tell me? Eh?" He slapped his desk *pow*.

"Lawd Gawd, Missa Ray," Sidney wailed. "As Gawd is me judge, sah, I *nevah know* say him deh dere."

"Cut de shit Sidney. Since when a littel dutty criminal like yourself mean more to you dan me? Since when?"

Sidney studied the floor.

"You t'ink I nice nuh?"

"Oh no, sah, Missa Ray," Sidney said with sincerity.

Jones's fist slammed down on the desk again. "Tell me dis," he roared, "you think a damn little dutty criminal like yourself can help you more dan me? You t'ink so? Answer me, goddammit! You t'ink so?" The veins in his neck and temples throbbed.

Sidney almost straightened up. His little eyes opened briefly to look at the policeman. Then he slumped again and looked at the floor. "No, sah," he whispered.

"Den why de raas unu hiding him for? Eh? Unu t'ink 'im smarter dan me because 'im have a hundred place fe hide an' I doan catch 'im? Is not because 'im smart I can' fin' 'im you know? Is because *unu* fool. *Unu* traders stupid. Unu believe that because all my men busy chasing Rhygin we feget 'bout you? Is so unu believe, nuh? Free trade an' glad times, eh?"

"No, sah." Sidney shook his head in vigorous denial.

"Damn right, no. Ah goin' pay de whole a unu back. You hear me."

Sidney's look of distress was genuine.

"Hey, listen. I done chase Ivan. Done." Maas' Ray glared at the little hustler, whose eyes glimmered with interest. "Man hunt done, tell de traders. From now on, clamp down! Jam dung!" He slapped the table. "Every man I have goin' be on *unu* ass. Everyt'ing jam dung! You understan'? Tell you confederates dem. No mercy. *No mercy!* Every cutter, every seller, every trader, every café, every rum shop—all jam dung. Every Gawd place where a stick a ganja sell, every sufferah, every badman—if unu so much as spit on de sidewalk, cuss one badword, much less have ganja. Even a *chalice* on you. You raas in jail, full term. Hard labor. You got it?"

Sidney nodded glumly.

"Unu doan know *dreadness* yet," Maas Ray promised. "As of today, until you bring dat raas bwai to me, not an ounce of ganja coming in this town. Not a wrap, not a leaf, not a stick, not even a damn *puff* . . . We goin' see how much unu love Rhygin when unu belly empty."

He fell silent, breathing hard and glaring at Sidney who studied his mangled cap and looked, if that were possible, even sorrier and more abject than when he had entered. "Sergeant, tek out dis little shit an' lock him up," Maas' Ray said.

"Come." The sergeant grunted, grabbing Sidney by the pants and jerking him upward so that only the tips of his toes made contact with the floor.

"No. On second thought, let 'im go! Sidney, you carry de message! Tell de traders dem say I doan care *who* I get. It can be dem or it can be Rhygin, unu choose. When puss no have cheese 'im nyam pear."

Sidney, of all a dem, Sidney? Poor, perjured, sniveling Sidney? Sidney who used to would sell 'im mother to keep on his good side? Who slunk trembling to his house late at night whenever he had something he could trade for a little credit with the police? No, maybe the little rat didn't really know that Rhygin had been in the hut. Anyway, now he knew. He'd take the message. And in a day or two at the most he'd have Rhygin. Let MI go on with their sweeps, the sufferahs would fight for the credit of turning Rhygin over. He should have done this long time ago.

The new policy was less than three hours old when the first evidence of its effectiveness came into his office. It was not, however, what Maas' Ray had expected.

"Missa Hilton been callin' you all morning Super," the sergeant said.

"Him say what about?"

"Only say him want an appointment, sah."

"Tell him I'm here, nuh."

What could Hilton want? Probably to bawl about the banning of the record. Too bad. A week ago he'd asked him to cooperate, but no. Him flood Kingston wid that damn record mek us look even more foolish. Now him going put on his taxpayer and good citizen hat so come complain? Mek him come, man. Maybe him learn something.

"Look Hilton," he'd appealed, "de damn bwai kill four of my men. You can' be pushing his record."

"Cho, I doan business wid dat." Hilton had laughed. "But, when you ketch him—ah wan' borrow him before you string him up. Him can cut a few more quick sides fe me. Hah, hah."

"Missa Hilton say him coming right over, sah," the sergant said.

Now that was interesting. Mr. Boysie Hilton, businessman, sportsman, playboy, coming to Central Police Station at five o'clock in the afternoon? It must be important to take him away from the tourist women dem in the Sheraton bar.

But when Hilton entered his usual expression of cynical amusement was in place.

"You a hard man to catch up with."

Maas' Ray shrugged, studying Hilton's face.

"When Ah coulden fin' you," Hilton said slyly, "Ah figah say you mussa gone tek a bath."

The detective looked uncomprehending.

"Yes man, I figure some Shepherd fix you up wid a bath in oil-of-mus-ketch-Rhygin."

"I know you didn' come here to mek school boy joke, eh?" Jones's voice betrayed his deep dislike and annoyance. Then he caught himself and continued in a mocking drawl. "De great Boysie Hilton, in police station? I figure say Sheraton burn down, or is could be police protection him looking? Wha' happen, you 'fraid Rhygin come colleck fe 'im record?"

"If I thought unu could protect yourselves," Hilton sneered. "Anyway, so unu ban de record?"

"Only after asking for and failing to get your cooperation, Sir."

"So . . . de police telling people what dem can listen to on de radio now? Nice."

"Yes, if it glorifies crime, sure."

"Come on Jones . . . Is jus' another little dutty criminal you going to ketch anyway. What's de big deal? So de record gets de sufferah dem a little excited—so what?"

"Look Hilton, I really don't have time . . ."

"You bettah damn well make it den." The two men looked at each other. "An' listen good buddy," Hilton continued. "It was a damn fool mistake to ban that record. *That* is what tells the masses that *unu* desperate. That's what makes dis little bwai a big deal—when Babylon start to mess with de hit parade."

Jones laughed. "Hit Parade, you not serious Hilton?"

"You better believe it. That stupid ban of yours made him a hero. An' even more stupid, Ah hear you out to shut down de ganja trade."

"Oh, you have an interest in that too?" Jones asked.

"Not de same interest as you," Hilton said evenly. "Only in the sense that anything that brings money to Wes' Kingston interest me. Ganja is de only t'ing dat bring money into shantytown. Not only that, it cool de people out too. You know what you doing? No money—no ganja—no music? Ah tell you, you bettah ketch 'im fas'."

"What you really saying, Hilton?" Jones seemed conciliatory and even interested.

"Jus' dis. I been doing business among quashie fe years now. I have six stores an' a studio right down deh. During dat time nobody evah tek as much as a record jacket outta one a dem. Dis mornin', four of me store windows shatter. You hear me, shatter, an' that damn sign RHYGIN WAS HERE. Nutten like dat evah happen before."

"You t'ink is him?" Jones asked, his interest quickening.

"It doan matter, a raas. In fact if it was him I wouldn't care so much. 'Im feel say 'im have grievance. But, suppose is not him? Then, dis is only de beginning. De raas beginning. I down deh wid dem every day. I study dem. Dem changing. Dem insolent now. Why not? Dem have star-bwai, a hero. A little raas sufferah like demself who police can neider kill nor ketch. Dass de trouble."

Jones shuffled some papers. "Come on, Hilton. If you want police protection come out and ask."

The businessman was on his feet, fury thickening his voice. "Doan tek dat damn tone of voice wid me, sonny," he roared. "Your blasted police can't even protect demself. First' unu mek de bwai turn unu fool. Den you so 'fraid for 'im you ban de record. Now, you out to shut down ganja trade. So tell me? When dem hungry an' can' even get a spliff to draw? What you t'ink dem going' to do, eh? When white rum full up dem head an' wind full up dem belly, an' reggae lock down an' dem see de police fartin' in de wind, eh? You talking about warfare, sonny. Social warfare. An' you better believe it. No, you better ketch him quick. . . . Because once quashie get desperate enough to trade without you, law and order finish in shantytown. Wha' happen? You doan believe it can happen, nuh?" He lapsed into a bellicose silence, glowering at the policeman.

Jones smiled. "Well Mr. Hilton, we thank you. Your police force is always glad to get the views and cooperation of civic-minded citizens. . . ."

"You stupid raas," Hilton said, and stormed out.

The bland smile disappeared from Maas' Ray's face as soon as the door closed. He was a great deal more impressed by Hilton's visit than he had let on. Whatever else he was, Hilton was no weak sister. It had to be more than a few broken show windows, doubtless heavily insured, that had brought him in. What he said made sense—the last thing he needed was any kind of a riot in shantytown. Jesas, dat would be a bitch right now. An' is exactly what good to happen wid all these damn soldiers racing round in their Land Rovers routing hungry, irritable, ganja-less sufferahs out of their shacks. No, he'd better do some thinking about that. As a matter of fact a riot would probably make Major Marsher happy as a rapist in a convent. Shit, he would do it, too. . . . But at the same time a lesson—a hard one—was absolutely necessary. And his men, they needed something to keep their morale up— and their mouths shut. A show of force yes, but a carrot too. A fat one. An', Ah believe I know jus' what can do it too. Maas Ray's frown disappeared and was replaced by a deep, boyish, satisfied smile. He rang the sergeant.

"Where we holding Smith?"

"Sutton Street, sah. You wan' me sen' fe him?"

"Yes, bring him to me. Oh sergeant, hold that—I'll go pay our friend a visit."

"Yes, sah."

Jose was missing some teeth and his face was puffy. He looked up warily when he heard Maas' Ray's footsteps approaching the isolation cell. He stood up, his face sullen and watchful.

"You can relax Jose, 'tis only I. But, you don't look so happy? Who were you expecting, Rhygin? Him can' get you here, y'know."

"Missa Ray, is not my fault, y'know, sah—"

"Shet up. Wha' happen, you want medal now?" He gestured towards Jose's face. "All things considered, you get off easy—dis time. My men don't like you, y'know, and apparently your own traders doan seem to like you much better. You know dem trading widout you now?"

"Dem desperate, sah, an' ungrateful too. How I to control dem when I lock up—"

"Stop you whining. When you was out you was too damn busy running from Rhygin to control nutten." He saw Jose wince and anger flood his face. "But you lucky, damn lucky I suffer fools gladly. I have a job for you—nothin' dangerous, even you coulden fuck it up. In fack you might even get back your little hustle. I want you to tek a message to the traders tomorrow. A simple message, nutten too complicated. Listen, I want you to tell dem . . ."

As he spoke, Jose's interest grew. The woebegone expression left his battered face. By the time he was finished Jose was smiling, somewhat painfully, but smiling. "Dat mus' work Maas' Ray, it can' fail, sah."

RHYGIN VERSHANN

Slowly and with great effort he crawled to the mouth of the cave and peered through the pile of dried bramble that hid the entrance on the hillside. All he could see was distant rusty roof-tops and, far away, the sea. He didn't think it prudent to move the brush too much. This was his third day there and the confinement and loneliness were wearing him down. He alternated between bouts of lightheadedness and periods of clarity combined with paranoid suspicion. The shoulder didn't hurt, in fact it had no feeling of any kind. Dat raas Pedro, leff me yah fe dead, y'know, he thought peevishly. No! Pedro woulden do dat, not Pedro. But whe' 'im dey? Is no 'bout a week now, I doan see him? Suppose Babylon hol' Pedro? I finish den.

A puff of wind from the valley below brought the smell of woodsmoke and bursts of drumming and chanting from a Ras Tafari camp. When the wind was right he could hear snatches:

> *An' dere we wept,*
> *When we remember Zion . . .*

Sometimes the songs comforted and strengthened him. Filled his belly with courage. At other times they made him sad and very lonely, thinking he would surely die there alone in the little cave. But the drumming was great, strong, intricate and very passionate. Pedro said that the master drummer of Ras Tafari, Count Ossie, and his son "Time" were holding a grounation for his people. Sometimes when he was dozing, the beat came to him and carried him back to his granny's mountain. No question but the drummer they called "The Count" was a master. Like Bamchicolachi come back, in some ways even greater . . . He wished he could hear it better.

But where Pedro deh, eh? Even if something happen to him, don't him would sen' somebody? Even if is only Elsa one him could trust. Still, if him doan show by tomorrow, have to mek some kind of move . . . If it weren't for the shoulder, that would be easy. But it was swollen and constantly oozed a yellow matter that stank. And he was always thirsty. Not hungry though—his belly was always nauseated and the thought of food made him retch.

> *'Ow can we sing, King Alpha song*
> *In a straaange laan'?*

The piled-up newspapers were already yellowing. He never tired of seeing the headlines. It was often too dark to read the stories, but he knew them by heart. The picture was a little disappointing. The face came out dark and blurry but the pose was great—a gunslinger stance beside the Honda, crouched low, alert on the balls of his feet, pistols covering two directions. Dass me, de real me. Rhygin to raas. Shoulder soon bettah an' is me back, y'know. Maybe it gettin' bettah too, no pain fe a long time. But it didn't look better and when he awoke last time flies were crawling in it. Frightened and cursing he had slapped at the flies. It was then he realized that he didn't feel anything in the shoulder. The puffy flesh felt like dead meat under his touch, hot and nerveless.

> *Dry your weepin' eyes, ooh*
> *Dry your weepin' eyes . . .*
> *Ah say dry up your eyes*
> *Fe go meet Ras Tafari . . .*

The mournful cadences, muted by distance, lulled him into a doze. He was in bed in Miss 'Mando's house and the faint melody was coming from Mother Anderson's balmyard. He was at a shelling match in Maas' Nattie's yard. Old Joe Beck was telling a story the words to which he could not hear and so he was crying, quietly. In the middle of the story, three white Dreadlocks walked naked through the company. No one saw them but him. He was on the darkened stairs of the old hotel, running, dodging, shouting and snapping off shots at yellow flashes in the dark. Then, there were scenes from movies he had seen—familiar westerns but a mysterious, black cowboy astride a Honda kept riding into the scenes, changing the ending. Every time he appeared, guns spitting and engines roaring, the crowd in the theater would erupt into cheering. A new scene came on, D'Jango was about to make his move. The crowd was watching for the black cowboy but a cold arrogant voice cut into their excitement: *"Show cut. Unu believe me now say show cut?"* The black cowboy did not appear.

He started up, feeling robbed of his dream. He was back in the hot cave, thirsty and yet trembling. From the camp below he heard familiar words faintly on the wind:

> *For de enemy is around you*
> *Seeking to devour you . . .*
> *So long Ras Tafari call you,*
> *So long . . .*

He had a transistor radio that Bogart had given him. Sometimes he held it against his ear and played it very low. But his song was never played anymore. For three days he hadn't heard it once. Also the news didn't mention him much either. He'd ask Pedro what was going on—the song had been Number One on the Hit Parade. And the request shows had been great. All the young gal dem calling in requests. He even knew the names and voices of some of them. Pearl, Pearl from Milk Lane. He remembered her, voice soft and husky with promise.

" 'Ello sah. Dis is Pearl, from Milk Lane. Yes, is me again. Ah want to hear dat song one more time. De one by Rhygin, de fastes' gun in Wes' Kingston. Give 'im me love an' tell 'im say, he hee, 'im can put 'im gun dem under my pillow any night, he hee."

But no more song and no more Pearl. No more requests at all. Maybe Pedro could explain what was going on. One day hundreds of requests, next day nothing. But . . . Ah did tell Hilton it was a hit. Maybe him believe me now? Wonder if Hilton tek bush like Jose . . . An' Preacha and Longah, bet dem nah sleep too good now eider. Dem doan see nutten yet. Wait till my shoulder better an' watch my comeback. Hey, dass it, "Return of Rhygin" to raas, starring Ivanhoe Martin. Smiling he dozed off.

Someone was calling his name. He awoke quickly, reaching for the guns.

"Doan shoot Jah, is Pedro."

He recognized the voice but said nothing, holding his pose, guns ready.

"Is me one man. You inside?"

"Come man." But he kept the guns trained on the bramble as Pedro moved it.

"So you ready den." Pedro smiled seeing the guns. "But you can put dem up." As he entered the little cave he gagged suddenly and the smile left his face.

"Wha' happen?" Rhygin asked.

"Nutten," Pedro lied, composing his face and trying to catch his breath. "Bwai, is buck a buck me toe. Ah bring some stuff. De beer dem still col'."

"Raas," Ivan said. "T'irsty a kill me."

"How de shouldah?"

"Gettin' bettah—no pain."

Pedro's eyebrows went up. "Mek me see it. I bring some medicine suppose to draw it down." He knelt and examined the wound catching his breath sharply when he saw it. He pressed it gently and there was a gush of pus.

Rhygin thought he saw a quickly suppressed look of horror on his face. "How it look?" he asked.

"Coming on—but it a go need a doctor," Pedro said.

"Hey, I hear on radio dat some people sayin' dem ketch me?"

"You believe dem?" Pedro asked, and was happy to see him smile.

"How Ah can' hear de record?"

"Minister ban it. Seem dem 'fraid it."

"Fe true? So is not de people . . ."

"Nevah de people, man. Marcus Garvey himself coulden draw de followin' whe' you have. De more dem ban de record is de more de people talk."

"Righteous breddah." Rhygin's eyes began to shine. He took a long pull at the beer. "So how de trader dem?"

Pedro had turned his back and was busy taking things out of his bag. He didn't seem to have heard the question. "See a gallon a water here. Few limes. Some bread an' fry fish. A nice pear an' a bag of irie irie collie."

"Ah ask you, what 'bout de trade?"

"Well—" Pedro hesitated and seemed to be choosing his words with care. "Some a we still backin' you."

"Some a we?" Rhygin asked.

"Yes, Ah doan too like what Ah hearin'."

"Like what? Talk man."

"Well, I doan see him personal, y'understan'—but dem say Jose come back. 'Im offer some a de breddah dem a rake off ina de export business."

"But dat is what I was after!"

"Ah know. Well it look like some a dem will get it—dat is, if dem turn you in."

"Who know whe' me dey?"

"Me one. So dat cool. But now I can' too sure which a dem is fe you any more. So fe de time, is me one."

"What 'bout Midnight Cowbwai an' Duffus?"

"Oh yes, Cowbwai sen' dis fe you. But dem say Babylon pick dem up dis mornin'. Ah say, breddah, Babylon *ragin'* out deh. Like when you trouble wasp nes'. Dem a kick down man door, bus' man head. Every man dem grab gone a jail. Maas' Ray sen' message say dem nah chase you no more. De trader dem fe turn you over. Preshah drop."

"Now dat dem get a raise dem good fe do dat yes—or feget me altogeder."

"No man," Pedro spoke quickly, loudly, "some a we still support you fe get rid a Jose altogeder. But . . . you have fe try get way fe a spell."

Ivan scowled and his voice rose to a dangerous level. "Ah nah runnin' a raas, Pedro. Ah not runnin'."

"Shh, hol' down man," Pedro whispered. "You know a bwai call himself Sidney Greenstreet?"

"Is me ol' time walkin' partner from de ranch."

"You trus' 'im?"

"Yes man—at leas' 'im used to be a ri-chus breddah."

"My feelin' dat too. Anyway him get a work 'pon a ship whe' sail go Cuba. 'Im come to me an' say dat de captain drunk-a-ready, and de mate is a conscious white man. De mate say dem wi' pass by Lime Cay on Wednesday so pick you up an' carry you go Cuba. 'Im say you will get a big welcome dere." He looked at Ivan anxiously. There was an unhealthy greenish tone to his skin and his eyes had a glazed glitter that made him appear demented. Even now that Pedro was somewhat accustomed to the stench from the rotting shoulder, he could barely breathe. He could see that Rhygin was examining the proposal. It was the best chance that had come along. He was relieved to see a slow smile creep across his friend's face and into his eyes.

"Yes, yes," he said beaming, as the possibilities struck home, "revolutionary to raas. Yes, Pedro mek we do it! An' I could get treatment fe de shouldah too.'

Pedro's worried expression lifted. The two men grinned at each other and laughed out loud, happy laughter that spoke of a deeper relief than either would admit.

DREADLOCKS VERSHANN

Ras Peter sat silent in the back of the room, his great maned head slumped onto his chest above his folded arms. He seemed asleep except that his deepset smouldering eyes followed each speaker. There was nothing studied about his posture. He was exhausted, both physically and emotionally.

At first dark he had rowed a delirious Rhygin across the harbor to Lime Cay and come back again against the current. He walked home to find Man-I in relapse. A weeping and distraught Elsa had met him at the door. The boy was feverish and moaning in obvious pain. Just at that moment, an excited Fudgehead had appeared with a summons to an important meeting. He knew that next to Sidney, Fudgehead was Jose's most valuable informer and henchman, so he knew that Jose must have sent him.

He knew he had to go. It was impossible to say which was

worse: the sound of his son's anguish or the angry condemnation in Elsa's face.

"Ah goin' by de hospital so send an ambulance," he promised, "an' den Ah be right back. De meetin' nah tek long." She turned away silently.

Less than half the traders were present. Babylon was kicking down doors at gunpoint. It was, as Stagecoach said, "Outright, blood claat, war." At first Jose seemed nervous and without his usual arrogant confidence. He ran the meeting, but listened quietly as Sidney gave his report, describing his interview with Maas' Ray word for word.

"An' 'im say to tell unu," he repeated faithfully and with emphasis, "dat not a leaf, not a spliff, not a puff coming in town unless we give him Rhygin." Then he lapsed into silence, his preternaturally mournful expression giving away nothing.

"But," Stagecoach said, "*me* no know where Rhygin deh? Who know?"

It seemed to Ras Pedro that questioning heads turned in his direction. He kept silent. Certainly Jose was staring at him.

"See it deh," Jose began. "If unu doan know, den unu bettah fin' out. You see Midnight Cowbwai? You see Duffus? You see Bulloh? Everyone you doan see deh a jail. An' dass jus' de start. Ah say Maas' Ray *mad* to raas. 'Im is like a madman out deh, a raas *madman*. Ah say, de man dread can' done. 'Im dreadful a way. An' if 'im no get Ivan den de trade finish. Unu can kiss unu pickney goodbye cause unu a go dead a jail." He paused to let that sink in.

"Like a roarin' lion, so is de wicked ruler over de poor," Ras Pedro said into the silence. "But oppreshan is only fe a season."

"Still an' all," Jose continued in a more optimistic voice, "it coulda worse. I been talkin' wid de high-up man dem in de trade. I tell dem say you traders deserve a break, y'know. I tell dem say bettah mus' come. Dem agree. Dem say, so longst as we settle dis Rhygin business an' lif' de heat off de trade—den we can get a break ina de export. Dem say from dat time deh, de new rate is like dis." When he slowly and dramatically announced the new deal there were gasps from the group. Even Ras Pedro, despite himself, was impressed.

"An' besides dat," Jose continued, his face shining with cupidity and great drops of sweat, "in case anybody ferget, dere is de question of de fifteen t'ousan' dollar—" But even he could not bring himself to do more than mutter the last word, "reward."

"An' Judas went out," Pedro invited, "an' hung 'imself."

"Dat a blood money," Stagecoach said. "We can' jus' give up Rhygin like dat?"

"Business a business, ol' man. My belly empty. My pickney belly empty, too," Fudgehead said.

"Trade can' resume til dem get Rhygin," Jose repeated staring at Ras Pedro who returned the stare silently.

"Business a business," Fudgehead repeated. "What you say Pedro?"

"Pedro doan say nutten?" Sidney said.

"Preshah mussa no reach 'im yet," Fudgehead said. "My baby hungry."

"Unu hear I." It was a quiet voice and from a totally unexpected quarter. Little Sidney was not known to share his opinions with anyone. His ratlike little eyes missed nothing, but when he spoke it was usually for money or credit. Inarticulate, beaten-down Sidney, street scuffler, peddler of information and anything else that fell into his hands and would bring a price. A man of no courage and little respect, who was afraid of everyone and was protected in the world only by a low cunning. At first he looked at the floor in the silence. Then he looked up, and at each man in turn. Pedro would have sworn that his gaze was steady and direct.

"Unu know say I doan know whe' Ivan deh," he said slowly. "But now Ah wish to Gawd say Ah did know. But is right say I shoulden know, for I is a informah. Is so I survive from I small. But even if I did know where Ivan deh—" He looked squarely at Jose. "Babylon coulda kill me an' I woulden talk."

Praises to Jah, Pedro exulted silently. Sidney fin' 'im heart.

But Sidney wasn't finished. "All a unu smell big money. Ah see dat inna unu face. Nutten no deh, renk as when a poor man smell money. . . . Is de worse t'ing dat, for is nutten 'im woulden do fe get it. Me know dat . . . for me poor all me life. De high-up man dem know it too, for dem rich all dem life. Yesterday, a man box-box me up ina me face. . . . Another one call me, an' Rhygin too, a little dutty criminal. An' is true. . . . But me is not so dutty. . . . Me is not so small. . . . Me is not so criminal dat me no know who abuse me, who scorn me, who down-press me all me life. . . . Ol' time people say, 'every fish nyam man, but is shark alone get blame.' Jose say Rhygin is stranger—not one a we—well, dem say 'when tiger wan' nyam him pickney, him say dem favor puss.' . . . All a we is little dutty criminal to dem—alla we. Mek Ah tell you. . . . If dem high-up man a go pay all dis money fe de life a one dutty little criminal, den dem really a buy somet'ing much big-gah. You evah see dem give way money yet? . . . Somet'ing much more dem want, man, an' dat is what Sidney who sell everyt'ing a'ready, *will not sell*. Unu can do what unu want, but dis little dutty criminal nah go sell. Sidney nah sell Rhygin so. . . . Nah sell 'im so. . . . Nah sell 'im so."

His voice tapered off. He fell silent, his ferret head cocked to one side as if he were listening to the echoes of his own speech. Then a tentative smile began, and spread and spread. Beaming with peace and pride, Sidney sat down. The silence was resonant and somehow loud in the room. Then Pedro said softly, "Derefore get wisdom . . . an' wid dy gettin' get understandin', Selah." With tears running down his jaw and into his beard, he left to go see about his son. He knew the meeting was over.

"G'wan, unu will nevah trade again," Jose threw bitterly after him.

But he didn't even care.

19

Presshah Drop

An it came to pass . . .
dat out of Rema dere came a great wailing: Rachel
weepin' for her children and would not be comforted . . .
— Ras Pedro Lament

DAUGHTAH VERSHANN

Elsa sat on the bed and held Man-I in her arms, alternately crying and cursing and wishing for something she could do. The boy's pain seemed reflected in her eyes. She stroked his head and crooned.

"Never min', Man-I. Nevah min'. Ambulance soon soon come."

"Jesas. You mean dem no come yet?" Pedro said, entering the room. " 'Ow 'im doin'?"

"Same way. You can almos' feel de fevah eat way de flesh."

"Bwai, Ah hope dem soon come. 'Ow dem tek so long eh?"

"Because we no live a Red Hills or Sky Line Drive," she said bitterly. "If we did have de Honda we coulda tek 'im weself."

"Ah pray to know say 'im in de hospital," Pedro said. "Ah can' stan' to hear 'ow 'im have fe bawl. Ah can' stan' it, y'know."

"When 'im come out, it goin' be de same t'ing all ovah again," Elsa warned. "He needs propah care—*all* de time."

Ras Pedro opened his hands in resignation and seemed about to cry.

"When de trade goin' start up again?" Elsa demanded.

"Elsa, police terrible out deh. Up to tonight dem lock up Duffus an' Midnight Cowbwai."

"So . . . you doan know why?" she said with some heat.

"You know?" Ras Pedro asked.

"Is mus' Rhygin dem want," she said. "Don't it?"

"Ahuh. Dem want 'im bad bad. Most a de bwai dem ready fe resume trade. Much bettah price too. But some a we no wan' give up Ivan."

"Ivan dead," she said. "Is Rhygin time now."

"Well, some a dem no wan' give 'im up."

"Dem mussa no have pickney," she snorted. "What you say?"

"I say no," he said firmly but looked neither at her nor his son. His head fell forward as he inspected his hands, the dreadlocks casting shadows over his face. He was silent for a long time. The only sound in the room was their breathing and the whimpers of the sick child.

"When," he began apologetically, "after Ivan get 'way—after a period, dem will forget an' de trade will resume. Dem can' stop de herb."

She sucked her teeth scornfully.

"Den . . . what you say, Elsa?"

She looked at him with hard eyes that showed neither pity nor softness. "You know what I say—every game whe' I play I lose . . ."

The sirens approached at what sounded like uncommon speed. They stopped in front of the house. A puzzled frown creased Elsa's face, but before she could speak the door splintered and the room filled up with cops. Man-I sat up screaming but Elsa cradled his head into her bosom. Ras Peter rose and took one step toward the door before the leader stepped up to him and slapped him hard across the face, so quickly and violently that he reeled across the room.

"Move an' Ah blow 'way you blood claat," the cop said. He followed Pedro close and grabbed his collar, twisting it so that the muzzle of the .357 Magnum came up under Pedro's ear and forced his head to one side.

"Shape. Just shape," he begged, "so Ah can scatter you brains 'pon de wall. What *unu* waiting for?" he said to the other cops. Search de place." He dragged the stunned Pedro outside and flung him into the back seat of the car.

Pedro fell against a body. Through a haze he saw that it was Sidney, apparently unconscious and bleeding from the nostrils.

"So . . ." the sergeant said, "you a de one hidin' Rhygin? Well, one a unu goin' dead tonight. You or Rhygin—me no care." He sat beside Pedro keeping the hammer cocked.

Elsa, hugging the boy, watched the destruction of the place. The police, except one, didn't even look in her direction. If they felt any shame or remorse it certainly didn't inhibit their impulse toward destruction. Man-I didn't cry, but seemed in shock.

"Please, corporal?" Elsa said. The man didn't answer but he looked up. He was the youngest and seemed less hostile, gentler somehow, than the rest.

"What?" he muttered. "We have orders to search."

"Not dat, sah. Dat no mattah—is de bwai."

"What about de bwai?" The corporal looked suspicious and tense.

"Ah believe him dying, sah. Please could you drop us at de hospital?"

The young man looked surprised. He looked intently at Man-I for the first time, then back at Elsa, "You lyin'," he said uncertainly.

"As God is me judge, sah. See fe youself, sah. 'Im sick bad, sah."

Very hesitantly he crossed the room holding the Uzi submachine gun clumsily. Some of the men watched him. "Gwan wid de search," he ordered and looked uncertainly at the child. "Well . . ." He looked around as if for guidance. "Is against regulations. I will ask de sergeant, maybe. Come on. Search over," he barked to the men and fairly ran out of the little house.

"Ah pray to God," she shrieked after them, "dat one day somebody leff you pickney fe dead so."

One of the men stopped and raised his hand, starting back. "You faastie bitch, you—I soon . . ."

"You, get over here," the corporal shouted.

Elsa stood in the door staring at the man who had threatened her. She didn't care what happened, the hatred she felt wouldn't be silenced.

"Yes," she taunted, "you ha' strength fe box up woman. Why you no go box Rhygin? Go put you han' inna *him* face, nuh?"

The entire party froze. The nearest man, who still had his hand raised, shouted, "Mek Ah blow way dis bitch" as though asking for permission.

"To the cars," the corporal ordered. *"Move!"* Muttering and swearing, the police left.

She sat and comforted the boy in the wreckage. She rocked him until he was calm and promised him, "You nah dead Man-I. I swear you nah go dead so. Even if is me one you have leave ina dis worl'. Ivan gone. Ras Pedro who nevah hurt nobady, him gone too. But you, you a go live. Ah doan care what I have fe do. You a go live. No you nah dead. Nor live ina no suffering eider. Ah swear dat to God—a sell me soul an' body firs' . . ."

Somewhere about four A.M., she could not be sure, the ambulance came.

"Raas. Is hurricane dis," the driver swore when he looked around. At first he would not let her ride with Man-I. "Sorry sister, rules is rules. Tek a taxi, nuh."

Elsa had her mouth open to scream, but closed it. She smiled and walked over to the driver. "Den honey . . ." She grinned, fondling his sleeve and trying not to smell his rummy breath. "Den is what time you get off duty. Nobody have to know, y'know—an' later . . ." She stroked his arm and rode to the hospital with the boy.

By the time she watched them wheel Man-I into the emergency room she was dry-eyed and numb, somewhere beyond feelings of fear or pain or even anger.

"Wait here mi love," the nurse said gently, "we ten' to him right now."

Elsa nodded and sat. The still little figure under the white hospital sheet could have been a stranger. The waiting room was bare with lusterless white walls and wooden benches. Despite the hour there were more people there than she would have expected. Pain and physical distress, it seemed, kept no hours. The astringent smell of hospital antiseptic stung her nose and eyes.

"Me nah cry doh, y'know," she said to herself. "Time fe dat over now. Poor lickel t'ing . . . Ah wondah if 'im evah a go see 'im faddah again? An' what 'im a go come back to? Maybe—is bettah 'im dead?" The thought came to her dully, meeting no resistance and registering no meaning so that it was some time before she realized what she had allowed herself to think.

"God forgive me," she muttered guiltily. "Man-I going to alright."

She saw before her the splintered door and broken furnishings and was grateful to feel stirrings of anger driving out the tiredness. "Dem really nevah ha' fe do it. None a it. Ah glad say Rhygin—"

A hand fell familiarly on her shoulder. "Ah bet is me you waitin' fe, mi love," the driver said, grinning.

She looked at the hand and then at him.

He squeezed her shoulder gently. "Ah off duty now," he cajoled. "Doan you wan' see me?"

"You sure say *you* wan' see *me*?" she asked in a voice that made him look a little more closely at her.

"How you mean? Don't arrangement mek?" He squeezed again possessively.

"Well . . ." she said slowly as if in thought, "we can' go my yard. As you see everyt'ing in deh mash up."

He seemed to ponder that for a moment. "Ah true," he said with the air of a man suddenly remembering something he should not have overlooked. "How dat happen doh?"

"Babylon," she said.

"You lie!" he exclaimed. "Wha' mek dem do it?"

"So dem stay." She shrugged as if skirting the issue.

"No, dem mus' have reason," he persisted. His hand was not so gentle now.

She gave a tired sigh.

"Dem was looking fe somebody. Alright?"

"It look like a raas fight—who?"

"Me man. De guy I live wid!"

"De baby faddah?"

She nodded. "Dem no ketch him eider," she added.

"Who him? What 'im name?"

"Why? What difference . . . ?" She tried to look evasive.

"I always like know who fa garden I a dig in," the driver said, smirking widely. Then he looked threatening. "Ah hope you nah tell me no lie, y'know, gal?"

"You t'ink say I mash up me own t'ings?"

"O.K. So who Babylon did want?"

"You no know 'im—wha' difference dat mek?" She smiled at him flirtatiously, genuinely beginning to enjoy herself.

"Ah jus' like to know," he said, smiling his ram-puss smile.

"Ah doan believe you know him. 'Im name Ivan—but most people call 'im—Rhygin?" She smiled into his face. "Wha' happen sah? Ah t'ink you wan' see me?" Mek you change you min' so sudden? She laughed.

BABYLON VERSHANN

"Pedro, Sidney . . ." The weary voice had the edgy tiredness of someone losing patience with a child who was both obstinate and stupid. "You understan' say I *have fe* get Rhygin? Say I *mus'* get

'im? Is him or me, y'know, you understan' dat? How 'im to win?
You hear dem say hungry belly mek dawg lick sorefoot? Monkey
nyam red pepper? If unu doan help me, you can' trade again,
y'know? An' unu good to dead too. It doan look like unu understan' how dis situation serious?

"Understan' better dan you," Pedro said.

The sergeant struck him across the face with a web belt,
knocking him to his knees in a corner.

"So . . . unu nah talk?" Maas Ray asked mildly.

"Maas' Ray—Sidney no know—nutten," Pedro whispered
hoarsely. " 'Im can' tell unu what 'im doan know."

"Even if Ah did know—" Sidney began.

"Shut up," Maas' Ray said, looking at Pedro. "But you is de
one who know eh? Lick 'im again. You nah talk? Reach 'im
again."

" 'Im tryin' fe say somet'ing, sah," the sergeant said.

Maas' Ray approached and leaned closer. The only expression
on his face was one of concentration. "Speak up now."

Pedro mumbled brokenly, the words coming hoarsely and
slow.

"Shit!" Maas' Ray swore and stood up.

"Ah believe say 'im mad, y'know, Super," the sergeant
muttered.

"Very God of very God . . . preserve us from peril . . . defen' us
from de enemy. . . .

" 'Im tek dis fe joke? Lick him raas again. See if 'im pray
again."

"What 'im say now?"

"Nutten, sah."

"Lick him raas some more!"

"Who de Lord lovet' . . . he chastiset' . . . an' scourget' . . .
every son . . . he taket' . . . ."

"Ah really feel say 'im mad, sah," the sergeant said.

"Mad me raas. Ah say to lick 'im."

". . . in Ras Tafari . . . Very God . . . of very God . . . makah an'
creatah . . . God of God . . . Light of Light . . ."

"See sah, 'im mad."

"Lick 'im, Ah say. No, wait! Give me de knife. See how him
preach when him head shave."

" 'Im a laugh, sah—you wan' me lick 'im again?"

"Wait, 'im dead to raas?"

"No sah, it look like 'im faint. Ah goin' get some seawater."

"Do Jesas—mek a fin' Pedro ina de house when Ah reach." She brought good news: Man-I was stable. "Pedro? Where you deh?" But she knew, even as she called, that there would be no answer. The house was just as she had left it. But Pedro have fe tek de boat an' carry Ivan go de ship. If 'im can' go, Ivan mus' dead. Both a dem a go dead. An' fe what? Ah wondah whe' de boat deh? Maybe I could—" But she had never even been in a boat. She was not sure where Lime Cay was or how far it lay. "Botha dem may even dead a'ready, de way Babylon dreadful now. Poor Man-I . . ."

In the bedroom the broken bed lay at a sharp angle, covered with her and Ivan's torn clothes. She slumped against it. She had no idea how many hours passed as she sat there thinking.

When she arose it was to search through the rubble until she found the exercise book in which Pedro kept his records. With many pauses and erasures she wrote until she had filled nearly a page with a steady even script. She read it over, made a few more corrections, then looked for some clothes. She dressed herself carefully in the red satin blouse and miniskirt about which she and Ivan had argued. She had never worn them before. The buttons had been ripped from the tight blouse so she knotted the ends and went into the street.

Preacher came to the door looking surprised and much older than she remembered. He was unshaven and his face was puffy, his eyes watery.

"I've brought you what you always wanted," she said before he could speak. "Go pay the taxi-man, please."

As he passed her in the doorway she thought she smelled a faint odor of stale rum. Maybe is so we all a go come to, she thought, but when he returned he seemed more his old self.

"You're not welcome here, dressed like that," he said.

"Cho Preacha, admit say you like it, nuh," she teased, and spun provocatively. "Besides it mek you a prophet, don't it?"

"God forgive you Elsa," he rumbled.

"Cho forget dat," she said and grew serious. "Read dis—an' copy it in ink and den sign it." She thrust the exercise book toward him.

Startled, he accepted it and squinted at the page, then at her.

"Read it," she commanded.

He put on his reading glasses and ran his eyes hurriedly down the page. "But . . . I doan understand. Who dis Man-I Peterson? Why you—"

"You doan ha' fe understan'. Jus' copy it—in ink."

"Come into de office, nuh." He wrote carefully, muttering the words as the pen raced over the paper. "Received this information from . . . for the care . . . an' education of said Man-I . . ."

"Alright," she said, reading it. "Now sign it."

"You quite sure?" he asked timidly.

"Sign it," she said, looking at the floor and biting her lip. "Then I'll tell you."

STAR-BWAI VERSHANN

The little island—actually, a big sandbar—was flat, sandy, and very dry. There was not a single cloud and the sun was merciless in the clear sky. The only sound he heard was the steady lapping of the water among the mangrove roots. Except for the thick curtain of mangroves in the water, the only vegetation was clusters of stunted sea grape trees whose sparse desert leaves offered areas of shallow shade. Patches of scrubby beach grass held the dry sand between their wiry roots. The only other sign of life were soldier crabs—queer primeval creatures bearing on their backs the shells of dead snails—which scuttled around the scummy sand at the water's edge.

It was so clear that he could see—when he was lucid—the trees on the mountains across the bay. They looked cool and green. The bay was a mirror with no current or slightest breath of wind disturbing its eerie smoothness. Earlier he had seen a boat pass. A squat, ugly little vessel, its unpainted hull completely covered with red rust. There had been two figures on deck, but the ship had not altered course or slowed its already sluggish pace. He started to fire a shot, but he couldn't be sure it was the promised ship. He knew that Pedro was not coming.

He was thirsty. He had dug a shallow trench and watched it slowly fill with clear water. It had looked cool and clear seeping through the sand, but when he tasted it, it was bitter and very warm. He couldn't tell, and didn't care, whether the sickly sweet smell came from the mangrove swamp or from himself. He lay in the thin shade of the sea grapes and allowed his mind to drift: Pedro would be there . . . he always was . . . They would meet the boat . . . a clean well-lighted ship . . . He was still Rhygin. Looking at the two pistols lying in the sand he drifted off. . . .

Something, some slight persistent thing aroused him. He opened his eyes and didn't know where he was. The glare from the sea lacerated his eyes like pins of fire. He had to close them. Where were those shades now that he needed them? What had awakened him? It was nothing much, for he felt no sense of danger. There it was—a slight tug, barely felt around the wounded shoulder. Without moving his head he peered through squinted eyes. It was a soldier crab, one that seemed bigger and was certainly bolder than the others. He had never seen any this close. It looked like one of those jerky mechanical monsters in a horror film. Four legs and two claws protruded oddly from the captured shell. He wondered idly if the crab had killed the snail. Then he saw what had awakened him. The clumsy pincer, moving with an awkward mechanical motion, stabbed into the bandage, closing over a piece of the yellow-encrusted cloth. The tug came as it withdrew. At first he thought the crab was trying to tear away the bandage to get to the flesh. Then he saw a small yellow granule sticking to the point of the claw. The claw brought it up to a lipless slit in the shell between the legs. The motion of the mouth reminded him of the toothless mouth of an old man gumming his food. The crab was not attacking, it was only feeding on the dried pus. Firs' de snail den now me, he thought. But . . . if dem was bigger, man would really have fe 'fraid dem. He shifted his shoulder and the tiny crab scuttled back and stopped, waving its outsized pincers at him in mock menace.

His attention was caught by the sound of a motor approaching on the harbor side. He scrambled to his knees and picked up his pistols. He stuck one in his waist and held the other in his good hand. He half ran, half staggered to the top of a low dune and lay in a clump of grass watching the bay. He noticed idly that the beautiful blue barrel of the pistol was flecked with rust. He no longer heard the engine. Then the police launch, with its motor cut, glided from behind the mangroves and in on the beach. Men leaped into the water and swarmed, running onto the beach, diving head first into the sand. They seemed to burrow down and lay motionless, not even raising their heads. They were less than a hundred yards from where he lay.

"So what dem a wait for—is *Sands of Iwo Jima* dis to raas? Is mus' Iwo Jima dem t'ink dem deh."

He had to fight the laughter that rose up in him. Were they real—or another scene from a movie? They certainly seemed in no hurry to move. If he just lay in the thick grass they would never find him. Not cowering on their bellies like that. He realized with a great astonishment that Babylon, with all their long guns, were afraid of him. Eight, or more like twelve, with long-range guns crawling like so many turtles in the sand.

"Me one, an' dem 'fraid me . . . Show doan over a raas! Starbwai can' dead after all. . . ." He rose to his feet shouting and staggering in the loose sand. "Cho—done de army business!" he challenged, laughing. "Who is de bad-man unu have? Sen' 'im out, nuh—one man who can draw. Sen' 'im out!"

He stood rocking in the shifting sand, bawling out his challenge and squinting against the gun's glare.

"Sen' out you fastes' gun—de bes' man unu have. Sen' 'im out!"

The police raised their heads—but were frozen either by fear or disbelief at this apparition.

"What de raas unu waiting for!" Maas' Ray screamed. "Is him! Shoot!"

A sudden brief silence followed the echoes of his scream. Then, the fierce thunder of automatic rifles. Rhygin crumpled forward and rolled down the dune. The fierce clatter continued long after he was still, except for the impact the bullets made. They continued to pump lead into the dune with the frenzied intensity of a gang of apes battering with clubs the dead body of a leopard.

"STOP!" Maas' Ray bawled. "Cease fire, nuh."

Ras Peter, eyes dull, face lumpy and bruised, limped into the yard. Elsa saw him enter and ran out shouting.

"Pedro, to God, you alive! But you hurt?"

"No, I man doan hurt." He didn't look at her but limped over to the mango tree and sat down.

"But Pedro," she wailed. "You head—"

"I man doan hurt," he said. "I man nah feel nutten."

"I glad," she said, wiping the tears from her face, "I glad."

On the police wharf a group of men were milling around excitedly watching the launch approach.

"You sure dem get 'im?" one asked. "How dem so quiet?"

A corporal caught the rope and pulled the launch up to the dock. "So unu get 'im. Unu get 'im," he shouted excitedly. "Whe' 'im deh."

A man gestured toward the stern at what appeared at first to be a pile of bloody rags.

"Dat? Dat a de great Rhygin?" The corporal's boyish voice seemed disappointed. "Cho, is jus' another likel dutty criminal." He turned his head and spat carelessly into the water. "Is what smell so, eh?"

Sitting under the mango tree, Ras Peter heard the forbidden song begin on a neighbor's radio and knew that something had happened.

> *because, de harder dey come . . .*
> *is de harder dey fall*
> *one an' aaawl . . .*

The voice of the announcer Numero Uno was hoarse, breathless with suppressed excitement.

We interrupt this program to bring you a special news bulletin. This afternoon a party of specially selected police sharpshooters from the Harmon Barracks led by Detective Superintendent Raymond Jones—acting on a tip from a well-known cleric . . .

Ras Peter put his hands over his ears and shouted, "Tu'rn it off! Ah say to tu'n it off!" But of course they didn't. "It done," he said. "It really done now."

In the house Elsa started to cry silently.

In Trench Town gulley a small boy lay in ambush behind a tree. He lay still, listening for the sounds of the posse. From a distant shack he heard the familiar rocking beat and the words.

> *De oppressah is tryin' to keep you down . . .*

"Wait," the boy said. "Ah t'ink dem ban dah song deh?" But he had little time to wonder. He had to deal with more urgent matters, the approach of the posse.

"Bram, Bram, Bram!" He leapt from cover, guns blazing.

The posse returned fire. "You dead!" the sheriff shouted. "Cho man, you dead!"

"Me Ah Rhygin!" the boy shouted back. "Me can' dead!"

He again swept the posse with withering fire before dancing back under cover. His clear piping voice sang out tauntingly, "Rhygin was here but 'im jus' disappear . . ."

Over the gulley, in the shacks and hovels of Trench Town, for the space of half an hour, silence reigned.

AYEH, JAMDUNG.
SEE IT DEH,
BOOK DONE.
SELAH!

Glossary of Jamaican Terms and Idioms[*]

A

a, *prep.* to, as in "Go a shop," from Spanish.

Accompong, *n.* name of Maroon warrior, Capt. Accompong, brother of Cudjo; also name of town. From the Twi name for the supreme deity.

a go, *aux w/v.* going to do, as in "Me a go tell him."

alias, *adj.* (urban slang) dangerous, violent.

asham, *n.* parched, sweetened, and ground corn. From Twi *osiam* (same meaning).

ackee, *n.* African food tree introduced about 1778. From Twi *ankye,* or Kru *akee.*

B

Babylon, *n.* westernized Jamaican society, the government and institutions, an oppressive force; the police, as agents of.

bankra, *n.* large basket. From Ashanti *bonkera.*

balmyard, *n.* place where pocomania rites are held, healing is done, spells cast or lifted.

batti, *n.* (slang, familiar) the buttocks.

boasie, *adj.* proud, conceited, ostentatious. Combination of English *boastful* and Yoruba *bosi*—proud and ostentatious.

bungo, *n.* racially pejorative. Crude, black, ignorant, boorish person. From Hausa *bunga*—bumpkin, nincompoop.

* Author's Note: For much of the etymological information, I relied very heavily on the excellent *Dictionary of Jamaican English,* by Professors F. G. Cassidy and R. B. Le Page, published by Oxford University Press.

bredrin, *n.* brothers or brother. From biblical *brethren*.

bullah, *n.* flat round sweet-cakes, food of masses.

C

chalice, *n.* (see chillum). A chillum passed ritualistically between bredrin becomes a *chalice;* sacramental.

chillum, *n.* elaborate water pipe for smoking ganja, from Hindi *chilam.*

cho, dismissive, exclamation.

coo 'pon, *v.* (origin unclear) Look! Look upon.

coo yah, *v.* (origin unclear) Look here.

coolie, *adj.* of East Indian descent, as in "coolie man" or "coolie gal."

collie, *n.* (urban slang) ganja.

cromanty, *adj.* from *Corromantee,* Blacks from the Gold Coast believed to be rebellious.

Cudjo, *n.* name of famous Maroon warrior; man born on Monday. From Fante, Twi *kudwo.*

cutchie, *n.* clay pipe for smoking ganja.

D

deggeh, *adj.* sole, lonely, measly as in "one deggeh dollar I have." From Ewe *deka*—one single.

deh, *pron.* there

dereso, deso, *pro.* (place; emphatic) there, as in "Look dereso"—"Look there."

dey, *v.* to be, exist, as in "No yam no dey—"There is no yam." From Ewe *de,* or Twi *de*—to be.

dey 'bout, *adj.* be about, available. "No ganja no dey 'bout."

dey 'pon, *aux. v.* to be engaged in action or continuing activity. "I dey 'pon haste"—"I am in a hurry"; "I dey 'pon dying"—"I am dying."

dreadlocks, *n.* the tangled uncut or uncombed hair of a Ras Tafarian. The wearer of such hair; also "Nyaman" or "Locksman."

dungle, *n.* legendary West Kingston slum surrounding a garbage dump, now cleared. From English dunghill.

duppi, *n.* the spirit of the dead capable of returning to help or harm people. Subject to the power of obeah and its practioners. From Bube *dupe*—ghost, spirit.

F

faastie, *adj.* (see faastiness), impertinent, rude, impudent.

faastiness, *n.* effrontery, impudence. From Surinam Creole *fiesti*—nasty, unpleasant.

fe, the infinitive "to," as in "Have fe go"—"Have to go." "Look fe it"—"Look for it;" "Him ready fe kill"—"He is ready to kill."

fi, possessive. "fi me"—"mine"; "fi you"—"yours."

fenneh, *v.* to feel physical distress, pain, and to show effects therefrom. From Twi *fene*—to vomit; Fante *fena*—to be troubled, Lumba *feno*—to faint.

G

ganja, *n.* dried buds and leaves of female plant of cannabis sativa. From Hindi *ganja;* also herb, weed, collie.

ginnal, *n.* trickster, con-man, an Anancy figure as in "Sunday Ginnal"—a preacher or clergyman.

H

head man jancro, *n.* albino buzzard with white feathers, usually around the neck area.

I

irie, *adj.* (Rasta talk) powerful and pleasing.

ilie, *adj.* (Rasta talk) literally, "highly," valuable, exalted, even sacred.

I an' I, *pron.* (Rasta talk) first-person singular.

I-man, *pron.* as above.

J

Jah, *n.* short for "Jah Ras Tafari," common way to refer to the divinity. Probably from Hebrew *Jahweh*—God.

janga, *n.* small river shrimp probably from Doulla *njanga*—crayfish.

jancro, *n.* literally John Crow, buzzard.

Jamdung, *n.* (urban slang) name for Jamaica; literally, "Jam"—to press, dung, down. Ironic reference to social and economic condition of the masses.

Jack Mendora, part of narrative formula for beginning or ending a tale. It indicates that the story is not aimed at any particular person. Meaning lost, ety. unknown, probably African.

jon connu, *n.* (John Canoe). Bands of elaborately costumed and masked dancers appearing around Christmas. They resemble the ancestral dancers of West Africa, but the ety. of the word is unclear.

K

kass kass, *n.* quarrel or contention. From combination of English curse or cuss, and Twi *kasa kasa*—to dispute verbally.

Kumina. *n.* Ecstatic dance for the purpose of communicating with ancestors. From Twi *akom*—to be possessed, and *ana*—by an ancestor.

M

maas, *n.* from master or massa. Now freed from its class origin; a respectful and affectionate form of address to an older man.

Maroon, *n.* free black warrior-communities which successfully resisted British hegemony during eighteenth century and early nineteenth century. From Spanish *cimmaron*—untamed, wild.

Menelik, Ras, *n.* Ethiopian nobleman who rallied his troops to resist Italian aggression. Defeated Italians at Adowa, 1896.

myal, *n.* a form of benign magic opposed to obeah, hence myal-man. From Hausa *maye*—wizard, person of mystic power.

N

nah, *adv.* will not. Emphatic as in "Me nah do that."

nagah, *n.* pejorative for black person, lit. "nigger."

nago, *n.* Yoruba person, practice, or language. From Ewe *anago*—Yoruba person.

nuh, interrogative at end of sentence; literally, "Is it not so?" "Not true?" Also imploring, literally "please," as in "Do it for me, nuh?"

nyabhingi, *n.* legendary worldwide secret society of blacks alleged to be led by Haile Selassie and devoted to the ending of white domination by war. Said to mean "Death to whites"; a group of Ras Tafarian "warriors"—*Nyamen*.

nyam, *v.* to devour, eat ravenously. Apparently African in origin especially in double (emphatic) form "nyam nyam."

O

obeah, *n.* the practice of, the art of, using the power of *duppies* to influence human events. The practice of malign magic. From Effik *ubio*—a charm buried in the earth; or Twi *obayi*—magic or sorcery.

P

pattu, *n.* the screech owl, bird of ill-omen. From Twi *patu*—owl.

pickney, *n.* (Afro-American pickaninny) child or (pl.) children; probably originates in West African pidgin from Pg. *pequenino*—small child.

pocomania, *n.* ecstatic, revivalist, Afro-Christian religious movement usually attributed to Span. *pocomania*—small madness. This derivation is questioned by some scholars who attribute it to Twi origins: *po*—small, and *Kumina*—dance of ancestral possession, therefore "small Kumina."

Q

quashie, *n.* peasant, country bumpkin, coarse and stupid person; racially pejorative generic term for blacks; originally Twi name of a boy born on Sunday.

R

raas, *expletive,* extremely impolite. From the English "your ass."

rahtid, expression of surprise, or to be enraged. From biblical "wrothéd."

Ras Tafari, *n.* original title and name of Haile Selassie I of Ethiopia. Hence *Ras Tafarian,* member of cult holding Haile Selassie I to be God incarnate.

rhygin, *adj.* spirited, vigorous, lively, passionate with great vitality and force; also sexually provocative and aggressive. Probably a form of English *raging.*

royal, (rial), *n.* offspring of some other race and black, as in "Chiney-Rial," "coolie-rial"; humorous, as in "monkey-rial."

S

samfie, *n.* a confidence man, formerly one who tricked the gullible by pretending to occult power. Probably African.

sankey, *n.* religious song of a particularly lugubrious tone, sung in the long or common meter. From Ira David Sankey, evangelist and hymnalist.

shampata, *n.* sandal of wood or tire rubber, secured by string or rubber straps. Span. *zapato.*

shepherd, *n.* leader of a revivalist cult; also proprietor of balm-yard, healer and prophet.

T

Tacumah, *n.* character in Anancy tales. Said to be a son of Anancy. Twi *n'ticuma.*

tambran switch, *n.* a flail made from the wiry, flexible branches of the Tamarind tree, braided and oiled. Effective and much feared in the hands of Babylon.

tallowah, *adj.* sturdy, strong, fearless, physically capable. From Ewe *talala.*

tata, *n.* father. Affectionate and respectful title for an old man. From many African lang. Ewe, Ge, N'gombe, *tata—* father.

Tafari, Ras, *n.* (see Rastafarian). name and title of Haile Selassie I, before coronation as Negus of Ethiopia. (Ras Tafari MaConnen)

U

unu, *pron.* you, plural. In usage close to Afro-American *y'awl.* From Ibo *unu,* same meaning.

Y

yaah, *expletive,* emphatic conclusion. "You hear me," as in "Don't do it, *yaah.*"

yabbah, *n.* earthenware bowl or vessel. From Twi *ayawa,* same meaning.

yah, *adv.* here, as in "Come yah!"